She tried to remember the night before, but everything was foggy. It was clear until . . . when? Why had Gwen told people she had too much to drink? She hadn't really drunk much at all. She went through things, and her mind again touched on that incredible sex. Had she actually slept with Gwen?

Well, okay, they had *slept* together, but had Brett done her? Brett couldn't even remember getting undressed, but all she was wearing now were her black silk boxers and a white T-shirt.

She remembered her back being clawed, so she went to the mirror, turned around, and lifted her shirt. She couldn't see any scratches, nor could she feel any.

Titles by Therese Szymanski

Available from Bella Books

When the Dancing Stops

When the Dead Speak

When Some Body Disappears

When Evil Changes Face

When Good Girls Go Bad

Editor: *Back to Basics: A Butch/Femme Anthology* (from *Bella After Dark*)

Included in *Once Upon a Dyke: New Exploits of Fairy Tale Lesbians*

When the Corpse Lies

A MOTOR CITY THRILLER

THERESE SZYMANSKI

2004

Bella Books, Inc.
P.O. Box 10543
Tallahassee, FL 32302

Printed in the United States of America on acid-free paper
First Edition

Editor: Anna Chinappi
Cover designer: Sandy Knowles

ISBN 1-931513-74-0

Acknowledgments

Any book requires the hard work and help of many people.

I'd like to especially thank Carol Napoli, a very talented grief and loss counselor, for her helpful suggestions and all the reassurance she provided; Joy Parks for her hard work in reading and making suggestions to the first draft of this book; Anna Chinappi for fixing me and helping to keep the pace moving; Barbara Johnson for keeping me going—telling me I actually could write this (when not giving me the serial-killer psychopath test); my big bro' Kathleen DeBold for her wonderful jacket copy; and Judy Eda for her always excellent proofreading.

Oh, and yeah, I'd also like to thank Bella Books' Linda Hill for making the first deadline on getting this book out the door! (And Becky Arbogast for her humor and questioning me on things.)

About the Author

Therese Szymanski occasionally releases her inner bad girl. A writer/designer/computer geek, she was born in Michigan and now lives in the nation's capital. An award-winning playwright and Lammy finalist, she believes in erotic freedom and maximizing the erotic content of life.

Reese's friends are afraid she has become a hermit. Or already is. She volunteers hundreds of hours annually to The Mautner Project (www.mautnerproject.org), and has had her stories appear in a variety of anthologies from Bella Books, Naiad Press, Alyson Publications, and Haworth Press. She edited Bella Books' first anthology, *Back to Basics: A Butch/Femme Anthology*, from Bella's new imprint, Bella After Dark. She was also involved with Bella After Dark's second book, *Once Upon a Dyke: New Exploits of Fairy Tale Lesbians*, where she wrote an incredibly sleazy lesbian fairy tale, wherein she let forth her sense of humor for the first time since her plays.

She enjoys skiing, working out, being a hermit, doing freelance design, and watching *Buffy the Vampire Slayer* (she's still in mourning over its finale). She's also still in mourning over not having any attachment to the theatre, since an evil day in '98 . . .

And, like many other authors she knows, truly hates writing bios.

Prologue

Six Months Ago

"Baby, it'll take me a bit longer to get home, but don't worry," Brett said into her cell phone once she got into her car. The snow was coming down so hard and fast she didn't want to risk shorting out either her phone or herself in the blizzard.

"Yes it'll take you a bit longer to get home, and I won't worry because you're staying in Lansing tonight," Allie said.

"What do you mean?"

"I've been watching the Weather Channel and there's no way you're making it through tonight. I've booked you a room."

"You actually trust me alone in a hotel all night by myself?"

Allie laughed. "Not really, but I'd still rather have you alive than dead."

Brett drove through the blizzard and finally checked into the hotel. She was mighty glad Allie had the foresight to book the room because the place was packed. Apparently a lot of folks were snowed in that night. Although the Lansing airport didn't have a lot of traffic, it still had enough to fill up Lansing's hotels, especially on top of everyone snowed in because driving was suicidal in this weather. Even to native Michiganders.

The only seat Brett could find in the restaurant was at the bar. At least she could get a bite to eat there.

She casually scoped the bar, half-heartedly wondering if she could score in such a heterosexual haven. It wasn't that she really wanted to pick someone up, she just felt as if she should at least think about it. She was considered a stud in many circles, and she had to live up to her rep, if nothing else.

She liked it when women found her desirable. It made her forget, at least for a moment, all the degradations her family put her through when she was growing up.

She cut that thought off at its throat. She'd grab a bite to eat, then go up to her room and enjoy having the remote all to herself tonight. She might even get some nasty porno that Allie wouldn't even consider watching. Not that after all her years in the adult entertainment industry it did much for her either. But doing something Allie wouldn't approve of made her feel like her old self—the self that had two women loving her when all she heard growing up was that she was shit, and nobody would ever love or want her.

Sitting at a bar and checking out the scenery made her feel more like the old Brett. There were a few women who were obviously working girls, but Brett never paid for it. Plus that would prove nothing. On the other hand, a few yards away two women sat with a man. One man, two women. Brett liked those odds.

"I don't understand why I have to do everything," one woman loudly whispered across the table to the other. "I thought we agreed that we need to . . . find someone to take a fall for what needs to happen."

"Yes, we did. But it takes time to work out something like that. It's not that easy. It has to be foolproof, you know."

"Yeah, I know. That's why I sent a couple of fools on the mission." She looked up at the bar and saw a woman sitting with her back to it, checking out the room. The woman's gaze stayed on their table for longer then warranted. The tall, dark butch obviously saw something she liked. The woman smiled. "And again I'm gonna save the show, make things happen, and tell you what to do."

"Hey!" her two companions said simultaneously.

"Whatever. Okay, here's what you're gonna do," she said to the other woman. "You see that tall butch at the bar?"

"It's all guys at the bar."

"Oh, God. There's one woman. She's in a black suit with a black shirt and a dark red and black tie. She's the best dressed person at the bar." To the other woman's blank stare she continued, "Jesus, use the bar mirror if you must. She's the only one up there without a pot belly."

"That's a woman?"

"Yes. What I need you to do is go up there and flirt with her."

"But I'm not into women. Are you sure that's a woman?"

"Yes, I'm sure, and it doesn't matter. You're not going to spend the night with her or anything. What you need to do is flirt with her—remember, until I told you, you thought she was a cute guy."

"But now I know—"

"Doesn't matter. Flirt with her, get her business card. We need her e-mail address, so make sure you get that. It should be on her card, but double-check that. Make sure it's there. And see if she's on some sort of Instant Messaging software. Really check that out. I'd like to be able to use that."

"What do I do if she asks me up to her room?"

"Tell her you're with friends—who are a couple, and you're just crashing on our second bed during the snow storm."

"Okay." The woman began to stand.

"Hold on."

"What now?"

"Undo another button on your blouse."

"Huh?"

"Just do it. And can you tighten your bra at all so you have a bit more cleavage?"

"I don't know—"

"Okay, so we get up like two good friends using the restroom together."

"Why?"

"Oh, God. How did I ever end up with you two?"

"Listen," the man said, "we're the keys to making this all work, so you'd better not keep talkin' like that."

"Whatever. We're going to the bathroom together so I can help fix you up so she'll be sure to be interested."

"I'm confused," the man said.

"What's new?"

"Why are we doing all this?" he asked.

She leaned over the table to him. "Because I've seen the future—and a sweet future it is—and this woman is going to make it happen." She nodded to her female companion. "I know what that woman wants, and you're close, but a bit more cleavage and a longer slit up your skirt will cinch the deal."

"You can tell all this just by looking at her?"

"No. I know her. And I know just how we'll set her up."

The man looked toward the bar. "I didn't know you swung that way."

"I don't! She's just . . . an old employer, okay? Her name's Brett Higgins."

"What did you do for her?" the man asked with a leer.

"It doesn't really matter. What does matter is what she'll be doing for us."

"Jesus, she must've really pissed you off. What'd she do? Kick you out without giving you breakfast or coffee first?"

"It doesn't matter. Let's go."

The future, and past, rushed before her eyes. She remembered working her way through college as a dancer at the Paradise Theatre. About ten years ago she'd been trying to pay for her own schooling by working there. Brett never blinked at her, instead paying five times the going rate for a lap dance with one dancer. One particular dancer. And it was always she that Brett threw the money at—never once considering how maybe others could use that money as well.

It pissed her off.

Storm had nothing on her. She didn't know how far she'd go for all the money and extra bookings Storm got, but she'd probably do whatever Brett wanted. After all, it'd be better than having fat, ugly, balding men pawing her for a lot less.

And Storm never even really knew all that Brett was offering. She was sure that Brett wanted her to stop dancing, but Storm's pride got in the way.

Sure, Storm was trying to get through college, but so was she. She had as much right to Brett's extra tipping as anybody else. But Brett only had eyes for Storm.

She wondered what happened with Storm.

In the bathroom, she slit her friend's skirt higher and adjusted her bra, breasts, and blouse, and thought about Brett.

"You sure you're not a lesbo?"

"Yes. But I know what'll get her attention." She knew Brett. She'd occasionally wondered what happened to her, but seeing her here, now, she was sure—Brett was still at the Paradise. She'd get her e-mail address, and maybe her IM name, and work from that. And some online research. Brett wasn't heavy into study and research.

She was perfect for the frame. And it did help that Gwen really was a lesbian.

This was going to be a cakewalk. Brett already had a criminal record, and she was known for sleeping around. What she had in mind would be perfectly believable. The best defense Brett could come up with would be to dump the body in a river or lake. Lord knew there were enough large bodies of water in Michigan in which to hide a corpse.

All she needed to do was establish enough contact between Gwen and Brett to make it a believable murder. She'd have to find out more about the Brett in the present to create that detail, but she was sure she could do it.

After all, Brett was Brett, and there was no chance she'd changed enough to make that impossible.

Of course, during her months of baiting and tricking and researching Brett, there was nothing more pleasing than when she figured out that Brett had a history with even the Lansing Police.

Cakewalk. All the way.

Chapter One

Day One

She had assured everyone that Brett would follow along with everything—she was like a trained chimp. All the months of hard work had come down to today—the day she would prove she knew Brett just as well as she said she did.

She crossed her fingers and really hoped she was right because she was their only way to cover themselves.

I like women who are women. I like a nice girl dressed naughty. I like high heels and short skirts.

Brett liked flirting with women, and making them want her. She liked being wanted. She liked being needed. She knew she should be happy with Allie—after all, she was beautiful, smart, and sexy as all hell.

I like a butch who knows what she needs. Who takes control. Who is willing to own me.

But Brett also enjoyed the conquest. She was hoping to get that out of her system through her online exploits. Unfortunately, seducing a woman online was nothing compared with feeling a woman's heated breath on her neck when she pulled her in close to dance with her. When she felt the woman's skin against her own as the woman gave up everything to be with her.

Brett was a predator, and she knew it. She liked the challenge of drawing in someone new. She knew part of it was that these women wanting her was self-affirmation.

But she was trying to keep all that under control. She was still amazed that you could have real conversations, just like in real life, except typed, online. Almost as amazed by that as by what people were willing to say, and do, online—all through the incredible technology of Instant Messaging (IMing, as she had learned it was called).

She hoped she could get the rocks off her flirtatious spirit by doing the online thing. She hoped cybersex would curb her desire to possess other women in more intimate, personal ways.

I like handcuffs. Restraints. I'd like to tie you up, spread-eagle, so I could do whatever I'd like to you.

She owed Allie her total and complete devotion. But she couldn't help noticing the way a dress would cling to a woman, sweeping between her legs and showing off her curves better than a bikini.

She was still a bit afraid of computers. But she had known she needed one for her various enterprises, and now she could not even imagine doing things the old ways. She couldn't cope with the idea of keeping hard-copy ledgers, journals, and records any more.

Brett, you know you can always do whatever you'd like to me. But I'm at work right now. I have to behave.

And she also knew how much the entire Internet thing helped her with her research.

She had done some reading, and subscribed to some magazines, to try to learn this dread machine better—and how to use it more efficiently. She had realized early on that if she screwed something up, she could always buy a new computer, and she kept multiple backups of any really important files.

What do you want me to do to you?

And what took her online were the articles she had been reading in her magazines and the realization that she could explore her ideas much more easily online. Currently, she was looking up ways of expanding the business. She knew a lot of people were online. She also knew that there were a million and one porn sites on the Web, and there had to be a reason for all that, right?

Anything you want. Everything you'd like.

She had started by looking for information on how to expand her legal enterprises. She was wondering about creating porn herself; after all, that was always a lucrative industry. She was exploring options of putting out her own magazines, or maybe videos. But then she realized the potential of the Web, and saw that she could start a Web site. Charge people for looking at the pictures. And maybe have live interaction with the girls. She could do the phone sex thing online, or maybe film live girls stripping and put that on the Web. The opportunities were endless.

Gwen, close your door.

But she was teaching herself everything. And she was learning mostly like she usually did—by exploring. She had learned women that way. And guns. And many other things, in fact.

I can't. Please, Brett, I'm at work. Don't do this to me here!

She remembered the first time Rick DeSilva took her to a firing range and put a gun in her hand. She had taken the tiny Beretta, pointed at the target, and shot. She knew how these things worked, so it took very little for her to learn it. To get it down.

Rick had eventually reached into his shoulder holster, pulled out his .357, and put it into her hand.

I want to fuck you. Now.

"Use both hands. This is a big gun and you'll feel it," he said.

"I can handle it," she said, wrapping her hands around the hefty weapon. Her hands felt like they had finally found home. She looked at the target and imagined it was her father. She squeezed the trigger and felt the power of the big weapon. She nailed the target in the heart. Then she looked at Rick. "Why are we doing this?"

Please, Brett, I'm at work. Even thinking of your hands on me here is a problem . . .

He wrapped her hands around the gun. "I'm giving you a promotion. You'll need this. That is, if you're up to it."

Close your door. Close your door and sit at your desk. No one will know anything.

She whipped away from him and faced the target, holding the gun in one hand. Before Rick could stop her, she pulled the trigger, blowing away the target's brains, while keeping her arm steady. "I'm up for anything."

Done.

Imagine me under your desk, pulling down your stockings . . .

Since then, while researching, she had been distracted by the acquisition of new knowledge in this cyber world—specifically with meeting and playing with new women online. She slowly realized she could use this new tool to relieve her predatory instincts.

. . . exposing your most intimate parts to me . . .

She had even gone so far as to masquerade as a boy and seduce straight women. She had done the cybersex bit, and enjoyed the power she had over women. She had even gotten blow jobs online, which always cracked her up. Occasionally she'd come out to a straight woman as being a woman. Usually she didn't. When she did, the woman was usually rather pissed.

I like it when you're wet for me. When you're ready for me. You are, aren't you?

It was fun.

Oh, God, yes.

It fed her dark side.

I'm fingering you, feeling how wet you are. I know you like getting off at work, you like the idea that I'm taking you at work . . . possessing you there.

There was one woman, though, Gwen, who had a bit more of Brett's attention. Gwen was some sort of a computer whiz. Brett knew she could e-mail her with any computer problems she had and get them solved. Beyond that, Gwen was . . . Gwen was incredible. She was everything Brett ever fantasized, just like Allie was. And she even spelled correctly, and could write.

You're wet enough for me to finger first, stroking your softness, and then slowly enter you with first one finger, then another, and another . . .

Gwen was the perfect woman. Especially since Brett didn't have to deal with her on a day-to-day basis.

I slide my entire fist up into you.
You like that, don't you baby?

Cybersex was a really nice way to help fight off the urges. After all, it wasn't really cheating.

"Hey there," Allie said, walking up behind Brett. Startled, Brett barely had time to hide the IM screen. "Almost done?" Allie asked, wrapping her arms around Brett's neck.

"Yeah. Just about finished. You need to use the machine to look for jobs?" Allie was looking for a new job while taking classes at a local college. Unfortunately for Brett, one of the classes she was taking was Women's Studies, which again made Allie believe that everything Brett did for work was wrong and bad. Brett did what she knew, and if she didn't do it, others would. There has always been pornography and prostitution, and there always will be.

"Yeah, looking for things to fill my time with."

Brett flicked off the monitor, knowing that the IM would hop to the top when Gwen replied. She turned and faced Allie, pulling her onto her lap and wrapping her arms around the drop-dead gorgeous blonde. "I can fill your time."

"Oh, you think you can, huh?" She straddled Brett's legs, opening herself up for her butch. Her arms snaked around Brett's muscular shoulders as their lips came together. No matter how bad Allie thought Brett was, she still wanted her and liked what she did to her.

Brett might not be politically correct, but she knew how to get her woman off. She knew what Allie liked; and what Allie liked, wanted and needed wasn't always PC either. After all, PC was no fun. Brett pulled Allie in tighter. She had been getting hot talking with Gwen online, and now that was taken from her. Allie would do just fine in her stead.

Allie moaned against her lips. "Brett, you're working."

"And your point is?" Brett ran her hands over Allie's curves, enjoying the swell of her breasts against the palms of her hands.

"Shouldn't you be working?"

"You know what they say: All work and no play makes Brett not too productive." Brett enjoyed the firm length of Allie's thighs fitted inside tight denim. She pushed her thumbs into the seams of Allie's jeans, right against the crotch. Allie moaned at her touch, as she pushed her thumbs in hard, playing with Allie.

Then she pushed Allie's thighs open even further.

"That's not what they say." Allie groaned when Brett's hands snuck up inside her shirt, pushed her bra up, and squeezed her hardened nipples.

Brett ripped Allie's shirt and bra up and off. "All work and no play leaves Brett and Allie really horny?" She licked Allie's collarbone, nibbling lightly at her neck. She felt the smooth skin of Allie's torso and wrapped an arm around her waist, pulling her in tight.

Allie lightly ran her tongue over Brett's ear, sending shivers speeding through Brett. Brett explored one of Allie's breasts, gently caressing the silky softness before finding the hardened nub of her nipple and feathering light touches over it.

Then she took it between her thumb and forefinger and twisted it tightly, squeezing hard. Allie was pushing herself into Brett, as if trying to ride her waist. Brett brought up her other hand to fondle Allie's other breast, again lightly teasingly at first, then grabbing the nipple and squeezing it as hard as the other.

"Oh, God, Brett," Allie said, taking one of Brett's hands and putting it on her zipper.

Brett slid the zipper down, then reached in to finger Allie's underwear, running her fingers inside the elastic. She dropped her hand down inside Allie's jeans to cup her over her thong.

Allie pushed herself up against Brett, shoving Brett back in her chair, stretching herself out on top of her. She was pushing herself into Brett, against her fingers, rubbing herself against Brett.

Brett brought her fingers out of Allie's jeans, shoving both her hands down the back of them to cup Allie's ass. Her mouth was connected to Allie's, their tongues dueling, tangoing.

Brett suddenly stood up, holding Allie with one arm around her waist while the other shoved her jeans and underwear down.

They loved each other, were in love, but tonight wasn't about love, it was about sex and fucking and all those hot animal things.

Brett lowered Allie to the floor and stripped off the rest of her clothes. She lay on top of her, grinding her hip into Allie's hot cunt, riding her, as she sucked at her neck, marking her. Allie arched up against her, wrapping her legs around Brett, pulling her in tighter. Her hands were under Brett's shirt, clawing at Brett's back.

Brett moved down Allie's body, licking and nibbling her way over creamy, flawless skin. She reached into her pocket and pulled out a couple of lube samples, ripping them open. She ran her fingers over Allie's wet heat, causing her to wriggle across the floor in need.

She coated her fingers with the slick stuff and entered Allie, one finger at a time, fucking her, slowly, until she had her entire fist buried inside of her. Then she slammed her fist into Allie, then pulled it out. In and out she went, enjoying the heat and sight of Allie, enjoying the feeling of Allie clenching around her fist inside, bearing down harder and harder on her hand.

She lay on her stomach between Allie's legs, her fist still embedded deep within her, pushing herself down the hardwood floor, even though she had to bend her legs at the knee to fit her length on the floor around the furniture. Then she brought her tongue down on her girl.

She moved her fist around inside while she feasted on Allie's tender flesh, licking and sucking and fucking her woman. Allie's moans became screams as she yelled out Brett's name . . . as she tightened her legs around Brett's shoulders, pulling Brett into her, forcing her deeper and tighter.

"Brett! Brett! Fuck me!"

Gwen Cartwright rubbed her tired eyes and looked at her watch. How did it get so late? She leaned back in her chair, staring at her monitor. She was so close, she could almost feel it. They were almost done—but every time she could see victory within her grasp, they found more problems, and they were only just about to enter the beta testing stage of program development!

Good thing she always built in extra time to any software development plan. She had learned early on that it was necessary.

She stood and stretched, looking out her window-with-a-view. Sure, she had the view, but she never had time to notice it. Maybe once this project was out the door, she could enjoy her hard-earned window office. As well as other things that had come into her life lately.

She smiled, still fueled by the latest praise from her bosses at this past week's meeting. Throughout the past year she had continually amazed them at what this single application could do. They had had no idea how far this one program could go, how much was possible.

And they had been even more excited when they realized she could bring it in not only on time and on budget—but also with some of the functionality put into add-on modules that people would have to pay even more for!

She turned to look back at her monitor. She hated leaving when she was so close to debugging this current glitch. She knew she was close; she could practically taste it. The solution was like a tickling in her brain—teasing her, if only she could think her way through it.

Usually standing and taking a breather could clear her mind, make her see the problem and solve it. Not tonight, though. That little bit of magic wouldn't work. Her brain was just too tired.

Sleep was in order. Definitely. But first she had to check her e-mail. She hadn't checked it since first thing this morning. After all, The Powers That Be might've suddenly decided the program should also be able to walk the cat and vacuum the goldfish. Stuff she'd rather worry about tonight, while she lost sleep, than be hit with in the morning when it was too late to develop a fitting argument against it all.

There was an e-mail from her boss with the simple subject line, "Oh Shit!" Gwen mentally picked up a fire extinguisher and looked at the message, figuring that regardless of how sleepy she was, she'd be able to fix this in a few minutes and avoid much needless freaking out. She glanced at the few words in the message and went to the Web link in it—a link to a recent article in a trade publication.

"Oh, shit," she said, reading the article. She rarely had time to read either the newspapers or the trade publications, but now she read this article, then ran over to her pile of unread publications and began searching through them, all thoughts of sleep and praise gone.

An hour later, after glancing through the trades, she went to her filing cabinet and frantically flipped through the files, but she couldn't find the ones she was looking for. She took a deep breath and started at the top of the cabinet and worked her way back through it, more slowly. Then she went through her in and out boxes and everything else on her desk.

The files were missing. She went out to her assistant's desk and did a quick search. She didn't feel right searching her stuff, but she needed those files.

She went into her office, closed the door, and dialed her assistant's number. When there was no answer, she left a simple message and hung up.

This simply couldn't be possible.

Allie suddenly sat up in bed, coming from a deep sleep. She had to go to the bathroom. She crawled from Brett's reassuring arms and got out of bed. Because of the bit of moonlight coming through the blinds, she didn't need to turn on the light. She had read somewhere that turning on lights would further awaken someone. Both herself and Brett, possibly.

Allie always knew that Brett was intelligent, courageous, and, beneath her black hat, good, but recently she was again questioning what Brett did for a living. Back when Allie was seventeen, Brett was a walk on the wild side, and Allie was just happy Brett didn't go near things like child pornography and prostitution.

Now Allie looked at her sleeping lover, in her forest green silk boxers and white T-shirt, wrapped around a pillow, and thought about how simple, serene, and innocent she looked. How wrong that image was—or perhaps how right it was. Brett tried to do the right thing, but still she went on managing the theatre and bookstores, and was even looking into further ways of making even more money from . . . well . . . pornography.

Allie knew many women danced for easy money, for drugs, for an escape . . . but still, Brett was enabling their behavior. But if she didn't, someone else would. And at least Brett tried to help those who wanted her help. Like Storm. Like Victoria.

Brett had raised herself above a crappy upbringing. But was what she was doing now really that good?

Allie knew Brett would blame all her new thoughts on the Women's Studies course she was taking, but Allie knew these questions had been brewing inside her head for a while. She went to the kitchen to heat up some milk to help her sleep, but decided that a Scotch would be easier.

Some of Brett's bad habits were making their mark on her.

Chapter Two

Day Two

Brett was sitting at her desk, feeling the thrumming of the music coming up through the floor from the theatre underneath where the noon show was in progress. She was feeling good and hot and cocky. She was feeling like Brett Higgins ought to feel.

She was ready to take on all the projects she had ideas for and just see how they'd end up. Get them up and running, and then keep the ones that were truly profitable. Of course, it wasn't great business judgment, but right now, it was sounding like a darned fine idea. At least it was better than the projected profit/expense analyses she was doing for each of the individual enterprises under consideration.

Her computer beeped at her, indicating she had an IM to distract her from her spreadsheet again. Chatting online with various women got her hot and made her feel like her old self again—her unhousebroken self, that is. Which probably wasn't a really good idea, all things considered.

Brett, dear God, I hope you're online!

Brett saw the screen name FemmeChick423 and smiled.

Yes, dear Gwen, I am.

She had been hoping Gwen would pop on at some point. She mostly ignored IMs from other girls, preferring to focus on work, but she always answered Gwen.

I hope you can help me. I'm in trouble.

Brett immediately sat bolt upright in her chair. Somehow, through the words they had exchanged online without ever meeting face-to-face, Brett had developed an attachment to this pretty, yet unknown woman.

How can I help?

She couldn't imagine anything happening to the dear, sweet femme she had spent so many hours chatting with.

I don't know. It might not be anything, but I'm scared.

Brett stared at the words. She didn't like the thought of Gwen being scared. It wasn't right, and it wasn't something Brett would allow.

Tell me. I know about a lot of things one should be scared of.

During their hours of cyber chat, they had shared thoughts, feelings, and all the stuff Brett could never tell anyone in real life. Somehow it was just easier online, without having the person be in your life, without having the person be able to judge you. It was easy with Gwen.

And telling these things to Gwen made it easier for Brett to slowly open up to Allie about some of the things, although after telling Gwen, Brett sometimes no longer felt the need to tell Allie. Which wasn't a good thing. It was like using the false courage of alcohol to numb sensations.

But for now, Brett waited for Gwen's reply.

Have to go now.

One thing Brett liked about Gwen was that she didn't use all the annoying euphemisms so many did online. No *U* for *you*, nor *R* for *are*. She actually IMed in complete, correctly spelled sentences.

But she sometimes also pulled away suddenly—and without explanation.

Brett leaned back in her chair, staring at the screen. She saw that Gwen had signed off. She wondered what was up. Gwen had never before sounded so . . . intense . . . had never before had such a problem.

She wondered what was going on.

She clicked over to review the last few e-mails Gwen had sent her. There was no indication of any brewing evil. She glanced over all the e-mails Gwen had sent her, looking for a few in particular.

She found the first she was searching for. She opened the attachment and waited in eager anticipation as her computer brought forth the first picture Brett had ever seen of Gwen.

Gwen had described herself, and what she had detailed sounded luscious, but Brett hadn't been ready to believe. Given her brief online experience, she became more convinced when the first picture Gwen sent was of herself fully clothed.

Brett now looked at that picture on her computer screen.

Gwen was simply looking up at the photographer, as if the picture had been a surprise. She appeared to be having fun. She was sitting at a table, a Kahlúa and cream or something similar in a glass in front of her; her soft, slender fingers lightly touching the glass. Condensation had formed on the side of it.

Gwen wore a red dress with spaghetti straps. Brett loved such thin straps when they were so obviously holding up a girl's dress. Not only did she find shoulders and collarbones incredibly sexy, but the idea of so little between her and seeing all of the woman was just a tease. It was like a slit up a skirt—a slit could show devilish hints of flesh while so much of the rest was covered. A slit could make a glimpse of firm leg seem forbidden. Like Brett was doing something illegal, which made it an especially tasty treat.

Thin straps had the same effect. Knowing that sliding these tiny pieces of fabric off of shoulders could uncover a girl just really did it for Brett. So little between her and paradise.

Gwen's dress in the picture also showed cleavage. Brett couldn't understand how so little could get her so hot. Cleavage was shown for a reason—to make the observer hot. The glimpse of cleavage was an extremely intimate act that Brett not only saw but felt as a heat washing over her.

Although Brett knew Gwen hadn't had all that in mind when the picture was taken, she knew Gwen had sent her this particular photo for a reason.

The next picture was one Gwen had taken of herself, with a timer she insisted, when Brett had repeatedly asked her for more pictures. Brett had asked because she wanted to see more of Gwen's life, but Gwen had taken this request somewhat differently than Brett's intention.

In the picture, Gwen posed naked, though she'd covered all her private parts by sitting on the couch with her legs up next to her and her arms crossed over her chest.

Brett got heated up over the first picture, and this one had her studying the curves of Gwen's body and imagining what was hidden. She also imagined what it would be like to stroke that soft flesh with her fingertips . . .

She wanted to feel that woman beneath her.

Brett reminded herself that Gwen's hair looked bleached blonde. She wasn't a true blonde.

Brett had a fatal attraction for femme blonde Scorpios, and Gwen was all of the above, even if she had to fake part of it.

But in the final picture, the picture Brett didn't get until they had been chatting and e-mailing for more than two months, the photo Gwen had insisted had been taken for Brett and Brett only, Gwen was again seated on her couch, but this time she had parted her thighs slightly, proving Brett's assumption that she wasn't a true blonde, and she didn't cross her arms over her chest.

That she looked a bit awkward in the photo made her all the more endearing and believable to Brett.

Brett looked at this picture and her eyes wandered over the full, pouty mouth; down the smooth, soft shoulders that begged for her lips. She knew the smallish but pert breasts would be soft in her hands, and she just wanted to feel every part of this woman and kiss her way across the silky skin until she was on her knees between Gwen's legs, running her hands over Gwen's beautiful body, feeling its softness, and always being able to look up into Gwen's green eyes as Gwen's breathing deepened and became ragged.

She wanted to make Gwen love her.

At that thought, Brett stood up and ran her hand back through her short, black hair. She paced her office like a caged animal. She felt like a caged animal.

She shouldn't feel like that. She loved Allie and really did want to spend the rest of her life with her. Oh, God. It had been so long since she had thought that. It sent a shiver up her spine. She was scared. She had only ever loved, and been loved by, four people in her life—Allie, Frankie, Storm, and Rick, and two of those people were now dead. Probably because of her.

She was afraid of getting Allie killed. She was afraid of hurting Allie, but she knew she would, eventually. She was a bad guy, and she'd screw up this love like she had the others.

And being loved for more than just a night scared the living bejesus out of her.

She poured herself a Scotch and looked at the computer screen, at the three images of Gwen. She studied them and realized that . . .

. . . well, no . . .

. . . but it was . . .

It was almost as if Gwen could read her mind. Over the past few months/years/decades, Brett had realized that naked women didn't do it for her. Or at least, not just any naked woman.

It used to be that the sight of so much nude female flesh would take her breath away, but then, when she had spent so much time in the pornography industry, after so much time around naked women, she realized it took a bit more to get her engine running. She could now look at a naked woman inches from her and not flinch.

It was either feelings and emotions or teasing and imagination that got her motor running these days. She suddenly realized how slightly teasing clothing—like cleavage, bare shoulders, and slits in skirts—could get her going more than a full-nude assault could.

She closed the nude pictures and stared only at the one of Gwen looking up at the photographer, then sat down to write an e-mail.

Gwen,

Let me know what's going on. If you're in trouble, let me know. After all, I'm only 1.5 hours away from you.

Brett

When she hit Send, she realized just how close in proximity they were. How easy it would be to check up on Gwen. After all, Brett had already told Allie she'd have to go back up to Lansing, the state's capital, to get the business licenses for any new endeavors she might take up. She'd had to go up there a few times lately in order to research various aspects of her possible new business ventures.

But then she realized how little she knew of this girl. This woman. She hit the Home button on her Web browser, and then plugged in +"Gwen Cartwright" and put her mouse over the Search button.

While the browser searched, she went back to her spreadsheet.

Over the next several hours she kept looking and refining her search results. She found out a bit about Gwen, and it all fit with what Gwen had told her. Gwen had been telling the truth. She was who she said she was, lived where she said she lived . . . that is, if it wasn't someone else pretending to be Gwen. But everything in the trade journals confirmed what she had said.

Gwen ran her hands back through her hair. She would rip it out if she could. But she'd be sorry for it because she was rather fond of her long blonde locks.

The bugs were driving her nuts, as was the idea that a competitor was so close to them—without her knowing!

She just needed some time away to work all this out. It had started crashing down around her ears last night, but she had been too exhausted to really pay attention.

Now she just needed time and space to work it all out.

She went to her car, figuring she needed to get out, but couldn't spend much time away. She just needed the light of day to dispel all her fears. So a drive-thru would do. Besides, she did need to eat.

But as soon as she walked out to the parking lot, she felt as if someone was watching her. She dismissed the feeling, simply putting it off as paranoia. She was working on a project, one that no one else could know about, one that was so secret she had to hide it from everyone else.

There was a great deal at stake here, the least of which was her 401(k).

She told herself no one knew, and no one was spying on her. But she kept looking in her rearview mirror, and a car *was* following her.

Whoever it was might be going wherever she was going. Not surprising. It was lunch hour after all.

She checked her mirrors and quickly traveled across two lanes of traffic to pull into a fast-food restaurant. The car pulled into the lot just beyond and the driver didn't get out. It was as if he was waiting for her. Watching her.

Gwen pulled out of the drive-thru lane to haul ass out of the parking lot.

Her tail picked her up.

No way could this be coincidence.

Gwen knew she needed a public place. She headed for Okemos. There was a nice, indoor mall there. Gwen needed an indoor mall with lots of witnesses. In a suburb. Things were noticed more quickly and easily in the suburbs. Trouble was dealt with out there.

The car followed her.

She cruised around the lot, trying to find a parking space as close to the entrance as possible. She wanted to be able to immediately run into the security of a lot of people. She slammed into a spot, shut off her engine and fled toward the mall, locking her car and stuffing the keys into her purse en route.

"Almost there," she murmured to herself under her breath. Then she felt a hand on her arm.

She screamed.

"June?" the man said. "Oh my God, June Cunningham! It's been years!"

Breathing heavily, she pulled away from him. "I'm sorry, you have me confused with someone else."

~

I don't know who else I can turn to. I know I've told you that I want to meet you, but this isn't merely a ploy. I need help, and you're the only friend I can think of who might be able to help. And God knows I need help.

I think somebody's trying to kill me.

And no, I don't know who; and no, I don't know why.

Please say you'll meet me.

Love,

Gwen

Brett quickly typed her response:

When and where?

And then she waited. She continued filling in her paperwork, developing the schedule for the dancers for the next month and calling them up to ensure they didn't have a scheduling conflict.

She then called Allie. Thankful she got the machine, she left a message saying she would have to run up to Lansing. If not today, then within the next few days. She'd try to do it all in one night this time.

The last time she'd gone to Lansing, she'd had to stay overnight at some hotel because she had been snowed in. The day had seemed fine and clear earlier, but it was Michigan, so the weather could change quicker than a femme could change her mind.

She hoped she could help Gwen without having to spend the night. She knew she couldn't be trusted around the woman for long.

It was when she was calling her suppliers to place orders for all the bookstores and the theatre that her computer chimed, indicating she had new mail. She was on the phone with Geri at a new lesbian sex-toy distributor (only lesbians would ever combine toys with music!) when it went off. She flipped over to her e-mail and said to Geri, "I'm sorry, Ger, gotta go. I'll call you back if I need anything else."

"I'm serious, Brett, you oughta lay in a good supply of these strap-on dildos. Nobody else offers one with a butt plug, and I know they're gonna be a hit! Imagine being able to do your girl in both places at once."

"I'll keep that in mind, Ger. At the very least, I might get one just for me."

"Yeah, I'll bet, Brett. I know you'd like this one."

I'm tied up here at work until at least 6. Can you do 8 at the Hilton in downtown Lansing? I need to see you as soon as possible, but

I don't want to keep you waiting because I know somebody will want to keep me late after that last meeting.

Brett, I am so grateful for you even considering this.

If you can help me, I will do just about anything for you.

Gwen

Brett looked at her Day Runner, then typed back:

Done. Wear red so I'll recognize you. Though I know I'd recognize you in Pooh sleepers (complete with footies).

Brett knew all the horror stories about meeting people from online, but she figured she was the one they should be afraid of. After all, she'd be packing her .357. She could take care of herself.

Chapter Three

Brett picked up the phone to leave Allie another message. Unfortunately, this time Allie picked up.

"Hey, hon, turns out I do have to go to Lansing tonight," Brett said, looking over the to-do list she kept on a legal pad by her computer. She was looking for any reason to explain her trip to Lansing.

"I hope you're not planning on getting snowed in up there again."

Brett glanced out at the clear sky. "I don't think there's any chance of that, babe." About the only months you could guarantee it wouldn't snow in Michigan were June, July, and August. But today looked safe.

"What's so important that you've suddenly got to take care of anyway? Wouldn't it make more sense to head up first thing in the morning so you can just do everything in one day?"

"It's only an hour, hour-and-a-half drive—"

"Hour-and-a-half if you drive the speed limit."

"Since when do I do that?"

"So what do you need to do anyway?"

Brett sighed. "Harry from New York is in town. He got in earlier, and his dinner appointment canceled on him, so I've got a chance to pick his brain." She hoped Allie would buy this lie.

"Like he's going to help you become a competitor."

"Give him a few drinks and he'll give me the keys to his warehouse and a truck to haul the stuff."

Allie laughed because she knew how true it was. Harry ran his father's business, producing adult magazines and videos. "I don't see how he stays in business the way he is."

"It's only with us that he has more than one or two. It's our golden touch, babe. Either that or your long legs." Harry had been really hitting on Allie the last time they got together.

"So shouldn't I go with you?"

"Oh, do you want to?" Brett was counting on Allie's reawakened feminist consciousness to stop her. And the fact that she had always hated getting ogled by males.

Allie paused. "Not really."

Brett knew Allie wanted to know for sure whether Harry was involved with the Mafia in New York, but also didn't like how the jerk acted. She kept telling Brett not to worry because she could take care of herself, but Brett knew she'd really like to see Brett twist the bastard's dick in a vise. So she switched the subject so Allie wouldn't change her mind. "Geri's got some new toys she wants to show me, so I figured I'd meet with her first, then maybe stop by the capital to look into a few more licensing questions I have, and—"

"Why don't you just get a lawyer to look into all of that for you? Wouldn't it save you a lot of time and trouble?"

"Yeah, but I don't trust lawyers. They're evil. When it gets down to it, I'll get one. I just want to know what I'm talking about so I'm not just relying on some uptight little lump of slime. Too many people rely too heavily on lawyers. I prefer knowing about things myself, and just use them for the fancy language." She never signed a contract, or any dotted line for that matter, without reading everything first.

"Okay. So go. You would anyway. In fact, you were probably hoping just to get the machine and leave me another message, weren't you?"

"Um, yeah, well . . ."

"Just don't drink and drive."

"You know me, babe. Good little law-abiding citizen here."

"Now."

Brett grinned. "Yeah, now." When she and Allie first met, Brett didn't stick strictly to the right side of the law, and even these days she didn't all the time either. The difference now was that when she broke the law, it was for a reason Allie could understand—like stopping bad people from doing bad things. After all, Brett was good at dealing with trouble. She handled things—that was part of who she was.

"Brett?"

"Yes, dear?"

"Are you cheating on me?"

Brett laughed. "No, I'm not. I haven't slept with another woman since we got back together." She hoped a little white lie like that wouldn't count too much against her in the overall balance of things.

"Are you sure?"

"Positive. You're the one I love."

Brett hated herself when they hung up. She wanted to call Allie back and tell her the truth—that a friend was in trouble and she had to help her. But she knew she couldn't answer all the questions Allie would have about who Gwen was, and why Brett needed to help her.

Although she kept justifying to herself that cyber wasn't cheating, she knew she didn't really believe that, and she couldn't bring Allie even further into the seedier aspects of her life.

She knew she had to help Gwen, and that she loved Allie and didn't want to lose her again, but she couldn't help but remember her feelings and thoughts when she cybered with Gwen. She wanted to know what Gwen was really like, and just what her skin tasted and felt like. She hoped she could control the second part of her urges, and just have Gwen as a friend. Besides, Gwen was a successful corporate type—someone that Allie supposedly aspired to be, living a nice, normal life—something that Allie wanted.

Brett used to want the same thing, but now she knew that was never meant to be for her. She sat back and remembered one of her IMs with Gwen . . .

I love necks, collarbones . . . I love off-the-shoulder dresses that show off those things . . .

I love wearing those things. I don't often, but with you . . .

Would you wear them?

Yes.

Would it be just for me?

There was a pause, and then Gwen typed:

Yes and no. It would be for both of us. I wear suits to work. But I'd like to feel like a woman again, and I'd like to feel like a woman for you.

I'd make you my woman.

I know you would.

You want to be controlled and taken, don't you?

Yes, Brett, yes . . .

I see you across a crowded room, and slowly undress you with my eyes . . .

Yes . . . I see you.

I walk toward you, my eyes glued to yours. Looking right at you.

Yes.

In this crowded room I come to you. I pull you into my arms . . . pulling you into me . . . bringing our lips together . . .

I am yours.

I kiss you. I pull you into my arms, pulling our bodies together as one. My leg is between yours, I am pushing you against a wall, grinding into you . . .

Brett . . . I want you.

I reach up under your dress, slipping my fingers into your panties . . . and I feel how wet you are.

Oh, God, Brett. I want you inside me . . .

I slide my fingers into you. Becoming one with you. Are you naked yet?

No . . .

Take off your clothes. All of them.

Brett, I can't. I mean . . .

There's no one there, is there?

No. I'm alone.

Then strip. I want you naked, now. Take off your clothes, and tell me what you see. Look in a mirror.

{Pause}

I'm naked.

Read this, then do it. I want you to go to a mirror and open yourself up. Imagine that I'm there with you. That you are doing it for me.

Brett shook her head, pulling herself out of the reverie. From all she knew, she had helped Gwen to many a climax, giving her every fantasy she never even acknowledged or knew she desired.

And it all made Brett feel like such a fucking stud.

And she liked the feeling.

"So, she's on her way up here?" the man said, sitting back in his chair and toying briefly with the dark hair on the sides of his head. She hated his pretentious haircut. He had done it just to look like some TV star—short and spiked on top, short on the sides. She bet he used a gallon of hair gel every day.

She looked at her watch. "I'm not sure if she's en route yet, but if she isn't, she will be soon," she replied as she ran a hand through her long, blonde locks.

"I can't believe she's fallen for everything just like you said she would," the brunette woman said, taking a sip of her coffee.

"I told you I knew her," the blonde said. "We just have to make sure everything goes according to plan tonight. Are you two ready?"

"Like a hooker picking up a trick in a Jag," the man replied.

The blonde stared across the table at him. "I don't appreciate such remarks."

"Hey, I was just trying to be colorful."

"We'll be ready on our end," the brunette said, her hand going up to her eyebrow. The blonde had noticed that this woman often unconsciously fingered the small, almost unnoticeable scar that crossed her impeccably plucked eyebrow right in the center. She also knew her ex-boyfriend had given her that scar when they were dating. She wasn't sure, but she guessed the incident involved an argument and a beer bottle.

"Will you be on yours?" the man asked.

"I've been ready for this for months. You don't know what a pain in the ass this has all been. I'll just be glad when it's all over." The blonde smirked, shaking her head over some of what she had done to get to this point. She never would have believed how much fun it had actually been. It was amusing to lead on the prey.

"It'll be over soon, and we'll all be a lot richer," the man said. "Just don't screw it up tonight. We so cannot afford to screw anything up now."

The blonde sat back in her chair. Each time the three of them got together, they met at a different cheap diner. They didn't want anyone to remember seeing them together at any point. Or all going to a particular house. "She's so stupid, playing right into my hand like this. It's so fucking unbelievable."

"Hey, I don't like the way you're talking—it's like you can't believe it. And that means you're not sure tonight'll go like you figure, either."

"It'll be fine. She's done everything to script so far, and she won't change now. Remember, I knew right from the get-go exactly what she'd do at every stage. It just disgusts me that she has. But now that we're here, it's unquestionable that she'll continue merrily along."

After the blonde left, the man and the brunette met again at a rather sordid bar. "Are you sure we can trust her?" the woman asked.

"What do you think?"

"It worries me that she's even questioning . . . anything."

"Right now, nothing can be blamed on us. We're still free and clear. What should we do?"

"It's scary."

"But we're in this for the big payoff, which is still to come. We want the money, we gotta hang in there, and see this thing through."

"But can we trust her? Not only trust her, but trust everything she thinks is gonna happen?"

"What I think is this: We watch our own backs. If something starts to go wrong, we make sure she takes the fall. All this shit is just to make sure her own ass is covered. I don't give a crap about that. But right now, she's the one who holds all the cards, so we gotta go with it and play along with her little game."

The woman again fingered the scar in her eyebrow that the man across the table had given her. "I have to admit, it's all gone exactly like she said it would. I just don't like that she was so . . . so amazed tonight about it all. It makes me uneasy."

"Remember, right now we're just covering her ass. We're playing along for the money, but we gotta do just what she's doing—cover our own asses. If anything goes wrong, she's the one who's gotta pay."

The woman grinned at him, wanting to reach across the table and take his hands. She restrained herself. "But we'll take our share of the money."

"Oh yeah. That's what we're in this for, anyway. Just follow my lead and listen to what I say."

Chapter Four

She stepped out of the shower, running her hands through her wet hair, drawing it back from her face. She picked up the hair dryer and put it on the lowest setting, carefully drying her hair around her comb, wanting to coax subtle curls into just the right places.

When she was done, she critically assessed the results in the mirror before carefully spritzing a light perfume in a few key areas, including on her neck and wrists. Then she pulled silk stockings up her legs and attached them to a garter before putting on the dress she had bought for this occasion, letting it drape gently over her body. She'd not bothered with underwear.

After all, she didn't want any panty lines. She smirked at her own funny, knowing the real reasons she was going without underwear.

The red silk fell over her curves like a second skin. It felt nice, good, sexy. She slid her hand from the neckline, which exposed just a teasing hint of cleavage, down over her ribs and to her hip. She liked the way it felt, and was sure others would as well. But there was just one other person she wanted it to feel good to.

She carefully applied light makeup, making sure to use mascara to draw more attention to her already long lashes. When she was finished, she looked in the mirror to assess the results and was pleased.

Her shoes were next. She knew she needed a thin, long heel to draw special attention to her legs. She finally decided on four-inch black heels to play into her black stockings.

The dress's spaghetti straps drew attention to her shoulders and cleavage and yet gave an air of vulnerability, and although the skirt went down nearly to her knees, it had a slit up to her hip, and she wanted to draw attention to that. She thought the stockings and heels did that.

But she needed the finishing touches. She carefully selected a light gold cross and a bracelet. When she brought her arms back to fasten the necklace around her neck, she sniffed the perfume she had applied on her wrists and then the body wash she used. She was suddenly glad she so carefully selected her scents.

She assessed herself in the mirror, pulling her hair back over one shoulder, and liked the way she looked. She was sexy, she was hot, and she could have her pick tonight.

And she knew just whom she wanted.

As a final thought, she added a gold anklet to her left ankle, and then picked up her purse and went to her rendezvous, almost wishing she could have as much fun as she wanted tonight.

Brett walked into the hotel bar and glanced around. It was filled mostly with traveling businessmen, the kind she knew all too well from her work at the theatre and her other establishments. Men traveled on business and got their rocks off in whatever way they could.

The few women in the bar, some of whom Brett knew were professionals, were surrounded by men. But still, the bar wasn't crowded. She noticed some guy leaning over one of the booths, and wondered briefly who he was cruising, especially since there were no other guys there. Either it was someone uninteresting or . . .

As the fellow stood up, Brett closed in and noticed the red dress the woman was wearing. It wasn't so much what it covered as what it revealed that caught Brett's attention. When the man walked away, Brett could see the teasing slit up the woman's left leg, and she stared at that limb, all the way down to the woman's gold anklet.

When she looked up, she realized the woman was staring at her. Probably wondering if she was whom she was waiting for, maybe even trying to figure out if she was male or female. Brett met her eyes, dropped her head a bit to the left, and grinned. The woman matched the photos, and was wearing red. Brett had been trying to prepare herself for Gwen wearing Pooh sleepers with footies, but the reality took her breath away.

The woman didn't look away. Brett stood tall and made her way to the booth. She bowed her head slightly, and looked into her eyes. "The fair Lady Gwendolyn, I presume?"

Gwen smiled at her. "Brett Higgins?"

Brett sat down across from her and signaled for a waiter. It was an art she had perfected through the years—getting a waiter to notice her in a crowded bar. "The one and only," Brett said, pulling out a Marlboro Light, which she played with for a few moments. She let the predator out, and slowly undressed Gwen with her eyes, imagining pushing those thin straps from her arms and drawing the simple piece of material down. Then she met Gwen's eyes, letting her know what she could do to her tonight, if Gwen wanted.

"How did you know my name was Gwendolyn?"

"I looked you up on the Net." She looked up at the waiter. "I'll take a Glen on the rocks, and another of whatever she's having." She sat back, pulled out her Zippo (It was gold with a devil on it. Some woman had given it to her, though she couldn't remember which one.), lit her cigarette, and noticed the cross that lay between Gwen's breasts. "You didn't think I'd just take you at your word, did you?" She met Gwen's eyes. "After all, you hear all sorts of horror stories about what happens when people meet on the Internet." She knew a lot of femmes who enjoyed having their attributes noticed, but you should never stare at them. Notice the attributes, then meet their eyes.

Gwen smiled at her. "As if you'd ever have anything to worry about."

Brett shrugged. "I figured we'd be meeting in a public place, but since you were so . . . discreet . . . about your problems, I decided it would be in my best interest to know a bit more about you. The trade journals and local papers are rather fond of you."

Gwen looked down at the table. "I just do my job, and I do it well."

"So I've noticed." The waiter placed their drinks in front of them. Brett handed him some cash. "Come back when we need more." Once he'd left, she looked across the table at Gwen. She always paid with cash to leave no trace of her being somewhere. She reached across the table to pry Gwen's hand from her drink and take it into her own. "What's the problem?"

"I told you: I think someone's trying to kill me."

"Why do you think this?" Brett had let her inner romance-sex monkey loose, but she knew she had to restrain herself. She was here on a mission, to solve a problem. She needed to help this woman.

"I'm in charge of a very important project at work. I'm a software engineer, and we're developing a new program that could be worth millions, even billions. The other night, after we got done chatting, I checked my e-mail one last time before leaving work. I saw an article that showed one of our competitors seems to be working on a similar product, and might even be able to get it to market before we do."

"Okay, I'm with you so far. You didn't know anyone else was working on it?"

"There was no reason to think it. It was all my idea. I'm leading this project, and it's a royal pain, but we're just about to hit beta phase . . . Do you know what beta testing is?"

"It's . . . well, like a test run of a new program?"

"Yes. Anyway, earlier today, I went out to lunch, really needing some air and sunlight to get my brain working again. I thought I could just roll down my windows, go through a drive-thru, pick up some lunch, and feel much better."

"So what happened?"

"I saw someone following me. So I pulled around the drive-thru and back out onto Michigan, and, well, basically drove like a bat out of hell."

"Were you being followed?" Brett knew Michigan was a major thoroughfare in Lansing and East Lansing.

"Yes. I mean, whoever it was pulled up into the parking lot just beyond the B.K. I had pulled into, and when I pulled out, he did, too. He followed me all the way to Okemos, where I went to the mall."

Brett sat back for a moment, studying the beautiful woman who sat across from her. She knew B.K. stood for Burger King—after all, she used to work for Mickey D's in high school . . . and she didn't like to think of her father's reaction the first time she had called McDonald's Mickey D's, so she looked up from where she was running her fingers over her glass of Glenfiddich and into the seductive paradise of Gwen's eyes. "You thought it was a good time to start your Christmas shopping?"

"Well, no. I thought an indoor mall in the suburbs was the best place to stay safe."

"Good thinking."

"Some guy stopped me on my way into the mall."

"What happened?"

"He thought I was someone else. He might've saved my life, though. While we spoke, I saw the car that was following me cruising around, so I managed to have this man walk me into the mall. I IMed you from the Internet café inside."

Brett stared down at the ice in her glass, absently rubbing the condensation along the outside. She looked up and into Gwen's eyes. "So why would someone want to kill you?"

Gwen put her head into her hands. "I thought if anyone would believe me, it would be you."

Brett reached across the table and placed one of her hands on Gwen's. "I didn't say I didn't believe you. If I'm gonna figure this out, I have to know the whole story. I need to know what's going on."

"Brett, we've talked a lot between the lines online, but I think I know a bit about you, just like you know something about me. I think we understand each other."

Their hands dropped down to the table, still entwined. "Yes, I think so."

"Mostly these days you hear about CEOs going bad and such, companies going under and all that, but . . . I'm working on . . . I'm in charge of . . . developing a new product worth an awful lot of money. A competitor is neck and neck with us on it. A competitor I didn't know about two days ago. If we're both about to go into beta testing on it, getting rid of me will ensure that they will make it to market first."

Brett had read about such things as corporate espionage, and in fact, she knew about people killing others over much smaller things than millions—perhaps billions—of dollars. This was entirely possible. She had been totally disgusted by the headlines of late, those that told what CEOs got away with.

"I hate to say this, but . . . I'm not sure what I can do about this. It's really not my territory, or neighborhood. This isn't what I know."

Gwen grasped her hands more tightly. "I didn't know who else to contact. Who else to ask. I mean, all my friends are business people."

"And what do you think I am?"

Gwen blushed at this. She actually blushed! "I know you're in business. But . . . you seem so self-assured, so knowledgeable. You seem street smart. I'm a computer geek. I work for computer geeks—well, that and clueless white collar types. You're the only person I knew who might be able to give me any sort of advice about this." She caressed Brett's hand. "Plus, I wanted to meet you."

They separated when the waiter brought fresh drinks. Brett

absentmindedly handed him more cash. She was totally taken with the woman a few feet from her. She needed a few moments to collect herself.

"Please excuse me," Brett said, standing. "I'll be right back."

Brett went to the bathroom, garnering a few strange looks from women when she went into the ladies' room. She quickly did her business, then splashed cold water on her face and dried herself off. She wet her fingers and fixed her hair, checking out her tie and the diamond stud in her ear in the mirror.

She looked good.

Gwen was examining her face in her compact when Brett returned. She quickly snapped it shut and slid it into her purse when Brett approached.

Brett slid in opposite her, picked up her glass, cradling it between her hands. She wanted to make love with Gwen, but knew she shouldn't. She wanted to turn everything they had gone through online into reality, especially with how sexy Gwen looked tonight, and with how unsure of herself she had been feeling. "What do you want me to do?"

"Tell me what I should do. From our conversations . . . well . . ." Gwen looked away, as if she was trying not to think about the intimacy of their conversations. "You seem like a woman who knows how to handle herself in any situation. You seem to know what to do in dangerous situations."

"I can handle myself," Brett said, taking another sip of Scotch. "Have you thought about hiring a bodyguard?"

"I'd feel ridiculous," Gwen replied, leaning forward against the table so Brett had a nice view of her cleavage. "Tell me, am I overreacting?"

"I can't tell you that. I've known people to kill for much less."

Gwen sat up and looked around. "You know, I feel much safer with you here. I mean, I still look around, and worry, but I know you can protect me." She leaned forward and looked deep into Brett's eyes. "I know what you can do. I know what you're capable of."

Brett tried to blow it off. "Well, yes, with me here, you don't have to worry. I've been in some situations before . . ."

"Tell me, are you armed right now?"

"Excuse me?"

"I'm sorry." She released Brett's hands and focused on her drink, some sort of frothy, fruity thing. "From everything you've said, I just thought, maybe . . . Well, I mean, I've thought you'd be good at fighting, but I also thought . . ."

Brett reached across the table and took Gwen's hands back into her own. "You're safe with me."

"I do feel safe with you."

That was Brett. The big, strong protector. That was who she was. Who she was meant to be. After all she had been through, it was a role she knew how to play.

"Even before . . . the past few days . . . I wasn't feeling safe. But now I do. I know this might sound silly, but chatting with you online over the past few months, I feel as if I know the real you—including the parts you hide from so many. Who you really are. And though I have to fill in some blanks, and sometimes look you up online—"

"You've looked me up online?"

"You didn't think you were the only one who Googled, did you?" Gwen asked coyly.

Brett smiled softly and drained her glass. The waiter was there with a fresh one a few moments later, but he turned and left before Brett paid him. She got up and handed him some cash, then returned to the table. Gwen was still smiling. "I like a woman with brains," Brett said.

Brett felt Gwen's stocking-clad foot sliding up her pant leg. "Maybe just feeling safe for one night would make things a lot better."

"Either there is, or there isn't, a problem. Me being here makes no difference."

"It does. There is a problem, but you make me feel safe. I really don't think anyone is going to try anything with you here." She ran her hand up Brett's arm, seeming to enjoy the feel of the muscles there.

Brett ran a hand through Gwen's hair. She wasn't feeling all that well, in fact, she was really tired. But she had to get home tonight to Allie. This was only her third drink . . . when was the last time she ate? God, didn't getting older suck? She needed more sleep than she used to, and had to eat more, and sleep more . . .

"You don't look too good," Gwen said, sliding into her side of the booth, so their thighs pressed together.

"Just suddenly very tired . . . Don't I know you from somewhere?" Suddenly, Gwen seemed very familiar from somewhere before . . . but Brett couldn't place . . .

"Why don't you come up to my room?"

" . . . need to get home . . ."

"You can't drive like this."

"Why do you have a room anyway? Don't you have an apartment . . . don't you live near here?"

"I didn't feel safe there."

Brett let herself be led from the booth. She tried to hold herself upright, though she kept her eyes closed a lot so things didn't swivel and spin quite so much. Gwen led her. She trusted Gwen.

After all, Gwen wanted her help.

"She's just had a bit too much to drink," she heard Gwen say.

"I'm fine. Just going upstairs with Allie . . . Gwen . . ."

"Ssshhh, baby," Allie . . . no Gwen . . . whispered to her. "Maybe you're coming down with something."

" . . . didn't drink enough to . . . where are we?"

"We're just going up to my room. You can lie down there."

"Just for a moment. I need to get home to Gwen. No. Allie. I'm with Allie."

"I know, baby. Don't worry, you'll get home to her." Then again, to someone else, "She's just had a bit too much to drink."

Her hands were so soft. Time wasn't right, it was . . . floating. Whoever she was. It was. Time. Yeah.

Brett heard there was only one bed, and she was okay with that, since it was soft. And the hands on her body were soft, too.

It was so nice, and she felt herself slipping away . . . not having to move or do anything was so nice . . .

Soft. Oh so soft. And silky. Brett's hands had their own mind. They roamed of their own free will. She thought about opening her eyes, but didn't want to lose this moment. Some moments were meant to be savored, like those pre-dawn barely awake moments.

Allie was naked. Brett liked it when she slept naked, and only on occasion let her crawl into bed wearing anything but maybe a necklace (crosses were so sexy between naked breasts). Tonight she was naked. Brett caressed her body, gently exploring her curves, feeling her and wanting her.

She wasn't even fully awake yet and she was horny. She wanted Allie. Now.

She ran her hand over the curve of Allie's ass, urging from her a low groan. Hearing that, she moved Allie's arm to the side to expose her breasts. Brett pulled down the covers and started to lightly run her fingers over them, gradually arousing the nipples to hardness.

Brett continued with her gentle ministrations until Allie was rolling over to meet her touches, and urging her to do more.

Allie was still asleep, and Brett was enjoying it.

Brett's hand dove down into the curls between Allie's legs, enjoying the wetness that was there.

Brett liked making her woman wet.

Dressed in silk boxers and a T-shirt, Brett crawled on top of Allie and their lips met. She spread Allie's legs, pushing her body into hers. Allie's arms twisted around her neck, pulling her mouth in closer.

But the kiss was . . . different. It was nice, but . . . different.

The body was nice, too, but . . . different.

Brett pushed down her boxers, pulling out the large dildo she was packing. She touched Allie between her legs, feeling her slickness, feeling how wet she was, wondering if she needed lube.

She didn't. Allie could take her. She marked Allie's neck, sucking and biting even as she pushed up into her woman, as she became one with her. And then she rode her like a pony. Allie's hips were bucking beneath hers, as she slid in and out, as she penetrated her, became one with her.

Allie held on to her, forcing her in and out, taking her, accepting her, keeping her legs wide . . . sucking her neck and sliding her hands under Brett's T-shirt to scratch her back . . . She clawed her back, riding the points between pleasure and pain, drawing blood, making Brett cry out . . .

And Brett loved every moment of it.

Allie slammed the phone down. It was two in the morning and Brett still wasn't home, nor was she answering her cell or pager. Allie knew how Harry liked to drink, and knew how Brett liked to drink. So maybe she should be happy that Brett wasn't drunk and driving.

Or maybe she should just be hoping that Brett wasn't dead or in a hospital somewhere. She really hoped Brett wouldn't drink and drive.

But still, she couldn't shake the feeling that Brett had been hiding something all along. Brett was up to no good. She was with some other woman.

No, hope that Brett isn't hurt or worse.

Allie leaned her head against the wall and stared at the phone, trying to decide. Then she picked up the phone and dialed again. The phone rang and rang.

After the ninth ring it was answered.

"Yeah?" a man answered groggily.

"Frankie?"

"Allie? That you? Wazzup?"

"It's Brett. She's not answering anything and I don't know where she is!"

"Didn't she go up to Lansing?"

"Yes, she did. But she didn't call me to tell me she was spending the night or anything!"

"Allie, calm down, this is Brett we're talking 'bout. She's fine."

"Then why hasn't she called me?" she nearly whispered.

Suddenly, Frankie sounded very alert, and Allie felt very bad for waking him. "I'll find her and let you know. Keep your line open."

Allie hung up the phone and leaned her forehead against the wall. She didn't want anyone to know how worried she was about Brett—how much she was sure Brett was hiding things from her—especially Frankie. Why couldn't Kurt have picked up the phone? Why couldn't she have spoken with Kurt? Kurt knew what it was like to try to train a wild animal. He and she could relate to each other. After all, he was with Frankie.

Allie was worried. Part of her feared that Brett was dead or injured, but another part, the larger part, dreaded that she was in bed with another woman.

Allie wasn't sure which would be easier to live with.

When Frankie called back about an hour later, he hadn't learned anything. "I tried all the usual places, and nobody's seen or heard from her all night. Nobody at the bookstores, theatres, or anyplace knows anything. And she's not answering her cell or pager. I've checked with some friends, and she ain't in no hospital or morgue, either."

"I already knew most of that." Allie was relieved to find out that she wasn't in the hospital or worse.

"So you said she was goin' up to Lansing."

"Yeah, that's what she said."

"Did she say why?"

"She said she was meeting with Harry—"

"I didn't know he was in town."

"That's what she told me."

Frankie chuckled. "Okay, so you know how much Harry likes drinking and all that."

"Yeah, I know how he gets."

"And you know how Brett can get, too."

"Yeah, I do."

"So Brett probably got drunk and is finally doing something smart and spending the night up there. Tell you what, if we ain't heard anything by mornin', then I'll get worried. I mean, she wouldn't want to call and wake you, or even admit she'd gotten toasted."

"You're probably right, Frankie."

"Or she just coulda had car trouble, and she wouldn't want to bug you with that either. Or admit that she couldn't fix it herself, 'kay?"

Allie allowed a slight smile to touch her lips. Brett really wouldn't want to admit that she couldn't fix a car.

"It could be nothing, okay?"

Or it could be everything. "Yeah, okay, Frankie. You're right. I'll call you in the morning if she's still not here."

"Hang on a sec, Al," Frankie said.

Kurt came on the line. "Girlfriend, are you going to be able to get any sleep tonight? Should we come over?"

"No, Kurt, I'm sure I'll be fine."

"Well, drink some warm milk. It's really good if you mix in some almond syrup, but you have to be careful heating it up so it doesn't burn—but it'll put you right to sleep."

"I will."

"And if you have anything like valerian, or Tylenol PM, that'd be good, too."

"Thank you."

Kurt lowered his voice to a whisper, "Baby, Frankie's probably right—she's just drunk and playing it smart for a change. She's passed out cold, alone, in a hotel room."

"I hope so, Kurt. I really do."

Chapter Five

Day Three

Allie woke up with a ringing in her head. Oh, the phone. It was ringing.

"Yuh?" she said, answering the phone.

"It's Frankie."

Allie immediately shot awake and looked at the vacant spot next to her in bed. "She's not here."

"Let me know if you hear anything, and I'll do the same."

" 'Kay."

Light. Way too much light. Brett rolled over and flung an arm over her eyes, trying to keep it out. That didn't work too well, so she rolled over and burrowed under the pillows and blankets. She curled up next to Allie, flinging an arm around her.

Allie was kind of cold. And sticky.

Brett felt rather haggard, hazy, and lazy. Basically, she felt as if she'd had incredible sex the night before. She grinned when she remembered that she had. She didn't remember using oils or playing with food, so why was Allie all sticky? Usually Allie was dead set against using anything sticky in the bed. "I am not a plate," was something she often said. The few times she did allow such things in bed, she immediately showered and changed the sheets after, saying she couldn't sleep with everything sticking to her.

Brett's mind was drifting, phasing in and out. She couldn't focus. It also seemed as if she'd had too much to drink the night before. She had a pounding in her head, and her stomach wasn't quite right.

Hold on. When had she gotten home? The last thing she remembered was the sex. Fabulous, orgasmic, mind-fucking-blowing sex. God, it had been incredible.

But . . . before that . . . before that . . . How had she gotten home? She had met Gwen at the bar, they had drinks, and then . . . things got blurry.

She raised herself up and forced open her eyes.

She felt her heart leap into her throat.

Most of Gwen's head was blown away. Blood and brain tissue covered the pillows, blankets, wall, as well as both their bodies. Brett could only see a few strands of blonde hair through all the mess.

Brett leapt from the bed, shaking so hard she dropped the .357 in her hand so it landed with a thump on the floor. She reflexively cut off the scream before it came out, and ran for the bathroom.

When she finished vomiting, she showered to get the blood off herself. She let the hot water practically burn her skin. Still shaking, she got out of the shower and looked at herself in the mirror. Her eyes were bloodshot, she was pale, and her mouth tasted like moldy moose meat.

She had to get a grip. She looked around at the various cosmetics

Gwen had left lying around. She saw the toothpaste and reached for it, then stopped. She picked it up with the washcloth, put a lot on her finger, and brushed her teeth with her finger. She swallowed some of the mint-flavored dental paste to try to get rid of the bile in her throat.

She took a gulp of air, trying to find the woman she had once been. It took several deep breaths, and she had to force herself to remember how it had been growing up, what her life once was, to discover the coldness again. When she looked in the mirror, pulling herself up to her full height, the eyes that met hers were cold, hard.

She went out into the room and looked at the body in the bed. Her face was gone. A .357 could do that. A .357 could be used to hunt game, including moose and deer. She reached down and picked up the gun. It was hers, and there was exactly one round missing.

She pulled the top sheet off of Gwen and stared at her naked body. It was a very nice body, under all the blood. She was a bit surprised to see the triangle of golden-blonde curls between her legs because she would've sworn Gwen was a bottle blonde.

She grabbed a towel from the bathroom and wiped down the areas of Gwen's body she had touched that morning, erasing her prints from the body. She rolled her over and looked around for any other clues as to what happened and to erase any other traces she might have left.

She tried to remember the night before, but everything was foggy. It was clear until . . . when? Why had Gwen told people she had too much to drink? She hadn't really drunk much at all—only three glasses of Glenfiddich. She went through things, and her mind again touched on that incredible sex. Had she actually slept with Gwen?

Well, okay, they had *slept* together, but had Brett done her? Brett couldn't even remember getting undressed, but all she was wearing now were her black silk boxers and a white T-shirt.

She remembered her back being clawed, so she went to the mirror, turned around, and lifted her shirt. She couldn't see any scratches, nor could she feel any. And she thought she'd remembered riding the woman, hard, with a dildo—a dildo she wasn't wearing, and didn't see anywhere.

She looked back at the woman in the bed. She had nice, long legs. She would have been fun to fuck. She also had long, red nails.

Brett had already wasted far too much time. She had to figure out what to do and do it. She could call Frankie and they could get rid of the body—pretend none of this had ever happened. She could call the police and report this, but more than likely, she'd be their prime suspect, and they'd have some damned good evidence to prove it. How could she explain any of this?

Now, if she and Frankie got rid of the body and anything turned up, it might look even worse for her. But she *could* make sure no one ever found the body. That's what the old Brett would have done—gotten rid of it and forgotten it all. But no matter how much she dragged up the old Brett to get through this moment, that wasn't her anymore.

But still, she couldn't just call the police. She had to do what she could to cover up her involvement until she found out what really happened. Plus, she wanted to know what actually happened—after all, the only acceptable rationale behind all of this was that Gwen had been right—someone was after her, wanted her dead, and they had framed Brett for her murder.

That pissed Brett off.

And no matter what she did, Allie'd be pissed off. She wouldn't, couldn't, believe Brett had gotten herself into this much shit. There was no reasonable explanation for how she did get into this. The *how* would piss Allie off as much as anything else.

She grabbed a fistful of tissues and went through the room, wiping down all surfaces while searching for any evidence that she'd been there. Since she couldn't remember a lot, she didn't know what she had touched, so she wiped everything down. Then she had to find all of her own clothing and possessions.

Brett went through what was apparently Gwen's purse, still using tissues to carefully avoid leaving prints. Using the standard-issue hotel pen and pad, she jotted down Gwen's full name, address, social security number, and any other important info she found in Gwen's stuff. She stared at Gwen's driver's license for a few moments, amazed that the government could take pictures of people from outer space with satellites, yet could still take such horrid ID pictures.

She left almost everything, only taking Gwen's pass card for work. She wiped down everything again, then pulled on her trousers. She planned on carrying her jacket, shirt, and tie over her arm so she wouldn't be quite so identifiable as the woman who had drinks with Gwen the night before.

There were no signs that anyone else had been in the room during the night. Gwen's clothes, few that they were, were tossed about the room, as if they had been pulled off as they entered. As if Brett had stripped her when they got there.

Brett's clothing was also haphazardly astray.

She shoved the tissues she had used into her jacket pocket, the hotel pen and pad into her back trouser pocket, then picked up the towels and washcloth she had used. She glanced over the room one last time. She'd like to strip the bed of sheets and blankets, but she knew she couldn't get rid of those easily. She was bound to have left hairs on those and probably much more.

She needed to buy some time to figure out who did this before the cops caught up with her. She put the "Do Not Disturb" sign on the door as she left, and glanced at the lock. The lock didn't show obvious signs of tampering, but management, maids, and likely others had key cards for it. Almost anyone could get in and not show evidence of it. She looked at the room number, 314.

Brett dumped the towels in the maid's cart as she walked by. She kept her eyes down and tried to look shorter than she was.

She wanted to kill whoever did this. Allie wouldn't like that much, though. And it really wasn't Brett's style any longer.

She'd just teach them a lesson.

⁂

Brett went down to the parking lot and got her car. She paid for parking with cash. And she handled the parking ticket with her sleeves over her fingers. She was sure there was some way she'd be traced back to this, but she wanted to make it as difficult as possible.

She drove right to the worst part of town. Lansing wasn't a big town, so it wasn't hard to find. Especially since she had gone to school in East Lansing and lived and worked around the area a bit since then.

She parked her car, spit on her fingers and ran them through her hair. She was still in her trousers and white T-shirt. Her wallet was in her pocket, as was a pocketknife. During daylight, that was all she needed. She glanced around the pavement until she found what she was looking for.

She climbed out of her car, setting the alarm, and walked over to the dark, shifty-looking guy leaning against a building. "Works, I just need the works."

"Ya mean the entire starter kit or what?" He looked her up and down and apparently decided against calling her anything like *babe*.

"I mean the works. I don't need no drugs, just the syringe, etc."

Then she went to Quality Dairy, a convenience chain located in the middle-of-the-mitten that was Michigan and picked up some junk food, packing materials, and latex gloves.

Brett drove to the back of a parking lot, where there were no people around. She tied off her arm and after sterilizing the needle with her Zippo, drew some of her own blood. She pulled off her sock and packed the vial in it, then wrapped that in tissue. She went to a Kinko's she remembered from college, put it all into a box with the packing materials, and sent it overnight to Randi McMartin, with a note asking that she have the blood analyzed for any chemicals.

Whoever was after Gwen must have followed her to the hotel. It made sense that both of them would have been drugged, but Gwen was the one who almost carried the much-larger Brett to her room.

And why had Gwen told everyone she'd had too much to drink?

Gwen was followed, Brett's drink was drugged, and Brett was framed for murder.

Since there was no sign that the room had been broken into, then whoever it was must be someone Gwen knew. A friend. Someone she would have told where she was staying.

But she had said she couldn't trust anyone.

And *her* drink hadn't been drugged.

Brett no longer trusted Gwen. The only problem was that Gwen was dead. And Brett killed her.

No. No, no, no, no. She did *not* kill Gwen.

Someone else did. And Brett had to find that someone else, because everyone else would be convinced that Brett *had* killed her.

Nothing made sense. Gwen had to have been followed . . . or the murderer had to know where she would go and have contacts there . . .

Dammit.

Being in a whole shit load of trouble was what she deserved. Even if she hadn't actually done anything. Cybersex did feel too much like cheating to not be sex, she admitted to herself. And she had gone to meet Gwen. Only her meeting didn't end with her being chopped into little pieces by an axe-wielding maniac—it had ended far worse than that.

All these thoughts sent her brain swimming in circles. It was a whirlpool that took her into the darkness. The only way out was to overcome it.

She had to keep a level head and just deal with it all. She knew what she had to do next. She had to search Gwen's place before the cops got there. She had to find out who was following her. She had to figure out who killed Gwen.

What did she know about the blonde? They had met in a chat room. Brett hadn't been there long when Gwen sent her an Instant Message, starting a far more personal chat. Brett tried to remember what had made Gwen IM her like that, but couldn't.

As she drove to Gwen's place, she pulled out her cell phone and called Frankie. She told him quickly and succinctly that he needed to get on her work computer and thoroughly and completely delete any e-mails and pictures connected with Gwen, and she gave him her e-mail address and IM name. She warned him that he'd need to find a computer expert to help him because he was worse with computers than she was, and even she knew that though you deleted things, they could be retrieved by someone who knew what to look for. She also warned him that the cops might soon confiscate all the computer equipment in the building.

"What's this about?" he asked.

"I'll tell you later. Just make sure my work computer is clean—and, if you can get away with it, check my home computer as well."

Brett parked the car a couple of blocks from Gwen's house, then grabbed her briefcase from the backseat, as well as the newspaper she had picked up earlier. She emptied her briefcase, donned her shirt, tie, and jacket, slid her lock picks into her trouser pocket, and got out of her 4Runner.

She walked down the street toward Gwen's house, trying to look respectable and self-assured. She quickly cased the joint and, not seeing anything indicating the presence of an alarm system, or any sign of life, she pretended to knock on the front door. During that time, she pulled on a pair of latex gloves and her picks and did the locks hard and fast—unlocking both within one minute.

It was a simple house, with living room, kitchen, and a half-bath on the first floor. Also on the first floor was a door to the basement, and the bottom of a staircase leading up to the second floor. Brett decided to start there.

There were four rooms on the top floor. One was obviously Gwen's bedroom, one was a guest room, then there was a bathroom and a home office.

Bingo.

Gwen was a computer geek. All her secrets would be in that room. Brett turned on the computer and looked around the study while she waited for it to boot up. She wasn't exactly sure what she was looking for after all—except for some reason someone might want to kill Gwen.

She opened Explorer, which Allie had shown her how to do, and started looking around to see what she could find. When she tried to sign onto Gwen's AOL, it asked for a password, but none of her guesses worked. She did find an Outlook e-mail account, so she glanced through that.

It seemed to be Gwen's work e-mail account, and there wasn't much in it. Brett did find it interesting that every time someone asked Gwen what she was working on, she'd only reply that she really couldn't say. She said it was important and big, though.

Brett continued to search around on the computer for another five minutes before resigning herself to the fact she wouldn't be able to find anything useful on it. She glanced around the workspace, saw blank CDs, and prayed she knew how to work the computer well enough to copy to them.

She figured it out and began hurriedly copying everything she could onto CDs. She focused first on things that looked like personal files and documents, then moved onto everything else, since she wasn't sure how everything worked on these machines. She just hoped she could find someone who could read the files for her. While the files copied, Brett returned to her hunt.

First she searched the office. Next to the computer were a few desk trays on top of which were printouts of some of the e-mails and IMs Gwen and Brett had shared. Brett picked those up and put them into her briefcase. She then went into the filing cabinets, looking over credit card and bank statements.

Gwen spent a bit of money, but didn't appear to have any debt—instead she paid off her credit cards monthly and had about ten grand in savings. She made a reasonable salary, if the regular direct deposits into her accounts were in fact her pay, which Brett was inclined to believe.

She took the work ID and keys she found in the desk.

When she entered the bedroom she picked up a pillow and

sniffed it. The scent was almost like she remembered. She walked around the room, looking at the pictures—family photos that Gwen must have taken, because she wasn't in them. Pictures of friends without Gwen. Pictures of Gwen with another woman.

She ran her latex-covered fingers over them, thinking about how these people would be grieving once they learned that Gwen was dead. She wondered if this other woman was Gwen's girlfriend. She wondered what she would do if anything happened to Allie.

She remembered how Victoria's death had affected her. She had closed herself off from the world when it happened, and only Allie had been able to bring her back, been able to make her really feel and live again.

She looked at what she assumed was a family portrait because everyone in it shared similar features and realized there would be a lot of people mourning Gwen. She wished she had been able to help the woman, but instead, she might have helped her get killed.

She shook her head and forced herself to focus. She had to be the old Brett here—get in, get the job done, and get out.

She found Gwen's perfume. Her soap. Her stockings.

There were two toothbrushes in the bathroom, but one was more used than the other. Brett sighed again for the girlfriend, but continued through the house, realizing there were some really nice things there—nice perfume, lingerie, and electronics.

By the time she was done, she had a handful of CDs and a fistful of papers. And then, after checking carefully through the window, she left via the back door, locking it behind her with her picks.

Chapter Six

Brett had to keep moving, especially if she wanted to use her cell phone. It would be harder to run a trace on her while she was moving. She pulled onto a highway and drove. She pulled a business card out of her Day Runner and dialed the number on her cell phone.

"Detective McMartin," a voice on the other end said after the third ring. Randi was a cop friend of Brett's and Allie's. Or perhaps it would be more appropriate to refer to her as Brett's ex-arch nemesis. As a detective on Detroit's special organized crime force, she had tried for years to get Brett behind bars.

"Randi, it's Brett. I've got a problem."

"Don't you always?"

"Someone's trying to frame me. I think somebody slipped a mickey into my drink last night, because most of the night is a blank."

"What do you want me to do about it?"

"I'm sending you a sample of my blood. I'd like you to have it checked."

"Again I ask—"

"It's already been shipped."

"You can't FedEx blood products."

"It'll be the least of my problems."

"You know you won't be able to use it to prove anything, right? I mean, there's no way of proving when it was drawn, etcetera."

"I know, I know, but it'll help *me* to know. And I need to know for sure that I was drugged."

"Brett, what's going on?"

"You got a pen and paper?"

"Yeah. What's going on?"

Brett gave her the hotel and room information.

"What are we going to find there, Brett?" Randi asked.

"A dead body."

"What the hell—Brett! Brett!" Randi screamed into the dead line.

Brett next called Frankie, quickly telling him to meet her at a restaurant she knew outside of Ann Arbor. The place did a steady enough lunch trade so they wouldn't be unduly noticed. Plus, it was about equidistant from where they both were at right now.

"Okay, I'll meet you there," Frankie said, apparently figuring he shouldn't ask her too many questions over the line. "But you oughta give Allie a call. She's real worried about you."

"Shit. Will do. See you there."

For this next call, Brett pulled into a rest area so she wouldn't continue to piss off other drivers on the busy interstate. Allie picked up on the second ring.

"Hey babe," Brett said. "It's me."

"Thank God! Brett, where are you? What's going on? Where have you been?"

"Everything's okay, dear. Harry kept me out late, and then the car broke down on the freeway in the middle of Goddammed nowhere. My cell phone was dead, and I knew you'd kill me if I hitched a ride."

"So what did you do? Sleep in the car?"

"Well, no. I walked back along the freeway to the last exit, but since I was in the middle of nowhere, there wasn't a phone there, so I kept going till I found a gas station. They towed the car back, and it was way too late to call you."

"It's never too late to call me, Brett. You should've known that. I was up all night pacing and worrying!"

"Well, I got into a cheesy little motel, and then had to check on the car this morning."

"Do I need to come get you?"

"Naw, they got it fixed and all, but since I'm so close to Lansing, I figured I'd head back up there to finish off a few things I gotta do." Brett was suddenly realizing that once their charge-card statements came in, Allie would know all of this was a bunch of horse shit, because there wouldn't be any hotel or garage charges, but by then, everything would be all right. Or she'd be in jail. Although they didn't have joint accounts, Allie handled most of the bill paying, using their respective checkbooks.

"But you'll be home tonight?"

"Oh, yeah, no problem. I'll see you then, babe, okay?"

Brett pulled back onto the freeway. She knew Randi could have already put out a tracer on her cell, but she was sure Randi would make sure there was something to check into before she went all-out on Brett's ass.

That was one of the reasons Brett had told Randi about the body instead of calling the Lansing police.

"Heather."

Heather Johnson looked up when Tim Donohue said her name. She flipped her long blonde hair back over her shoulder. "Yes?"

"Have you heard from Gwen today?"

"No, actually, I haven't. She left yesterday after work, saying she was meeting someone for drinks, and I haven't seen or heard from her since."

"So she was here yesterday afternoon?"

"Oh, yes."

"Hm. I tried reaching her, but couldn't."

"She did really seem to be focused on something."

"Well, can you try to track her down? It's really important. Try everywhere and everyone you can think of."

"Will do, Mr. Donohue!"

"Heather, how many times do I have to tell you? Call me Tim."

Randi sat and stared at her computer screen. The call from Brett had left her disturbed. She knew she should call Allie, but also knew she shouldn't. She shouldn't keep going after Allie. After all, the woman had given her leave to pursue others. Plus it appeared Brett was finally beginning to trust her, and that might lead to some major leads for her, which, considering Brett's associations, could be a major boon to Randi's career. Also, she couldn't forget all Brett had done to show her she was now on the right side of the law.

Just because she wanted Brett's woman didn't mean she should be gunning against her. If Brett said she was framed, she should start her part of the investigation believing that. But that was not something she would usually do. Everyone always said they were innocent.

So that left Randi wondering if she should investigate this lead of a body in a room in Lansing herself or give the lead to the Lansing cops. It was in Lansing, so it wasn't really her jurisdiction. But since her domain was organized crime in Detroit, and it seemed as if somebody who was perhaps in organized crime in Detroit was involved, she would logically have interest in the case.

She'd call Lansing with this anonymous tip, then go up and introduce herself to whoever was in charge. If there was a body, they'd be all over the place by then.

"Nice place, how'd you find it?" Frankie asked, walking up to Brett's table and sitting down.

"Woman I was dating a while ago worked in Dexter. We'd meet here sometimes. Lucky me, it's still here."

"What's going on?" he said, picking up the menu and glancing over it.

"I've been playing around online while doing some research on where we, as business partners, can go next."

Frankie grinned at her. "Cybersex?"

"Yeah."

"I've always wondered about that." Frankie was about as computer literate as a chipmunk.

"It's weird. Anyway, Gwen from Lansing, whom I've become particularly close to, e-mailed me that she was in trouble. She asked me for help." She glanced at the waitress who'd materialized beside their table. "I'd like a chicken Caesar salad and a Miller Lite," she said.

"Bacon cheeseburger medium rare with Swiss and mushrooms, and a Miller Lite," Frankie said. Something about their demeanor apparently told the waitress they didn't want to be disturbed further because she immediately left without saying another word.

"Miller Lite?" Brett asked Frankie.

"Kurt's trying to get me to cut down on unnecessary calories. He's also trying to get me into aerobic exercise and shit."

"Let me guess, the really old cheese in the back of the fridge doesn't count as a green."

"Nope. So you hooked up with this Lansing woman." Brett and Frankie had known each other for so long and worked together on so much that they could often talk in short cuts.

"We met for drinks. We didn't hook up. At least I don't think we did."

"Explain."

"I'm pretty Goddammed sure it was just a dream but . . . everything from last night is so vague and foggy . . . Frankie, I met her for drinks, and at some point everything kinda got weird. I remember her leading me up to her room, telling everyone I was drunk . . . and I kinda remember fucking her, or Allie, but see . . . If we had sex like I remembered, then I shoulda had some major scratches down my back, 'cause I remember feeling the blood dripping down my back from her nails."

"And you don't have any scratches."

"Not a one. And I also was packing in my memories, but I wasn't in real life. There wasn't a dildo in sight when I woke up." She could tell Frankie this because she knew he'd understand.

"So what happened?"

"I woke up this morning with my . . ." She stopped, looking around, suddenly realizing someone nearby could be listening in.

"You woke up with your dick in your hand," he said, referring to her gun as something else.

"Yeah. And . . ." No one seemed to be watching, but she leaned closer to Frankie and watched the volume of her voice. "Gwen was in bed next to me, her head all but blown away."

"So what'd you do?"

"Wiped everything down, took a blood sample and sent it to Randi, told her about the body in the room. I've been on the move since this morning. I also investigated Gwen's house."

"Why the fuck didja tell her?"

"What was I supposed to do? Call up Ski and let *her* know?" Brett said, referring to Lansing Detective Joan Lemanski, with whom she'd had previous contact, and not at all good.

"Called me. We coulda made it so that body never was. She'd a been just another missing person."

Brett shook her head. "Frankie, y'know that shit just comes back to bite you in the ass. Plus, I'm trying to be a good guy these days, remember? Besides, this is a frame so someone would've made sure it got traced back to me. I thought about everything this morning, Frankie, before I figured out what I had to do." She leaned back in her chair. " 'Sides, someone is trying to frame me, and I want to know who, 'cause they're gonna pay for it."

"Why McMartin though?"

Brett shrugged. "I needed someone I could trust to get my blood tested 'cause I need to know. Plus, I knew she'd give me some time and might help since I cut her in on it so early. I know how bad she wants to burn my ass, but I think she'd know I didn't do it."

The waitress delivered their food. "Is there anything else I can get you?"

"Not right now," Brett said. "Just bring us the check when you got a minute."

Frankie began wolfing down his burger, liberally coating his fries in catsup. "You talk to Allie yet?"

"Yeah. Called her on my way here."

"She was real worried last night. And this morning." Frankie had always liked Allie, and always cautioned Brett that she should never do anything to lose the woman she loved.

"Yeah, I know. But last night I was drugged, and this morning my mind was elsewhere. I called her and everything's copacetic. For now." Frankie didn't say anything, so they continued eating in silence for a few moments. "I know she's gotta learn something at some point. I know I can't figure this all out in one day, but I need to know more before I 'fess up to it all, y'know?"

"I don't know too many folks in Lansing, but I'll see what I can find out."

"I'll use your pager to keep you up to date."

"Keep moving around. That'll confuse 'em. Let me know where to find you."

"Not on voice mail."

"We'll work it out. We always do."

"Yeah, we do."

He looked up to meet her eyes. "Be careful, Brett. You've got a lot to lose."

She met his gaze across the table. She knew he was talking about Allie, and her love. But she decided to respond otherwise—that she could be locked up for life because of this. "I've been on the lam before, pal. You know that. I know how calls can be traced and all that shit. Granted, I haven't run recently, but I'll watch it. The cops have new ways to trace people, and track phone calls and all that shit. Just remember, I know how to look out for number one."

"Do that."

Brett had been feeling so much today—guilt, anger, remorse when she woke to find the corpse in bed with her. Then hate and anger, with all the prior emotions still there, underneath, when she realized someone else had taken away that life and tried to blame her for it. And she almost grieved for Gwen and her loved ones when she had been in Gwen's house.

But Frankie made it all so simple. With Frankie she could be about business and nothing more. Their relationship wasn't about emotions, it was about business. And this was business.

She breathed a sigh of relief at this escape from everything she had been feeling.

Randi showed up at the hotel, which was already swarming with cops. She took the elevator up to the third floor and approached room 314. It didn't take long for a uniform to stop her. She flashed her badge.

"Who's in charge here?" she asked.

"Detective Lemanski," the uniform replied, gesturing toward the room. "Ski!" he yelled toward it.

Randi stepped over the crime scene tape and went in search of Ski, carefully watching where she stepped so as not to disturb any potential evidence.

"Can I help you with something?" a woman said, blocking Randi's path.

"Yeah, I'm looking for Detective Lemanski."

"That's me."

Randi again pulled out her badge. "Detective Randi McMartin,

Detroit Special Organized Crime Squad. I'm the one who called in the anonymous tip."

"If you called it in, how can it be anonymous?"

"I got the tip from an anonymous source. Figured it was your jurisdiction, so called it up here."

"So why are you here?"

"It came from a reliable source."

"How can it be reliable if it was anonymous?"

"I thought I recognized the voice. And if I was called on my direct, that means they knew who I was."

Ski nodded. "Who're you covering for?"

"Nobody."

"Yeah, right."

"Call Detroit and check me out. I'm on the up and up."

"Then whose voice was it?"

Randi shrugged. "Say the name, and I'll tell you if you're right."

Ski pulled out a notepad. "Brett Higgins."

"Got it in one. Since it was her, I figured I ought to check up on it."

"Do you know where she's at?"

"Not a clue."

"Are you lying to me?"

"No. From how the call sounded, I would guess she was calling from her cell. She knows the routine well enough that she'll be hard to find at this point."

Ski studied Randi for a few moments. "Who is Higgins?"

Randi shrugged. "We've suspected her of organized crime dealings for years. I've led investigations into her activities. She's come up clean." She met Ski's eyes. "I don't like her, but she hasn't steered me wrong in several years. And she's stayed clean. I don't like what she does, but it's all legal. Now."

Ski pulled out her cell and turned from Randi. Randi stood there, looking around, knowing Ski was checking her out. She couldn't believe Ski had come up with Brett's name so quickly. If Brett had really had anything to do with this, she would be almost untraceable.

Ski turned back to Randi. "Everybody calls me Ski." She led Randi into the heart of the crime scene. "The room was in Brett Higgins' name, though she left without checking out. The room's been wiped clean, but the corpse has been preliminarily IDed as one Gwen Cartwright." She nodded toward a purse on the chest of drawers by the TV. "The ID we found in there matches the body. We're still early on, but it appears the murder took place last night, sometime between when Higgins was seen with Cartwright at the bar, and the time we found the body. Oh, and a fairly powerful gun did this. Just about wiped her face clean off." Ski turned to Randi. "Now tell me, why the hell did Higgins call you about this?"

"Because she says she was framed." Randi liked Ski's frankness. The woman already had her respect, which wasn't easy to get.

"Really."

Randi shrugged. "Only reason she would've called this one in." Ski seemed to be playing it straight with her, so she'd give her the same back.

"Yeah, right. Sounds like you're protecting her."

Randi shrugged.

"So you want to give me a description of this Brett? I need one to put out an APB."

"You can get it from her driver's license."

"Yeah, well, since you're obviously so close to her, I figured maybe I oughta check with you first."

"She's five-feet-ten. Black hair starting to gray. Her eyes are probably listed as green or brown, but they vary with her mood. Look for a rather butch woman."

"Sounds like you know her well."

"I was gunning for her ass a few years ago. You get to know something about somebody you're following, watching, as closely as I was her." They kept meeting each other's eyes to check if the other was lying. Randi liked what she saw in Ski's eyes. The detective was being straight with her, but there was something more, something in the depths of those hazel eyes. Ski's long, dark hair was pulled back from her face in a ponytail. Randi could tell that hidden beneath the blazer and loose trousers was a rather nice body.

Ski had been staring at her since she gave the description. It threw Randi off. "Are you sure that's all?" Ski all but whispered.

Randi got back down to business and pulled out her business card. "Please call me if anything develops."

Ski handed over her own. "You do the same. But I won't hold my breath."

"What do you mean by that?"

Ski led Randi from the crime scene to the emergency stairwell so they'd be away from the other cops. "You're not telling me everything."

Randi shrugged. "Brett's bad news. I don't like her. I'd love to see her caught for something, and put away for a long, long time." She met Ski's eyes. "But I won't let an innocent person take the rap for something she didn't do. And I honestly don't think she did this."

"You just said she's bad. Why wouldn't she do this?"

"Because if she did do it, you wouldn't find the body for weeks, if ever. And she would not have called me to tell me there was a body in this room."

"So why did she call you?"

Randi shrugged. "We know each other. She knows I know her M.O. And that this isn't it."

Ski pulled her into the stairwell. "We're off the record now. Tell me everything you know."

"I don't know shit yet. She called me, and I called you. And no matter where she goes, because of who she was and is, I can find out about any investigation on her." She looked up and at Ski. "And my gut tells me she didn't do this."

"Well, then, prove it to me."

Chapter Seven

Ski returned to room 314 and spoke to a uniformed officer. "We need to check the records on this room. I want to know who had access. And make sure we check every single surface for prints. Also check the hotel laundry, see what was put in it after eight last night." She called the station and had them put out an APB on Brett. "I want her caught."

She drew a few quick sketches of the room, but her mind was elsewhere. The brief description McMartin had given of Higgins had matched a suspect Ski had on a previous murder case she had worked.

She turned to one of the officers. "Get me a picture of this Brett Higgins."

"If she's got a driver's license, we can pull that up."

"Can you get it faxed here for me?"

"Sure."

With just a nod, Ski sent him on his way. She wished she knew if she could trust Randi.

Randi got into her car, and called Greg Morrow on her cell. She briefed him on all she knew.

"Randi, what do you want me to tell you? You'll just do whatever you want anyway."

"You know that isn't true."

"Yeah, I do. But where Higgins is concerned—"

"Okay, so maybe you might have a point. But I'm supposed to keep an eye on her anyway, and I really don't think she would've reported this to me if she was involved."

"So you don't think she's involved, but you want to look into this anyway. Randi—"

"Remember when not too long ago I told you I'd seen her, and you insisted she was dead?"

"We all thought she was—including you!"

"Yeah, well, I did until I ran into her looking not-quite-so dead. But you still didn't believe me, Greg."

"There were reasons for that, Randi. Higgins has always gotten under your skin."

"I know her, Greg. And we both know she looks guilty on this from a mile away, but you and I both know she isn't. I can help here."

"But that isn't your job."

"But if she had anything to do with this, it is. She called it in to me. And asked me where she could ship a blood sample."

"Why the hell would she do that?"

"Because she knows I'll get it tested, and will tell her the truth. I don't know shit about this, Greg, but I think she's innocent."

"It didn't happen in Detroit. We need closings here," he said, referring to the fact that many homicides in Detroit were open cases.

"I know."

Greg was silent. He knew Randi put in a lot of unclocked overtime hours. And still put in for enough regular OT that her record was pretty firm. "I don't like this, Randi. You're obsessed with her, but you're a good cop."

Ski hated working a case with this many reporters around, but at least it gave the case a high enough profile to have enough people assigned to it. Given all the possible connections in the case, she didn't have enough time to check out all possible leads, so having patrol cops do initial interviews helped a lot.

It didn't take much time to discover that the room was originally booked with Gwen Cartwright's credit card, but then was paid for with Brett Higgins's card. The two were seen leaving the bar together, after a few drinks. Gwen had half-carried Brett out, insisting she was drunk. Two key cards had been assigned for the room. They had found one with Gwen's possessions. Brett apparently left with hers still on her.

There had been calls placed from the room, after Brett had left the bar with Gwen—to the Paradise Theatre, to Frankie's house, and to Brett's residence—but there were no prints on the phone. In fact, the entire room had been thoroughly wiped clean. Apparently, somebody didn't want any to be found.

Patrolmen were interviewing everybody who had access to key cards and the room.

"Hey, Ski, here's that picture you were looking for."

Ski took the paper and looked at it. The woman in the picture had been her chief suspect in a murder a few years ago—but then she was calling herself Samantha Peterson. Even then Ski had known there was something suspicious about the darkly dangerous butch.

In her mind, this was looking to be a pretty cut-and-dried case.

Randi called Allie on her way back to Detroit. She didn't waste any time with pleasantries. "Where was Brett last night?"

"She was in Lansing, having drinks with one of her distributors, Harry somebody from New York. Her car broke down on the way home, and she had to walk to the nearest gas station. Her car got towed, and she spent the night in a motel. Why?"

"When was the last time you heard from her?"

"Late this morning. Randi, what's going on?"

"Allie, Brett's wanted for questioning for a murder in Lansing."

"What?"

"Brett's wanted for questioning—"

"I heard you, but who? What? What the fuck do you mean?"

"Apparently she had drinks with Gwen Cartwright last night, who was found dead this morning in a hotel room."

Allie took a deep breath. Brett hadn't mentioned a Gwen. She had only mentioned Harry. "There's gotta be some kind of mistake. Are you sure, Randi?"

"Gwen was last seen leaving the hotel bar with Brett. The room was paid for with Brett's credit card."

"No . . ." Allie whispered.

"She lied to you, Allie. People saw her with Gwen. A lot of people."

"Yeah. I know. I already knew."

"What?"

"She's cheating on me, isn't she?"

"Yeah. It sure looks like she is."

Allie didn't know what to say. The tears were streaming down her cheeks. She had to work hard to control her breathing. She was hurt, she was sad, and God-fucking-dammit, she was pissed as hell!

"I don't think she did it, babe."

Allie couldn't speak. She knew her voice would crack. Brett had spent the night with another woman. Allie leaned against the kitchen table, trying to regulate her breathing so Randi wouldn't know she was sobbing. She removed her hand from the mouthpiece.

"She called me to tell me about the body. I think she was drugged, Allie."

"It doesn't matter," Allie finally said. "She fucking lied to me, and cheated on me, and . . ." She stood up, picked up a frying pan from the stove, and slammed it against the wall. Repeatedly. "Goddammit!"

"Allie, she called me to tell me where to find the body. She's got to be innocent. She wouldn't have contacted me otherwise." Randi was apparently trying to calm her down, but Allie wasn't having any of it.

"Of course she's innocent, Randi—but she cheated on me! She lied to me and went behind my back, and, Goddammit, who the fuck is Gwen Cartwright?" Allie looked at the mess in the kitchen, thinking that maybe she should've used a clean pan to bang the walls, instead of the one she was using to cook dinner. She kicked the wall.

"I'm coming over," Randi said.

"No, don't."

"Okay, fine, bye," Randi said, hanging up.

Allie knew Randi would come over anyway. She couldn't face her with Brett's betrayal so fresh on her mind. What she'd really like to do was get stinking drunk and destroy all of Brett's possessions. Instead, she picked up the phone and dialed a number.

Frankie picked up on the second ring. "Hello," he said in his deep baritone voice.

"Frankie, I just got off the phone with Randi." She reached up into the cupboard above the stove, looking for Brett's Glenfiddich.

"Oh."

"What's really going on, Frankie?" She found the bottle, and then a glass.

"Brett did call you earlier, right?"

"Yeah, she did, and fed me a bunch of lies." She poured a shot and downed it. She felt much better. Not really.

"Allie—"

"Don't feed me another load of lies, Frankie. I need to know what's going on."

Frankie glanced at his watch. "Listen, it's about time for me to take off. Kurt and I ain't got no plans tonight . . . why don't I go pick him up, we'll pick up some grub and come over."

"You're just buying time to figure out what you're going to tell me."

"Yup."

"And you want Kurt here to help you out."

"Guilty as charged."

"So why should I go along with this, instead of just making you tell me right now?"

"Because I wouldn't tell you anything right now. Or I'd hang up on you. Besides, you don't want to be alone right now."

Allie sighed, looking at the Tuna Helper all over the kitchen. If she was gonna get good and drunk tonight, she should eat something. It would help with tomorrow's hangover. "Okay, fine. I want almond boneless chicken." Besides, she didn't want to be alone with Randi tonight. Or did she?

It didn't matter, because Frankie had already hung up.

"Oh, Allie, are you okay?" Kurt said when he and Frankie arrived, dropping the food onto the table and running to wrap Allie in a big hug.

Frankie put the beer and wine he was carrying into the fridge, and put a bottle of Scotch onto the counter.

"What's going on baby?" Kurt asked, still holding Allie and stroking her hair. "Mr. Talkative over there wouldn't tell me much of anything."

"Oh, Kurt, Brett's been cheating on me!"

"Oh, and yeah," Frankie said, "she's also wanted for a murder she didn't do." Frankie went about pulling out the various cartons of Chinese food, which he opened up and put serving spoons in. He also laid out plates, napkins, and condiments.

"We'll figure all this out," Kurt said, pulling away from staring at his lover and the bombshell he had just dropped, and went back to soothing Allie against his shoulder.

"Did you bring me almond boneless chicken?" she asked. "I haven't eaten all day, I've been so worried and frustrated. And then angry."

"Yeah, babe. I did." Frankie walked over and pulled both Kurt and Allie into his arms, holding them tightly. "We'll figure this out. Brett didn't do it. It's all gonna be all right, 'kay?"

Allie pulled away. "No, it won't be. Nothing will ever be the same again. Frankie? Don't you understand? She cheated on me and lied to me!"

Frankie ducked down to her height, meeting her eyes and holding her forcefully by the shoulders, so she couldn't pull away. "Allie, Brett didn't cheat."

"How do you know that?" Allie pushed herself from his grip.

When Frankie didn't reply, Kurt looked at them both. "Brett told him. And Brett never lies to Frankie."

"Did he tell you that? He doesn't seem too talkative right now."

"No. He didn't. But I know," Kurt said, looking between the two. "Brett never lies to Frankie, and he doesn't lie to her."

"I want Frankie to say it," Allie said, looking up at Frankie, who was now standing again at his full height.

"What Kurt said."

"How the fuck did you do that?" Allie said, rounding on Kurt.

Kurt shrugged. "Fall in love with a taciturn man, you learn to read the silences and expressions."

"You haven't been with him nearly as long as Brett and I have been together!"

"Allie, the two of them are complementary. Just like you and Brett are."

"Then who the fuck is Gwen Cartwright?" Allie asked, confronting Frankie.

Frankie stood stock still, but turned his head away. "Brett was trying to control herself by flirting online. Gwen asked her for help. She thought her life was in danger." He then looked right at Allie. "She didn't do it, Allie. You know that."

"Maybe she didn't kill anyone, but that doesn't mean she didn't cheat on me."

"Who told you she did?"

There was a knocking at the front door. All three of them turned to look. Frankie and Kurt hadn't closed the door behind them, so Randi poked her head in.

"Hello? Anybody home?" she asked, then saw them. Then saw the food. "Great. You got ABC?"

"I'm so glad we got extra of that!" Kurt exclaimed, pulling away from Allie and Frankie. He was such a fag, always trying to lighten the mood and make everyone happy.

Randi had apparently realized she had walked in on a moment, so she busied herself with putting together a plate of dinner. Kurt, Frankie, and Allie followed suit.

Once they were all gathered in the living room with dinner and drinks, Randi recapped the situation for them, telling them all she had learned from Ski and her own preliminary investigation and interactions with Brett.

"So when I get her package tomorrow, I'll be able to see if she was drugged."

"Hold on, what did you say that detective's name was?" Allie asked.

"Ski. Joan Lemanski," Randi replied, putting her plate down on the antique chest that served as a coffee table. She pulled Ski's business card from her pocket and handed it to Allie.

"Oh shit," Allie said, studying it. She had seen that same card a few years before.

"What's up?" Frankie asked.

"Ski . . ."

"You know her?" Randi asked.

"Yeah. A few years ago, when we were up in Alma, Brett and I were taking a walk and saw some guy shot right in front of us. We saw who did it, and chased after him, but lost him. We called the police, but by the time we all got back there, there was no body."

"Well, you just said you lost him," Randi said.

"No, I don't mean nobody as in no one, I mean that the body—the dead one—was gone."

"So what happened?" Kurt asked, picking at his food as if it was popcorn.

"The cops thought we were nuts. But then Brett started her new job at an ad agency, and discovered her new boss had been murdered." Allie put her plate down, apparently no longer interested in her food. Instead, she picked up her wine and took a sip. "Ski was the detective there when we reported the missing dead body, and she was also the investigating detective for Chuck Bertram's murder. He was the guy we saw get shot." She looked at everyone, taking time to look into each of their eyes so they would understand the full impact of what she was saying. "She ended up thinking Brett was behind it."

Randi sat back, holding her beer. "So that explains that."

"What?" Frankie asked, his mouth half-full of noodles.

"Ski seemed . . . disturbed . . . when I described Brett to her."

"Brett does seem to have that effect on women," Kurt joked, getting up to refill drinks.

"No. It was more as if she was remembering something."

"It's not going to take her long to remember Brett. Especially once she gets pictures and such." Randi handed Kurt her glass. "But I think she already was on the trail, so you can probably expect her to come calling real soon."

Allie stared down into her nearly empty wine glass. Kurt came up with the bottle, offering her a refill. Allie pulled her glass away. "Actually, I think I'm about ready for some of that Scotch."

Kurt knelt in front of her, putting her glass and plate on the chest behind him, and pulling her hands into his. "You sure?"

"Yup. Think it's time for Scotch."

"What's going on, baby?"

"Scotch. Need Scotch." Allie stood to get it herself.

Kurt followed her, and indicated for the others to remain where they were.

Chapter Eight

Randi and Frankie reviewed all that they knew at that point, which showed that to any outside observer, Brett was clearly guilty.

"Her running doesn't help matters at all," Randi concluded.

"Oh, like she's got any choice," Frankie said. "If they got her, they'd stop looking anywhere else. All they'd see is her."

"Frankie, c'mon, you've got to admit, her lying to Allie doesn't make her seem any more innocent."

"Randi," Kurt said, "Brett was just trying to do a friend a favor."

"That's not like Brett and you know it," Randi said.

"Then you don't know Brett," Frankie said, still sitting, but obviously upset.

"We all know Brett only looks out for number one."

"Randi, how can you say such a thing after all this time?" Allie asked, standing and looking down at Randi.

Frankie stood, too. "She's put her neck on the line to save both you and Allie and a lot of other people as well."

"Hey, now, we don't need any more murders around here," Kurt said, pulling Frankie away from Randi.

"Okay, you two have me there, but—" Randi began.

"Damned right we do!" Frankie said.

Kurt grabbed Frankie and pulled him down next to him, using gentle touches to calm him down. But Frankie still sat like a predator, ready to lunge at its prey.

"—explain to me how she met this woman to begin with."

Kurt silenced Frankie with a motion. "She was online doing research."

"Okay, so somebody started IMing her, some woman. Why did Brett respond? How did she become so involved with this stranger she met online?"

Kurt smiled. "Have you ever been online?"

Randi shrugged. "Sure, yeah, of course."

"Have you ever chatted online? Maybe in a chat room or with instant messages?"

Randi sat next to Allie again. "No chat rooms, but yeah, sometimes I IM with other cops. Detectives. We discuss points of the cases we're working on and bounce ideas off one another."

"And how'd you meet all these folks?" Frankie asked, reaching a bear-like hand to take a mouthful of his drink.

"Some are cops I've worked with, some I've met at conferences or such. Y'know, just around."

Kurt glanced at Frankie with a grin. "So it's not that you've been fooling around in the Frisky Dyke Detectives chat room?"

Randi laughed. "I only chat and e-mail with people I know from real life. I mean, anybody can pretend to be anyone on the Net, and there's not much way of proving them wrong until you actually meet them."

Allie suddenly looked up and stared straight ahead, as if lost in thought.

"So you're saying you've never cybered with anyone?" Kurt asked Randi.

"Of course not. I mean, what's the point?"

Frankie, seeing where Kurt was going with his line of questioning, finally relaxed against the back of the love seat, laying his arm along the back of it, ready to enjoy the show.

"Do you read erotic fiction?" Kurt asked. "Maybe some sleazy lesbian mysteries?"

"I don't see where it's any of your business."

"Cyber is like interactive erotica. Sometimes really badly typed erotica, but it's still got its bonus points. Your partner can be your dream, your fantasy. And if there're pics involved, then make it pornographic interactive erotica."

"But the pics are never real. Even I know that. I mean, you can send pics of anybody you want!"

"That's it," Allie murmured. "Brett said it was Gwen, but how do we know it really was Gwen?"

Frankie nodded. "Brett said it was Gwen Cartwright."

Randi wrapped an arm around Allie. "It's pretty obvious it was. Between the items found in the room, the credit card originally used to book the room, and the overall statistics of the body, it's pretty much a given. Plus, Gwen's missing, her car was in the lot of the hotel, and the list goes on. I'd be more surprised if it wasn't Gwen than if it was."

"Whaddya mean about the body? Can't they just tell?" Frankie asked, leaning forward and resting his elbows on his knees.

"The woman got shot in the face with what was probably a .357, so no, they can't do a visual ID quite that easily. Fortunately the employer has her fingerprints on record, so they should know for sure tomorrow. And of course we'll also check dental records, but that will take a few days."

Frankie looked over at Allie and shrugged. "It was worth a thought."

Allie sighed and leaned back, right into Randi's waiting arm, which curled around her shoulders and brought her in tight.

Frankie looked over at Kurt, who turned toward Allie and said, "Maybe we should spend the night?"

"I'll be all right," Allie said, curling in closer to Randi.

"Yo, Allie, I'd really like to be here if Brett calls in or anything," Frankie said, standing and stretching.

"Really, I think it's best if Frankie and I spend the night," Kurt said. "We'll just sleep in the guest room. Don't worry, we won't be any trouble at all." He made no move to get up. He sat watching Randi and Allie.

Randi met his eyes. She knew that he and Frankie were staying to ensure she didn't.

Frankie reached down and offered one of his paws to her. "Randi. Let me help you out. Glad you came over and all, thanks for everything. But we should all get to bed soon. After all, tomorrow's sure to be a real big day."

Randi stared up at him for a long moment before reluctantly accepting his outstretched hand. "Yeah, I guess I ought to get going." As she stood, she collected her things and then headed out the door, saying, "I just hope if Brett's on the run, she really knows what she's doing. I mean, they're watching for her—watching her ATM and charge transactions and everything."

Allie knew Randi was giving them a warning to pass along to Brett, but Allie also knew that Brett already knew all about covering her tracks. After all, this wasn't the first time Brett had been on the lam.

As soon as Allie had gone to sleep, Frankie left a message on one of Brett's pagers with all the information Randi had shared, including the name of the Lansing detective who was on the case. He made sure Brett knew who had passed on the info, and told her to let him know if she needed any more cash, or was going to activate one of her aliases.

He hoped she wouldn't do that because she really needed to clear her name and be herself again. Plus, he and Allie really needed her in their lives.

Brett knew she couldn't keep driving around town in her car. Even though the cops might think she would get as far away as quickly as possible, they were still likely to be looking for her. She knew Allie and Randi would tell her to turn herself in, insisting that they would be the ones who would prove her innocence—that the police would really get to the truth of the matter.

But it's real hard for someone to put their faith in the cops when one doesn't trust them nor have a very good history with them.

She couldn't use her credit cards to get a room. She couldn't stay in her car, or even really continue using it. But she couldn't go home, or to Frankie's, or the Paradise either. Those would be the first places the police would look.

Then she realized there was one place the cops wouldn't think of immediately, a woman who would probably relish housing a wanted (but innocent) woman. Who would also believe in her innocence.

Alma was such a small town, she figured she couldn't hide her vehicle there. So she found a nice, nasty area with a working pay phone (an almost impossible task), made a call and quickly arranged where she would dump her car and where she would be picked up. Her car would most likely be stolen, but that was a small price to pay. And, maybe if the cops spotted her car, that would help throw them off her trail.

The last time Brett had been on the lam, after a while in California, she and Allie had moved back to Michigan, to Alma, a small town hours from Detroit out in the middle of nowhere, north of the middle-of-the-mitten. There, besides purchasing a house with its very own ghost, they had also acquired a rather eccentric college professor as a neighbor.

Maddy was a sweet older woman with a habit of speaking in riddles and an uncanny ability to sometimes see bits and pieces of the future. Maddy had been thrilled when she discovered the darker side of Brett's and Allie's pasts.

Now Brett was climbing into Maddy's girlfriend's blue Camry. Brett figured Leisa lived far enough away from the Motor City to not feel compelled to drive American. Because of Maddy's office hours, she couldn't come pick Brett up, but Leisa, a high school teacher, could come right away.

"I'd ask you how you were doing, but I already got the briefing," Leisa said as she drove back toward Alma.

"Um, Leisa, glad to see you and all, but please don't drive directly back to Maddy's. Drive around for a bit—going around blocks and making sudden turns. Without using your turn signal."

"Were you followed?" Leisa said, glancing anxiously about.

"I don't think so, but I want to make sure we're clean." Brett nonchalantly looked around. "Don't act suspiciously. Just drive." Leisa didn't appear to have familiarity with this sort of thing, all action flicks and spy-TV shows notwithstanding. "I'll tell you when to head home."

Brett wasn't sure if she was more worried about the cops or whoever had framed her. Regardless, she figured caution was a good callword for today. Or until the end of this. And she really didn't want to get Maddy and Leisa into the middle of such a situation—though knowing Maddy, there was nothing she would enjoy more than finding herself in the midst of trouble and possible adventure.

"About time you two got here!" Maddy exclaimed, charging them as soon as they entered. "I was starting to worry when it took so long."

"I wanted to make sure neither the cops nor whoever's framing me followed us."

"Oh, yes, I'm quite sure that is a good thing. Since you are trying to hide." Madeline Jameson, a slightly plump woman with wavy red hair and glasses had attired her rather short figure in a Red Wings' jersey that clashed with her hair, and a pair of tan painter's pants. Brett was just surprised the trousers weren't green. Through the years, Brett had wondered if Maddy dressed to promote her entire image as a slightly eccentric English prof. And Brett wasn't sure Maddy hadn't been a virgin when Leisa seduced her.

Maddy handed Brett her car keys. "We will do whatever we can to aid you in your plight," she was saying, "although I am quite sure you will attempt to avoid that as much as possible."

"Maddy, I just really don't want you or Leisa in jail for helping me. And that really is a risk."

"Oh, pshaw," Maddy said with a wave of her hand. Brett was positive she had never actually heard anyone use that word in conversation before. She was sure Maddy had used it purposely. "I haven't spent a night in jail in years. It would be a welcome break in habit." To Leisa's and Brett's confused looks she explained, "I *was* an activist during the Sixties you realize. You will use my car and I'll walk to work. It isn't as nice a vehicle as you're accustomed to, I'm sure, but I don't really need much, since this is such a small town."

Normally Brett wouldn't like to force someone to walk to work, but everything in Alma was in easy walking distance, even for a girl from a city with no public transportation. In Detroit and its suburbs, if you needed to go two blocks for a quart of milk, you'd drive. If you had a car. And almost everyone did.

"I can't thank you enough for this, Maddy—"

"You can stay in the spare room. I put fresh sheets on the bed as I paced and worried about you two. If the police decide to investigate my residence due to my prior involvement with your activities, I have created two different places in which you can hide."

"You've just been a bundle of energy, haven't you?"

"I assumed if you were on the run, I would need to assure you of adequate hiding places in case the police showed up with a warrant." Maddy always said everything so matter-of-factly that Brett just had to smile. She wasn't sure if she could ever say or do anything to really make Maddy embarrassed, or to even throw her off balance. "I have cleared up the attic so if you need to use it, you can get up there easily. Lots of places to hide and easy access to the outside. If you open the window at the back of the house, you can climb across the roof to the big oak in the back yard and crawl down it."

Brett smiled at how well Maddy had thought this through. "And what's the second choice?"

"The basement. The man who owned this house before me said his wife left him and took their daughter with her. He actually killed them both and hid them in the basement. He had pulled out part of the wall, carved out a space behind it, and entombed them there." To Brett's and Leisa's shocked looks she added, "It took the police a while to figure it out, but the cleaning woman noticed a strange smell in the basement and turned him in. After his wife supposedly left, he employed her to clean, cook, and do the laundry. What he didn't know was that the housekeeper's father had been involved in the funeral business, and so she was familiar with the smell of decaying flesh. After a few weeks of trying to find any dead rodents or such in the basement, she realized that the brickwork in an area of the basement didn't fit with the rest of the walls. Anyway, when I moved in, the police had crashed through that wall, so the brickwork had to be redone. I found an out-of-town contractor to do the job, thinking that perhaps someday I might need to hide something. He did a very nice job of it."

She was slowly leading Brett and Leisa down to the basement to show the area off. The brick exactly matched the rest of the walls. He *had* done a fine job. "It's bricked over, Maddy. I really don't see how this could help me."

"Brett, my dear, I realize you think, most of the time, that I'm quite off my rocker, but I knew at that time that this particular secret might one day come in handy. And in today's world of crazy terrorists—" She pressed a brick three times in a row, and the section opened. "Because of the murders, the house was a steal. So I was able to invest in having the bricklayer and carpenter fix this for further use. They hung the bricks on a swinging door, so it could be opened and utilized rather like a safe. In fact, I could put a safe in here if I felt the need to."

The space wasn't large, but it was big enough to fit two bodies into. Brett could easily fit into it.

"Of course, the downside to this is there is no easy escape route. But it might be an adequate hiding place. Give you some water and a soft pillow, and you're all set."

"Maddy, you're incredible!" Brett said, grinning at her.

"People were murdered in this house?" Leisa asked.

Chapter Nine

“If you need to switch cars,” Leisa said, handing Brett her spare set of keys, “you know where I work. I’ll know what happened.” Leisa Kraft taught at Alma High School. Leisa was buxom, with hair the color of molten gold and incredibly intense sea-green eyes; she was just a smidgen taller than Brett. She was a bit heavier than Brett usually liked her girls, but certain attributes more than made up for that. She was quite a bit younger than Maddy, but Brett and Allie had seen the connection between the two the first time they met Leisa.

Of course, Brett only noticed that connection when she took her eyes off of Leisa.

Apparently it took Leisa and Maddy a bit longer to work through things, especially because of the age difference, but they had found each other at last and now even lived together.

Brett and Allie had helped them both in the past, so Brett didn’t feel too bad accepting their assistance with this matter. She just hoped they didn’t end up regretting it.

"Would either of you care for anything to eat or drink?" Maddy led them into the kitchen.

"Um, baby, actually I think both of us kind of missed dinner," Leisa said, walking up behind Maddy and wrapping her arms around the much-shorter woman.

Maddy turned around and stood on her toes to give Leisa a quick kiss. "Then I'm glad I anticipated as much." She walked into the kitchen, glanced at her watch, picked up a pair of oven mitts, then opened the oven and pulled out a pot roast. She quickly tested it, then put it on the waiting hot pads on the counter. "Dinner is served. Help yourselves. I'd carve, but I'm terrible at it."

"Maddy, I think I love you," Brett said, her mouth watering. She hadn't realized how hungry she was till she saw and smelled the succulent beef garnished with onions, carrots, and potatoes.

"She's mine," Leisa said with a grin, picking up a knife to start cutting. Maddy held a plate for Leisa to place the tender slices on. They functioned as if they knew each other's thoughts and actions.

"I've anticipated that no matter how feminist and politically correct Allie might become, she would be unable to turn you into a vegetarian," Maddy said over her shoulder to Brett.

"Me butch. Me eat meat. Me drag girls back to my cave." Brett said with a grin as she slid a few slices of the tender beef onto her plate, along with carrots, onions, and potatoes.

Maddy put down the plate of meat she was holding for Leisa and reached into the fridge. She pulled out a big bowl of salad. "Ah yes, I see. But I also know that Allie would never forgive me if I let you go repeatedly without greens." She put the bowl in front of Brett, in the center of the table. "Take some. Eat it. You might enjoy it." Her tone brooked no insolence, so Brett followed orders.

"Brett," Maddy said. "You didn't go into many details over the phone. I would like to know more about that in which you are entangled."

"Girl asked me to help her out. I came up to Lansing for her. Somebody drugged me. Somebody framed me. When I woke up she was dead. The cops think I did it, so I need to find out who really did. Or else get used to life in jail. That's it."

"Hold on, back up. Maddy just told me what to do, I didn't ask why or anything. I got a very brief overview, and your further explanation makes me think of a lot of questions," Leisa said. "Would you mind actually explaining a bit?"

"I just did."

"No, Brett," Maddy said, "you just gave us an outline I would give even a freshman an F for."

"It's better if you don't know what's going on."

"I'm housing a fugitive, Brett. We're already involved," Maddy said.

"We need to know what's going on so we can help you," Leisa said, leaning on the table, ignoring her food, and looking earnestly at Brett. Brett looked down at her food. It was difficult to sidestep Leisa's piercing eyes. "It's the least we owe you, Brett."

Leisa knew how to play Brett. Brett could do favors, but couldn't accept them. She could help folks, but couldn't accept help. Leisa just phrased it as a payback, and Brett knew and understood owing people well—after all, it happened all the time in the business world.

"You told me not to contact Allie, Brett dear," Maddy said. "Why?"

Brett put down her fork and went to the fridge to grab a beer. "I don't want to get her involved."

"She's got to be worried about you," Leisa said.

Brett turned around with her beer and leaned back against the counter to face the women. "But she'll be pissed about me gettin' myself into a situation like this—being framed and all."

"You couldn't help it," Leisa said. She had given up on eating and was just staring at Brett, whereas Madeline continued eating as though this was the most normal thing in the world.

"I came up here to help a femme who had been making moves on me online. We met for drinks. I went to the john and somebody slipped a mickey into my drink. At least I think they did, it's the only logical explanation. I went up to her room thinking I had drunk too much, but knowing I hadn't, and fell asleep. The next thing I knew, it was morning and I was in a bed with a naked dead woman and my gun was in my hand. What about this is going to sound innocent to the cops or Allie?"

"Do you love Allie?" Maddy asked.

"You know I do, Maddy. I'd do anything for that girl." Brett thought of Allie's smile, of the way she really listened to what Brett had to say, of how she'd wake up and hold her when she had a nightmare, and of the way her eyes lit up when Brett did something unexpected but nice, or romantic, for her. She really did love her girl. And miss her.

"Then she will trust and believe in you." Maddy stood and approached Brett like a determined mother. Or a college professor, weeding out the truth amongst the many lies hidden in students and English lit. "I already know that, Brett. You just need to explain everything to us—why you made certain choices and followed the path you chose."

"I'm not a nice person, Maddy. You got to understand that. I'm a really bad person. That's why I do what I do," Brett growled at the ceiling, getting frustrated with this questioning. "I don't deserve Allie."

"Brett, dear, you're not a bad person. You help people. You helped Liza Swanson, and many, many children at Alma High School. You have also risked your own life to save others. You just do not wish to acknowledge the good in yourself. You have an image in your head of who you are, and are having a difficult time changing that image."

"You went to Lansing to help that woman," Leisa said.

"You don't understand. I got online, and started surfing and all that other shit, for business, yeah, sure. But I met Gwen because once I was online, I started flirting."

"So you were trying to be true to Allie," Leisa said.

"Yeah, but I wasn't. Listen, I had cybersex with Gwen. We fucked online, okay? I wasn't true, I wasn't faithful, I wasn't good. I was bad." Brett knew these two would pull it all out of her, and just admitting her guilt up front would make it all a lot simpler. She couldn't hide anything from them, after all.

"It's not like you had sex with her—" Leisa started saying.

"Why?" Maddy asked.

"I had sex online with her, okay?" Brett said to Leisa, then to Maddy, "What?"

"Why?" She slowly stepped closer to Brett. "Why did you meet her? Why did you meet women online?"

"They were there. We flirted. It felt good. I liked it. I was just researching and it all got out of hand."

"You were controlling your impulses through a more acceptable outlet. Brett, you simply need affirmation of your desirability, but you chose to try to find it through online means, so you would not be tempted through an actual physical presence of someone you might find desirable."

Brett stared at her, sorting through what Maddy had said, but finding it impossible. "Huh?"

"She said you were trying to be good. After all, we've had prezes who think actual sex doesn't mean anything unless it means shoving a real dick up a real pussy. Considering that, cybersex doesn't mean anything. So you were trying to be good," Leisa interpreted for Brett. No wonder these two were together!

"I was, and then it all went . . . bad. Way wicked bad."

Maddy put a hand against her forehead. "You . . . you came to Lansing to help a woman."

"Yeah, she e-mailed and IMed me that she was in trouble. I came. I lied to Allie and came."

"And then you were set up."

"Yeah, I mean, somebody drugged my drink. I felt like I had been hit upside the head with a very large and heavy object, or at least a half-gallon of bad Scotch, but I'd had just like a drink or two. I had to have been drugged!"

"Sounds—" Leisa began.

"You say you went to her room because you were drugged. Has it occurred to you what that really means?" Maddy asked.

"Okay, fine, I was tempted. And I did think about what I was wearing and all when I went up there, but . . . I really did go there just to help her. I wanted to fuck her, but I really wasn't going to." Brett went into the living room and sat on the couch, head in hands. "I love Allie, I really do," she whispered to the floor.

Maddy sat next to her and put an arm around her. "It means you did not go because of your own choice." She tried to pull Brett into her arms.

"I chose to go to Lansing. I got myself into this, and I will get myself out of it." Maddy's arms around her slowly pulled her down. The calming fingers over her hair allowed her to slowly melt into Maddy's motherly embrace.

Brett let Maddy hold her as if Maddy were her mother—had her mother been a storybook one, instead of one from *Dante's Inferno*. Her own mother didn't even have the strength and courage to be a wicked stepmother or evil witch. But still, even with Maddy, Brett wouldn't cry. She learned at a young age not to cry.

Leisa sat on Brett's other side. "You know, it's almost as if you're just trying to live up to your reputation—or your perception of what you should be."

Brett smiled. "Actually, I think I'm probably just a big old flake who is incredibly self-centered and egotistical."

"Well, that, too," Leisa said with a grin. She ran her hand casually through Brett's hair. "You're really cute when you're all self-deprecating."

Brett enjoyed having both these women touching her with such love and devotion, without any sexual connotations. They didn't expect anything from her, and it felt nice. She didn't feel a need to perform. Why hadn't she kept up better contact with them?

"You do not believe you deserve to be happy or successful," Maddy said. "So you commit actions that will be detrimental to those things. You are sabotaging yourself. I believe you can be a good person. A faithful lover."

"Either that or you're a drama queen," Leisa said, apparently knowing Brett needed some comic relief so as not to bolt from the room. "You need to be at the center of bad things or else you're bored."

Brett pulled herself together and grinned at Leisa. "From the bit I know of myself, I'm guessing you're probably closest to the spike. But that's all irrelevant, 'cause what's important now is what I should do next."

"Not necessarily," Maddy said. "It is also important to determine exactly what the cause of this situation is, or else it is bound to occur again."

Leisa reached around Brett to put a hand on Maddy's shoulder. "Honey, you may have hit the nail on the head. If we sit here and keep working on why this happened, so it doesn't happen again, the cops will, sooner or later, show up, arrest Brett, and throw her in jail for the rest of her life, and then she won't have these issues anymore. Perfect solution!"

Brett stood and began pacing. It felt weird to be between two lovers. "So what do I do?"

"Okay," Leisa said. "You came here 'cause you're apparently sure the cops wouldn't really give you a fair shake, which is probably true, given your reputation."

"So you cannot turn to the police for help with this situation," Maddy said.

"Um, I think we covered that when I called and said I *needed a place to hide from the cops*. I believe the question now before the judges is what I should do next."

"What *we* should do next," Maddy corrected.

"Seems to me that you're the one with all the experience in this sort of thing—being on the lam, investigating a crime, committing crimes while investigating crimes—" Leisa said.

"I resemble that remark!"

"So tell me, general, what do we do?" Leisa said.

Brett sighed. "Okay. I will need your help." She pulled out one of her business cards and wrote a phone number on the back. "I just picked up this pager today, so it's clean—at least for a while. If I'm ever away and the cops show up, page me with 1313 to warn me."

"1313?" Leisa asked.

"Nice random number that no one would plug into my pager."

"How did you come up with it?" Maddy asked.

"Most people think of thirteen as unlucky. I'm different. I think it's a lucky number. Repeated, it's twice as lucky," Brett replied. "Anyway, page me with that number if you need to warn me. Try not to leave me voice-mail unless it's urgent. I don't want to have to check it too much. I'll know to check it right away if I see 1313." She turned to Leisa. "I need you to call Frankie tomorrow—from your work. Give him this number and find out any new intel. Let him know I'm with you. I'm sure they're tracing my credit and ATM cards and don't quite trust if they're tapping or tracing calls from and to Frankie's, my home, the Paradise, etcetera, so we've got to be careful about calls. For all I know, they might end up watching here as well. Leisa, you're my safest point of communication because you came into the picture after Allie and I left Alma. If Frankie or anyone has info to pass on to me, they should go through you or Maddy, preferably at work. Oh, and use a pay phone somewhere to call Randi McMartin, Detroit PD, and find out the results of my blood test."

"You think you might be pregnant?" Leisa asked, confused.

"I sent her a blood sample today. Shipped it overnight. So call late in the day to see if she knows anything—but do it anonymously." Just then her old pager went off. She automatically reached for her cell, but remembered she had destroyed it so she would not unconsciously use it, like now.

Leisa picked up her own cell from the coffee table. "Use this. It'll be safer than Maddy's home phone."

"Thanks," Brett mumbled as she went through the digits to access her voice mail, then listened to Frankie's lengthy message, occasionally jotting down notes. After she hung up, she looked at Maddy and Leisa. "I have to stay away from home, Frankie's, and any of the places we own, as well as any place I am known to frequent.

And I definitely cannot drive my car any more. Maybe I'm being paranoid or too cautious, but—"

"It is better in this circumstance to err on the side of caution," Maddy said.

"What do you need now? Have you found anything out yet?"

"Well . . . I do need a computer. Please tell me you have one?"

"Yes, we do," Maddy said. "Do you require any assistance? Leisa seems to be quite capable in that arena."

"I don't want to get you involved," Brett repeated.

"We already *are* involved," Leisa said. "What can we do?"

Brett sighed and sat down. "Do you have anything to drink?"

"Scotch, wine, bourbon, beer, vodka and there might even be some tequila," Maddy said, standing. "What's your poison?"

"What type of Scotch?"

"Um, let me look . . ."

"Make that another beer." Brett figured if Maddy didn't know what type of Scotch, it really wasn't worth drinking.

"You sure?"

"Yup." As soon as Maddy returned, Brett twisted off the cap and took a deep sip. Then she looked up at the women sitting across from her, almost snuggling on the sofa. She sat back in the overstuffed chair. She recapped her morning, and how she had drawn her own blood, then finally to how she had broken into Gwen's home. She pulled the CDs out of her briefcase, along with all the other materials she'd stolen. "And so, if either of you knows anything about how I might be able to take a better look at the stuff on these disks, that would be rather helpful."

Leisa glanced at Madeline, who said, "Putting on the coffee."

"Hey, look, listen—we can always get to this tomorrow," Brett said, feeling guilty. She felt bad enough calling on their hospitality and help, but she didn't want to keep them up all night when they had to work tomorrow.

"It's nothing," Leisa said, taking the CDs and heading toward the study in the back of the house.

"Really, she does mean that," Maddy said, placing a hand on Brett's arm to stop her from following. "We put the coffee on late quite a bit, actually. Whenever we have a lot of papers or exams to grade, for example. Or when she has just purchased a new game for the thing she connected to the television."

Brett glanced at the TV. From what she had seen, the house was now a conglomeration of Maddy's and Leisa's possessions. She figured they had weeded some out along the way, but the big, flat-screen TV was definitely Leisa's. She quickly identified Leisa's new gaming system. She smiled. Somehow she could see the very precise Maddy being adamant over killing stuff in some game. The woman was probably a complete gaming addict. Brett made a mental note to never take her to a casino.

"Let's set you up for the night in the spare room and by then the coffee should be finished, and you can join Leisa. Although we have more beer if you prefer that. I picked some out today, knowing your predilection for such." Madeline led the way upstairs. "Alas, I didn't know your preferences in Scotch. We just have a futon in the spare room, but I understand it is quite comfortable." She pulled towels from the closet and continued, "Leisa is unsure of her computer skills, although she is quite skillful with all electronics. She has no formal training, but she has read quite a lot about it." Maddy gestured toward the wall of books in the spare room. Many of them were computer manuals. "She really has a genius about it all. Your disks are in safe hands. Leisa will decipher whatever can be found on them."

"I just copied stuff, Maddy. I had to be quick and could only do what I did because of what Allie's made me learn. I don't know anybody who could really work with what I brought so I'm glad for any help."

"Don't lean over her shoulder. Let her simply do what she does. She works best if not questioned."

"Got it, boss."

Chapter Ten

When Brett took Leisa her coffee, bringing another beer for herself, Leisa was flipping through files on one of the CDs. Brett put the coffee next to her and pulled up a chair.

"From what you've said, I'm looking for reasons anybody might want to kill Gwen," Leisa said, still staring at the screen.

"That's good. Find anything yet?"

"Not directly, no. But I do need an answer to a question to know at least a little thing—what's Gwen's e-mail address and screen name?"

Brett told her. After all, she IMed and e-mailed enough with Gwen to know them by heart.

Leisa smiled. "Interesting. You see, I've found that there are two different AOL accounts set up on this computer."

"And that means?"

"Nothing by itself, but you see, one account only has you on its Buddy List and e-mail address book. Just you."

"Really?"

"That's not that interesting by itself. A lot of folks have more than one identity on AOL. That's one attraction to that program—different screen names and such. You can be who you want to be, when you want."

"So you're saying she played me? At times she focused just on me?" Brett was confused. Then she remembered how Gwen had started IMing her from out of the blue.

"I'm not sure what I'm saying, yet." Leisa turned to look at her for the first time. "What I do know is that although some folks have different screen names and identities online, that isn't what Gwen had."

"What do you mean?"

"I mean the different names aren't all tied into one account. Well, some are, but the one that focuses on you is not on the master directory. The actual program—the software—for that screen name is tied to a different account, which is hidden. You'd only ever access that account if you knew what you were looking for, or were a big ol' computer geek."

"I'm thinking maybe Gwen was. It seemed as if she was. Especially taking into account what she did for a living and all."

Leisa turned around in her chair to fully face Brett, who stood leaning against a bookshelf. "You've got a lot of files on these disks. It looks as if you also scanned in some stuff."

"Yeah, I did." Brett shrugged. "Didn't know how else to make copies without anyone noticing I'd taken anything."

"It's gonna take me a while to go through them—to look for any further incongruities like these, or anything else that is hidden. And I have to look through your screen shots and all the scans. I might pull Maddy in to help."

Brett nodded. "Yeah, all-hands-on-deck sort of thing. I understand."

"Brett, you're in a lot of trouble."

"I had kinda clued in to that."

"So what do you plan on doing about it?"

Brett sat down, staring at her beer and slowly peeling the label off it. "I need to figure out who really killed her."

"How do you plan on doing that?"

"Shit. I need a real plan, don't I?"

"Yeah, that might help about now."

Brett stared down at her beer, and Leisa stared at her.

"Brett, I have to ask . . . I mean . . ." Leisa said.

"Spit it out already."

"You described what happened this morning to us, but . . . you seemed . . . unsure."

"What do you mean?" Brett stood and began pacing, only occasionally looking at Leisa.

"You said it was your gun, and that you seemed to have dreamt . . . well . . . fucking Gwen. Do you remember what happened? How much do you actually remember?"

Brett leaned her head against a bookshelf. She couldn't believe how many books these women had. "At some point everything became blurry. I remember getting to the room as well as I remember doing Gwen. But see, that's the thing . . ."

"What is?"

"I woke up this morning in the room, so that means it actually happened. But . . . about the sex . . ."

"What?"

"I remember her nails ripping open my back. I remember blood, I remember the pain of it. God, it was fucking hot."

"And . . . ?"

"And I looked at my back today, and it was unmarked."

"I don't understand."

Brett lifted up her shirt, showing her back to Leisa, in its entirety.

"I don't see anything."

"That's the point. I did not have sex with her. Or, at least, the sex I remember was just a dream. And I remembered drilling her with a cock, and there wasn't one in the room."

"God, you were fucked up."

"No shit. So what do I do now?"

"You woke with your gun in your hand and her dead, apparently by a bullet from your gun. The door was locked, and you were on the inside."

"Yup."

"You're fucked."

"You're helpful."

"I try to be. Maybe what you need to do is approach this problem like I approached the computer tonight."

"What do you mean?"

"I started with the basic thought that somebody wanted Gwen dead, so the key is to find out why. Once you have motive, you might come up with some suspects. You told me she was in tech. What was she working on?"

"I'm not sure."

When Brett finally went to sleep, leaving Leisa still at the computer, she remembered she was doing the right thing. After all, Maddy had told her that Leisa worked best alone, with no one questioning her. Brett needed her very best work.

And Leisa had given her things to think about. Leisa had got her thinking in the right directions about how to look at all of this—how to properly investigate it. Brett had looked into some things before, but then . . . she was either undercover, investigating at her own will, looking into the past, or looking into things that pertained to her but didn't center on her.

Whoever did this had pinpointed her before it all went down. Someone had picked Brett out to frame and that pissed her off. Big time.

She was too worked up to sleep, but she couldn't exactly go for a drive, or pace around in someone else's house. She wanted to check on Leisa but couldn't. Leisa needed her time and space.

So she lay in bed and tried to replay everything that led up to last night. She remembered her growing emotions and her fear when Gwen was in trouble. She remembered Gwen suggesting they meet in person.

She remembered everything. How hot Gwen looked, how she wanted to do Gwen and feel that nubile body under her hands, how she wanted to hear that gorgeous woman scream her name.

But it was all just about sex and being wanted. And she had that with Allie.

She remembered being dragged to the room and remembered her dream.

It was insane. She couldn't tell fantasy from reality. It all blurred into one, the colors streaming together like a wet watercolor painting.

Maddy was right. The futon was nice. But still she tossed and turned, haunted by her past. She wasn't sure when she fell asleep, but she did know when she woke up. She couldn't remember the dream, but she woke sweating and gasping.

She glanced at her watch. Ten a.m. Maddy and Leisa were already at work. She made her way downstairs, hoping for coffee, or maybe a soda at the very least. She hoped Leisa had left a note about anything she had found.

On the kitchen table she found something different. Something she didn't want to see or know about.

It was the paper, opened and displayed to the front-page story of Gwen's murder and its continuation. Brett glanced over it, seeing her name prominently mentioned. There was no way she was getting out of this. She was going to spend the rest of her life in jail, unless she went on the lam. But she deserved a life in prison, with all that she was and all she had done.

And if she was asked to tell the truth, the whole truth and nothing but the truth, and if she did, she would have to admit that, yesterday morning she did think, for a bit at least, maybe she did do it.

And then she stopped looking at the text and finally looked at the pictures—pictures of the coroner removing the body from the hotel, of the room, and of Gwen.

Brett picked up the paper, in case she was wrong. But even from the fuzzy black and white newspaper photo she knew.

Gwen Cartwright was not the woman she had dinner with the night before. She had no idea whom she had met with, but the one thing she knew for certain was that she had never in her life met the woman in the photo.

Chapter Eleven

Day Four

"Look what I've got!" Leisa cried, walking in the front door and seeing Brett staring down at the newspaper. "Wigs, hair dye, make-up, clothes . . ."

"You're supposed to be at work."

"I made the calls I had to make. Then I got sick." She coughed convincingly. "I just had to help you."

Brett dug through the bags. "Where'd you get this stuff?" she said, frowning.

"Stores and . . . well . . . the clothes came from the Salvation Army. I know it's not your style but—"

"It works. And it's probably a good idea." Brett knew she'd never use any of this shit. Allie'd put her in disguise once, and Brett hated the feeling.

"I didn't know what you'd need, so I probably got too much. But I went to different places for all this. Oh, and I picked these up." She pulled out a bag full of all the newspapers she could find. "I hate to break it to you, but apparently you're the prime suspect for murder."

"Big surprise there." Brett dug into the newspapers, hoping they'd provide more clues for her to work from. They all showed the same Gwen Cartwright in the pictures—a woman she'd never met, but who was strangely familiar, nonetheless.

Leisa poured herself a cup of coffee. "Have you had breakfast, or can I make you something?"

"Uh . . . I dunno . . ." Brett was skimming the articles, looking for anything she hadn't known before.

"To which question?"

"I don't know." Brett realized what she'd said and looked up. "I'm sorry, what did you ask?"

"Would you like me to make you breakfast?" Even now Leisa was nice and kind. She and Maddy were perfectly suited for each other.

Brett realized showing her face around town more than necessary was probably not a wicked good idea. Yet her stomach grumbled.

Leisa laughed. "I'll take that as a yes." She began pulling out pans, eggs, sausage, butter, and all the other bits. "So, do you know what your plan is for today yet? I mean, you do have a plan, right?"

Brett had returned to reading. "Um yeah . . ."

"Well, is this part of the mystery? Me figuring out what you'll do next?"

"Oh, sorry, I was just reading. What did you say?"

"I asked if you have a plan—if you know what you'll do next?"

Brett stared down at a page from the *Detroit News*. "Yeah. I want to figure out who I had drinks with in Lansing."

Leisa was ready to crack the eggs into the pan. She stopped in mid-gesture. "How do you like your eggs?"

"However you make 'em is fine. If you do something like sunny-side up, I like toast with them. If they're scrambled, I'm fine."

Leisa went about the preparations for breakfast. "I thought you had drinks with Gwen?"

"I thought so, too." Brett picked up a newspaper and showed it to Leisa, interrupting her cooking. "This is *not* the woman I had drinks with."

"I don't get it. Who is this woman then?"

"I don't know. And that's the point."

"No, I mean it. Why are you shoving this paper in my face?"

Brett took a deep breath and leaned back against a counter. "All the papers are saying this is the woman I allegedly killed. This is not the woman I met the other night."

"Um, Brett?"

"Yeah?" She was still staring at the papers.

"Did you ever see pictures of her before?"

"Yeah. I did."

"So . . . ? Well . . . Um . . . Didn't you notice something yesterday morning?"

"Leisa, didn't I tell you . . . oh, I guess I didn't. Okay, babe, get this, it was bad enough that I thought I had shot her . . ."

"Okay."

"I carry a three-fifty-seven. It was in my hands when I came to."

"And that means?"

"A three-fifty-seven can be used for large game hunting. It's a regular show stopper."

"And that means?"

Brett looked at Leisa full on, meeting her height for height. She spared nothing. "I woke up with a corpse. She was dead. Her face had been blown off." She began to think about the corpse she had seen. The exact damage that had been done to it.

"So how did you know it was her? It could've been a maid then." Leisa was apparently not thinking about the carnage Brett had seen that morning.

It's easy to analyze if you can't quite imagine the scene. If you blocked it from your brain. Which was a lot easier if you had never seen it. "We were in a locked room. She had the same size, shape, and build as the woman I met the night before. Her hair was exactly right . . . what was left of it, that is . . . I mean, I didn't really study her . . ."

"So? I'm confused."

"So am I." Brett sat down and closed her eyes, trying to remember the few brief moments she had looked at the body. Someone had apparently gone to a lot of trouble to make her practically unrecognizable. Brett would've sworn that the overzealous killer or killers had shot the woman at least twice in the face. She'd had no face.

She didn't like to think about it.

But she did wonder why they hadn't scorched her fingertips as well.

"I was brought in to appear as if I killed this woman. The real Gwen Cartwright. But I didn't. I never even met her," Brett said. "The real Gwen Cartwright, that is."

"Okay, so I'm still confused," Leisa said, splitting the scrambled eggs with cheese into two portions. Brett pulled the bagels out of the toaster and slathered cream cheese on them while Leisa portioned out the sausage patties.

They sat down together to dig in. There was silence as they both ate.

"What exactly do you mean?" Leisa said after a bit. Brett liked a girl whose appetite was as big as hers.

"Okay, so it's clear I was framed. But I don't get it. Why me? And why did they make it so easy to identify her? None of this makes much sense!"

"You've been—"

"Holy fuck!" Brett said, dropping her fork and bagel and hitting herself upside the head. "I can't believe it took this long to remember!"

Leisa jerked back. "What?"

Brett grabbed a newspaper and pointed to Gwen's picture. "This is the woman I couldn't identify in the pictures at Gwen's place! I didn't know who she was . . . but . . . now . . ."

"What?"

"I saw pics of Gwen and her family and friends. I thought she was behind the camera, but she was in front of it." Brett sat down. "Shit, this is even more twisted than I thought. Someone really set me up."

"Who?"

"Yeah, that's what I've gotta figure out." Brett ignored the rest of her breakfast to pace. "Okay, so I saw the woman I met somewhere—knew her from somewhere. But where? Was she in some of the pics at Gwen's? But, y'know, she looked a lot like Gwen really does . . ."

"So was . . ." Leisa stumbled, apparently trying to grasp the implications of what Brett had just said. " . . . she the one who set you up?"

"Probably."

"What are you going to do about it?"

Brett leaned against the table and looked right at Leisa. "I'm gonna find her and I'm gonna make her pay."

"What I don't understand," Maddy said when she came home during a break in her schedule, "is how the police positively identified her if her face was obliterated?"

"Her place of work had her fingerprints on file," Brett said. She and Leisa had read all of the newspaper reports on the murder and then gone online and watched television to see if they could find out any more basic information. "What they did was ensure I wouldn't recognize who I was in bed with. They wanted me to think I had killed Gwen Cartwright."

"Why do you think that?" Maddy asked.

Brett had been running it through her mind for a while now, and thought she had some ideas on it. "They blew away her face so *I* couldn't recognize her. God, there was nothing left, so I figured no one else could easily, either. I just didn't think about checking her fingerprints, after all, most people don't have their fingerprints on file."

"What do you mean?" Leisa asked.

"You get fingerprinted for lots of different reasons, like if you join the military, are arrested, or need to be bonded or get a security clearance. But a lot of people never get fingerprinted. Probably more people in this country aren't than are. I just didn't think to look . . ." Brett's words fell off, as she mentally kicked herself for not really checking out the situation when she was right there. But she was freaked, and sickened and . . .

"So whoever did this knew her body could be identified," Maddy said.

"Could the woman you met have been the one the real Gwen was afraid of?" Leisa said. It was as if they knew where Brett's thoughts were going and were trying to stop her from diving into that font of abysmal thought and self-contemplation.

"No," Brett finally said, shaking her head and responding to Leisa. "I thought about that, but the woman I met online sent me pictures—and those pictures were definitely of the woman I had drinks with."

"Didn't you say you searched her stuff?" Leisa asked. "I mean, you got her address off her driver's license, right?"

"Yeah, I did, but . . . driver's license photo, y'know? I just thought it was really bad." She thought for a moment. "Actually, seeing her picture in the paper, it really was a very bad picture. They can take photos of people from satellites miles away, but just try to get the secretary of state to get a good picture. Sheesh!" Michigan was an anomaly that way. Where other other states used motor vehicle administrations and departments of motor vehicles, licenses in Michigan were issued by the secretary of state.

"So your first point of business is to discover just who it was you met in Lansing?" Maddy asked, focusing Brett's thoughts.

"Yeah." She shook her head. "I wish I could get back into Gwen's house, but that's impossible now."

"Why?" Leisa asked.

"I'm sure the cops are there, and will probably have a stakeout after they've gone through the place. Too risky."

"No, I mean, why do you want to go back there?"

"I'm sure the woman I met with was in some pictures at her house, but I'd like to make sure."

"Then you think fake Gwen was someone the real Gwen knew?" Maddy asked.

Brett thought about the woman in the pictures on her computer at her office. That was the woman she had met for drinks. And she was sure that woman had also been in some of the pictures at Gwen's, because she remembered wondering if the other woman was Gwen's girlfriend, whom Gwen had never mentioned. It was definitely her. "Yeah, I do. In fact, I'm sure of it." She tried to remember which picture she had thought that about precisely—was it a picture of fake Gwen and real Gwen together?

"So that means an acquaintance of hers set you up," Maddy said. "I must wonder, however, why an employer would have an employee's fingerprints on file. Isn't that somewhat unusual?"

"If Gwen's employer kept her fingerprints on file, that means they fingerprinted her to begin with, which must mean she was doing something for them that had some consequence. I want to know what that was." Brett was rediscovering her anger and purpose, which was what she needed at this point.

"You said you investigated her online," Leisa said. "She was high enough up in the company to mean something, so—"

"No. You don't get fingerprinted without reason," Brett said. "Usually a security reason."

"You think Gwen's job is the reason she was killed?" Maddy said. "Or, more precisely, what she did at that job? Where did she work anyway?"

"It's a possibility, one that I'm not about to overlook at this point." Brett pulled Gwen's security card out of her pocket. "I think I need to visit CompuVisions."

"CompuVisions?" Leisa echoed. "Sounds like an eyeglass place."

"They do software development."

Maddy suddenly looked up from the article she was perusing.

"With the number of lawsuits of late based on software rights, online sharing, and free-market share, that could be a lethal profession to be in."

Maddy reached to take the pass card from Brett. Brett snatched it away. "What do you think you're doing?" Brett asked.

"You cannot expect to be allowed to freely roam her work area in order to investigate this. Your image is in enough newspapers to make you someone to watch out for."

"Well, your girlfriend has brought me an ample supply of disguises."

"Brett, by your very height and demeanor, you are always noticeable. Have you considered that the very woman who set you up might in fact be working there right now?"

Leisa picked up her car keys. "I need to let Frankie know about this latest development and—"

"'This latest development?'" Brett asked, putting her hand on Leisa's wrist.

"Yes," Leisa said, brusquely pulling her arm from Brett. Then she faced her. "You've told us the players, and that he should be kept appraised of all things. I think this is a particularly hot item for him to be aware of. Isn't he a friend, and isn't he helping?"

Brett looked down. "Oh, yeah." She wasn't used to people doing so much for her.

"Brett, you're in a lot of trouble here, and you told us who, how, and when to contact people. You told us you want our help." Leisa looked directly at Brett, who looked up from the floor to meet her gaze. "You have to trust that we will do what we have to do. We do want to help you." Leisa turned and left.

Maddy took the pass card. "You asked us to help, and that's what we are doing."

Brett put her hand around Maddy's. "Maddy, I know I need your help. Both of you. But I don't want you more involved than you have to be, not unless I need you to be."

"I've helped you before."

"For which I am truly grateful, but . . . I'll pull you in when the need arises. I don't want anyone else in this until I need them. It's too dangerous."

"You need us, Brett."

"Yes, I do. And I'm using you as much as I can at this point."

"Brett, I know you've always had to do things yourself. You had to survive and make it happen. But now you have friends who are willing to help."

"My life has taken some bad turns, Maddy, and I don't want anyone more involved than needs to be, don't you understand?"

Maddy stared at the desperation in Brett's eyes for a moment too long, then said, "I do. I understand what this could mean. Accomplice to murder, arrest, interrogation, jail."

"I don't want anyone in jail who's innocent."

"Neither do I, dearest. That is why we're trying to help you."

"I don't want anyone involved who doesn't need to be."

"You brought us in, Brett. And we want to help you, or else we would have turned you away."

"You help me because you think it's all a big game, some adventure."

Madeline forced Brett to look at her. No small chore since Brett was much taller, but Maddy was determined. "No, we do not. I never have. We agreed to help you because we know you are innocent. A bit misguided, and not knowing your true path, but innocent nonetheless."

"But I'm not innocent, Maddy. I thought about cheating on Allie."

"Brett, dearest, your soul is a deep, dark hole. You are a good person who constantly lets herself be held back by the past. Because of it, you feel you deserve whatever comes to you. In fact, you make some things happen because you feel you deserve it."

"Oh, for fuck sakes Maddy, can you speak English for once?"

"Part of you wants to be punished, or die, because of your past. And so you set yourself up to pay for it. But underneath it all, you're a good person who wants to do good and have a good life with a loving woman." Brett sat down on the sofa, and Maddy knelt before her, taking her hands in her own. Brett enjoyed the warmth of Maddy's hands in her own cold ones. "But you sabotage it because you think you're not worthy. And that, my dear, is how you end up in trouble."

Maddy got up and walked away from Brett, then turned back to her. "Well, that and the fact trouble seems to follow you like the serial killer in a bad horror movie stalks the babysitter. Between the two, you're doomed."

Brett grinned. "Thanks for the brilliant prognosis, doctor."

Leisa came rushing in the front door. "Brett, I have some bad news. I spoke with Frankie, and he told me about Ski and Randi and what's going on down there."

Chapter Twelve

Allie had barely been able to sleep the night before. She woke up early for breakfast, and to retrieve the morning papers. They subscribed to several, including the *Detroit News/Free Press* and the *Oakland Press.*

Frankie and Kurt woke and only took coffee for the road before they were out the door.

She was alone. Allie was often alone. She often felt lonely these days. It was nothing compared to the desolation after her folks died because now she had Brett, but she was still oftentimes alone.

Their friends were mostly Brett's friends. Well, and Randi, who hung around because she lusted after Allie. And Allie knew that. Allie had intentionally cut the strings between them earlier, but still Randi came around. And she liked that Randi continued to be there for her.

But when she thought about Brett, Allie clenched her thighs together, trying to hold down the lust that hit her loins. She looked back down at the newspaper, studying the picture of Gwendolyn Cartwright, whom Brett supposedly murdered and, Allie was sure, probably had sex with. She wondered what Brett saw in Gwen. Why Brett went to her, instead of Allie.

What could Gwen give her that she couldn't?

Allie held her head in her hands and cried. The tears dropped onto Brett's picture in the paper. She loved Brett, dammit, so why wasn't this working? It didn't matter if Brett hadn't killed Gwen, and Allie was sure she hadn't, but something had happened between them, and Allie didn't know how to accept that. React to that. Go on from there. Her head was pounding. She needed Motrin. Or something stronger. But she needed to keep her wits about her.

There was a pounding on the door. It took her a few moments to understand the knocking, to understand when it went from just knocking to pounding.

She got up and opened the front door.

"Detective Joan Lemanski, Lansing Police. We have a warrant to search these premises." Waving the warrant, Ski pushed her way in, not that Allie put up any resistance.

"Search everything," Ski said to the uniforms who accompanied her, then looked at Allie. "Allison Sullivan? I have a few questions for you." Allie realized Ski recognized her.

"Would you like a cup of coffee?" Allie asked. She was trying to keep her cool. God, she hoped Brett hadn't left anything around here!

"That would be good."

She poured them each a cup, and then set another pot to brewing. "We particularly like Kona coffee," she said conversationally as she tried to think of how she could warn Frankie. "But you have to make sure the bag says one hundred percent Kona, or else it's mixed with something else."

"Kona?" Ski asked, sitting down with her cup.

"It's Hawaiian. Doesn't have the nasty aftertaste. No bitterness at all. Are your officers going to rip apart the house?"

"They might, if they have to. It depends on you."

"What do you need, officer?"

"Detective. Joan Lemanski. But you already knew that, *Allie*. You live with Brett Higgins?"

"Yes. We're lovers." Allie remained standing, shuddering at the sounds of things falling and crashing throughout her house. Inside she was having a fit, freaking out, the whole big shebang. But she knew she had to keep her cool.

"Are you aware that *your lover* is wanted for murder?"

"She hadn't mentioned it to me, but as you can see, I noticed it from today's newspapers."

"And so the papers are the first you've heard of it?"

Allie thought about lying, but she had seen the glimmer of recognition in Ski's eyes when she opened the door. She knew Ski recognized her—and more importantly, Ski really wasn't that surprised by it. Ski had already figured out that the Brett Higgins she was tracking was the Sam Peterson she had investigated a few years earlier.

Ski was playing with her, and she didn't like it. And Allie knew Brett had been set up, hadn't killed anyone, and she knew that made Brett crazy. And she felt a little bit crazy herself right now.

Allie put her foot on the chair rung between Ski's legs, forcing her to suddenly open them further, and leaned in to her. "Ski," she whispered, "Brett wasn't guilty the last time, and she's not this time either. How many times do we need to make you look like a fool before you're gonna understand she's innocent?"

Ski stood, pushing Allie's leg aside and making her momentarily unbalanced. "We can rip your house apart. We can tear it all to shreds, especially with the new Patriot Act laws—"

"Good, then I hope you'll find and kill that 'coon that's living in the wall, 'cause it's driving us nuts. Keeps pounding around like a ghost." Allie was speaking in a normal voice now. "Brett just about scared the neighbors to death one day when she went gunning for it."

"And what was she gunning for it with?"

"Her legally registered three-fifty-seven. God love the NRA!"

Ski's red face belied her true feelings when she calmly said, "So you're admitting *Brett* was Sam Peterson?"

"I'm not admitting anything. I'm telling you Brett is innocent, and we have nothing to hide."

"Confiscate the computer and anything that goes with it!" Ski yelled toward her men. "They met online. We found e-mails on Cartwright's computer, files that indicate they had a *very intimate online relationship*." Ski tried to gain the upper hand by moving toward Allie, forcing her to back up to the wall.

Allie had been preparing herself for the worst, and she had finally bottom-lined it to the fact she knew Brett was innocent. Anything she and Brett had to work out, any of their problems, really had nothing to do with this. "It doesn't really matter, does it? Since Brett didn't do it." Her back was against the wall, and Ski's leg was between hers. She needed to turn the tables on her. She pushed away from the wall and looked Ski directly in the eyes as she began moving toward her. As soon as they touched, Ski's thigh against Allie's crotch, Ski began to back away.

"Maybe if I read you some of what your lover wrote, you'd have second thoughts."

"Not at all." Allie did not want to hear anything. She could not hear anything. "Brett is very talented. As I'm sure you'd like to know." She knew from previous encounters something about Ski, and . . . Ski wanted to torture her. She wanted to take Allie to the brink and trick her into saying something incriminating, even though Allie really didn't know anything. Not even where Brett was.

But the longer Allie could detain and distract Ski, the more time it would give Brett. "How long has it been since you've gotten laid?" Allie whispered, stalking Ski. "You were horny then, you're even hornier now. One of us has gotta be your type. Which one?"

Ski was cornered. Her face was flushed.

"We've searched everywhere, detective," a uniform said, entering the kitchen. He saw Ski with her butt against the stove and Allie with her leg between Ski's and quickly said, "Coffee. Good."

Ski slid away from Allie. "Let's take the computer with us." She turned to Allie. "It will be returned once it is examined."

"I'm sure."

As soon as the cops left, Allie called Frankie. She kept it short and to the point.

He was ready for them. That's why he and Kurt had gotten up early. "I got it covered babe. I'm used to dis shit," he said.

After hanging up with Frankie, Allie tapped her fingers on the phone for several minutes. She wanted to talk to someone, but couldn't call any of the obvious people. She didn't know where Brett was, but she didn't want to contact any of their out-of-town friends because Brett might be there.

She had nowhere to turn.

She took her coffee and the phone out to the porch, hoping to think of someone she could call.

She wanted to call a fellow student from one of her classes, but there was no one who could really understand this. This was twisted and warped and fucked. She could only imagine what anyone from any women's studies classes would tell her: Get out while you still can!

But she wasn't ready for that. And she didn't want that. She couldn't live with that.

And Frankie was undergoing police interrogation, and God knew what Kurt was going through . . . and she knew, just knew, Brett was with Maddy and Leisa.

She looked around the quiet street, amazed at how suburban it all appeared. There was her neighbor, two doors down, washing his car. He stopped to spray his dog and scrub the beast down, laughing all the time.

Allie wanted such a carefree life. Unconsciously she wandered toward him. He looked up at her and said, "Oh, God, I hope your girlfriend isn't planning another terrorist attack on my dog again, is she?"

She knew the neighbor and the dog were terrified when Brett tried to hunt the raccoon living in their walls. Allie hadn't been putting Ski on about all of that. Brett had been pissed when she heard the pounding and thought they had purchased another haunted house, so when she realized it was something she could easily stop with a well-placed bullet, she took matters into her own hands.

Allie did the same and called the Humane Society to capture it and a contractor to fix whatever hole the critter had gotten in through. Now she said, "No, I just saw you two and thought I'd come say hello. Brett's out of town. I'm Allie."

The dog leaned against his legs, all but cowering from Allie. "Behave!" he yelled. The dog must've weighed almost what he did. "I'm Fred," he said, putting out a hand, once he'd wiped it on his shorts.

Allie shook it.

He picked up the hose and started spraying the dog off. "Sorry, I just don't want the soap drying on it," he said.

Allie couldn't blame him for being nervous. It was morning, and, well, Brett *had* been running around with a rather large gun not too long ago.

"So you're home from work today?"

"Yeah. I go to Illinois tomorrow. Gotta new roommate for Astro here." He reached down to pet the lab, whose entire body wiggled every time his tail wagged.

Astro finally came up to Allie, asking for attention. She immediately dropped to her knees to lavish the appropriate worship on him.

It made her feel better. Allie wanted to beg Fred to loan her Astro for a while, just a few days, till it all blew over. Allie was sure Astro wouldn't judge her or Brett by anything that was going on around them.

Sometimes it was nice to find someone outside of it all, just to take you away from it. Even though Fred and Astro didn't know what she was going through, Allie suddenly didn't feel quite so lonely.

Brett went to Lansing to help someone. That was all that mattered now. Well, that, and that she was innocent.

She looked up at Fred. "So when do I get to meet the new roommate?"

"I dunno. I'll check with her. Hey, maybe we can find a date to do a dinner party—her, my boyfriend Martin, Astro and you. Your girl can come just so long as she leaves the cannon at home."

Allie laughed. "It's a deal. I'll frisk her before we come."

Fred laughed uproariously at that, and Allie realized her unintentional double entendre and laughed with him. She was going to enjoy this neighborhood.

Chapter Thirteen

When Ski arrived at the Paradise Theatre, Frankie was standing in the box office with a couple of dancers and the teller. Even at this hour of the day, there was one dancer on stage and another ready to go on.

"I'm Detective Joan Lemanski of—"

"Yeah, yeah, I been expectin' y'all. Glad you let me sleep last night and all."

"What do you know?" Ski asked.

"My partner Brett is suspected of murdering someone. I read about it in the papers. She didn't do it, by the way. But you're here with a warrant and all to take a look around." He took the warrant from her, not looking at it. "Not that you need it. We like to cooperate with the police here."

Chicora Leigh grabbed Ski by the lapels and brought her close. "You're a nice one."

Frankie pulled her off. "She's a cop."

"I know that. But she's still cute."

"We follow the law here. And you're free to take a look around if you'd like." Frankie towered over most of the cops, and with his prizefighter's build could probably take them all out without even thinking about it. "Our offices are just upstairs. Ask me if you need any help." He sat down in the teller's chair and kicked his feet up on the desk. "Just don't wreck anything."

When the uniforms had gone upstairs, Ski looked at Frankie. "You've already covered everything up, haven't you?"

Frankie shrugged. "Ain't nothin' to cover." He was following Brett's script, the one he'd learned watching her for so many years.

"Do you know who I am?"

"Yes ma'am, you're a detective." He glanced around. He wanted to let loose on her about how ridiculous this was, but he needed to watch his every word.

She looked at him as if he couldn't pound her into the ground with a single swat. "You're hiding something."

"No ma'am, I ain't hiding nothin'. I been waitin' down here since I got here—ask anybody." He waved around at the other employees, who all nodded.

She glanced around the box office, quickly glancing through the drawers and finding nothing of interest—just office supplies and sheets of paperwork, containing nothing more interesting than doodles, contact numbers, and schedules. Frankie wheeled himself around her in the chair, allowing her full access to everything.

She knew there was nothing to find here. He was being far too accommodating.

"So you're pretty tight with Sam . . . oh, sorry, you know her as Brett. She was just Sam Peterson the last time I investigated her for murder." Ski watched for any acknowledgment of her statement from Frankie. There was none. He had his role down pat. But he had learned from the master, after all.

He shrugged. "We go back a while."

Ski pulled out a notebook, even though she didn't need her notes for what she was about to say. "Yeah, I found that out. Once I knew who I was really looking for. Let's see . . . You were already working for Rick DeSilva back in 1991 when she came on board here, at the Paradise Theatre."

Frankie smiled. "She came on pretty fresh out of college, with her little degree and shit."

"Didn't think much of her at the time, did you?"

Frankie put his feet on the ground, still leaning back in the chair with his hands on the arms of the chair. "No, officer, I didn't. I'd seen smarmy college types before and didn't think much of 'em."

"So it pissed you off when DeSilva took her under his wing like he did?"

Frankie stood, towering over her. "Not at all. 'Cause by then she'd earned it."

"Is that why, after she sold you her part of the business, you hired her back?" She knew he had to have a weak point with Higgins, was sure he'd have to be pissed about something with her, and she wanted to find out what that was. She knew this giant of a man could tell her something she wanted to know.

Frankie stood, watching her, not fidgeting, squirming or anything. He gave her a few moments to continue, then said, "Me and her are a team. We work well together. Things ain't the same without her." He took a step closer to Ski. "I was glad when the cops gave up tryin' to find anythin' on her, 'cause then she could come back home, where she belonged."

Ski thought she saw her opening, and went for it. She looked out the window to the auditorium and gave a cursory glance at the dancer onstage. "Big guy like you, being around all these naked girls all day long, must get you all worked up."

"Not really, they're not my type," Frankie deadpanned.

"So you like your women a bit rougher . . . a bit tougher . . ."

"Oh, I like hot chicks with long legs and big tits . . . women with smooth skin and full lips . . . Yeah. I like those. They make me a lot of money, after all."

Ski was caught briefly off balance. But she compensated. "So you like the darker side . . . you like what Brett has to offer with her boldness, her lean, hard body. You know there's something inside it all that only you can touch . . . reach . . ."

Frankie smirked. "Sounds like you've thought about it a bit yourself, detective."

She had just been trying to think of what Frankie would want, but was really running out of ideas. "I'm just trying to imagine how you see her." She pulled her notebook out and began to flip through it, as if searching for something, while she regained her composure.

"Why don' you keep searchin' then? 'Cause, since you've researched us so thoroughly, maybe you might see why Brett 'n I make such a good team in bizness."

"Why don't *you* tell me why you make such a good team?"

Frankie laughed and turned away. "You don' know shit."

The clerk opened the door to the straight side of the theatre and Victoria stepped in. "Hey, Frankie. Where's Brett?"

"Tempest—Victoria—this is Detective Joan Lemanski with the Lansing Police."

Victoria was dressed in her latex catsuit and six-inch stilettos. The zipper on her catsuit was pulled halfway down, revealing a lacy red bra and toned abdomen. "So you're here gunning for Brett, huh? Well she didn't do it! Whatever it is."

Ski saw the opportunity and dove for it. "So, you're friends with Brett, huh? How well do you know her?"

Victoria's eyes went from Ski to Frankie and back again. "I just started dancing here a few months ago."

"You seem to care a lot about Brett, nonetheless."

"She's my boss. If something happens to her, I'm out of work."

Ski carefully positioned herself to see if Frankie was giving Victoria any hints. He wasn't. "So work is all you care about?"

"I like keeping a roof over my head and paying my bills on time. These gigs help me out." Victoria wasn't used to being questioned like this, so she was nervous.

Ski looked at Frankie and the clerk. She put a hand on Victoria's elbow. "Where can I talk to her alone?"

Frankie nodded toward the stairs. "Upstairs."

Ski led Victoria up and found an empty office. "Make yourself comfortable."

"Don't think that's possible," Victoria said, leaning against a wall and looking at a clock. "I've got a show soon, so let's make this quick."

Ski stood in front of Victoria with her legs spread and her arms crossed. "You seem like a bright girl—why're you stripping here?"

"Because it pays well."

"There are a lot of other places to strip in this state, places that aren't so degrading." When Victoria didn't nibble, she continued, "Why do you strip?"

"I already told you." Victoria stood straight, facing off with Ski. "It pays the bills."

"So you enjoy taking your clothes off for a bunch of guys who try to jack off on you?" Ski was getting closer, almost stalking Victoria.

Victoria turned her head from Ski, then looked back to her. "I've got a high school diploma. This is an easy way to make good money."

"For your fix?"

Victoria went behind the desk and sat in the chair, propping her feet up on the desk. "You want me to be something I ain't." She stretched back languorously, then teased her hand down her torso, toward the zipper. She inched it down until it showed the top of her thong. Then down to its end. "And you want me for who I am."

Ski pulled her eyes from the display. "The only thing I want is to learn what you know about Brett."

Victoria stood, with much of her body on knowing display, and stalked Ski, pressing her back against the door. "You're after Brett. You want to know what she likes." She put her hands on Ski's waist, then pushed them upward. She kissed Ski's chin, then whispered into her ear, "You want to know the truth?" She put her hand on Ski's shoulder holster, but Ski beat her to it. Victoria put her hand on top of Ski's.

Feeling breathless, Ski pushed Victoria away. "I want to know the truth. What is she hiding?"

Victoria stalked away, letting Ski get a good long look at her ass outlined in latex. She turned her head toward Ski. "Nothing."

Ski's eyes came up. "Nothing?"

Victoria came toward her again. Not touching, but close enough for it to feel like touch. "I came to Michigan to kill Brett. I thought she was the reason my sister was dead. She wasn't . . . isn't . . ."

"You say that almost as if you're just repeating what you were told."

"It wasn't Brett. I can't explain it. But it wasn't."

This time it was Ski who went to Victoria. "You're in love with her."

"No. I'm not." Victoria answered too quickly.

Ski glanced at the clock. "I think you need to be onstage." She turned and left the office. She went directly to Brett's office to help her officers there, and heard Victoria go back downstairs for her show.

Ski double-checked the officers' work, glancing through to make sure they hadn't missed anything. Then she made sure they took Brett's and Frankie's computers and peripherals. She didn't want to have any computer left behind, any drawer unsearched.

On her way out, she looked through the box office window to watch Victoria naked onstage, working the audience into a frenzy.

After her show, Victoria tracked down Frankie, who was alone in his office. He was trying to restore order to the mess the cops had left. "Frankie, just what is Brett into? What has she done?" Victoria reached up to grab Frankie by the collar and, despite his size, to push him back against the wall.

"She hasn't done anything, really. She's innocent!" Frankie backed himself into the very far corner. Victoria followed.

"So why was that cop grilling the both of us?" She stuck her long nails into his neck just where his carotid artery was, making him wince.

"Brett's in trouble, okay, and . . . I can beat the shit out of you easily, so why am I putting up with this?"

Victoria pushed her nails in further. "Because you let yourself get into this position in the first place. And you can beat me easy, but my nails are long and sharp enough to kill you."

"I got that," Frankie said. Then he cupped his hand around Victoria's and pushed it down, proving she really couldn't harm him. "What I meant was that we both love that big bull and will do anything for her." He pulled her tight against his chest, hugging her.

Suddenly, they pushed away from each other.

"That didn't just happen," they said in chorus.

And then they looked at each other.

Frankie was the one who broke the silence. "You're in love with her."

"So you know I'm not gonna turn against her." Victoria headed out of the office toward the stairs.

"Yeah, I do. Now." Frankie followed her.

"I'll get over it."

"Ya sure? I hear falling for her is incurable."

Victoria stopped and turned back toward Frankie. She hated to look up at him, but she did. "You saying such big words would be funny—if this wasn't so unfunny a situation." She took a step up, toward Frankie, facing off with him, as much as she could.

He leaned down and pulled her body against his, just so she couldn't escape. He put his mouth near her ear and whispered, "Chill. It's none my bizness, and I don't care. Get over it though, 'cause she's with Allie now."

Victoria pushed away finally. "I know that!" Her face was red when she looked at Frankie. Then she turned and rushed away down the stairs.

When Victoria was done with her last show of the day, she dressed and left. She had recently purchased an old Honda Civic. She wasn't sure where Brett was but given the news stories and what she knew about Brett, she had a general idea of where to drive. She figured she'd develop more of a plan on the way.

It was an hour-and-a-half drive from Detroit to Lansing. While Victoria drove, she thought about every detail she had heard on the news and read in the paper. She recalled every word Ski had said, but it didn't bring her any nearer to where she needed to go. She figured she'd go to the hotel where the murder had occurred and hoped she recognized someone—hoped that would take her where she needed to be.

She put her foot to the accelerator and looked at her watch. She didn't know Michigan that well and had never been to Lansing before. She dug into her glove box, hoping she had a map of the state so she'd know she was heading in the right direction.

She wanted to cry. She wanted to lay her head down on her steering wheel and cry, but she couldn't, because she was driving. She remembered Brett telling her about her sister and . . . one late night . . . over much Scotch . . . admitting to having thought she had seen her sister as a ghost . . .

Victoria didn't care about much else, but she brooded over the rest of the conversation to try to remember where it was that Brett had thought she had seen Pamela's ghost. Alma came up in her mind, and Victoria pinpointed that bit of her memory and forced it to the front.

Alma . . . Alma . . . A house in Alma . . . Brett (and Allie) had lived there.

Where was it?

She had to find Brett.

Brett was in Alma. Victoria grew sure of that, and so she went there, looked up names in the phone book until she found the one that she was searching for.

She had learned something from her time with Brett. To make sure she wasn't being followed, Victoria drove around randomly so she'd see if she was being tailed and perhaps lose someone she hadn't noticed.

Nothing was suspicious.

Still, she parked her car three streets from her destination and walked to Maddy's.

Chapter Fourteen

Victoria knocked. And then knocked again. Lights were on in the house, so someone was home. She glanced in through the windows, trying to see any movement but saw none.

She went back to knocking, thinking about other places to knock, or try, while glancing about, sure that Allie and Brett must be inside, having sex, when—

The front door opened. "Get in here quick, child," a wild looking woman with wicked red hair said, yanking her inside.

"Maddy, she's okay," Brett said, laying a reassuring arm around her.

The wild-haired woman, Maddy, looked at Victoria. "No. She's not. She wants more than you can give." She glanced up at Brett's eyes, then said, "But no, she holds no particular grievance against you now. She is safe in this matter."

Brett looked at her. "What are you saying?"

"You already know." Maddy turned and went up the stairs.

Brett couldn't believe Victoria had found her. She pulled the soft woman into her arms. "Were you careful?"

"I watched for tails, I parked several streets over . . . Brett, I just had to know you were okay!" Victoria snuggled closer into her arms.

Apparently, Madeline had stopped only a few stairs up. She watched them from that vantage point. "Brett." Her voice drifted down as a soothing melody. A Brahms' lullaby. "I opened the door and thought she was a ghost. I, too, had seen her image before." She kept her distance, yet persisted. "She is not who she seems."

Brett looked back at Victoria, and all the ethereal crap stopped. She knew where she was now, and Maddy's seeming ability to see inside of her, to see through her, no longer held sway over her.

"I'm just glad you're okay," Victoria said, pulling Brett even closer. "I just needed to know that. What should I do? What can I do?"

"How the hell did you find me?" Brett led her over to the sofa.

While Victoria explained, Brett studied her features, her body, her voice, and her eyes. Storm, Victoria's older sister, whom Brett had loved, still loved, had always been such a comfort to Brett, and right now, Brett just wanted to feel the softness of Victoria's lips under hers.

Even though Pamela Nelson, whose stage name had been Storm, died a decade before.

Ski sat back at her desk, looking at her computer monitor. She had all the files from both Gwen Cartwright's home and work computers. She had let CompuVisions identify which files were highly classified programming items, and she didn't have those files copied. She had glanced over them, and they only seemed to contain indecipherable computer code.

CompuVisions said these files only had to do with a hot new computer program they were developing. Ski spent a while with the CEO looking over those files.

Earlier in the day she too had found the second AOL account on Cartwright's home computer.

She thought about everything she knew. Cartwright's home lock hadn't looked tampered with, and although she had her team fingerprint everywhere, she was sure Higgins' prints wouldn't be found there. None of Brett's friends had yet heard from, or seen, her. Or so they said. The police had located Brett's vehicle in Lansing, but it was clean, and the only thing they learned from it was that she had apparently ditched it. Brett didn't talk much to her neighbors, and no random remarks had been made to give any clue as to her whereabouts. Ski had alerted the police in Alma to the fact that Brett was known to be there on occasion, but so far they had no indication she was hiding there.

Ski pulled out a folder with details on Brett and the people closest to her. Allison Sullivan had helped protect Brett previously, even though she was a former police officer. Frankie Lorenzini had a record of his own. Although Lorenzini's boyfriend Kurt—Ski still couldn't believe Lorenzini was gay—was clean, Ski didn't trust him and didn't think he knew Brett that well anyway. Apparently he had only started dating Frankie in the past few months or so.

She had so misplayed Frankie earlier that day.

Brett had stayed just inside of the law for quite a while, but several years ago, she went on the run and managed to disappear without a trace. Until Ski ran into her, in Alma. But even Ski hadn't discerned her true identity at the time. The woman knew how to disappear and remain hidden. When she had run, the first place she went was California. If she had gotten that far this time, Ski knew she probably didn't have a chance in hell of catching her. The woman was a pro.

Ski looked at the open-and-shut case she had going against Higgins. Every path led directly to her. On top of everything else, ballistics discovered the murder weapon was a .357, Brett's weapon of choice. She'd bet a year's salary ballistics would match the bullet to Brett's gun. And now she had the e-mails in the hidden AOL account on Cartwright's home machine.

Ski picked up her folder on Chuck Bertram's homicide, reviewing her notes from the case. At the time, she thought Allie was good at talking with the police, was totally devoted to her lover, reasonably quick on her feet, and willing to do anything to help cover for her girlfriend. When Ski spoke to her, the woman had looked upset, very upset, as if she had been crying a lot. Ski had pretty much discounted her, thinking nobody could be such a good actress, but looking over Allie's personnel file from when she was with the police department made her think twice. As did looking over the notes she had assembled on Allie's role in the other escapades the two had gone through in the past few years.

In fact, since going on the lam, the two had solved a cold case, with Brett getting shot in the process; solved a murder and put a crime boss in jail while causing a big pile-up on I-94 when Brett jumped from one moving vehicle to another to save Allie; gone undercover at the request of some friends to help some high school kids, something that ended up with Brett jumping off a building to save someone who wasn't even a friend—Randi McMartin who, for years, apparently wanted nothing more than to see Brett behind bars; and worked together to stop a serial murderer in Detroit, something that required Allie to go undercover as a stripper. Ski found herself wishing she'd seen that, especially after her encounter with Allie that morning.

Ski sat back for a moment, thinking about Allie, then about Allie onstage, stripping . . . taking it *all* off.

But see, that was something, Ski thought, sitting bolt upright. Somebody killing strippers in Detroit was bound to be bad for Brett's business. She flipped back through the various cases Brett had been involved with. By all appearances, the only time they did help people just to help them was when they went undercover at Alma High School. But still, at times, during these things, they *did* help others. Like Randi McMartin.

There really was no reason Brett saved McMartin, except . . . There was no reason.

But Brett was such a professional, there was no way she'd leave such a huge trail pointing directly to her if she had done this. But with Chuck Bertram's homicide she had said something similar—that she never would've reported the murder at the Capitol had she actually killed him. It would be pretty stupid. So stupid it couldn't be her.

Of course, she was innocent. That time.

But hadn't McMartin said something similar to Ski as well? That by itself was somewhat interesting. The woman had spent years trying to take Brett in, and now she was sticking up for her? Had Brett risking her life for McMartin made that much of a difference?

She again looked through the e-mails. She would be surprised to discover that if Brett had broken into Cartwright's house, she had left such evidence behind. But maybe Brett hadn't known enough to really look through the computer files in order to find them. Ski chuckled at this. Brett seemed to know so much, she couldn't imagine her not being a techno weenie too.

She pulled out a notepad, detailing steps she could take to locate and apprehend Higgins, because she really couldn't think of any other lines of investigation. She really had to find the friends who brought Allie and Brett into the situation at Alma High School. After all, they must be reasonably close friends to be able to ask Brett and Allie to risk their necks for something like that—and for Brett and Allie to do it. So she'd go have a talk with them. She'd just have to keep checking back at Brett's known locations, and talking to those involved again and again, until one of them cracked.

She glanced at her watch. Ten o'clock. She thought about making some calls but realized she should just go home and get a good night's rest. Tomorrow was a full day.

She knew she was avoiding something, even as she packed her briefcase and headed home. Once she got there, she poured herself a bourbon on the rocks, pulled Randi's business card from her wallet and flipped it over. Randi had jotted her home number on the back just in case Ski had information to share. Ski also thought that meant in case there was anything she wanted Brett to know. Which seemed to show Randi knew how to get in touch with the elusive criminal.

Ski had problems seeing Randi as the enemy, though. From what Ski had uncovered, Randi was a dutiful and dedicated detective. Maybe she should talk with some of Randi's coworkers? Find out even more about her.

But still, she picked up the phone and punched in the digits.

Randi McMartin was apparently as restless as she, because she picked up on the second ring. "Yeah."

"McMartin, it's Lemanski, up in Lansing."

"Oh yeah? How's it going?"

"I'm sure you know. Not well. I can't find Brett."

"Not all that surprising. She's a slippery one."

"As I think you well know." Ski didn't really know what to expect from this call. She was hoping for honesty between fellow officers, but it appeared McMartin wasn't on board with her plans.

Over the next hour, Ski and Randi played cat and mouse, but Randi had given Ski everything she asked for—she admitted to hating Brett, trying for a long while to put Brett behind bars (where she thought she belonged), and they went back and forth over aspects of the case. Ski had a few more drinks, and she thought she could discern that Randi had, too.

Ski and Randi got along well—each giving as well as getting. Ski figured Randi could get a message through to Brett—but not as well as Frankie could.

Ski really figured she could trust Randi when Randi admitted her obsession with Brett—Randi was convinced Brett either killed her brother, or had him killed. And that was why she had been obsessed with Brett for so long. She wanted revenge. But only when it was really due.

And Ski had to admit that Randi's belief that Brett was innocent of his murder made her start to think twice about Brett as the culprit in Gwen's murder. Could her focus on Brett be preventing her from investigating other suspects?

Ski asked Randi what had changed her mind, figuring it was that Brett had saved her life, but Randi said that she realized her brother had become a drug-addicted criminal, and Brett believed rapists and murderers ought to die. Randi said she wasn't defending Brett as much as she was going for the truth.

The only new information Ski learned was that Higgins had sent Randi a blood sample on the day of the murder, and it showed she had Ketamine, an animal tranquilizer some people took for recreational purposes, in her blood. It was also known as a date rape drug.

"She liked to party?" Ski asked.

"Yeah, but not that way. And considering KT can knock you out, I doubt Brett would use it. She likes to be in full control, if you know what I mean. And she likes her women conscious."

Ski could very well believe that. "No recreational drugs of any kind?"

"Nope, nothing except caffeine, nicotine, alcohol, and Chap Stick."

"Chap Stick?"

"Watch her. She's always putting it on. It's like a drug to her."

Ski heard the sound of ice cubes going into a glass and something pouring over them. She was thinking another drink sounded like a damned good idea. "So she's not into drugs? Not at all? Not even pot?"

"No. She doesn't snort, smoke, inhale, straight-line, or otherwise ingest any illegal substances as far as I've ever seen or known. A few years back, I thought she might be involved in the distribution of drugs, but these days she's clean of everything, even poppers. And believe me, I've been looking for anything to burn her ass with."

"What did you do with the blood sample?"

"I've kept it secure for the chain of evidence. I handed the sealed envelope over to the techies. I was never alone with it. In fact, one of them signed for it. And it's all well documented."

"How do you know it's hers?"

"I don't, but if we ever need to, we do a DNA match. It still proves almost nothing, because she could have taken the drug after the fact, or weeks before. And there's no record of when she took the blood sample. She could have samples stored in her refrigerator for all we know, just for times like these."

Ski tried to corner Randi one last time. "I found e-mails to and from Brett on Gwen's home computer. Rather revealing e-mails." Thinking of them almost made Ski blush.

"Yet another dead-end straight to Brett. Now, I'm not saying you don't sometimes come across open-and-close cases, but from somebody like Brett? I don't think so. Let me ask you this, Ski, do you just want to catch somebody, anybody, or do you want to catch the murderer?"

"I want whoever's responsible. But give me someone other than Brett to pursue, somebody who also has motive, opportunity, and means, and I'll go there." Ski suddenly remembered her own meetings with Allie and her earlier thoughts of the woman stripping, and she suddenly had a feeling about what Randi might be thinking about. "Are you in love with Allie?" she finally whispered.

The silence before Randi answered told Ski the truth. "No."

"So are you helping Brett because of Allie?"

"God no," she finally said. "I'd like more than anything for Brett to go away for a good long time."

"So you can have Allie." Ski kicked her feet up, leaning back on her sofa, enjoying this. "Are you protecting Brett to stay on Allie's good side?"

"Brett knows I'd like to see her gone."

"Even since she saved your life?"

"Yeah. Allie and I had a big blowout when Brett saved my life. She told me Brett had changed, but I didn't believe it. I still wanted to follow her till I found something, anything."

"So what happened?"

"I realized I was wasting taxpayers' money. And that I should stop. Ski, I can't say this any more plainly: I don't know where Brett is, and I don't know anything about this case that I haven't told you. She might have been having an affair, I don't know. What I do know is that she's now playing by the rules, staying just enough inside the lines to avoid prosecution or even arrest. She would never do this like this."

"You're in love with Allie."

"I thought I was. I'm getting over that now."

"Are you sure?"

"Yeah, I am."

"Randi, I'm a cop, too. I know." Ski didn't know when this had become a personal call.

"You're calling from your home, aren't you?"

"Yeah. I worked late, going through all my notes, and looking at the decedent's computer files. When I got home I realized I could probably still call you."

"Find anything interesting?"

"Huh?"

"In the computer files?"

"Just some e-mails to and from Brett."

"Well maybe you can look at other people Gwen e-mailed?"

Ski suddenly realized something. "I don't have the files here, but from one of Gwen's hidden home AOL accounts, the only person mail went to or from was Brett."

"Oh really?'

"Yeah." Ski reached for her briefcase, searching for anything to prove differently, but couldn't find anything. She pulled out a pad and wrote a note to herself.

"So you called me to see if I was hiding anything?"

"Yeah . . ."

Randi imagined herself and Ski in the stairwell, remembered how close they were, and the ferocity with which they spoke to one another. She remembered realizing Ski was just like her. She remembered Ski's eyes, and body . . .

"I'm trying to make sense of this case, and you're not helping. I should've just signed online to see if anybody there could help me."

"But you didn't. You could've and didn't. You called me." Randi found herself sitting bolt upright on her sofa, realizing that maybe there was another reason Ski had called, other than work.

"You know the case."
"But you called me." Ski was not hard on the eyes. Nope, not at all. Randi looked at her drink, thinking this second bourbon should be the last, but still she got up for another. "I like your dimples."
"What?"
"I've been watching the news, and you making statements to the press, and smiling and . . . well . . . I like your dimples."
"I don't have dimples."
"Whatever." Randi realized she'd crossed a line. And then she was glad she had. "You're cute. You called me late at night, on my home phone, so . . . you get the nonprofessional me." Shit, she couldn't even really flirt well anymore. No wonder Danielle had let her go after a handful of dates.
"My notes won't include this part of the conversation."
"Good. So can I ask what you're wearing?"
"I can't believe you just asked that."
"What are you wearing, Joan?"
"Nobody ever calls me that."
"I am. Does it offend you?"
"No," Ski whispered.
"So what are you wearing?"
"You've been drinking."
"So have you. What's your point?"
Ski was sitting on her own sofa. She wanted desperately to unzip her trousers and finger herself in response to Randi's soft and husky tones, but she realized that even somewhat drunk, the cop might realize what she was doing. She wondered if that was a bad thing.
"Joan?" Randi asked.
"Yes?" Ski finally whispered back.
"When this is all over I'd like to . . . to . . ."
"What, Randi?"
"When this is over . . . maybe we could meet some night for dinner? Drinks? Maybe a movie?"
"Yes."

Chapter Fifteen

Day Five

The next morning Brett insisted that everyone go to work, just as usual.

"Listen, the cops haven't come knocking yet," she told Madeline and Leisa, "but if you two keep playing hooky, that's gonna be a red flag to anyone who's paying attention."

"Well," Victoria said, "we already know the cops are watching the Paradise and all, so—"

"No. You might be seen or identified. We need everything to be the same as usual so as to not attract any undue attention. You need to go dance." Brett didn't add that she mostly just wanted to ensure Victoria's safety.

"I must admit, Brett does have a point," Madeline said. "We all need to get to where we should be."

"What are you going to do?" Leisa asked, packing up her briefcase for work.

Brett sat on the sofa and looked at them. "Whoever IMed me and e-mailed me pretended to be afraid of someone. Said someone was following Gwen. When I researched her on the Web, it seemed to indicate that she works in software development, and that can be a very secretive dog-eat-dog world. So I'm thinking I should check out her workplace. It's the only thing I can think of to investigate."

"But if it's so secretive, won't they have security?" Leisa asked.

Brett pulled out the security card she had lifted from Gwen's stuff. "Well, I'm kinda hoping they haven't thought to deactivate this yet."

Leisa smiled, looped her arm with Madeline's, and said, "Well, then, we'll leave you to your investigation. Call if you need us." She looked at Victoria. "Would you like us to drop you off at your car on the way?"

Victoria paused a moment, staring at Brett's set face, then said, "Yeah. I'd like that. Thanks." She turned and followed Maddy and Leisa to the car.

Brett went to the window and watched them leave, assuring herself they weren't followed and the house wasn't being watched. She went upstairs and looked through the disguise items Leisa had procured for her. She didn't want to admit to anyone that she was even considering using this tacky array of items.

She really wanted to just go dressed as a man, but since most people thought she was a guy anyway, she'd be too easily recognizable. Though, when she picked up a short blonde wig, she wondered if she could pull it off—dressed as some sort of outrageous California surfer dude. Except she wasn't in California.

She walked into Maddy's and Leisa's bathroom and rifled through their drawers, finally finding what she was looking for.

She had watched Allie put on her makeup enough to figure out what most of the stuff was for. Maybe she should have had one of the girls stick around to help. To her, it was more complicated than it looked. Too much and she might look like a slut. Brett definitely didn't want to look like a slut.

"Christ, this is so whacked," she said to herself in the mirror. Brett tried to remember the details of applying women's makeup. She rubbed foundation all over her face and neck. She picked up what she thought was blush and brushed it on one cheek, then the other, then did it all over again. And again. She realized she looked like a circus clown, washed her face and started all over again.

The doorbell rang.

Brett went to the front upstairs window and tried to peer out. One brief glance told her all she needed: A police cruiser was parked in front of the house. She wondered if she should hide in one of the safe places, but decided to take a chance. After all, they hadn't even spoken with Maddy or Leisa, so would have no reason for a search warrant.

Instead, she reached up and cracked the window just a bit. She knelt by it.

The cops rang the doorbell again, then started pounding. She was sure they were walking around the perimeter, looking for any sign of life within.

"Ski, I don't think anybody's home."

"There's a car in the drive," Ski replied.

Another, different, male voice. "I'm not seeing anybody in there."

More pounding, then the first male voice again. "I really don't think anybody's home. They are both teachers, didn't you say?"

"Yeah, but one's a college professor," Ski said.

Second male voice. "Then maybe we should just go see them at their jobs."

"I won't need back-up there," Ski said. "But you might be right."

Brett waited while she heard two vehicles start up and drive away. Then she waited five minutes before glancing out the window, to find it clear. And she returned to the bathroom.

There she saw the eyeliner pencils and reached for one. She almost wished the cops had broken down the front door. God only knew she'd rather hide from them than do this shit. Anyway, she had no idea how to use eyeliner. And figured she probably should've done it before she'd used the mascara. So much for that. She stared at her face in the mirror, trying to decide if she needed anything else.

Lipstick. Dammit. Brett liked her Chap Stick and had a feeling that it and lipstick were incompatible. She found several tubes of many different shades and decided a more neutral apricot would work well. Not that she had any idea about this shit.

Again she tried to mimic Allie's application of the strange stuff while wondering why Maddy and Leisa had so many different cosmetics. It didn't seem as if they wore much, though she could imagine Leisa using a bit more when she dressed up for a special occasion.

She found a bottle of perfume that was more like what Allie would wear than the colognes Brett would wear and spritzed lightly. Very lightly.

With that done, she went to examine the items Leisa had brought home. There was a long black wig, a long red one, and a long blonde one. She thought about her black eyebrows and was ready to reach for the black one, thinking about all the snide comments she'd heard about women with blonde hair and dark eyebrows, and then thought twice and grabbed the blonde wig and put it on the bed.

Then she returned to the bags, with the idea of blending into a software development firm. It would either be relaxed, or uptight and businesslike. Regardless, she figured she'd be less recognizable in a skirt or dress, even as she shuddered at the idea. She went through everything trying to find something she might be able to pull off. She found a neat black skirt that seemed to be about knee length on her, a black silk blouse, and a houndstooth jacket. They looked good together.

She stripped and put on the outfit. It fit, but a few problems remained. She hated to do this, but she found the appropriate panties, a real bra, and a pair of pantyhose in Leisa's drawers. Dressed again, Brett looked at herself in the mirror. One last look through Maddy's and Leisa's things produced the right finishing touch: A cute silver heart on a chain.

Brett's short hair gave her the drag queen look, so she picked up the wig and went into the bathroom. She looked at herself in the mirror, preparing to put on the wig and suddenly realized something. "Oh, fuck a duck."

She so didn't want to do this, but knew she had to. She went through the drawers until she found a set of tweezers. Oh, God, she *so* did not want to do this. Peering into the mirror she aimed for her eyebrows and plucked.

"Goddamn! That hurt! Fuck, fuck, fuck!" she yelled, jumping back. She peered at herself in the glass again, wondering if this was really necessary. Yup, it was.

She repeated, again and again, until it seemed as if the top part of her face was numb, it hurt so damned much. How did women do this? But her eyebrows were now much more feminine looking.

She wet her hair, gelled and slicked it back, then she put on the wig. She brushed it a bit more till she was happy with the result. She went back and found a low, very low, pair of Leisa's pumps. She and Leisa were apparently the same shoe size, which only made sense, since Leisa was no small girl.

She put on the jacket and studied herself in the mirror. She felt like a Goddammed drag queen. But she took a couple of steps and immediately realized another problem. She had no fucking clue how to walk in these things. She definitely looked like a drag queen when she walked. Maybe a cowboy drag queen even. She closed her eyes and tried to envision Allie walking toward her, all dressed up. And then she tried to mimic it. One foot in front of the other, hips rolling slightly.

This was so fucking ludicrous!

"Goddammit, if I had known this'd take so long, I woulda just dressed up like a stupid fuckin' California surfer boy!"

In a huff she grabbed a set of keys and her smokes and shoved them into her pockets. Oh, God, that didn't work. She found a small black handbag and threw her essentials in it. As a last thought she threw in the lipstick, because she was sure she'd screw it up by the time she got to CompuVisions.

She quickly drove to the building, checked herself in the mirror, and went for it.

At the building's front desk she signed in illegibly, then put her name down as Sarah Hannigan, and said she was visiting the third floor. The front desk guard seemed to study her a bit more than she liked, but she just tried to appear nonchalant about it.

She got onto the elevator and pushed the button for the sixth floor. She heard someone yelling for her to hold the elevator, but she just hit the door close button. Repeatedly. An arm was shoved through the door opening at the last minute, forcing it back open.

"Didn't you hear me?" the fellow accused, stepping in. "Je . . ." he cut himself off, noticing Brett. He gave her a slow once-over. A slow smile curled across his face. "I haven't seen you in this building before."

Oh, fuck. He was hitting on her. *A man was hitting on Brett Higgins.* She'd never gone to therapy, but she was sure she'd need years of it to get over this crap. "Um," oh shit, she couldn't even talk like herself. She felt like fuckin' Dustin Hoffman in *Tootsie.* She raised her voice an octave and continued, "I'm new here."

He glanced down at the floor numbers, finally remembering to push eight for himself. "So you're working at CompuVisions?"

She nodded. "Just started."

"God, and what a time to start. Didn't some bigwig there just get killed?"

Brett looked down at the floor, feigning innocence. "Well, yes, but I try not to think about it."

"I'm sorry. Well, I'm Jim Wilson, I work up on eight for Creativity, Inc. Maybe some time we can have lunch?"

Brett smiled at him. "I might like that."

"I didn't catch your name," he said when the elevator stopped on six.

"I'll find you," she said with a smile when she got off. Goddammed bra gave her cleavage. Made her really notice she had tits. They weren't that big, but . . . God!

She turned from the elevator and immediately confronted a stark white security door. It was in a short corridor where the only other access was a fire stairwell at one end. There were no windows. Besides seeing what she could find, she also needed to case the joint if she needed to break in sometime in the off hours for further snooping. She had to figure out how to get in and out, and where she needed to go.

She pulled out the pass card and slid it through the reader. The door clicked. At least something worked out. Brett opened it and walked into a busy office. She tried to remember to walk like a woman, keep her head up, but not meet anyone's eyes. She wanted to look as if she knew where she was going and had important business to attend to. She tried to fit in.

She took a tour of the floor, gazing over the many cubicles, offices, and rooms while examining pictures and people to see if anyone looked familiar. She also tried to identify the location of Gwen's office. Fortunately, Gwen really was a bigwig with a nameplate on her door. Unfortunately, she had an assistant of her own who sat right outside her door like a gatekeeper.

Brett didn't think it would be too easy to slip by her. In fact, it looked pretty impossible. The woman was already giving her the evil eye because of her loitering around the door long enough to read the nameplate.

When the girl made eye contact with Brett, Brett smiled and said, "Sorry, I'm new here, I need to stop by human resources. Would you happen to know where that's at?"

"Yes. Of course. Just go down this hall, and it's the second-to-last door on the left," she said, pointing with her hand.

Brett looked down long enough to see the name on her desk: Heather Johnson. Brett hadn't been sure until she heard the voice. When she first looked at her, she thought the young woman seemed familiar, but she didn't know until she heard the voice.

Heather Johnson was the woman she had met for drinks on that fateful night.

"Thank you so much," Brett said, meeting her eyes, careful to keep her voice at a higher pitch than usual.

There wasn't a flicker of recognition in Heather's eyes. But now Brett was positive.

"No problem," Heather said, turning back to her computer. She did look a lot like Gwen. They could have been sisters.

Brett left and, following Heather's directions, went to Human Resources. It was a bustling, cramped office, so Brett just smiled and went on her way. When she glanced back down the hallway, Heather wasn't at her station.

Brett walked back toward Gwen's office, knowing she was taking a huge risk, even as she quickly moved her lock picks from her purse and into her front jacket pocket. She went directly to the door and, after a quick glance around, tried the knob, which didn't turn. It wasn't a tough pick, so to any normal observer it probably looked like she was simply using a key.

Brett was good, damn good.

Brett took a quick look around the office, noting the layout and window. She pulled latex gloves from her jacket pocket and started typing on the computer, which immediately awoke as soon as she hit a key. It was a nice machine. She went right to the e-mail program and glanced at the last few e-mail messages sent and received.

She heard Ski's voice. The office was busy, but somehow that one voice stood above the others. Probably because Brett was waiting for that voice, or Heather's.

She peeked out the door and saw Ski with Heather heading directly in her direction. She could try to hide, but the chance was too great that she'd be cornered there—either trapped by Ski outside the office for most of the afternoon or else discovered in the office.

She quickly slipped out, locking the door behind her.

Ski had apparently caught Heather in the break room, because it looked as if she had a fresh cup of coffee. She led Ski over to the copy machine while they talked and she photocopied. Brett slipped around to listen in on them briefly.

"Listen, I'm trying to focus on my work here, okay? That's the only way I can make it from one day to the next, okay?" Heather was saying.

"I know you're upset, and you should be. I'm amazed you're already back at work, truthfully," Ski said.

Heather turned tearfully to Ski. "It's what keeps me going. I can't stop or else I'll feel. I'll remember and I'll . . . feel." Heather quickly returned to photocopying.

"But sometimes you just have to stop and grieve. You have to go through the grieving process. Your boss was just brutally murdered."

"I hope you'll catch the bitch that did it." Heather pulled tissues from her pocket to wipe at her face.

"Maybe you should go home. We could talk in private there," Ski said. "I'm sure they'd understand."

"I can't, don't you understand it? I can't just go home, because then I'll miss her even more. At least here . . . I miss her here, too . . . but here I've just lost my boss, not . . . not . . ."

Brett noticed people were clearing away from Ski and Heather now, giving them a wide berth.

Ski gave Heather more tissues. "I know she was more than a boss to you."

Heather looked up at Ski. "Yes . . . yes she was. I loved her. I can't believe she was cheating on me!" She was turning her face up toward the ceiling when she noticed Brett. Damn, the woman was a good actress. "Can I help you with something?" she asked Brett. Ski turned around to see who Heather was addressing.

"No, no . . ." Brett said, stepping back. "I just needed to copy something, but I see you're busy . . ." She continued backing off. Heather suddenly reminded her of someone else, but Brett couldn't place her. Without the wig and getup, Brett was now sure she knew Heather from somewhere before the restaurant. And the pictures. And everything else.

Brett suddenly realized that Heather could be the key to solving Gwen's murder. But she had no proof. She couldn't take this to the cops without something to hang it all on—there was a lot of evidence against her, and none against Heather except for Brett's word. She had nothing. But at least now she knew something. It was one piece falling into place.

Her eyes flickered from Heather's to Ski's. Ski was taking more interest in the interaction, and Brett saw a glimmer of recognition pass over Ski's face as she took a step toward Brett.

"Do I know you?" Ski said, following Brett. "Wait, who are you?" she called as Brett took off.

Brett walked swiftly between the few people in her path. Ski was catching up, so Brett slammed through the security door and toward the elevators. One stopped immediately and Brett leapt in it, tossing aside the two people waiting.

Each moment of the elevator's descent seemed like a millennium. Brett wondered if she ought to have taken the stairs.

Brett second-guessed and wondered if she should've just faced off with Ski. Maybe Ski would've taken her somewhere private to interrogate her. Then Brett could have tried her disguise even more. And if Ski saw through it, Brett could have slugged her and left the room for coffee, making her escape then, with no one chasing her. But Brett had seen recognition in Ski's eyes.

By the time the elevator reached the lobby, Brett realized her instincts were still sure. She knew there was a reason she kept following them.

Brett started walking through the lobby, trying to appear casual, but then she heard a door slam and Ski shouting, "Stop!"

Brett took off running, wondering if she could make it to her car before Ski caught her. Brett slammed out the front door, racing for her car as she saw flashing lights from down the street. Suddenly, a few yards in front of her a car slammed to a stop, nearly causing an accident.

The passenger door flew open as a woman yelled, "Get in!"

It was her only chance. Brett took it. The gas pedal was floored before she could get her door closed.

Chapter Sixteen

Heather wondered what had happened when Ski took off running after the new employee. She wiped at her eyes again, then, remembering her role, peered balefully around at the numerous coworkers staring at her. She shrugged in response and went back to her desk with her coffee and copies.

She put her head into her hands, picturing the woman Ski had raced after, imagining her asking for directions to human resources. Still nothing. The woman wasn't bad looking, but was nothing on Gwen.

Then she remembered Gwen laughing, Gwen playing softball, Gwen leaning over her computer until late in the night, focusing on her computer, on the program she was developing. She remembered the many nights she surprised a late-working Gwen with dinner, or coffee—long after Gwen had thought everyone had gone home.

Long after everyone had gone home. But Heather was there, or going back there, paying attention to Gwen.

She remembered the night she walked into Gwen's office, wearing only her tight black skirt, thigh-highs, pumps, and a leather jacket unzipped to reveal her cleavage. She pulled the zipper down for Gwen, down to her navel.

Gwen was the one to pull it down the rest of the way. Gwen turned her chair to face her and Heather straddled her hips.

Heather remembered the way Gwen had kissed her, held her, made love to her. Whenever she needed to cry she just had to remember all of that, and she could.

But she didn't love Gwen. After all, the woman was hot, but such a geek. Heather had to teach her how to really kiss, how to really make love and fuck, and how to let go and be taken to the heavens. But she was a good student. That much Heather had to give her.

She remembered Gwen screaming when she came and how she herself had screamed when Gwen made love . . . fucked her. The woman had gotten good.

She hadn't been Gwen's first, but she was the third. Gwen was hot, but too shy, and she didn't know how to dress until Heather found her.

Heather felt weird trying to seduce a lesbian at first. She'd always been with men. But then she knew what she had to do, so she studied Gwen, trying to figure out what pushed her buttons, and she realized Gwen was attractive, beautiful even, intelligent, shy, witty, and everything she always wanted in a man. Except she was a woman. A woman standing in her way to a helluva lot of money.

And although Heather had never been with a woman before, she knew what got her going, and sometimes she remembered Brett Higgins. Brett was so butch, so tall, and so hard, she was almost like a man.

Heather had to admit, Gwen turned out to be better in bed than any of the men she'd ever been with. But Heather figured Gwen knew what buttons to push on a computer as well.

But there was no love involved. It was a setup. She always knew what was going to happen, what needed to happen. Once this was all over, she'd have everything she ever wanted. She'd be loaded and that was what she always wanted, right?

“What the fuck?” Brett said as the little car took off, racing down the streets of Lansing with lots of fast stops and quick turns. She looked at the driver. “Victoria?”

Victoria slammed the brakes and went careening down an alley. Her eyes glued to the road, she said, “I almost didn’t recognize you.”

“You were supposed to go to work,” Brett said, putting on her safety belt and holding onto whatever she could find during Victoria’s mad driving.

“Yeah, well, the cops are already suspicious of the Paradise and everyone there anyway. Since Maddy and Leisa really *had* to go to work, I figured I should hang around to back you up. I called in sick to Frankie, and went to where I knew you’d go.” She finally slowed down on the driving and looked at Brett. “By the way, apricot’s not your color. You should’ve gone with something more along the lines of a true red.”

Brett looked out the window and away from Victoria and said, “And you don’t look as good as a blonde.” Victoria herself had donned a long blonde wig. “So how the hell’d you find me?”

“I kept cruising around. I saw you pull into the lot, and kept cruising around till I saw you come out running.”

“How the hell’d you recognize me?”

“I’d know you anywhere, Brett.”

Brett looked back at her and knew Victoria was in love with her. She couldn’t say anything. She loved her, too.

Victoria’s eyes took in Brett’s appearance and she said, “It did take me a moment to recognize you. That’s why you had to run to catch up to my car.”

Brett turned from Victoria and pulled off her wig. “Where are we going anyway?”

Ski chased after the car for a block, pulling her gun, but unsure she could disable the moving vehicle without any civilian casualties.

When the first police car pulled up, she pointed out Brett's escape vehicle and yelled at them to follow it. Now that both patrol cars were gone, she realized she should have caught a ride with one. She'd likely lose them by the time she got to her car parked at the back of the building.

But then another car squealed to a stop next to her. "Get in!" someone yelled at her. She took one look and jumped in. Randi took off after the patrol cars. "Who are we following?"

"I believe the elusive Brett Higgins," Ski said as she fastened her seatbelt. She was glad she'd caught this particular ride, because Randi drove more like herself. In fact, it didn't take Randi much effort to get past the two patrol cars and closer to their objective.

But both cars were moving too quickly for Ski to risk blowing out the car's tires. Any shot fired would mean the possibility of casualties, and she wasn't ready for that, yet. Right now, she was just chasing a suspect.

"Whoever's driving's a pro," Randi grunted, making yet another quick turn. "You say you think we're following Brett Higgins?"

"Yup."

"Hold on, I thought I saw a woman get into the car we're after."

"Isn't Brett a woman?"

"Yeah, she is, but she's no girly girl, and from what I saw, that's who we're following."

"It was Brett. I know it was!"

"You sound like you're trying to convince yourself."

"She wouldn't have run if it wasn't."

"Whatever." Randi floored the accelerator and followed until, "Goddammit."

"What?"

"Where'd they go, huh? Which way?"

"Shit. You lost them."

"We lost 'em, babe. You're here with me, after all."

"They were right there. How the hell . . . ?"

"I told you, Brett's crew is good."

"Who was driving?"

"I don't know. I couldn't get a good look at who it was," Randi said, trying to place what she saw with Brett's known associates. She shook her head. "I really don't know. Did you get an ID on the car?"

Ski shook her head. "There weren't any plates. Looked like a dark green Honda. Not much to go on. I can't even put out an APB on that—unless they leave the plates off." She pulled out her cell phone and did what she could, but from what she knew of Brett, it wouldn't work. The plates would soon be back on.

Randi pulled over into an abandoned lot and looked at Ski. "So you're telling me that femme was Brett?"

"Yeah. I didn't believe it at first either, but when I—"

"What?"

"I really looked at her." She couldn't exactly tell Randi that Brett's eyes gave her away.

"Ski," Randi said, regaining the other woman's attention. "Why was she there? Did you actually see her in their offices?"

"Yes, yes I did. I was interviewing someone and there she was. It took me a moment to place her, but she knew when I did. She took off running."

"But why was she there? She had to have known there was a high risk of running into the police there."

"I don't know . . . it doesn't make sense . . . She had to have recognized me, but she was still just standing there, listening to us . . ." Ski looked directly at Randi. "I know you have a theory, so let's hear it."

Randi looked away. "You don't want to hear it."

"What is it?"

"Brett went there trying to find a lead, a reason she's been set up. It's the only possible explanation."

Ski stared at Randi till Randi turned to look into her eyes. Then Ski looked away. And said, "If you want to protect Brett, give me another suspect."

"I don't want to protect Brett. I told you last night she should be locked away for the rest of her life. But she didn't kill Cartwright. This makes me even more sure." When Ski didn't reply, Randi continued. "What the hell was Brett wearing anyway?"

"Blonde wig, makeup, houndstooth jacket, stockings, black silk blouse, black skirt."

"Oh, good God!" Randi said. "Was there cleavage? Did the skirt have a slit?"

"Yes and yes."

Randi chuckled. "Didn't she look like a Goddamn drag queen?"

"Not at all. I thought she was kinda hot, actually."

"Oh, fuck me and the horse I rode in on—Brett Higgins with cleavage? And she was *hot*?"

Ski looked at Randi. "She has nice legs."

The two women looked silently at each other, and then burst into gales of laughter thinking of the image of Brett Higgins in drag. It seemed only natural when they fell into each other's arms.

When they finally, awkwardly pulled apart, Ski said, "I'd appreciate it if you could take me back to CompuVisions. What were you doing out here anyway?"

"After last night's phone call, I thought it might be good to check up with you in person."

"And you just happened to pull up when I needed a lift."

"Coincidences don't happen often, but they do sometimes happen." Randi looked at her watch, then pulled out her cell phone and called in to work, saying she wouldn't be in the office today, but they knew how to reach her. When she hung up she looked at Ski. "It's late enough that I think I can spare some time helping you out."

"What makes you think I need any help?"

"Honestly? Nothing. I'm just hoping to get a picture of Brett in drag. What a grand way to ruin her reputation."

"Do you really think Brett will go back there today?"

Randi focused on the road. "No. I know she won't. And she won't look the same again. But I've been trying to get her ass for the past decade, and I'd like to be in on any possible bust."

Ski smiled. "I was really surprised at her cleavage."

Randi fell on the steering wheel in laughter again. "Brett . . . cleavage . . ."

Ski allowed Randi to join her when she went back into CompuVisions.

"Heather Johnson, Detective Randi McMartin. She's been following Brett Higgins for several years. She asked to be in on the investigation. Did you recognize the tall blonde I followed?" Ski introduced the two women in the CompuVisions conference room.

"No, not at all," Heather replied. "She stopped by my desk earlier to ask directions to human resources."

Despite intensive questioning, Heather could provide no further clues. Afterward, Ski let Randi know she thought Heather had been Gwen's lover. Randi looked around the place, trying to figure out how Brett got in. They informed Matt Breske, president of CompuVisions, of the possible security breach. He immediately called the security company to have a new card reader installed, and issued new pass cards to everyone.

When they left Breske's office Ski turned to Randi. "Well, we've done all we can to secure this area."

"Okay, Ski, given that I keep saying that Brett didn't do this, we need to find another suspect, and—"

"Usually the murderer is someone the victim knows. So that makes Heather, as Gwen's lover, the most likely suspect. After Brett."

"Why don't we look into that aspect? See if we can find somebody who will say they are actually lovers? Were lovers."

Ski turned to Randi and put a hand on her arm. "I saw pictures of them together in photographs at Gwen's place. I don't think we need much else."

"But what if they had a lover's quarrel, or something like that?"

"I'll give you the next two hours. We can split up the people who sit near Heather, question them and see if they've overheard anything. You can play your involvement any way you like, just don't lie or do anything to fuck up my investigation. You in?"

Randi grinned. "Yeah, I'm in."

Chapter Seventeen

"Where *are* you going?" Brett asked Victoria, who was on the interstate heading back toward Detroit.

"Brett, turn on your brain. *I* tracked you down at Maddy's and Leisa's—just how much longer do you think it'll take the cops to figure as much?"

Brett pushed the seat all the way down, so no one would see her in the car. "Yeah, all right, fine. The cops showed up there this morning already."

"What happened?"

"They knocked and rang and looked around, but they didn't have a warrant, so they couldn't come in. But they'll probably be back. You still haven't told me where we're going?"

"Why do you think Pamela chose Detroit?" Victoria whispered.

Brett sat up and looked at her, sensing something important. "I don't know, why?"

"Get down!" As soon as she was sure she had evaded the cops, Victoria pulled down an abandoned alley, drove to a service station, and put her plates back on. Then she took off her wig and started driving again. "There was another reason," Victoria now said, taking an exit off the freeway, one Brett was unfamiliar with—Danesville. Brett *had* seen it driving to Lansing from Detroit, but still, she didn't know it.

Victoria was driving the speed limit, and Brett figured they were fairly safe, so she raised her seat so she could see where they were going. As far as she could tell, they were just adding a few more no's to "the middle of nowhere."

"What was the reason?" Brett asked, looking back at Victoria.

Victoria glanced at her. "I can't really have a serious discussion with you looking like that."

"Well, gee, don't make me feel any worse. You got any tissues around here?"

"We'll get you to a real bathroom and you can clean that crap off."

"Please tell me there'll be some real clothes for me to get into there."

"I'll see what I can do." Victoria was now following a dirt road, glancing down occasionally at a piece of paper.

"Have you ever even been here before?"

"No. I have not. But I called ahead." She turned down a dirt driveway and then to the house about a hundred feet in.

Brett figured no one would find her here. But she wasn't as close to the action as she wanted to be, either. Victoria seemed really tense and upset. Brett figured she ought to tread carefully since no matter how vehemently she denied it, Victoria had just saved her ass.

"We're expected," Victoria said, putting the car in park. She grabbed her bag out of the backseat and headed in.

"Wait!" Brett said, but the front door was already opening. She rushed out of the car.

"Victoria?" the woman at the door asked. Brett thought she

looked somewhat familiar . . . but Brett really didn't know that many older women, and this woman was at least sixty.

Victoria stopped her purposeful stride and approached hesitantly. Brett sidled up, watching. She knew something was going down, but wasn't quite sure what.

"Grandma?" Victoria asked, walking slowly toward the woman, who ran forward and pulled her into her arms.

The hug lasted several tear-filled minutes, and Brett just stood back and watched. Brett also glanced around to make sure they weren't being watched, hadn't been followed.

Finally, the older woman and Victoria stepped apart. "My God, look at you!" Then she touched Victoria's cheek with her hand. "I just have to look at you and know you've got to be my granddaughter." She then turned to Brett. "This must be your friend who needs help." She carefully looked Brett over. "Apricot really isn't your color, dear."

"Grandma, this is Brett Higgins. Brett, this is my grandmother, Rebecca Carson."

How could Brett have missed it even for a moment? The slight olive tint to the skin, the lustrous black hair, now shot through with silver, the well-shaped form . . . So this is where Pamela and Victoria Nelson came from. "Pleasure to meet you, ma'am. To tell the truth, I'm really not quite myself at the moment. I don't know who I am, but I think it's from my worst nightmare."

Rebecca stared down at Brett's extended hand without taking it. She looked back up at Victoria. "I hope you know what you're doing." She turned, wrapped an arm around Victoria's waist, and led her inside, leaving Brett to follow.

"Uh, grandma?" Victoria said, "I think Brett would be your eternal slave if she could have a shower? And maybe some other clothes?"

The Titanic's iceberg was nothing compared to how Rebecca Carson was acting toward Brett.

Rebecca led them upstairs and to what was obviously a guest bedroom. "I've put towels in the bathroom already. I think you'll find everything you need there. As for clothing"—she turned to look Brett over, starting at her pumps and working up—"I really don't think I have anything to fit . . ." Her words dropped off as she met Brett's eyes. "Her."

Brett almost laughed out loud when she realized Mrs. Carson had thought she was a guy in drag. She wasn't sure if the dyke Brett would be much better, but it still felt right. She pulled off her wig, shrugged, and said, "We can go get me some other clothes somewhere later. I just can't bear to put this outfit back on again."

Victoria laughed, apparently realizing the misunderstanding as well. "Grandma, why don't we leave Brett to her shower, and we'll see if we can find her something to wear? You don't have any eye makeup remover do you, for the mascara?" Rebecca shook her head. "Well then, just scrub with soap and hope for the best," she instructed Brett.

Letting the hot water cleanse her, Brett heard the bathroom door open and close, then open and close again. When she got out she saw that Victoria had dropped off something like hair gel for her, and she gratefully smeared it through her hair. In the bedroom she found boxers, a white T-shirt, black trousers, a bowling shirt, a leather belt, plain white socks, and a pair of black leather shoes.

She quickly dressed. The pants were a bit too long and too wide in the waist, but she cuffed them and belted them and, even though she felt weird in these strange clothes, especially the bowling shirt, it was a lot better than being in the clothes she had been wearing.

She headed back downstairs, stopping on the staircase to listen to the women in the kitchen. Unfortunately, Victoria was coming upstairs and caught her at it, before she heard anything.

"Trying to eavesdrop, huh?" Victoria said, running right into Brett. Her arms were now around Brett's waist.

"No, not at all. I just wanted to make sure I wasn't coming down at a bad time was all."

"Yeah. Right. C'mon." She pulled Brett down to the kitchen.

"Well, Gran, this is . . . Brett. Still not the real Brett, but much closer than you saw before."

"Oh, God! I can't tell you what a relief it is to see you now!" Rebecca cried out, quickly sizing her up. "I thought you were a really bad drag queen!"

"Um, no ma'am. I was just in disguise."

"Rebecca. My name's Rebecca," she said as she took Brett's hand and shook it. "Meeting my granddaughter for the first time today makes me feel old enough, so ma'am's just too much." She looked between Victoria and Brett and smiled. "I gotta tell you, women in our family just don't have a lot of luck with men, so I am so happy Victoria's found herself a nice butch. I mean, once I realized what type of clothes you'd like, I mean, after figuring out you were a woman . . . Goddamn, it was such a fuckin' relief, y'know?"

Victoria and Brett shared equally bemused expressions, which apparently Rebecca caught.

"Sorry, this has just been one helluva day. Okay, so Victoria didn't say much earlier, so why don't you two fill me in on what's going on?"

"Well, Gran, Brett's in trouble—"

"You already said that. I want details. And I do mean details. What would you like to drink? I've got coffee, tea, soda, milk, water, beer, Scotch, wine—"

"Scotch," Brett said.

"I like you," Rebecca said, pulling a bottle of Johnny Walker from the cupboard. She picked up a pack of cigarettes from the counter and lit one, turning back toward Victoria and Brett.

Victoria turned Brett toward her. "Pamela came to Detroit because she knew Gran lived in Michigan. She figured she might get help from her if she needed it. I looked Gran up on the Internet yesterday, and pulled up maps to her place online, before I came to see you. This morning I called her to see if maybe she might hide me and a friend who was in some trouble. While you were in the shower we discussed clothing, and anything you might need. And that you're a big, butch dyke, and not a drag queen." She turned back toward her grandmother. "Sorry, I just thought I ought to fill her in." Apparently Victoria and her grandmother had already done some bonding over the matter of Brett's clothes.

Rebecca was smiling. "No problem. So was Victoria right in her choice of socks?"

"It was either what you're wearing, or old men's black socks—long nylon things that go up to your knees."

"Black pants, black shoes, white socks. I'd feel like an old man either way. The others might look better, but I feel better with these. Whose clothes are these anyway?"

"My dearly departed husband's," Rebecca said.

"I'm sorry."

"Don't be. I'm the crazy old woman everyone avoids, 'cause they all know I really killed my husband. Those who were around then don't believe he could've just left in the middle of the night without a trace. So now I'm the weird old woman of the neighborhood, the one whose house kids avoid. Which is more than okay by me!"

Brett pointed at Rebecca's cigarettes. "Can I have one of those? I seem to have left mine in my . . . purse."

"Don't you just hate when that happens? I won't even try to light it for you."

"Good," Brett said, grabbing a cigarette and lighting it with her favorite Zippo. Taking a deep, thankful inhalation she was mighty glad she'd kept the lighter in her jacket pocket rather than the purse.

Rebecca broke into her nicotine-induced trance. "Let's go to the living room and catch up. I'd really like to know what I'm getting myself into and all. Please avoid my lack of manners 'cause—"

"You're the crazy woman everyone avoids," Brett finished.

"Except the local pastor. And God knows I wish he'd avoid me, too."

"Brett was framed for murder, and now she's running from the cops," Victoria said, grabbing a soda and leading them into the living room. She sat on the couch.

"Finally, some excitement! So you're on the lam now, huh?"

"Uh, no. Actually, I want to figure out who really killed Gwen, so I can prove I'm innocent."

"Not quite so exciting, but it has potential."

"I was at Gwen's place of employment, trying to get a lead, when a cop recognized me. I was running when Victoria picked me up."

Rebecca stared at them. "I think I need a bit more back story. I mean, you're fine staying here and all, but I'd really like to know what's going on."

"It's a long story," Victoria said.

Brett took a long drink of Scotch before she answered. The stuff wasn't her usual, but it sure tasted good. "Someone lured me to Lansing to frame me for murdering Gwen Cartwright, whom I'd never met or spoken with, except online. She drugged me and killed her. Now the cops are after me, and I'm trying to figure it all out, so I don't hafta go on the lam. Again. 'Cause goin' on the lam really sucks."

"Not that long, apparently," Victoria said.

"So the cops are after you for something you didn't do?" Rebecca asked.

"Yup," Brett said.

"Got it." Rebecca looked back to Victoria. She reminded Brett of both Victoria and her older sister, Pamela. "So how long have you been together?"

Brett, panicked, looked to Victoria.

"Well, um, we're not exactly together," Victoria said, putting her hand on Brett's.

"So what, exactly, are you?"

"Friends. We're just friends," Victoria said.

"How do you know each other, then?" She didn't seem happy with this new development.

"We work together," Brett said, then turned to Victoria, who was speechless. Brett looked down at her shoes, and realized she was feeling some sort of acceptance, and also realized she shouldn't. She wasn't accepted. She was not of the now. She turned to Rebecca. "You're Victoria's grandmother. Maternal or paternal?"

"Her mother's."

"Well, then, let me tell you, your daughter married a son-of-a-bitch."

"I knew that. It runs in the family."

"What? Ending up with evil no-good men?"

"Yes. Why do you think I didn't like you until I knew you were a woman?"

"So you were happy thinking your granddaughter—by the way, how old are you?—was with a woman?"

"Yes, dammit. For as long as we can trace our family tree, the women always hook up with bad men. I'm hoping a woman will help break the curse. And I'm sixty-six."

Brett stood looking down at Rebecca. But Rebecca was still facing off with her, daring her to . . . do something.

"Gran? Brett?" Victoria said, stepping between them, and separating them easily. "Sit down, drink, smoke, whatever." Once Rebecca was seated, Victoria knelt at her feet, holding her hands. "Gran, I'm a big girl now. We've never met before, and both mine and Brett's nerves are on edge wondering if we can trust you, and if you'll help us. After all, we don't know each other."

"What do you want to know?" Rebecca put down her drink. "That you look just like your mother? Just like she used to look like me?" She hesitated, wanting to take a drink but then changing her mind. "I look at you, and know you." She looked at them both. "Where is Pamela?"

Brett and Victoria exchanged a glance, and that was all it took.

"Your mother, my daughter, sent me pictures of you two when you were born. Weight and length noted on the pictures. She let me know I was a grandmother. Nothing more. Nothing. Tell me, were there just the two of you?"

"Yes."

"So where is Pamela?" She looked between the two women before continuing. "God. Did Jackson . . . ?"

"Why weren't you there?" Victoria asked, bending forward to hold her head in her hands.

Brett curled her body over Victoria's kneeling one, holding her. Burying her face in Victoria's hair. Trying to comfort her, hold her, make her feel safe.

"She left me, wouldn't listen and left me. She only sent me pictures when you were born, with no return address," Rebecca said, stroking Victoria's hair. "She wouldn't listen to me. Wouldn't understand or believe."

"Believe what?" Brett asked, still holding Victoria.

"We never understand that the men we choose are here just to destroy us, and all we love. Your grandfather didn't live long enough to destroy me, but he did enough to ensure the girls' mother hated us both. She ended up with an evil holy roller, the worst type of evil. So what happened to Pamela?"

"She ran away from home as soon as she could," Victoria said.

A look of hope flashed across Rebecca's face. "So she might still be alive?"

Brett crawled forward to keep a hand around Victoria's waist while taking Rebecca's hand. "She was murdered more than ten years ago."

"Where? How? She got away but . . . she's dead?"

"I'm sorry, yes. She was murdered in Detroit."

"She was so close and didn't come to me?"

Crying softly, Victoria placed her hand gently on Brett's shoulder. "Gran, she didn't get in touch with you for the same reason I didn't until now—from what Mom said, we thought you might be evil too. Or might turn us back over to them. Him."

With tears in her eyes too, Rebecca looked at Brett. "You knew her?"

"We were lovers."

"How . . . how did it happen?"

Victoria knew Brett felt responsible for Pamela's death—and until recently, Victoria was more than happy to let her be guilty. She didn't think her grandmother or Brett really wanted to get much into it, and it was bound to come between her grandmother and Brett. So she had to stop it all. "Gran, can we just not talk about this right now?"

Rebecca met Victoria's eyes for a moment, then nodded her agreement. "For now."

"For now," Victoria repeated, then segued, "So, do you think you can help us?"

Rebecca looked between the two women and smiled. "Yes, I think I can do that. You two can stay here, but I'm afraid I just have the one guestroom. Brett, you can have any of my husband's clothes you'd like. And if you know anything about cars, well, I've got a few in the backyard that you can trade parts between. In case you need some vehicle other than Victoria's or mine. Let me know if you need anything else. I don't have a lot of money, but what I have is yours." She cupped Victoria's cheek. "It's the least I can do after all these years."

"Thank you Gran!" Victoria said, wrapping her arms around the older woman.

Rebecca finally leaned back, wiping a tear from her eye. "Vicki, I saw that you brought a bag with you. Why don't you and Brett take that and anything else you need upstairs and get settled in while I make us dinner?"

"Sounds like a plan," Brett said, leading Victoria outside. As Victoria went through her car, looking for anything they might need, Brett said, "She seems like a real nice lady. I do have one question, though."

"What is it, honey?"

"Did you notice that first Rebecca said that her husband left, then later she said he was dead?"

"What do you mean?"

"Well, I'm just curious is all. I mean, after all, she seems to be the only woman in the family who's come to realize that men are evil to the family."

"Brett, I'm sure she figured it out after he left, and now she just likes to think of him as dead. I mean, you saw how she was about my sister."

"Doesn't matter. She's helping us, and I think it'd be a cold day in hell before the cops connected me to her. And she's got a good point about the cars. I mean, it might not be safe for us to use your car again."

"Well, that's everything, then," Victoria said, shoving a couple of maps in a bag.

"Can you get everything to . . . upstairs while I go look at the cars in the yard?"

"Sure, no problem." Victoria knew Brett hadn't wanted to say "our room." That was when Victoria suddenly realized she and Brett would be sharing a room—and a bed. She smiled to herself.

As soon as Victoria entered the house, Rebecca called out, "Vicki?"

"Yeah Gran?"

"Can you come in here for a moment?"

Victoria entered the kitchen and found her grandmother watching Brett through the window. "Whatcha need?"

"I like that girl. She seems nice and capable."

"Oh, she is. She's strong and, God, if you saw how she usually dresses—"

"Sounds like you have a bit of a crush, my dear."

"She's with someone else."

"A woman, I hope?" Rebecca again peered through the window. "I'd hate to think of a hot butch like her wasted on some man."

"Gran!"

"Plus, she looked awful in that get-up earlier." Rebecca turned back to face her again. "If she's got a girlfriend, why are you the one helping her?"

"I don't know who knew where she was at, but I think she doesn't want many people involved because it might put them at risk." To her gran's look she added, "I involved myself. And this morning she told me to go back to Detroit. I tracked her down later by myself."

"Well, after all that, I hope you make the most of your time here," Rebecca said with a wink.

"Um . . ." Victoria couldn't believe her grandmother was trying to help her hook up with a woman, and one who was involved with someone else to boot. "You said you needed help with something?"

"Oh, no. I just saw Brett in the backyard and figured I could have some time alone to chat with you—give you a little gentle prodding in the right direction."

"Oh, okay." Well, if all the men the women chose were evil, the choices would be either for Victoria to be with a woman, or be alone. Victoria started to head back upstairs.

"Oh, by the way, Vicki?"

Victoria turned back to the kitchen. "Yes?"

Rebecca was in the doorway looking at her. "Please let Brett know that the old woody station wagon in the backyard is the only one she can't move or do much with."

"Okay. Why?"

"That's the one I buried your grandfather under."

Chapter Eighteen

Ski and Randi had Heather in the conference room. They decided to team up on her after sharing their knowledge.

Heather looked up at Ski. "I'm not under arrest or anything, am I?"

"Of course not. We're just looking to clear up a few details. I want to make sure that once we find Higgins, we've got an iron-clad case against her," Ski said, following the plan she and Randi had concocted.

"Oh. Okay. I'm sorry, I didn't quite catch who you are?" Heather said, standing and extending her hand to Randi.

"Sorry, this is Detective Randi McMartin," Ski said, while Randi and Heather shook hands. "She's with the Detroit Police Department special organized crime unit. She's here because she's got a special interest in the case. She's been watching Higgins for years."

"Oh, nice to meet you."

Randi pulled a chair away from the oak conference table and straddled it. "Ms. Graham, we're wondering if you've ever met this woman?" she said, putting an eight-by-ten glossy, black-and-white picture of Brett on the table in front of Heather.

"Just in the news stories and everything. I mean, this is Higgins, right?"

"Had you ever seen her before the recent events?" Randi asked.

Heather picked up the picture and studied it. "No. At least, I don't think I have."

"Heather," Ski said, moving next to her. "We're trying to put together Gwen Cartwright's last day—trying to figure out exactly what happened to her. Do you think you could walk us through it?"

"The day started rather frantically. The night before, Gwen had discovered that a competitor was really close to where we were on the development of a piece of software just like the one she's been working on."

"And you didn't know about it?"

"No. We thought this was a totally unique, break-out application."

"So you suddenly found out about this other company and that was . . . ?"

"A really bad thing. There are two basic philosophies to developing software—you work somewhat off a competitor's product so you can provide it at a lesser cost, or you create something quite new and different, which requires a substantial outlay and hope you become the next Bill Gates. Gwen's project had that potential."

"I understand you weren't very upset when Cartwright disappeared that day. Was she often tardy or forgetting things?" Randi asked, leaning forward.

"No, not at all. Gwen . . ." Heather closed her eyes and took a deep breath. Ski handed her a tissue, which she gratefully accepted. "Gwen was very punctual. She wasn't the absentminded genius sort at all. She kept very good track of details, including meetings and such."

"How long have you worked for Cartwright?" Randi asked.

"Four years."

"I see here," Randi said, opening a file and looking at a copy of Heather's resumé, "that you have a B.S. from U of M in software engineering. Yet you were just Cartwright's assistant? Didn't you find that degrading?"

"Not at all. In the past few years there's been more than enough people graduating with different types of computer degrees." She shrugged. "I had a few offers, mostly from dot-com companies in San Francisco. I didn't want to move all the way out there just to have the company go belly-up, which I knew would happen. I thought about going for some quick, easy cash, but thought working for a company like CompuVisions would better help me in the long run. I was immediately assigned to Gwen. We hit it off, and she helped me learn more about having a real job and further develop my skills. I helped her as well and—"

"How?" Randi asked.

"How what?"

"How did you help her?"

"Okay, so sometimes when you're dealing with miles of code, there are bugs. Because of my background, I could help her find the bugs. Although I was her assistant, in a lot of ways we were more like partners. And each level she rose, she took me with her. You've seen my file, and so know that I make more than both of you put together. She looked out for me." She started crying again and wiped at her eyes with the tissue and smiled thankfully at Ski when she put an entire box of them before her. "Thank you."

"So when she didn't come back from lunch, you weren't concerned?" Randi asked.

"Of course I was!"

"Listen, Heather," Ski said, "some people around here seem to think you and Gwen might have something a bit more than your regular employer-employee relationship, and—" Ski said.

"She was my . . . my best friend . . ."

"Was that all you were?" Randi asked, standing over her.

Heather didn't even look up. "We were lovers. I couldn't let anyone know how upset I was when she didn't come back from lunch because . . . because . . . we've been hiding what we really are for so long . . ."

"You were involved with Gwen?" Ski asked. "Romantically?"

"For two-and-a-half years. She's the real reason I stuck around so long." She finally looked up at the two of them. "We've been . . . together . . . for so long, and having to hide it for so long . . . hiding it was second nature. We're not supposed to fraternize, you know."

"So when Gwen didn't return from lunch, what did you do?" Ski asked.

"I tried not to worry. I put on my calm, cool façade and went on. I hoped there was some reasonable explanation for her tardiness."

"Did you know Cartwright was e-mailing and IMing with Higgins?" Randi asked.

"No, I didn't. Was she?"

"Yes, I'm afraid so. It appears as if Cartwright and Higgins were having an affair, and that's what led to the murder."

"No. No . . . I can't believe she was cheating on me!"

"Heather, I'm afraid . . ." Ski began, but Heather ran from the room.

"Well, that didn't end the way I anticipated," Ski said.

Randi shrugged. "We can pick up questioning her later. Want to get some dinner?"

They walked together to the parking lot. "You've really got that bad cop thing down pat, don't you?" Ski asked, driving them to the restaurant.

"You've met Brett. Interview her, and enough of her cronies, associates, and those like her and you'll get it down as well."

"I didn't catch anything off, though. I mean, yeah, we now know they were lovers, but . . . I didn't catch anything really off, y'know?"

"I didn't either. But it's good to have her admit they were lovers."

Allie drove the road she knew well, following I-96 up to Lansing and then heading toward Alma. She needed to do something, after all. Everybody kept saying they didn't know where Brett was, but Allie figured Brett would want to stay close to the action in Lansing. She knew Brett was working the case, trying to figure out and prove who had really killed Gwen Cartwright.

There were a lot of hotels in and around Lansing. And East Lansing had a lot of dorms, but still, Allie figured Brett would hide out with friends, especially because she couldn't use any of her credit cards. And Alma wasn't very far from Lansing.

She couldn't believe Brett hadn't figured out a way to get through to her, to get a message to her. She understood the need for secrecy in this matter, and she even realized she might be leading the cops directly to Maddy's, but she had to know her lover was okay.

And she knew she could cry on Maddy's shoulder.

"Oh, baby, are you all right?" Maddy asked, opening her door as soon as Allie walked up.

"No, I'm not," Allie sobbed into her shoulder. "I don't know what's going on, I don't know where Brett is, I just don't know anything!"

"It's okay, it's okay," Maddy soothed, leading her into the house.

Leisa closed the door.

Allie looked up from Maddy's shoulder. "Is she here?"

"No, not right now," Maddy said, smoothing Allie's long hair.

"But she has been here?"

"Yes. She went out this morning to check out where Gwen worked."

"But she isn't back? Was she going anywhere else? Have you heard from her?"

"I'm sure she's fine," Maddy said. "Brett's a survivor, after all."

"There was a bit on the news that the police had spotted her, but she got away," Leisa said. "So she's probably just lying really low for now."

"Why didn't she tell me she was here?" Allie asked.

"She gave us a list of names and numbers to call in case of emergency," Maddy said. "We knew to get in touch with you if something happened. She simply wanted to ensure that you are not implicated in any way."

"Well what about you? Wasn't she worried about you?"

"We did create some contingency plans to hide her and protect ourselves," Maddy said.

"Allie, you two have helped us so much," Leisa said, "we had to help her. And we're close to Lansing, where Brett needs to be, and we figured the police weren't very likely to look here. Or at least, not right away."

"She's been talking to Frankie though, right?" Allie asked.

"Well, um . . ." Leisa said.

"Actually, I believe the police are a little more thorough than we expected," Maddy said, standing and walking to the front door. "Allie, remain where you are." She opened it just as Ski was about to knock.

"She has really good hearing," Leisa explained to Allie.

"Can I help you, detective?" Maddy asked Ski, remembering her from the last time they met.

"I think you know why I'm here, Ms. Jameson."

"Actually, I don't."

"I'd like to talk with you about your old neighbor, Brett Higgins."

"How very convenient," Maddy replied. "Seeing as her girlfriend is here already. Please come in, detective."

Ski walked in, followed by Randi. "This is Detective Randi McMartin—"

"We all know who she is, Ski," Allie said.

"She is assisting on the investigation because of her long-standing interest in Brett Higgins."

"Of course she is," Maddy said.

“Can I get anybody anything to drink?” Leisa asked, heading to the kitchen.

“No thank you,” Ski said. “Do you mind if we take a look around?”

“Yeah, I do,” Leisa said from the kitchen. “I’ve heard about police searches—how you rip everything apart and all that.”

“Ma’am—” Ski started.

“Leisa.”

“I don’t know you, do I?”

“No, we haven’t met before. I’m Leisa Kraft.”

“She’s Maddy’s girlfriend,” Randi said from the living room.

“Ms. Kraft—”

Leisa smiled. “Call me Leisa.”

“I promise not to wreck anything. I’m sure if Brett was here, she’s gone now, but just to be sure, we’d like to take a look around.”

Allie stood. “I’ll give you two a personal tour. I’m sure you’ll have questions for us, so we can talk at the same time.”

“Sounds like a fine idea to me,” Randi said. “If it’s all right with you two,” she said to Maddy and Leisa.

“It’s an acceptable solution,” Leisa said, looking at the two detectives with her arms crossed over her ample breasts.

Ski slowly nodded. “Give me a minute and we can begin.” She went outside to order the two police officers who’d accompanied them to watch the house—one in the front and one in the back. Brett would have a hard time escaping their notice, if she was even in the house.

“Let’s start in the basement,” Ski said when she returned. Randi kept her eyes open and listened to the questions Ski asked Leisa, Maddy, and Allie and the replies they gave. It was all pretty standard—no, they hadn’t seen or heard from Brett; no, they had no idea where she was; they were sure she was innocent; no, they knew nothing about Gwen Cartwright prior to this. Etcetera.

The only interesting find was several bags full of secondhand clothing upstairs. Maddy and Leisa didn’t say anything when Ski dug through the items and both Ski and Randi raised their eyebrows at the strange assortment of clothing and wigs.

"These look like disguises."

"Of course they do," Maddy said.

"I picked them up the other day thinking about Halloween," Leisa said. "I was with some students at the store and decided to plan ahead."

"You went with some kids to a store?"

"I was helping the drama group. They were mostly getting costumes for a play. We went to a secondhand shop."

"Mostly?"

"Well, some of them were doing some personal shopping as well."

"So you just randomly picked up some things?"

"Yes."

"I really don't think any of this would fit Maddy," Ski said, glancing at the small redhead and looking at the size of the clothes.

"I told you, it was for the drama department."

Maddy picked up an extremely loud Hawaiian shirt, and put it on. "Actually, I think this rather does fit me."

"Yup, that's just your style," Allie said, truthfully. To Ski's raised eyebrow she continued, "She really does dress that way."

"And a wig does fit everybody," Randi said, picking one up and placing it on Ski's head.

Ski frowned and tossed the wig onto the bed. "Whatever. All I know is Brett's outfit today was not her own."

"I really don't think these trousers are that bad," Leisa said, picking up a pair of pants and holding them to her waist.

When they were done searching, Ski sent the two uniformed officers away, and Allie pulled Randi into the backyard. Randi told Maddy and Leisa to keep Ski occupied.

"Have you heard anything from Brett, really?" Randi asked Allie once she was sure they were alone.

"No, I haven't. And that is the fucking truth. Now, what do you know?"

"The blood Brett sent me had ketamine in it. A rather strong animal tranquilizer used as a date rape drug. She's got Ski going bongos—and I do keep telling Ski that Brett obviously didn't do it."

"Did you just say 'bongos'?"

"Yes. I did. Deal with it."

Allie smiled. Randi looked terribly serious and noble while she paced and talked about what was going on.

Allie knew she needed to get rid of Randi immediately. She needed to finish her conversation with Maddy and Leisa, and figure out where Brett was, and how all this had happened.

"So you two really have no idea where she might be?" Allie asked Maddy and Leisa once they were again alone.

"No," Maddy said. "We weren't lying to the two detectives."

"When we left this morning," Leisa said, "all she said was that she was going to CompuVisions, and we should just act normal, so as to not arouse suspicion. We dropped Victoria off at her car and—" She shut up when Maddy gave her a sharp jab in the ribs.

"Victoria?" Allie asked. "She was here?"

"She showed up last night," Maddy said, patting Allie's back. "It really is all right. She left this morning. We drove her to her car. Nothing happened between them. They slept in separate rooms."

"And now Brett is missing," Allie said, pulling out her cell phone. "Frankie, it's Allie. Did Victoria show up at work today? . . . Oh really? . . . Really? . . . We have to keep this short, but you have to know some things. Randi and I talked . . ." Allie proceeded to fill Frankie in on her discussion with Randi, and then got Victoria's home number from him.

When she hung up, Allie immediately tried Victoria's number, and left a brief message on the machine, in case the woman was screening. When she got off the phone, she looked at Leisa. "I need to use your computer."

"Um, why?" Leisa asked.

"Victoria didn't show up at work today, so I'm guessing she's still with Brett. She hasn't been here very long. In Michigan, that is, so there aren't that many people she could know. I'm not sure what I'm looking for, but I want to jump online and see if anything grabs my attention."

"What, are you just gonna Google her?" Leisa asked, referring to the Internet search program.

"Well, yes, that and I'm going to also see if I can find her parents' phone number. I know a bit about Pamela and Victoria, and I'm thinking that if Victoria had any friends up here, her mother might know something about it."

"From what I know of those two girls and their parents, do you really believe you can garner such information from their mother?" Maddy asked.

"I, like Brett, can be quite the charmer when need be."

Leisa and Maddy watched, listened, and learned as Allie charmed Mrs. Nelson with her southern accent and sweet talking, eventually discovering that although Victoria had no friends in Michigan, and although there was not a single reason her runaway daughter would go to Michigan, Mrs. Nelson finally admitted that her mother, Rebecca, lived in Michigan. She gave Allie her name and offered the information that she lived in the middle of nowhere.

It didn't take long for Allie to find a phone number online.

Chapter Nineteen

When the phone rang, Rebecca answered it. She looked at Brett, then covered the receiver and said to her, "It's for you. A woman. Says her name is Allie."

Stunned, Brett looked at Victoria, then Rebecca. She stood and took the cordless from Rebecca, taking it into the next room. She didn't want the other two to overhear the convo she was about to have. "Yo, babe, how's it goin'?" she said into the phone once she made sure she had privacy.

"Brett," Allie said.

"It be me."

There was an extremely uncomfortable silence until finally Allie spoke. "You're not going to ask me how I found you?"

"Victoria found me. I thought she had gone home—had sent her home. But just when Ski found me, she was there to help me escape. She brought me here." Allie used to be a detective—if she figured out Brett was with Victoria, it really wasn't too surprising she had tracked her here.

"So, yeah, you were just along for the ride."

"What's going on, Allie?"

"Brett . . . Brett . . ."

"What, babe?"

"There's so much we need to talk about."

"I'd hope we could do that when I'm not wanted by the cops and, by the way, are you on a secure line?"

Allie faltered for a moment. "I'm not sure." Then, all business, she gave Brett all the information she had. Another brief silence, and then they said a cursory and strained goodbye, words that allowed that more would follow at a more opportune time.

Brett hung up the phone and walked back to where Victoria and Rebecca waited for her. "Gwen Cartwright was dating her assistant, Heather Johnson. Today I realized that Heather is actually the woman I had drinks with that night at the hotel. She was the one behind it, and she set me up. She's got to be behind it all."

"You said this woman approached you online," Rebecca said. "You met online. So how did she pick you out? How did she do this? Put it all together?"

"You're familiar with the entire online thing?" Victoria asked.

"I live in B.F.E." Rebecca shrugged, referring to the fact that she lived in Butt Fucking Egypt—the middle of nowhere. "And everybody here thinks I'm a murderess. I've gotta get my kicks somehow."

Brett sat back with her beer. "We met in a butch/femme chat room. She IMed me. We got to talking. She e-mailed me. She sent me pictures . . ." She looked at Rebecca, who had smiled as if she was leaping to conclusions about the nature of said photos. "Non-pornographic pictures!"

Victoria was getting the idea that her grandmother was extremely cool. After all, she had taken all of the information of Brett's previous crimes in stride—much as she had this current situation. Rebecca hadn't shrugged at all to know that Brett was wanted for murder. She just wanted to help her. That made Victoria glad, and made her wonder if she should've tried to contact her grandmother earlier.

"So you're saying this woman hit all your buttons, right?" Rebecca said. "I mean, if she had sent you porno pics, that would've turned you right off, right? Or at least that's the feeling I'm getting here."

"Well, yeah," Brett said. "I haven't been online that long, but even I know that if someone sends you naked pics from the get-go, most likely they're not theirs. Well, not unless you're in a gay male chat room. Those boys are such showoffs!"

"Brett, I know this is hard for you, but you've got to do it," Rebecca said. "For some reason, this woman picked you out of all the millions of people online to take the fall. There must be some reason!"

Victoria knelt in front of Brett, taking her hands. "Brett, I know this is hard. And I know it's not what you like to think about—but you have to remember every little detail."

Brett stood up, pulling away from Victoria. "Fuck. I was hanging out, and she IMed me. We talked a bit. She had a brain and was femme. I was intrigued. She e-mailed me. I responded. She sent me a pic—a fully clothed one. She was pretty. I liked what I saw. We talked some more. Online. E-mail and IMs. I liked her. That was all."

"Did she send you naked pics later? Did you cyber?" Rebecca asked.

Brett looked woefully at her. "Yes and yes."

Victoria couldn't believe it. "You do what you do, yet responded to porn pics online?"

"She played me! She did it on purpose, knowing that pulling me along like that would do . . . something to me!" Brett started pacing, trying to work it out.

But Victoria saw it all. "The only way she'd know how to play you like that is if she knew you."

"But how the hell does she know me?"

"That's what we've got to figure out," Rebecca said, standing. "From what you've said—that she made first contact, and played you and all, she must know you. Perhaps it's someone from your past?"

"You didn't recognize her at all?" Victoria asked. She couldn't believe Brett had put her off, shunned her advances, and then bopped babes online. Victoria wanted to ask what this woman had that she didn't.

Brett sat, put her head in her hands, closed her eyes, and tried to replay everything. Every moment. Tried to remember exactly how the woman had IMed her. Exactly why she responded. How she felt about getting the pictures.

"You were chosen for a reason," Rebecca said. "This Heather person picked you out for some specific reason."

"What were you doing having cybersex anyway? I thought you and Allie were like dancing-through-the-daisies happy and all that shit," Victoria said.

"Okay, fine," Brett said. "I was online researching different ways we could legally make money. I wanted to expand the business."

"So how did this research lead to cybersex?" Victoria asked.

"I . . . I don't know."

"You weren't just researching when you went into that room."

"No. I wasn't. I kept learning more about computers and all that. I got online to research and started surfing a bit. Then one night I thought about . . ." She looked up at Victoria, meeting her eyes just long enough for butterflies to find Victoria's tummy. "I thought about . . . other things . . . and then thought that playing online wouldn't be so bad. It wouldn't be like I was cheating or something." She abruptly stood and went to the kitchen, returning with another beer. "I was trying to be good. I went looking for conversation . . ." She walked up to Victoria. Right up to her.

Victoria could feel Brett's breath warm against her cheek. She wanted to lean up those few centimeters and touch those lips with her own. But she couldn't. It would be wrong. She wanted, needed, Brett for her own, not as a loan from another.

Just as her sister had needed her.

"You know Heather from somewhere," Rebecca said. "She obviously knows you too well for somebody who just met you. A lot of people would respond more, and better, to other forms of persuasion. Maybe it was someone who was upset with you for some reason?"

"Why?" Victoria said, still standing close to Brett. She couldn't touch her, but she wanted to.

"Why what?" Brett pulled away.

"Why were you playing around online?"

"Okay, you two work that out, and I'm gonna go to bed." Rebecca went to the foot of the stairs. "Sleep well." She went upstairs to bed.

"Why were you playing around online?" Victoria pressed the issue.

"I was drunk. I was researching, studying, learning, and I was drunk, okay?"

"So what happened?" Victoria had a feeling that something would happen if she just pushed Brett enough. She couldn't explain it, she just knew. And tonight she wanted to push her. "What happened?"

"Goddammit, Vic, I was drunk. And I'm drinking now!"

"What's going on, Brett?"

Brett sat on the sofa, sighed, and pushed her hands back through her hair. She stared up at Victoria. "You look so much like her. I look at you and want to believe I've gone back in time, and pull you into my arms, like I would her. You make me think she's still alive."

Victoria sat next to her. "I'm not my sister." She draped her arm along the back of the couch, behind Brett, and pulled her legs up under her as she faced Brett.

"I know, but it's still this huge, massive, mind-fucking blow-out, okay?"

"Do you want me to leave?"

Brett turned to her. "No."

"No because you want her or . . . No because you want me, here?"

"I know you're not your sister. I know you're you, Victoria. You're not my Storm. And now I can do things right. I want to make sure no more bad things happen to you. I want to protect you. I want you to . . . have all she wanted but didn't get."

"Like you?"

"What?"

"You heard what I said," Victoria said, straddling Brett's lap.

"Oh dear God, don't do that."

"Do what?" Victoria fanned her hair across Brett's face and leaned down to kiss her neck, nibbling lightly on her pulse point.

"That . . ." Brett gasped, her hands on Victoria's hips, as if she wanted to push her away. In reality, she held Victoria just right. "Sitting on me, like that, kissing me like that . . ." Her hands went down to Victoria's thighs, her strong thumbs feeling Victoria's inner thighs. Rubbing them.

"I need to know, Brett. Did you think of me when you went online to fool around?"

"Vicki . . . Don't do this . . ." Victoria was rubbing her body against Brett's.

"Then tell me, Brett." She grabbed the back of Brett's hair and yanked it back. Hard.

"Goddammit, woman." Brett wrapped her arms around Victoria and pulled her down for a long, hard kiss that sent electricity shooting throughout Victoria.

Brett pushed her onto her back and lay on top of her. Brett's hard thigh was wedged between her legs, pushing hard against her center. Brett's lips were on her, and Brett's tongue was in her mouth. She gasped for air. Her hands were on Brett's shoulders, and she could feel the muscles she had only previously admired from a distance. And Brett's tongue was in her mouth, surprisingly gentle . . . She could melt into this woman. And she started to, rising against Brett's hip, grinding against it.

When Brett suddenly pulled away, she moaned at the loss.

Brett looked down at her. "Goddammit, Vicki." Victoria could see the animal lust in her eyes. She lay back and reveled in the feeling of Brett's hands on her body. Brett closed her eyes and let one palm wander over Victoria's body—over her collarbone, down her breasts, first one, then the other, then over her stomach, and down so her knuckles were against Victoria's heat. She pressed down, so Victoria moaned, against her will.

Victoria hated herself even as she did it, but she did it nonetheless. She grabbed Brett's hand, the gentle yet powerful hand, and brought it up from her body, and kissed it. She entwined their fingers, sat up, and looked at Brett. "You know I'm yours. You know I love you and want to be with you." She leaned forward and touched her lips to Brett's. She gently tugged at Brett's upper lip, biting it tenderly. "I want you. But you have to want me, Victoria, not Allie and not my sister." She took Brett's hand and placed it on her breast. She gasped when Brett moved her hand, feeling her.

Victoria took Brett's hand, balled it into a fist, and kissed it. "You have to figure out what happened, who you want, and what you want."

Brett grabbed Victoria by the shoulders and pushed her back down on the couch. "You shouldn't play with things you can't control." She shoved her thigh between Victoria's legs and began humping the girl, who gasped at the contact.

Brett held her down—her legs cemented under Brett's more powerful ones, her wrists held beneath Brett's powerful hands.

Victoria moaned and arched into her, pushing herself against Brett. "Brett, don't." Her eyes turned liquid.

Brett knew the girl was close to climax, and she never left a woman in such need.

"Please, stop."

Brett pushed herself up and looked into Victoria's eyes, their bodies mere inches from one another.

Victoria willed herself to not follow Brett's movements, to not push herself against the woman she desired. "I want you, Brett. I want to be with you."

Brett grinned and lowered herself onto Victoria, who moaned and arched up into Brett, her body wanting the contact.

"But not like this." Victoria pushed at Brett and struggled under her. Brett let her go. Victoria looked down at Brett and then ran up the stairs to their bedroom. She closed the door and leaned back against it, her heart pounding wildly.

She wanted Brett so bad, in all the worst ways. She kept telling herself that she couldn't, shouldn't. But then she'd see Brett and realize she'd take her any way she could have her.

She had been so close, with Brett's hard, muscular body over hers, controlling her . . .

Pamela hadn't required Brett's full attention. And maybe that was part of what Brett had—her unfettered need to own and control. Maybe that was part of who she was, and if she got rid of that, she wouldn't be the same Brett—she'd be someone else. Brett as a panther, prowling and defending and fighting—that was who she was. Not some housebroken little kitty.

Brett wanted to follow her, but if she went to bed with Victoria, things would happen, and they couldn't. Not now. She sat up, staring at the dark TV screen, replaying every moment with Gwen in her head. No, not Gwen. Heather.

She needed to focus on something, anything other than Victoria.

She had to sleep on the sofa. She got up to look for a blanket of some sort. Anything to make it more comfortable. And yet she kept seeing Victoria, leaning over her, touching her, and straddling her lap.

She tried to remember how she met Gwen/Heather, and her mind went round and round, with all the images intermixed. She got another beer. She drank it. Then another. She wanted to go online, but Gwen wouldn't respond tonight.

She remembered having drinks with Gwen. Heather. She had drinks with Heather. She remembered every moment she could about that night. And it kept replaying in her head, and she lit another cigarette and replayed it again . . . and again . . . and again . . .

And she remembered.

There was a blizzard, and she was stuck in Lansing and she was cruising a woman at the bar . . .

And that woman was Heather Johnson.

She leapt from the couch, yanking herself from her near-dream state, and quickly thought about what she had just remembered. She walked outside to pace, to feel the cool night air, and she thought.

The woman who had set her up had IDed her during the blizzard.

There had to be a reason she had done that, and sent her friend after Brett, and if Brett could only unlock that . . . could only find that memory . . .

Soft arms enveloped her from behind. "Come to bed," Victoria whispered into her ear.

Brett turned to her and pulled her into her arms. "I want to."

"Then do it. Make love to me."

Brett picked Victoria up in her arms and carried her upstairs. She put her down on the bed and kissed her. "I love you," she said, pulling Victoria's top off her. Victoria shivered under her touch.

"I'm yours," Victoria said, closing her eyes.

Brett leaned forward, tracing her tongue along Victoria's collar bone, and down between her breasts.

"Brett?" Victoria said, grabbing her head between her hands. "I've never . . . I mean, I have, but not . . ."

Brett sat up and looked down at her, sliding her finger between Victoria's breasts. She had been lovers with Victoria's older sister for years. And she knew a few things about Victoria's life. She thought maybe she knew what Victoria wanted to say, but needed to hear it.

She lay down next to Victoria, running her hand through the girl's black tresses. She kissed her ear, then brought the sheet up to cover their bodies. She pushed herself up to look into Victoria's eyes. "What, love?"

Victoria closed her eyes. "I've never been with someone of my own free will before." Her body was tense.

Brett snuggled her arm beneath Victoria's head, so she was holding her. She knew Victoria was telling her the truth. She had watched her, after all. And now, she kissed her forehead. "Then why don't I hold you tonight?" She snuggled down next to Victoria, pulling their bodies close, and ran her hand over Victoria's soft hair, and down her bare back. She wanted to do more, but knew this was what they both needed now.

Victoria's body gradually relaxed, and she melded into Brett.

Much like Allie did.

Brett caressed Victoria, just touching and soothing, but running her hand over the nearly naked body beside her in bed made her think again about Gwen . . . Heather. Victoria was only wearing a pair of panties . . . Her body was much like Storm's. Brett had seen both women naked more times than she could count.

She remembered waking up with Gwen dead in bed with her. She remembered her naked body. She knew now that she hadn't slept with her . . . hadn't had sex with her . . . because if she had, then Gwen would've left vivid scratches on her back, and Brett didn't have any.

What she did have, however, was her memory of Gwen's naked body, and her memory of the nude pictures Heather had sent her. She couldn't believe after all these years of working around naked women she hadn't noticed it immediately.

Little differences, the size of breasts and nipples, birthmarks, the way pubic hair was cut, trimmed or shaved, the shape of thighs, the curving of hips and backs . . . Women could even have the same tattoo, but no two looked exactly alike. Their flesh color could change the appearance of a tattoo, as could the firmness of the flesh beneath it, and its exact location.

Heather had a tattoo of a stretching panther curving sinuously along her hip. It wasn't very big—maybe three inches long. You could look at it and see it almost as a black cat, but if you really studied it, it was a black panther.

Brett had studied the pics Heather had e-mailed her, and it took a few for Brett to even notice any portion of the tattoo. When she mentioned it, Heather seemed embarrassed, as if she hadn't wanted Brett to know about it. She admitted that it really hurt when the tattoo artist worked right on her bone.

Heather had said that she made sure to find a female artist. She had had enough of men looking at her and trying to paw her with their hands all over her.

Brett should have noticed it immediately. Heather's answers to her questions sounded a lot like someone who had worked in the adult industries. She had been a dancer.

And now Brett remembered the tattoo. Heather had worked for her at the Paradise.

How could she not have remembered before? That was why Heather had tried to hide the tattoo from her!

She wrapped an arm around Victoria's sleeping form and buried her face in the abundant hair. Black as a starless night. Long and luxurious. She took a deep breath. Victoria even smelled like Storm.

She reminded herself to remember in the morning that Heather used to work for her—and that she and Storm worked for her at the same time—even as she slid into a deep sleep.

Chapter Twenty

Day Six

Victoria woke the next morning warm and relaxed. She was in bed with someone who held her softly and lay beneath her. She panicked and tried to push away, but the sleeping figure grumbled and pulled her back down to a soft chest, and she fought for just a moment before the smoothness of the skin and body made her realize she wasn't with . . .

She stopped and looked down at whom she was with, as memories of the night before started rushing back into her head.

She lay back down into Brett's strong arms, curling back up into her original position—one leg tossed over Brett's, an arm wrapped around her waist, head resting on her chest. She hoped she hadn't spoiled it with her scrambling. She just wanted to enjoy it a little bit longer.

Just a few more moments . . . minutes . . . or hours . . .

But apparently she had disturbed Brett, at least a bit. Brett pulled her in tighter, and her hand began absentmindedly caressing Victoria's back and hair and down to her thighs and over her ass.

Victoria remembered the night before—how she had played with Brett and tried to seduce her and how Brett had stopped when she told her to.

She leaned up slightly, still within the secure confines of Brett's arm, and looked down at the dark-haired woman who lay there content, asleep, peaceful.

Brett seemed such a hard-ass, always driven, always moving, always doing. But there were other things about Brett Higgins—how her sister had described the woman in her letters and how sometimes Brett would wear Pooh ties. She only seemed to do that when she was in a playful or light mood, and if anyone brought it up to Brett, all she'd do was growl, "Pooh just is. Got it?"

She ran her hands through Brett's surprisingly silky and soft hair, and then traced the usually hard lines of her face: her cheek, her forehead, down the line of her nose to her lips. How could anyone ever look at Brett and not see that she was a woman? Her fingers lingered on Brett's lips. They were surprisingly soft. And full.

Brett smiled a bit in her sleep and sucked Victoria's finger into her mouth, pulling Victoria closer to her. "Oh, honey . . ." she moaned.

Victoria was now straddling Brett's thigh, and getting hot as Brett sucked her finger and ran her hands over her body, sliding down her underwear to feel her ass. Victoria suddenly became aware that the only thing she was wearing was that one tiny bit of satin.

Part of her wanted to run screaming from the room, knowing she was in bed with someone of her own free will, wearing only panties. But she was so turned on and enjoying every sensation Brett's hands sent rushing through her body. She liked the roughness of Brett's T-shirt underneath her naked breasts, of Brett's tongue on her finger, and she so wanted to take her underwear off.

She gently pressed herself against Brett, trying not to moan, and trying not to wake Brett. She wondered how far she could go, what all she could do, without waking Brett. She felt a rush of guilt, but she was still too turned on from last night, and sleeping all night like this, to think about it.

So she wouldn't. She shut down the rational side of her mind and tried to just feel. She knew her underwear was soaked, again, just like last night.

She didn't want to do anything with Brett if Brett was thinking of another woman. But for now, she could just fantasize. She thought about pulling slightly away from Brett and masturbating. Brett could catch her at it. That thought gave her another rush and she couldn't stop the moan as she ground against Brett's thigh.

She had to do something, and right now she really didn't care how embarrassed she might be if Brett caught her. She leaned forward and kissed Brett lightly, and then she pulled her finger from Brett's mouth, luring her to her own mouth instead, letting her suck on her tongue and mouth.

She reached down to try to peel her underwear from her body, but as she was inching the waistband down, the hand on her ass suddenly grabbed, pulling her hard against the thigh between her legs.

"Oh, God," Victoria groaned out loud.

"No, it's just me," Brett said, holding Victoria firmly against her. "Do you really think you could moan and grind on me without me noticing?"

"How . . . how long have you been awake?"

"I remember your fingers on my lips. So you want these off?" Brett put her thumbs inside Victoria's underwear, just along the seams. She didn't wait for an answer before she jerked her hands, ripping along both seams and then pulling them off.

The act of force, and the feeling of the tiny bit of material sliding over her cunt made Victoria moan again. She felt like putty. Brett still had on her T-shirt and jeans, and now she herself was naked. In bed. With Brett. And Brett's hands were on her ass, making her ride her thigh until she was gasping again.

Victoria wrapped her arms around Brett. "God, oh God, Brett . . ."

She rode Brett hard, and Brett pulled her to her, kissing her hard and deep, as if she meant it.

Brett rolled her onto her back, and Victoria's thighs automatically opened for her, allowing her to lie between them. She wrapped her legs around Brett, trying to force the pressure where she so desperately needed it.

"God, Brett, please . . ."

"Open your eyes. I want to see inside of you when I make you come." Brett pulled her body up off of Victoria, and then shoved her hand between their bodies when Victoria moaned and searched for her with her hips. Brett's fingers found Victoria's clit and grazed over it, flickering over it, touching and caressing before entering Victoria with two fingers.

Victoria gasped and closed her eyes. She felt Brett inside of her, and she tried to urge her deeper. Brett caressed her, inside, even as her thumb played against Victoria's clit and Brett kissed her jaw line and neck.

"Brett, Brett!" Victoria screamed, opening her eyes and looking up at Brett. She felt Brett inside of her, and touching her, and the orgasm reached its peak and kept going. And all Victoria knew was that Brett was inside of her and looking at her as she groaned and moved against her, within her, making it go on and on. And she couldn't believe it, and the pleasure kept coming and she came up, rising toward Brett and then falling back so Brett could hold her while she gasped for breath.

She knew Brett loved her. Brett had looked inside her, and she did the same during those moments. She wanted to save them and cherish them forever.

She couldn't think about it.

Brett's arm was under her neck, and Brett was on top of her, and she felt warm and loved and safe. She didn't want to open her eyes.

"Are you okay?" Brett asked, running her free hand lovingly over Victoria's cheek.

Victoria opened her eyes, and they felt wet. She was crying. "Brett . . ." She had so much she wanted to say, but she couldn't.

"Shhh . . . baby . . . it's okay." Brett wiped away her tears, then kissed her cheeks, forehead, and eyes. She still lay on top of Victoria. Victoria finally opened her eyes and looked up into Brett's. Brett was holding most of her weight up on her arms. She moved a bit to the left so her left arm held her weight and her right hand could touch Victoria. All over.

Victoria wasn't naive, and she wasn't a virgin. When she first thought about how handsome Brett was, she had thought about Brett forcing her, eating her out, fucking her. She had fantasized for months about Brett going down on her.

But now, now that she was here, with Brett lying over her, she only wanted to have Brett looking into her eyes. That was how she felt most open and exposed, when Brett looked into her as she came. And when she loved her most.

"Brett," she moaned.

Brett kissed her jaw, then her collarbone, and moved farther down. She gently kissed her right breast, licking her breast all around before she suckled on the nipple, and Victoria arched back up into Brett's wonderfully soft and gentle mouth.

She knew Brett was going to go down on her soon, and she wanted that. God, how she wanted that! She couldn't even begin to imagine how it would feel. And she started to tense up, just trying to decide . . .

"Baby? Baby? What's wrong?" Brett asked, looking up at her.

Victoria closed her eyes, though she knew the tears were flowing. She thought she had left tears behind. Her legs were still spread with Brett between them, and her body still knew what she wanted as she moved under and against the hard body on top of her, but she didn't know what was happening.

"I'm sorry, I don't know what I did," Brett said, sounding so much like a repentant child, Victoria had to look at her.

Brett's eyes varied from green to brown, and right now they were liquid brown with concern and . . . love? Victoria was lost in them.

Victoria was stopped until she felt Brett starting to move from her. Then she locked her legs and arms around Brett again, holding her against her. "Don't leave me, please don't leave me."

"I'm not, I'm right here, Vicki." Victoria had always hated the nickname, but she was finding she liked it when her gran or Brett used it. "I'm not letting go, okay?" Brett finished, holding her tightly.

Victoria pushed Brett up just enough so she could look into her eyes. Then she grabbed her shoulders tightly, not wanting her to get any farther from her. What she saw in Brett's eyes in those moments made her know why her sister had loved Brett so: Brett was unsure. She wanted to make love to Victoria, but was worried that maybe she wasn't good enough. "There are so many things I want to do with you," Victoria whispered, barely able to say such things. She was a stripper, she had lost her virginity to her father when she was nine, and still, these things were hard. "But . . . but right now . . ." She squeezed her eyes tight, holding back the flood of tears.

She was sure Brett would see this as a blow to her ego.

But Brett didn't move. She finally whispered, "Vicki?"

Victoria wanted to say something, but she was too embarrassed.

"Do you want to be alone?"

"No."

Brett stayed where she was for a moment, and Victoria knew she had lost her forever. Until Brett took a deep breath and finally said, "I want to make love to you again. Tell me what to do."

Victoria had too much fear and too much sadness inside to jump for joy like she wanted to. Instead she said simply and calmly with her eyes closed, "I like looking in your eyes . . . I like seeing inside you when you're . . . inside of me." Her body yearned, and she didn't know how she could make it happen without doing it herself. Her mind was throwing up so many barriers. But she couldn't be alone yet.

Brett again leaned to her left, and teased her fingers over Victoria's body, tantalizing her skin, and then her nipples, and tummy, and inner thighs. "Tell me what you want, what you need and if I do something wrong. Okay?"

Victoria breathed deeply, enjoying the sensations rushing over her. "Please, Brett, just . . ."

"What?" Brett asked when Victoria didn't continue.

Victoria opened her eyes to look into the liquid brown eyes inches from her own. She took a deep breath as Brett's fingers trailed over her, making her skin rise and dance underneath her touch. "Please, Brett, do what you just did and look at me when you do it." Her cheeks flushed even under this much of an admission. She stripped for a living, but still couldn't say what she wanted in bed. What she needed.

Brett didn't say a word, just trailed her fingers down between Victoria's legs. She looked right into Victoria's eyes while she touched and caressed her there. Whenever Victoria tried to turn away, Brett put her hand to her face and made Victoria look right at her. Into her eyes.

Victoria gasped, but finally, she was caught in Brett's gaze. As if they were one. Brett touched her, caressed her, and she looked into Brett, and Brett looked into her. And then Brett was inside of her.

Brett's fingers found their mark inside, while her thumb caressed her clit, and they breathed in and out the same air, their eyes never straying from each other.

This time, Victoria felt her walls crumble.

"Girls!" Rebecca called out, "breakfast's almost ready!" She had heard noises upstairs for a while now, and finally decided she might remind them someone else was in the house. She pulled out potatoes and shredded them down for hash browns. She knew she had a while till they were ready for breakfast.

She really didn't want to disturb Vicki and Brett, because she really wanted them to find each other and be happy—and she knew Vicki couldn't be happy with a man. But this Brett . . . Frankly, Rebecca didn't worry that she was a potential murderer, or had a rap sheet.

She started frying the hash browns, and then heard Brett behind her. Upstairs, the shower turned on.

"I thought you said breakfast was almost done," Brett said.

"I lied. I figured it'd take a bit for you two to come down here."

"Oh. Um . . ."

"Here, have some juice," Rebecca said, pulling out a carton from the fridge. "I've also got coffee."

Brett took a cup of coffee and turned toward the phone. "Can I use this?"

"Sure."

Brett dialed. "Is this line safe?" she asked. No hello or anything, just that. Rebecca had to listen. "Good. You already know I didn't do it. I was set up." Rebecca pulled out the eggs and cheese and milk. "Whatever. Listen, the woman I met at the bar that night was Heather Johnson . . . yeah, her . . . Yeah. Her . . . She was pretending to be Gwen . . . and I don't really care what you say, I gotta end this, so I'll just tell you that Heather knew me and deliberately chose me to take the fall for Gwen's death, so goodbye." Brett hung up the phone, then leaned over it, staring down at it.

"Should I even ask?" Rebecca said, walking up behind Brett and placing an ashtray, lighter, and pack of cigarettes next to her.

"You don't mind?" Brett asked.

"No, I don't. I wouldn't have done that if I did." Rebecca leaned against a counter across from Brett, arms folded over her breasts, staring at her. "What was that about?"

Brett lit a smoke and shrugged. "Just calling Randi McMartin, a cop I know, and think I can trust. I figured they wouldn't be tracing her line or this one, so it might be safe."

"You're sure you can trust her?"

Brett nodded. "I think I can. Anyway, from what you said last night, I figured I knew the woman who played me. We met during a blizzard in Lansing last winter when I was snowed in. And then I put two and two together to figure she worked for me about a decade ago. So I need Randi to check her out, maybe figure out why she wanted to set me up." Brett slammed her fist against the table. "I just don't understand why she did this to me!"

Victoria walked up to Brett and wrapped a casual arm around her waist. "Honey, in case you haven't noticed, most of the women who work for you wouldn't say no to you—and not because you're the boss."

"What do you mean by that?"

"Were you with Pamela or Allie when Heather worked for you?"

Brett shrugged. "I can't remember." She leaned back against the kitchen counter and stared up at the cupboards, thinking. "It was Storm. I was with Storm then. I remember Heather watching, staring, when I pulled Storm into my arms."

Victoria grinned and pulled Brett toward her. "Well, maybe this Heather had a thing for you, and got pissed because you wouldn't pay any attention to her."

"Oh, c'mon—that was like a decade ago—if I pissed her off so much, why would she wait so long to do anything?"

"Maybe she saw you in the bar and you were just convenient?" Rebecca suggested from across the room.

Victoria and Brett looked at her, and then Victoria turned back to Rebecca. "You might be right. But I think she'd be even more apt to jump on it the first chance she got if she had a thing for Brett years ago."

"Okay, so, whatever," Brett said. "I mean, great, we know who and kinda why, but there are other, bigger whys out there as well. Why did Heather kill Gwen in the first place?"

"Darned good question," Rebecca said. "But for right now, why don't we eat?" She set the plates down on the table and sat down.

Victoria and Brett joined her and they all loaded up their plates and began eating.

The sound of a car pulling into the driveway broke the silence. Before the car doors slammed, they were all on their feet.

"I'll be hiding out back," Brett said, using the kitchen door to disappear into the auto graveyard behind the house. "If you don't give me the all-clear in five minutes, I'll be taking off on foot. I'll make contact later." She quickly kissed Victoria and was gone.

Rebecca was already in the living room, peering out the window when Victoria entered. "It's not a police car, and they're not in uniform."

Victoria used the peephole to look first when the knock came. Then she opened the door. "Hello," she said.

"Victoria," Allie said.

"Come in," Victoria finally said. "Let me go get Brett."

"Where's she at?" Allie asked.

"Out back," Victoria said over her shoulder. Then she turned around, realizing her error. "Oh, Allie, Maddy, and Leisa, this is my grandmother, Rebecca."

Leisa smiled at Rebecca and said, "Wow, you must've started early!" remarking on how young Rebecca looked to have a granddaughter Victoria's age.

"I gotta get Brett before she takes off," Victoria said.

"I'll come with you," Allie said, taking a step forward.

"I'll just be a minute," Victoria said, all but running out the back door.

"Allie, is it?" Rebecca said, stepping forward. "I'm sure Brett will be very glad to see you." She knew there had to be some reason for all of the behavior she had witnessed—both last night and today. And now she knew why. She wanted to help Victoria, so she had to help cover with the woman she deduced was Brett's girlfriend.

"Oh, yes," Allie said, "I'm sorry. I just haven't seen Brett since this all started. I've barely even spoken with her."

Chapter Twenty-one

Victoria was thankful her grandmother had detained Allie. She needed a moment alone with Brett before they went back in. She walked out the door and said, in a loud voice, "All clear."

Brett peeked warily out from behind the decrepit Ford farthest from the house, then stood. "Who was it?"

"They're still here," Victoria said, approaching Brett. When they were just a few feet apart, she said, "It's Allie, Maddy, and Leisa." She reached forward and ran her hands down the edges of today's bowling shirt, which Brett wore unbuttoned over a white T-shirt.

Brett's face paled, and Victoria could almost see a look of pure panic. Brett put her hands on Victoria's shoulders, "Vicki, I—"

Victoria placed a hand lightly on Brett's cheek. "Darling, I won't do or say anything. Don't worry. Let's just get you out of trouble." Ever since Allie showed up, Victoria realized she was willing to do whatever was necessary to be with Brett. She was even willing to play today's Storm and let Brett be non-monogamous. She just hoped Brett would kiss her before she went in to Allie.

Brett couldn't be hers alone, at least not yet, and if she did anything to break up her and Allie, she never would be. Brett seemed the sort of woman who knew how to hold a grudge.

Brett glanced up at the house, checking the windows.

"Gran's keeping her in the living room."

"I'm sorry, Vicki." She pulled Victoria into her strong arms, holding her tight. She tenderly caressed her hair, and Victoria melted into her embrace, wanting the moment to last forever. "I'm not sorry about last night, or this morning. I'm sorry that all this is happening around us, and that Allie's here now. I'm sorry because . . ."

Victoria put her finger to Brett's lips. "Stop. Don't say it. I don't care. Just kiss me. Please, kiss me."

Brett tenderly laid her hand on Victoria's cheek, then kissed her. "I do love you," she said, when their lips finally parted. Her breath was warm on Victoria's cheek.

"I love you, too," Victoria whispered back.

"Oh, God, Brett!" Allie said, throwing her arms around Brett as soon as she and Victoria entered. "I was so worried, so scared! Why didn't you call me? Contact me? Let me know you were all right?"

"I didn't want you involved in this. Didn't want you implicated." Brett held Allie, soothing her, just like she had just done moment ago with Victoria. Stroking her hair softly, holding her, feeling Allie's heartbeat next to her own.

She also felt all eyes in the room on her. Especially Victoria's. She wished she knew what she wanted.

Well, actually, she did know what she wanted—Allie *and* Victoria. She had to keep the grin off her face when she realized she wouldn't say no to both of them at the same time. She just had to realize she was shallow and incapable of true love. That was what it had to be. She was just shallow. So she just had to figure out where happiness lay.

She met Rebecca's eyes over Allie's shoulder. This could end in all kinds of awful ways but maybe she would get lucky. She turned Allie to face Rebecca and said, "Allie, this is Rebecca, Victoria's and Pamela's grandmother, and Rebecca, I'd like you to meet Allison Sullivan, my lover."

"Victoria introduced us before she went out to get you," Rebecca said somewhat coldly. "It wasn't too hard to figure out your relationship with her."

Maddy apparently sensed a level of tension in the room, because she cleared her throat before saying, "I think we should gather round and figure out what exactly is going on, and what, exactly, we are going to do about it."

The detective/cop inside of Allie took over. "Okay, so let's all sit down, and we can all get caught up." She led Brett by the hand around to sit on the sofa by the coffee table.

"Good. Update time," Rebecca said, sitting in the overstuffed chair at the head of the coffee table. "I know I could use some updating. And a bit more knowledge of what precisely is going on here."

It took them about a half hour, complete with Brett continuously apologizing for her actions to Allie and justifying the steps she took every bit of the way, to go over the significant points of the matter.

"Oh, what a wicked web we weave, when first we practice to deceive," Rebecca said, once they reached a lull in the conversation. Brett was sitting on the couch with an arm gently and possessively around Allie's shoulders. Victoria had been pacing the entire time.

"Uh, yeah, I think I've learned that one now," Brett said.

"What is done is finished," Maddy said, sitting on the sofa opposite Brett and Allie with Leisa. "We must look toward what we must do in order to rectify the situation."

"I've been looking over everything Brett got from Gwen's computer," Leisa said. "I think Heather used the hidden AOL account on Gwen's computer to send a lot of the e-mails to Brett. She probably sent the rest from her own computers. I think Heather used her position as Gwen's lover to have access to her life. And e-mail accounts."

"Sometimes Gwen e-mailed me from her work computer," Brett said.

"I wouldn't mind getting a look at that machine," Leisa said.

Allie shook her head. "That would be tough. Apparently CompuVisions is well protected on the computer front—they were working on some new software application, so even Ski didn't get copies of everything Gwen could have done."

"Why not? Since so much of this involves computers, I'd think it would be a key part of the investigation?" Leisa said.

Allie shook her head. "I double-checked with Randi on it. She's working with Ski on this, and I think she's kinda convinced Ski that Brett really is innocent—and that Ski's thinking that maybe Randi's a conduit between her investigation and us. Gwen's e-mail and personal stuff would be stored on her own computer. The program she was working on, and more critical information and secure stuff, would be stored on the network server. CompuVisions' honchos apparently were open enough that Ski doesn't feel the need to get court orders for the release of the network information."

"Did you find anything else on Gwen's computer?" Brett asked Leisa.

"I went through all of her e-mails. I think she thought something was going on. She just didn't know what. It seems as though one of their competitors came out of nowhere with a product suspiciously close to what CompuVisions was working on. I'd like to check her work e-mails to see if anything else pops up there."

Allie again shook her head. "I don't think that's possible, but I'll see if Randi can get us the files."

"At least maybe you can get her to look for the things you're interested in," Victoria said, sitting on the arm of Maddy's and Leisa's sofa. This was the first time she had spoken. Brett looked at her and could see in her eyes the iron control she was holding over herself.

"Good thinking. Maybe she could at least get me the four-one-one on such things. Anything else I should ask her about?" Allie asked Leisa.

Leisa leaned back and stared up at the ceiling. "Have her look at the file creation dates. When I looked at her home computer, it looked as if somebody had been fiddling with her files—but sometimes computer geeks get overconfident and slip up on details."

"Got it," Allie said, writing in a pad of paper she had pulled out, just like the good cop she used to be. They trained her well.

Brett was well aware of Victoria's eyes focused on her. So she got up and began to pace, putting distance between herself and Allie. She didn't want to hurt Victoria more than she already had. "With all that security on their network and such, was CompuVisions working on any government contracts?"

"No," Leisa said, shaking her head. "I looked into that. If this was any sort of corporate espionage, it was based on the new program Gwen was in charge of."

"So if Gwen was the golden goose, why'd they kill it?" Rebecca asked.

"From what's been said about Gwen knowing about this other company, the game was up," Maddy said.

"Okay," Brett said, "I don't get all this computer mumbo-jumbo and such, but what I think I'm hearing is that maybe Heather used Gwen to gain access to this hot-shit computer program, sold it to their competitor, and then killed Gwen."

"Yes, I think that's about where we're going with this," Leisa said.

"It's the most likely solution, after all," Allie said.

"But again, we get to why kill the goose that laid the golden egg?" Victoria said, standing as well, and impatiently pacing.

"The program is nearly done. CompuVisions planned on releasing it in two months' time," Leisa said. "Alternities, their major competitor, could probably do the final trouble-shooting themselves, as well."

"And in that time, they could continue altering the code," Allie said, "to make it look not so much like they stole it."

"So Gwen was now dispensable," Maddy said.

"And a possible liability," Rebecca added. "So they were just waiting for her to hit the possible liability stage before dealing with her."

"Brett, do you realize what this means?" Victoria said, grabbing

Brett's arms when their paths crossed. "Heather knew back when you saw her that at some point it would end up with Gwen dying—so all those months ago she started plotting against you."

"So she's been planning on killing Gwen all this time," Allie said, standing and facing Brett and Victoria.

Brett put some space between herself and Vicki and moved closer to Allie. "She might have even hooked up with Gwen in the first place for all this to happen."

"I hope she got a fucking-Goddammed lot of money for it, at least." Victoria was standing against the wall, her arms crossed over her chest.

Brett felt as if she was caught between Scylla and Charybdis. "This all started years ago, then." She turned away from Victoria and toward Allie. "So every step, every word, has been calculated and premeditated." She turned away from both women and faced another wall, away from all of them. "For all I know, I might've just been in the wrong place at the wrong time." She pounded her head against the wall. "I hate this shit! Corporate-fucking espionage! What the hell is this? Killing someone for something like that?"

"Throughout history," Maddy said, "people have been killed for money. Surely you, Brett, must understand this."

"Power, sex, love, and money," Allie said. "All classic motives. After all, what is the life of one compared with all the money you can accumulate." She sat down again, not looking at Brett.

"Heather probably seduced Gwen to get into her life," Victoria said, slowly approaching Brett. "She wanted to have full access to everything Gwen was working on. She got that, and continued with Gwen to keep getting that information. Once Gwen questioned it, once Gwen might become suspicious, well, it was over." Victoria was just a step away now. Brett wanted to pull her into her arms and cry onto her shoulder, wanted her solace.

"They put the next part of their plan into operation," Rebecca said. Still seated in her lounge chair at the head of the two couches, like the chairman of the board. "They killed Gwen and framed you for it."

"In such a way they were most likely to prove that Gwen was the one doing the underhanded dealings with other companies," Maddy said. "With her out of the picture, it would be more understandable if she was playing on both sides of the fence."

"Dammit!" Brett cried, turning to the wall.

"Hold on, you said, 'they.' " Allie said, finally standing again. "Heather is the key, but she's not in this alone!"

Brett turned from the wall to look at her friends—new and old. Her lover stood like Odysseus, or maybe Jessica Fletcher, with an important discovery. "You're right."

"So the question is, what do we do now?" Maddy asked in almost a whisper.

Brett looked at Maddy as if she had just survived *Survivor.* Like she was the million-dollar winner. Brett didn't watch the show, didn't watch much TV at all, but who could not hear about some bits and pieces of TV lore? "Maddy's right. We need a game plan. We know something about what's happening, but not all of it. As we just realized, there's a fucking lot we don't know."

"So we have to find out what we don't know, because that's the only way out of this mess," Victoria said.

"It is the first step in proving Brett's innocence," Maddy said.

"I think that's what we all want to do," Victoria said, looking directly at Allie.

"They've done the entire 'Brett killed her' bit, but . . ." Allie said. "What about proving that Gwen was the leak?"

"CompuVisions isn't looking too closely at that yet," Leisa said. "But Heather must have some plot to ensure it does happen."

"I wonder if they were just trying to make me out to be Gwen's murderer," Brett said, "or if they also wanted to pin me for the info exchange as well?"

"I think we ought to make that not happen," Victoria said. "If they were planning on it, that is."

"So we really must get on top of this situation," Maddy said.

"Maybe they just hoped everything would lead to Gwen?" Leisa added hopefully.

"I so do not want to risk that," Brett said. "We need a plan. And now."

"That would be a good thing," Victoria said.

Brett vigorously paced. She couldn't look at those around her and become distracted. "A plan. A plan is formed on given knowledge. But we don't have a lot of that now, do we?" She turned to look at everyone, slowly, meeting each of their eyes in turn. "I've tried to shut each of you out. Tried my best to keep you safe. But you've tracked me down, nonetheless, against my wishes. But now you know what you're into—all of you can now be charged as accessories after the fact." She again slowly looked around the room. Looking into each woman's face for signs of fear, uneasiness, or questions, and found none. "Fine. I hate this. But if you're gonna put yours in with mine, despite my misgivings, then I'm gonna have to trust and use you. This is your last chance to get out before things become hairy." No one moved.

"I think we're all in this with you, Brett," Victoria said, placing a hand on her shoulder.

Brett stepped away from the warm touch. "I want to know what each of you is willing to do for me. I'd like to just do this alone, but having you all butting in randomly might cause problems—so if you're here, I want to know how far you're willing to go." Brett didn't like giving away her power, or asking for help. She didn't like delegating responsibility, or bringing others into her mess.

Allie looked around and then went to Brett, placing a hand on Brett's shoulder. "I think we're all in this with you."

Brett pulled back from Allie. "You don't understand. What I'm talking about now is not only death—if Heather's in this with others, and you all are trying to help me, they might come after you, too—but also about imprisonment. As in, for many years."

"Brett, I have already told you that I can do nothing else but help you," Maddy said.

"Maddy, all of you—I have helped people, usually against my will, but this isn't the case. This is about me. It's not about any greater good or such wild moral sentiments—it's about getting me out of a great big bloody mess that I got myself into, okay? And it might involve all of you ending up in the women's penitentiary acting out really bad triple-X flicks with your new best friends—Butch, and Bertha, and . . . and well, really big, bad scary bull-dykes. For several years!"

Maddy stood up, facing Brett. "Once upon a time you helped a girl named Liza."

"She was already dead. Just a ghost."

"But still you helped her."

Leisa stood up. "And you helped a high school teacher who just asked. You didn't want to, but you were there."

"I didn't really—"

"Ask Kathy or Becky or . . . there were a lot of people you helped there in Alma, Brett," Leisa said. "You didn't have to, and didn't want to, but you did."

"You did all you could to help Pamela. To give her a decent life," Victoria said.

"And she got killed, because of me."

"I would've killed myself months ago except for you," Victoria said.

"But also, because of me," Brett said.

"Yeah, you're the black hat," Leisa said. "You only help folks because of your own best interests. I've heard this tune and know the words by heart. But I don't really know you, and I'm still here."

Finally Allie put her arms around her lover's neck. "I'm always here for you. Because I know the real you. And I've seen you throw yourself off the side of a building to save somebody you didn't even like."

"Well, fuck," Rebecca said. "I just met you last night, and seeing all this, I'm ready to do whatever I can to help. 'Sides, it'll be more fun than being the evil murderess hiding in the woods."

"A well-deserved rep if ever I heard one," Brett said, pulling away, and into the safe place of no emotions. "I'm not so good at delegating," she continued. "But it looks like we really have to have a game plan. And I'm thinking it focuses on Heather. And maybe others. After all, she must've been selling this info to someone."

Chapter Twenty-two

Before heading up to Lansing, Randi stopped by the Paradise. She wanted to look into what Brett had said about Heather Johnson having worked for her at the Paradise about a decade before.

So far, she hadn't been able to track down anything to prove it. Technically, Heather should have had some sort of exotic dancers' license, but a lot of dancers never actually got one. The Paradise was one of the many places that never checked for such things.

And most of those who worked at the Paradise never claimed a penny of it to the government, so there were no social security, or federal, or state tax records to prove they had ever worked there. No paper trail.

Randi was sure that Brett was right on this, but she couldn't really confront Heather until she had some proof. She had seen the Paradise's records—they were sketchy at best—and she knew that since the time Heather had worked there, the Paradise had burned down along with any records, so it was highly unlikely that Frankie would be able to provide proof, but she would still check.

Randi had spent a while that morning going through computer files from Ski, looking for any red flags Allie had mentioned. Randi knew Brett was evil and self-centered and not worthy of a woman like Allie, but the woman had saved her life. And Randi was a cop. A good cop. And there was no place for personal feelings in her line of work.

She parked at the Paradise, and walked into the cashier's office. She flashed her badge. "I need to see Frankie Lorenzini."

The clerk looked at her warily. "Do you have a warrant?"

"No. I just want to talk with Frankie. Tell him it's Randi McMartin. Detective Randi McMartin."

The clerk kept an eye on her while he went to the desk and picked up the phone. He spoke in guarded tones so she couldn't hear what he was saying and couldn't even see his mouth enough to have a clue what he was saying. But he opened the door, allowing her upstairs to the offices.

Frankie greeted her at the top of the staircase without a smile or handshake. "Randi, glad to see you." He turned and went into his office.

Randi followed. She flung herself into one of his visitor's chairs and steepled her fingers beneath her chin, looking up at him.

Frankie didn't sit. He looked down at her. "Are you here about Heather Johnson?"

"Yeah. What can you tell me?"

"Nice girl, she was working her way through college."

"I've done some research, and I can't find anything to prove that she worked here. Can you?"

He shook his head. "When the Paradise burned, a lot of crap burned with it. And dancers come and go, so Brett and I . . . well, we weren't really into keeping track of them, y'know?"

Randi stood. "I figured as much, but I needed to check anyway."

"Good thing that somebody was thinking, though," Frankie said, when Randi was almost to the door. He put a box on his desk. "When Rick DeSilva kicked, Brett and I inherited everything. We figured if he was keeping certain business records, we should, too."

"Frankie, what's in there?"

"Take a look. You'll find it interesting."

Randi started digging through the box. "So this was some of DeSilva's stuff?"

"Yeah. I thought about Heather, and didn't think there was anything to show that she was ever here, but . . . then I remembered about the crap from Rick's that I took home with me."

"Was there more?"

"Yeah, but this box was just like this when I got to it." He sat in his chair. "Look through it."

It didn't take Randi long to find a picture of Heather, which was obviously a dancer's photo. Heather sat stark naked on the counter of what was obviously the box office of the old Paradise Theatre, with her legs open to show off her shaven pussy. Behind Heather's head was a calendar that showed the month and year—March 1993. Randi found a few other similar pictures that made it pretty damn obvious that Heather had indeed worked at the Paradise. She also found contact sheets that listed Heather, who danced under the name Explicit, as well as schedules that showed she danced at the Paradise for at least a year.

Wondering briefly why DeSilva would have kept these particular items, she asked, "Do you mind if I take these with me?" as she was putting them into a folder.

"Not at all. You know we always cooperate with the cops."

"Yeah. I know."

"I hope you're here to tell me you've arrested Brett Higgins," Heather said, entering the conference room where Ski and Randi waited for her.

"Actually, no," Ski said. "We're still looking for her."

"Well, I hope you've found something—especially since you let her get away at least once already. That was pretty embarrassing, huh?"

Randi had had enough of this, but she waited patiently for Ski to make her move.

"She was well disguised," Ski said.

"But I thought you had a past with her—I mean, you've met her before and all, right? I thought I'd heard you'd previously had her under investigation for another murder."

"You know quite a bit about me and Higgins, it seems?"

Heather shrugged and sat down. "She killed my lover. I wanted to learn more about her. In one newspaper article they mentioned that bit about Chuck Bertram's murder, and how she was the chief suspect for a while, and you had been in charge of the investigation. I just want to see justice done." She let a tear slip out of her eye, and pulled out a tissue to wipe at it. "Sorry."

Bingo, Randi thought, Ski had extracted a lot from Heather.

"So if Brett's costume that day was so lame," Ski said, sitting down across from Heather, "why didn't you recognize her?"

Heather looked confused. "I've seen some pictures of her, but it's not like I've ever actually met her or anything."

"Yes, just seeing pictures of somebody is a lot different than actually meeting them. But you have met Brett Higgins."

"Sure, now I have. But I still didn't get a really good look at her."

"So you're saying you've never met Brett Higgins before that day?"

"That's what I'm saying, yes."

"Ms. Johnson, when we first started investigating Gwen's murder, I had looked over your file. We discussed it a bit the last time we were here, but I've got a few more questions."

"I don't understand—are you investigating *me* now? Why? You know who killed her—why aren't you out there tracking down Higgins?" She stood up so she could look down at Ski.

"Calm down, Ms. Johnson," Ski said, standing to meet the woman eye-to-eye. "This is why this is called an *investigation*—

because I'm *investigating*. We're looking for Higgins, yes, but I'm also looking at all angles of this case—something may come up that might help point out where she's at, what she's up to, and what she might do."

Randi caught Heather looking at her, so she figured she'd better say something. "It's very strange that Higgins showed up here. She knows we're looking for her, and she shows up here?"

"It is very strange," Ski said. "And it worries us that maybe she's not done here yet."

Randi loved watching Ski work. The woman was good.

"What do you mean?" Heather said, sinking back into her chair.

Randi put a foot on the chair next to Heather and looked down at her. "There's something we don't know, and we've got to figure it out."

"Right now, for all we know," Ski said, "she might come for you next. And we really don't want to see anybody else die."

"She might come for me next?" Heather whispered.

"We don't know," Ski said. "Are you willing to answer our questions now?"

"Yes . . . yes . . . just keep her away from me." Heather looked scared. She was crying now.

Ski looked down at Heather's personnel file. "I see here that you received several college scholarships. Must've been quite the student."

"I worked hard in school. I didn't want to end up like my parents."

"What do you mean by that?"

"My parents were white trash. Dad used to work at a car plant, but he threw his back out, claimed workman's comp, and became an alcoholic."

"So did your scholarships cover all your college costs?" Randi asked, glancing through Heather's file. She didn't know a lot about scholarships, but since Heather said she had several of them, Randi was thinking that none of them were full-ride deals.

"No, they didn't," Heather admitted.

"So did your parents cover the rest of your costs?" Ski asked.

Heather laughed. "They could barely cover the cost of toilet paper! And they never understood why I wanted to go to college anyway."

"So how did you pay for college?" Randi asked.

Heather whipped around to look at her, as if she'd realized what she'd admitted. Then she tried to cover her tracks. "I lived with my folks and worked a bunch of little part-time jobs and such." Randi thought she saw a glimmer of panic in Heather's eyes. Brett wasn't wrong.

Ski and Randi looked at each other. Ski gave Randi the slightest nod.

"So where did you work?" Randi asked Heather.

"Fast-food joints, convenience stores, the usual."

"Funny. I just show you working at Mickey D's. No convenience stores," Randi said, putting down the social security form she'd printed out earlier in front of Heather. "And not for that long, either. At least, not while you were in college."

Heather didn't say a word.

"Earlier you said you've never met Brett Higgins," Randi said. She pulled out the photo she'd gotten from DeSilva's box, the one where Heather showed all her glory, and placed it on the table in front her. Randi tapped the photo. "Look familiar?"

Heather looked down at the picture. Then away. Her face turned crimson. She looked pleadingly at Randi, then said to Ski, "I've tried to forget that bit of my life. I needed to get through college, and that was the only way I could afford it! I didn't do it for that long, just enough to make it through school!"

"Heather," Randi said, forcing her to look back at her. "You're forgetting who I am. I'm a member of Detroit's special organized crime division, and I've been after Brett's ass for a long, long time."

"What are you talking about?"

"I've been inside every adult club in Detroit, and a few outside, and I know where this picture was taken. I was in this very spot eleven years ago. This picture was taken in the box office of the old Paradise Theatre, back before it burned down and was rebuilt."

Heather put her head down in her arms, which she crossed on the expensive oak table in front of her. Her shoulders shook as if she was sobbing. With a catch in her voice, she said, "I've tried to forget about it. It's not like having been a stripper's gonna help me get a good job, or have anyone respect me or anything . . ."

Randi looked at Ski, who smiled and gave her another nod. Randi pulled a few other pictures out of the folder. "Not that long, Heather?" She placed one picture, then another, and another in front of Heather. In the pictures, Heather's poses and jewelry differed. "Not a lot of white girls dance at the Paradise, and apparently, Rick DeSilva liked you. He kept enough pictures of you."

Heather stood and faced Randi. "I'm a lesbian. I'd think you two could relate to that—he wasn't my type."

The woman was hitting below the belt. But Randi could do the same. "You just said that you didn't work there that long, but these pictures tell a different tale."

"Um, Heather?" Ski said, tapping the pictures. "Are you seeing what I am? 'Cause I'd really not like to embarrass us all even more. Why don't you just admit how long you worked there? And that you did indeed know Brett Higgins."

The three of them looked down at the pictures. They seemed to chronicle her progression in pubic hair fashion from natural to bikini waxed to completely shaved.

"About a year," Heather said.

"So why did you lie about knowing Brett?"

Heather looked up at her. Randi figured she was trying to come up with the next lie. "I'm sure you've got yet another embarrassing photo of me to prove whatever it is you're trying to prove."

"You didn't tell us about being Gwen's lover and now you've lied about knowing Brett Higgins," Randi said.

Ski shrugged and walked away, as if to imply: People who lie are usually hiding something.

"Fine! I used to work at the Paradise Theatre. I thought I recognized Brett's picture, and her name, but I wasn't sure! It's been over ten fucking years, for God's sake!"

Randi placed a picture on the table in front of them. "That sort of ambiguity doesn't usually follow this sort of picture." The picture showed Brett with a naked Heather on one side of her, and a naked Storm on the other. "So are you going to tell us the truth now?"

"Okay, fine, I knew it was Brett, but she was always so dark and brutal. And no one here knows about my past, and it's not exactly the sort of thing I wanted to broadcast. I don't want everyone to know I used to strip, okay? Can you blame me?" She looked frantically between the two women, tears streaking her cheeks.

"Don't worry. Just tell us," Ski said, placing a calming hand on her shoulder and guiding her back down to her chair.

"You know how every dyke in Michigan is only one step away from every other one? I had figured we'd meet at some time, but just couldn't believe it when she came up in this."

"So you knew Brett was a dyke?" Randi asked, leaning over her.

Heather looked up at her. "Everyone knows she is. You just have to look at her to know."

"So did she do anything while you danced there to let you know she was? She come on to you?"

"You mean besides the affair she was having with Storm, or where her hands sometimes went?" Heather replied. All of this saved Randi from having to pull out the last picture.

"So let me get this right," Randi said. "You've hidden crucial information because of embarrassment?"

"Can you blame me? I'm being offered a promotion now, and having all this baggage that would make people lose respect for me. Employees don't respect explicit pornographic pictures of their bosses, okay?"

"There's a reason she's lying," Randi said through her mouthful of burger.

"Even I'm seeing that," Ski said. "She lied about Gwen, about her future, about Brett. You had a good battle plan for this, by the way."

"Thanks, it takes two to make a team."

Ski looked back down at her food and concentrated on dipping some of her fries into the ranch dressing she used instead of catsup. "Heather's alibi does stick, though. She was at work at the time Gwen was killed. The security log and cameras in the lobby confirm it, as well as the security guard and a janitor."

"Did she frequently work late?"

"Both she and Gwen put in a lot of hours, especially over the past few months. Usually together, but sometimes it would just be one or the other. Apparently, Heather really did help Gwen substantially."

"Did you figure out how Brett got in?"

"She used Cartwright's pass card. They've fixed that oversight now. But, knowing Brett, I'm thinking if she wants to get back in, she will."

"Really? I didn't know heavy-duty B-and-E was her thing, too."

"That last case I worked on her? This guy was found murdered at an ad agency. One night, I had a thought about something, and returned to the scene to check it out. Well, I thought I heard something, so I checked it out and was sure somebody was there. I can't remember what floor the office was on, but I swear to God, Randi, the woman jumped out of the fucking window and got away."

"I wonder if Brett actually likes herself."

"Why do you say that?"

"Because she keeps doing this stupid-ass shit that could get her killed, but she survives, almost by accident."

"It could just be overconfidence—she knows she'll figure it out, even if she doesn't plan ahead."

Randi shook her head. "Ski, I'm telling you—there was really no reason that either of us survived when she threw herself off that building to catch me. It was just dumb luck. And when you met her, she was on the lam—we thought she was dead, because we thought we buried her."

"I've looked through the files, so I know that."

"Yeah, well she was on top of a burning building and got a cop to shoot repeatedly at her, and then she leapt away. It was insane!"

"You know I'm watching Madeline's house in Alma."

Randi nodded. "I figured Brett might hide out there."

"So why didn't you say something?"

Randi looked up and met Ski's eyes. "It was just a feeling, nothing I could use to justify a stakeout." She dipped a fry in catsup, then put it in her mouth. "And, quite frankly, knowing Brett, if she was there, and you went there while she was there, she could still get out of it."

"You like her."

Randi looked up, and looked right into Ski's deep brown eyes. A lot of folks had brown eyes, but Ski's were exceptional. They were deep, with gold highlights. "I hate her guts. I despise everything about her," she said truthfully. She looked back down at the wrapper of her sandwich. She remembered when fast-food sandwiches came in Styrofoam containers. When did they switch?

"Randi, I know you're talking with her, or in contact with her in some way—I need to get to her, and you come closer to her than I am on a daily basis. She has to come in for questioning. You have to understand how frustrating this is to me!"

"I do." Randi reached out to touch Ski's hand. The contact was electric. "And I'd tell you if I knew where she was, but I honestly don't know. I've had thoughts, but they're more instinct than anything else. Nothing I could work for a warrant, so . . ." she shrugged.

Ski took Randi's hand in her own. "She's in contact with you, isn't she?"

Randi looked down at their connected hands. "Sometimes, yes. But she's careful. I know she's in contact with Frankie—and it's usually Frankie who calls me, and . . . Honestly?"

"Honestly. What are you thinking?"

Randi thought that what she was thinking about was how beautiful Ski was. But she couldn't say that. "I'm thinking that you hit the nail on the head when you said to Heather that it was suspicious that Brett was at CompuVisions."

"What?"

"She wouldn't go there, she wouldn't hang around Lansing, if she was guilty. I mean, there is a vague chance she's trying to pin the blame on someone else, but you know what I think."

"Yeah, I know."

Randi pulled her hand away and focused again on her lunch. "I just want to be a cop. You can't be a cop if you beat confessions out of the innocent, y'know?"

Ski pulled away. "You're starting to scare me, Randi."

"Good."

"What?"

"I should scare you."

"Why?"

Randi crumpled her trash noisily. She tried to ignore Ski, but Ski walked up to her.

Ski tenderly touched her lips to Randi's. "I'm still looking forward to going out with you."

That night, the Alma Police Department said they'd keep an eye on Maddy's house, so Ski went through the files on Brett's and Gwen's computers. Again.

There were e-mails from Brett's machine, e-mails from Gwen's work computer, and e-mails on Gwen's home machine. From what was written, it looked like Gwen and Brett were having a hot-and-heavy affair, and that Gwen had wanted it to become a relationship. Brett wasn't hip on the idea, but Gwen threatened to expose their relationship to Allie. Randi had told her that Brett had never actually had sex with Gwen, but these e-mails seemed to indicate differently.

Ski knew Brett had a history of violent behavior—her discussion with Randi earlier today confirmed that. Ski wouldn't put it past Brett to get rid of such a threat to her now-happy home life. But she didn't think Brett would be quite so obvious, unless it was a crime of passion, unless Gwen taunted and threatened her enough.

Especially after Randi's earlier revelations, Ski felt guilty about not giving her a complete copy of all relevant files from Gwen's computers. She was surprised Randi hadn't asked for the same things from Brett's computers.

Ski wondered how Brett had so many women, when she herself couldn't find just one good one.

She remembered her few close encounters of the Brett kind and had to admit the woman did have a certain charisma and charm about her. She could pull off any situation. She always knew what to do. And she was sure of herself, but not arrogantly sure, not until the right moment.

Then she thought about the earnestness in Randi's eyes when they were talking about the case, about how soft her hand was and how she had some little calluses at the bases of her fingers, as if she worked out. From what Ski could tell of her figure underneath the clothes, she probably did.

When Randi smiled, it was as if she didn't want to. The corner of her lip would twitch upward slightly, and she'd either restrain herself or allow it to become a smile. Ski wanted to make her go right for the smile.

She also wanted to think about how Randi's hands would feel on her body, and how their naked bodies would feel together. But not yet. The trust factor was on shaky ground.

Chapter Twenty-three

Allie knew following someone could be difficult and dangerous. But Brett had warned everyone about the dangers when she laid out the plan—even warning them that it wasn't as easy as the movies made it seem. She had also stressed that whomever they were following had already killed once, and would probably do so again if necessary, especially if cornered.

Allie knew Brett was innocent of murder. Brett had admitted to flirting online and doing the cybersex thing but said she had gone to Lansing just to help Gwen, and Allie believed her. She wasn't happy that Brett had lied and done the nasty online, but she witnessed how Brett could go out on a limb to help others. She wasn't a killer. Not these days.

What really surprised her was that Brett had so many people following her orders so blindly. A regular little fan club. At least she was Brett's lover, so she had a real reason to be here, but why did the others follow her lover, risking themselves while doing so?

She brought her wandering attention back to the matter at hand when she saw Heather get into her Lexus and start the engine. She looked to Leisa's car, and it appeared she had also noticed. Leisa pulled out of her space a little too quickly after Heather, so Allie waited until Heather was out of sight to follow.

As she followed Leisa and Heather, Allie was aware that Heather might have spotted Leisa, because she started darting in and out of traffic. She picked up her cell phone and called Leisa. "Stay on the line. I think she's spotted you. I'm gonna try to pick her up, so let me know where she's going." They should have had radios, but this might work. You always needed at least two tails, and these were not ideal circumstances, but she hoped it would work even though the others were amateurs. Allie quickly cut around a few corners, listening to Leisa's blow-by-blows on Heather's location.

Leisa would be better in this situation because she knew her way around the streets, but they were spread too thin as it was. Allie had to pray she knew them well enough to find Heather once she lost Leisa.

She sped down the streets, in constant communication with Leisa in order to get one step in front of Heather. Thankfully, Lansing wasn't a big town, but it did have access to several different freeways, so if they lost sight of Heather, she could disappear very quickly. Allie didn't want that to happen.

Shortly after Leisa lost Heather, Allie picked her up again. "Okay, now we do it in reverse. I'll tell you where we are, and you follow along on parallel roads. You *cannot* let her see you, or else she'll run again."

Allie followed Heather onto I-495, taking it down toward East Lansing. Allie had to make a quick judgment call—she didn't think Leisa would be able to follow on the freeway without being seen, so she had her follow on surface streets, telling her to take Michigan down to East Lansing. She could always have Leisa hop onto the freeway later.

She didn't need to. Heather went to a diner just outside the

Michigan State campus, which Leisa knew, so Leisa parked a few streets over and joined Allie in her car.

"She's in there, and it looks like she's meeting with a man and a woman." Allie peered through her binoculars toward the restaurant, then handed them to Leisa. Then she piled her long, blonde hair up on top of her head, and liberally applied makeup.

"What are you doing?"

"I'm going in there. I need to get pictures of those two, and eavesdrop."

"Hold on, Allie. She probably knows you, or has seen a picture of you. They don't know me. Wouldn't it be safer if I went in?"

"No. I don't want to risk it, risk you. I've done this sort of thing before, and I can handle myself." She checked the Beretta strapped to her ankle and the one stashed in her purse. Then she donned a brown wig, and Leisa realized that she had done her eyebrows to match her new hair color as well. "Besides, they won't recognize me."

Leisa was impressed. That wasn't one of the wigs she bought, this was a good one. Even she wouldn't have recognized Allie.

"While I'm inside, call Maddy and let her know where we're at and get an update."

"Will do."

Allie walked into the diner and took a seat at the counter with her back toward Heather's group, but a few feet away. She could watch them in the mirror, but unfortunately the diner was too busy for her to overhear much, which was probably the reason they picked that particular place.

Allie ordered an omelet and coffee and pulled a paperback out of her purse. She kept trying to listen in on their conversation even as she picked at her food. She didn't want to wait very long, so she palmed her digital camera, knowing there was a good chance she'd be made while doing this, but she needed to risk it. She went to the bathroom, quickly and surreptitiously snapping as many pics as she could while she walked past.

When she came out of the john, she snapped some more. She

paid her bill and left, getting out of there before they did, so as not to arouse any suspicions.

When she returned to her car, Leisa was in the driver's seat, Victoria in the passenger's, and Brett alone in the back. Allie got into the back and smiled at her girlfriend.

"I can't believe you just did that," Brett said, leaning over and giving her a light kiss.

Allie quirked an eyebrow at her. "Are you saying you're not upset in the least?"

"Yes, I am. You know I don't like you putting yourself in danger like that, but I know what you'll say to that as well as just about every single word of the rest of the argument."

"Brett, I—"

"And I'm also glad you're doing all this for me, especially with the circumstances. So thank you for sticking by me." Brett took Allie's hands in hers for a moment, then leaned down to kiss them softly and gently. "It means a lot to me."

Leisa could see Victoria's discomfort. She kept her eyes on the restaurant, except when she tried to nonchalantly look into the rearview mirror so she could see what was happening in the backseat. She frowned whenever she did that.

"So, Allie, did you find anything?" Leisa asked.

"There were a lot of people in there," Allie said, "so I couldn't really hear too much, but I did catch that her companions' names were Diane and Douglas. And Heather really didn't seem too happy."

"Is that all?" Victoria asked.

"I called Maddy when you left, like you said," Leisa explained. "Brett and Victoria got right out here."

"Frankie and Kurt are on their way," Brett said. "It just takes a bit longer to get here from Detroit."

"I'm sure you really followed the traffic laws to get here so quickly yourself," Allie said. Brett wanted to be involved with tailing Heather, but Allie had argued it would be too risky. She reached into her purse. “Anyway, Brett, baby, I’m finally glad you insisted on such an expensive digital camera. If we had gone with the one I wanted, I never would’ve been able to hide it in my hand so well.”

“You got pictures?” Leisa said, reaching for the camera.

“Why didn’t you say so earlier?” Victoria asked.

“Everybody was too busy cutting me off.” She leaned toward Leisa. “Did I get anything? I had to do it blind.”

“Let me copy this,” Leisa said, pulling a mini hard drive out of her purse. “I don’t want to risk losing anything.”

Brett trained the binoculars on their suspects to ensure they kept all three in sight.

“Do you know these people?” Leisa asked, passing the camera back so Brett could skim through the pictures. Allie reached into Brett’s right pocket to pull out her lighter. They couldn’t risk drawing undue attention to themselves by turning on an overhead light, but the small flame of Brett’s ever-present Zippo worked.

“Thanks,” Brett said to Allie, then to Leisa, “No. Never seen ’em before in my life.”

“We should get these pictures to Randi,” Allie said. “I’m glad they turned out. If we’re lucky, those other two might have criminal records.”

Frankie knocked on Brett’s window. She immediately lowered it.

“What’s goin’ on?” he asked. Kurt stood behind him, a hand on his shoulder, listening.

Brett handed him the camera. “Do you know any of these people?”

“Just Heather,” he said, glancing through the pics. “We got here soon as we could.”

“I couldn’t believe I was driving so fast,” Kurt said. “But Frankie told me to follow him, so I did.”

“Here’s the sitch,” Brett said. “Leisa and Allie will follow Douglas. Kurt and Frankie, you two take the girl, Diane. Victoria and I will take Heather. Maddy is call central. Keep the calls short. Use pay phones if you can.”

"Heads up, team," Leisa said, jumping out of the car. "We have movement. Allie, I'm going to my car, call me." She took off running.

Everyone looked at the diner and took off for their vehicles, leaving Allie unable to argue their teaming. She could see the sensibility of it—each team had one experienced person on it—but still, she didn't like Brett pairing up with Victoria.

Frankie hopped into his car and beat it over to the restaurant before he picked up his radio and contacted Kurt. As soon as he got Maddy's phone call, he called Kurt, grabbed the radios he and Brett used back before cell phones, and headed out. He gave Kurt the other one when they met at a fast-food joint just before getting on the freeway. It was then that he told Kurt to keep up with him.

Even though Frankie Lorenzini was a big man, he could run fast when he needed to. He reached his car before Kurt, and so when he picked up the radio he told Kurt he had their woman, and Kurt should just try to get to him. He wanted Kurt in the lead as tail, because he knew he was better at picking it up again, if need be.

Frankie was certain Heather was suspicious that she and the others might be being followed because Diane's driving was whacked. Over their radios, Frankie gave Kurt a basic lesson in tailing a mark as they continued toward Lansing.

Frankie grinned when he heard Kurt's words—"I don't think she's actually noticed me yet. Y'know, this is kinda exciting. I think I'm beginning to understand you even more." Kurt was doing good, real good.

In fact, Diane led them all the way to her house without making them.

He parked down the street, and relied on Kurt to get him the address of the house, as well as the license plate number of the car, which he called in to Maddy, so she could find out who Diane really was.

He carefully climbed out of his car and walked casually over to Kurt's. "I'm gonna go check this joint out," he said. "I'm turning my radio on low." He indicated to Kurt that he had it in his pocket. "Just click a few times if you see anythin' I should know about."

"Got it."

Frankie went down a few houses, to one with its lights out, and carefully stole through backyards until he reached Diane's. He looked in through a few windows till he found her—she was at the computer in her living room. It looked like she was checking her e-mail and writing replies. Then she checked her messages.

She picked up the phone, and by the way she impatiently tapped her fingernails, he figured she got an answering machine. She spoke for just a few moments, then hung up. Then she shut off all the lights and turned on the TV, sitting on the couch with her drink.

Frankie quickly cased the house, moving from window to window to assess the situation. He saw some blinking red lights by the phone in the kitchen that indicated she had some sort of security system.

After checking the vicinity, he quickly made his way across the street back to Kurt.

"Call Maddy, see what she's got, if anything, yet. Let her know Diane's alone, has some sorta security system, and is watchin' TV right now. Oh, but she did check her e-mail and messages when she got home, and responded to both. I don't think I can get into the house, but I'll risk it if I really need to. Find out what we should do. Give me three long clicks and two short if you hear anythin'."

"Frankie?" Kurt said, grabbing his hand before he could get away again.

"Yeah?" Frankie said.

Kurt wrapped an arm around his lover's neck and brought him down for a kiss. "I love you, be careful, you big brute."

Frankie smiled. "I'm always careful. But more so now that I've got you." He kneeled outside Kurt's window and took Kurt's hand in his own. "Kurt, y'know I love you. I hate bringin' you into this crap, but . . ."

Kurt ran his hands through Frankie's thick hair. "Oh, shut up you lout. I'm glad I'm here. I know Brett didn't kill anyone. So we have to help her." He kissed the top of Frankie's head. "I just know how hot-headed you can be, and I don't want you doing anything idiotic, okay?" He pulled Frankie up by his hair, so they looked into each other's eyes.

Frankie loved it when Kurt got butch.

Douglas was all but flying down the streets, apparently trying to lose any possible tails through sheer speed. Fortunately, Leisa was able to keep up. He led them to Potter Park in downtown Lansing.

Leisa and Allie parked next to each other about a block from the park.

"Go find a pay phone, and give Maddy the tag number of the car," Allie told Leisa. "You did get it, right?"

Leisa pulled out a notepad. "I think I'm starting to get this routine now." She had some information already jotted down—the make, model, color, and license plate number of Douglas's car.

"Good, you do that, and I'm going to see what I can come up with in the park. I won't be near my car, so be ready to follow if he leaves quickly." She jogged toward the park, stopping briefly at Douglas's car. She looked around and pulled out her keyring flashlight so she could read the vehicle identification number, which she wrote into her own notebook.

She carefully made her way through the woods, sans flashlight, trying to locate Douglas. She didn't want to walk boldly through the lit and open areas of the park, which would be a lot quicker, because then she could be noticed too easily.

Once she found Douglas, he was already meeting with two men Allie didn't recognize. She knew she couldn't get any nearer to them without showing herself and silently wished she had some of that top-secret gear all so prevalent in spy movies. She pulled her digital camera from her pocket and tried for the best pictures she could.

There was almost no light in this area of the park, but fortunately, unlike the restaurant, she could aim, focus, zoom in, and shoot.

Allie worked her way around through the trees, trying not to be seen or heard. The three men seemed to be uptight, as if they were watching for her. Allie figured that was just her own paranoia, but she trusted her instincts.

The men seemed to be threatening Douglas, and even though they were all yelling, Allie couldn't make out anything but random phrases that meant nothing to her.

She wanted tails on these other two men, and thought maybe one or two of the others could be diverted to follow them.

The trees in this area extended a bit nearer to where the men were, so Allie risked moving forward, using one tree, then the next and next, as cover. There were several feet between her and the next tree. If she could just give Leisa something to go with on these guys, she'd call her.

She rushed forward to the next position, but stepped on a branch—hard—while doing so. The men all looked in her direction and she stopped before rushing forward again. She hoped to God they hadn't seen her, but still put her hand around her gun before finally peering to see what was happening.

They were staring right at her location. She ducked back, trying to calm her breathing.

"What was that?" Douglas said. She recognized his voice from the restaurant.

"Probably some animal." Another man's voice.

"Maybe we should check it out." Yet another man's voice. And an awful sound that Allie recognized as a gun being cocked. She pushed her back up against the tree even tighter, trembling and trying to control her breath. She hoped they'd keep making noises so she'd know when they were close, when she had to do something.

She didn't want to think about what that something would be.

"Calm down." It was the second man. "We're all worried because that twit Heather thought somebody was following her. The last thing we need is to attract the attention of the police by hunting squirrels and raccoons in the middle of the night. We're done here, *for now*, and so we can just go."

"Fine."

"Okay."

Allie felt each beat of her heart as she slowly counted down from sixty. She only heard them walking during that time. She wrapped her hand around her gun, ready to use it, and cautiously peered out toward where they had been.

She was sweating, despite the cool chill of the night. No one was there. She stepped a few feet beyond the tree line to carefully peer around for any of the men. She kept stepping out until she saw two of them and the direction they were taking.

She dodged ahead to the opposite tree line and pulled out her phone. "There's three of them, try to follow at least one, get as many plates as you can," she said, hanging up before Leisa responded.

Allie darted through the trees to the other side of the park. She was running across roots and branches and other debris, trying to catch up. She yelped as she walloped her arm against yet another tree. Brett is gonna pay for this, she cursed silently. Her arm wasn't just gonna bruise, it was gonna swell.

She tried to focus on the mission and keep sight of the guy. She didn't know what she was going to do once the guy got into his car. She had no chance of trailing him on foot, and there weren't a lot of taxicabs cruising around Lansing, especially not in this neighborhood at this hour.

But she did get the plate number, make, and model.

Chapter Twenty-four

Randi was with Ski at work. She didn't want to leave her, and her cell phone rang moments before they would have parted ways. Allie had so quickly and concisely explained the multi-tail operation they had going that Randi couldn't risk the hour-and-a-half drive between Lansing and her own office.

It appeared something was going somewhere with this case, and Randi knew the importance of quick information in such a situation. So she went with Ski back to Ski's office, hoping she could hide what she was really doing.

What was she doing? Totally and completely helping a wanted fugitive, even through degrees of separation.

Randi and Ski sat at Ski's desk, going over details of the case. When Randi's cell phone kept ringing, she told Ski she was working a few cases back in Detroit and was merely following through on them.

Meanwhile, every time Ski left her desk for the bathroom or coffee or whatever, Randi pulled up info on her computer—getting as much information as she could on the people, plates, vehicle identification numbers and whatever else Brett's gang came up with. This information could really help if they lost their suspects, because home and work addresses could help them pick them up again. Of course, a rap sheet and more detailed information wouldn't hurt either.

"That really is Diane Jackson's home address. And that car and vehicle identification number belongs to her," she whispered to Kurt using another detective's phone. "She has a clean record for the most part. Just three unpaid parking tickets in East Lansing. She had a few speeding tickets, but those are all paid." She quickly hung up when she heard somebody near her. "I was looking for a binder clip," she told Ski, when discovered at somebody else's desk.

Later, it was Leisa who called her to ask for info on the car Allie had lost. Leisa herself had lost Douglas because he drove erratically.

Allie had seen Robert Stephanski leave the park. He was a badass with quite the rap sheet. Randi was able to quickly give Leisa his addresses and numbers, as well as the highlights of his criminal career, including that he was on parole from Jackson State Penitentiary for the past year. Apparently he had been clean since he got out and was working as a janitor at Alternities, a computer company that rivaled CompuVisions—but Leisa and Randi quickly figured that the income from that job wouldn't pay for the shiny new SUV he was driving.

This time Ski caught Randi in her conversation, but she was just sitting at the desk, Stephanski's profile already wiped from the screen, and Randi was able to finish her conversation with Leisa with, "That's about what I'm thinking." Then she closed with, "I'll get back to you about that last point," and hung up. She had written down another name and plate number Leisa had also given her. She figured she'd look it up as soon as she could, then call Maddy with the info. Leisa had told her Maddy was at home acting as call central.

Ski noticed she was fidgety, and when questioned, she told her she had a headache. When Ski went to get aspirin, Randi quickly looked up Douglas Beauregard. He wasn't as dirty as Stephanski, nor as clean as Jackson. He had some outstanding parking tickets in both Lansing and East Lansing, some speeding violations and a few DUIs. His license was suspended. She did find that his girlfriend—Diane Jackson—called in about alleged abuse, but never pressed charges. The only time he really served time beyond overnight stays was when he went to juvy, but that was only for two months when he was fifteen.

She quickly called Maddy with the info, including his addresses, not realizing Ski was listening in. "I'll let you know if I find out anything more, Maddy," Randi said.

Ski put a hand on her shoulder and whispered into her ear, "Busted."

Randi hung up the phone. She didn't turn to face Ski. "I was talking with Maddy. She called to ask me some things, and if you haven't noticed, we are friends. I tend to help friends."

"Even when those friends are wanted criminals?"

"Maddy's not wanted. And why were you eavesdropping and sneaking around anyway?" She turned to face Ski.

"You weren't very discreet you know," Ski said, perching on the desk near Randi. "Every time I left the room and came back, you were at somebody's desk, on the phone. And you hung up suddenly as soon as you knew I was there."

"I've only spoken with Maddy and Leisa tonight, honest."

"What did they want?"

"They gave me license plate numbers, makes, models, that sort of thing. I gave them the lowdown on the owners. They had first names on all but one of them."

"You know I could charge you for being an accessory after the fact. Tell me who they asked about."

"Sure. I'll bring up the records."

Ski smirked at her, then sat next to her as they started looking through the records.

⁂

When Maddy called Leisa with Douglas's address, Leisa had just been driving around, trying to find him again. It was pointless, but she had to try something. She didn't like to think she'd failed Brett and Allie.

She kept maps in her car, so she was able to find the address fairly quickly. It was in a bad part of town, and she was sure it was his place because his car was in the driveway. Enough lights were on in his shabby little house to indicate he was still awake. Unless he was just afraid of the dark.

She turned off the car and coasted as close to his place as she could before she parked and snuck over, glad she had dressed in dark clothing. She tried to look as if she were casually taking a midnight stroll until she reached his house. Then she went into sneaky mode around to the back of the house.

Leisa found herself in this situation because she liked and owed Brett and Allie. But there was also a thrill to all of this—it was excitingly dangerous getting to run around and follow people and peer through windows in the middle of the night. Who'd ever guess that a mere high school teacher could do such a thing? She carefully made her way from one window to the next, peering in, looking for Douglas. It was just . . . She was a humdrum teacher, living a nice, quiet life, and doing this, helping Brett, made her feel like she was the female James Bond. It was exhilarating, and she was loving it.

Douglas was in one of the front rooms, which looked to be some sort of den or office. But she wanted to remain hidden and knew the front shrubs wouldn't adequately cover her full figure.

But now, she crouched in the bushes and watched Douglas chat animatedly with somebody online. He had a drink next to him. Leisa guessed it was some sort of alcoholic beverage. She couldn't tell who he was IMing, but she could tell that he was. She tried to get comfortable in the shrubs because she realized she'd probably be there for a while.

⁂

Allie went to the address Maddy gave her for Robert Stephanski. There wasn't a car in the drive nor any sign of him. She wondered if she should try to break in, but unlike Brett, she didn't carry picks with her everywhere she went, and she wasn't as proficient with them as Brett—after all, it was generally frowned upon for cops, even former ones, to break into places.

She sighed and figured she ought to call in to let Maddy know he wasn't home. He should come back at some time, so she decided to stake out the house.

Randi stayed with Ski far into the night while she told Ski everything she knew. They researched all the people whose plate numbers Randi had been asked about, but only after Randi successfully pleaded with Ski to not immediately send patrol cars to all the addresses.

Besides, what could cops do in those situations? They could only perhaps ask Brett's team to move along. The only one they could do anything about was Brett. They couldn't do anything at all about the suspects, because there was no proof any of them had done anything.

And maybe . . . just maybe . . . Brett was leading them in the right direction. One that they should look into as well.

Ski yawned. Loudly. She couldn't help it. "I'm sorry, I've got to get some sleep." She put her head down on her crossed arms in front of her computer terminal.

Randi laid a tender hand on her back. "Yeah, we should get some rest. That would be good."

"I've got to go home."

"I should probably get home as well."

"What? You're exhausted. You can't drive all that way!"

Randi shrugged. "Okay, so I'll catch a motel somewhere along the way."

Ski looked at the bullheaded butch and decided she wouldn't let her stay in a motel. "No. You'll come home with me. You can sleep on the futon."

❧

Leisa sat in her car, now parked directly across from Douglas's house. With her binoculars, she watched him IM for quite a while before finally realizing he was just gonna drink himself to sleep while cybering with God knows whom. She called Maddy, assuring her that she was all right, then letting her know where she was and what was going on.

She was so focused on the recently darkened house that she shrieked and hit her head on the ceiling of the car when Frankie knocked at the window. Once she calmed down, she turned the key in the ignition and lowered the window.

"Yo. What's up?"

Leisa shook her head. "Not much. He finally passed out about ten minutes ago, and now here I sit, and wait."

"Nope, no more," Frankie said. "Brett wants you home and doing the computer thing to see what you can find out about all these bad guys we got running all over town now. I'm here to relieve ya."

"Oh. So I should go home."

"Ya done great, kid. I'm just here for the long, boring sleep part of this gig. You can do a lot more on that computer of yours. More'n any of the rest of us could."

Leisa was a lot happier after his pep talk—when she drove off, she didn't feel so much like she had been pulled out of the game for non-performance and felt more like she was being reassigned for other, equally important, matters. It seemed strategic.

Amazing that a guy like Frankie could do that. And with so few words.

Frankie went to his vehicle and watched Leisa drive off. Then he got out and did his own inspection of the house. All was quiet, just like Leisa had said. She'd done a good job.

Once he settled in, he picked up his cell phone. "Yo, bud, I need some stuff done. Buncha places, tonight. Get your crew together and come up to Lansing."

Brett went to CompuVisions, planning on breaking in to get better access to Gwen's and Heather's computer systems. But as she walked up to the front doors, the one security guard she expected to see there wasn't. Instead there were four. One turned directly toward her as she walked up and ran after her when she took off.

She ran for a good half-mile before stopping to breathe. She couldn't believe she lost her edge. That was not like her. She carefully made her way back to her car, then drove to a pay phone and called Maddy. She kept a hand on the .357 in her pocket, because no place in Lansing was truly safe after dark. And cops might find her. Although having a shootout with them was not her plan.

"Yo, Leisa, what's up? Find anything for me yet?"

If Leisa had felt like she'd been pulled out of the game, she definitely didn't feel like that anymore. Which would have made Brett happy had she known.

"Okay, so I've done some things tonight that aren't exactly legal," Leisa started.

"Oh, dear God, that's terrible. Someone in our group doing somethin' illegal?"

"I'm sorry."

Brett chuckled. "I was being facetious. I just hope you covered your tracks."

"Oh, yeah. Of course. Anyway, turns out that the head of security at Alternities, where Robert Stephanski works, is also an ex-felon. He was in Jackson when Robert was there. Plus, there's another employee there with Stephanski's same title."

"Two people with the exact same title?"

"Yeah, looks like both of them got the same jobs, over the same people. And they are management positions, so I'm guessing at least one is a made-up thing."

"Well, keep it up. Have Maddy call everyone and tell them to try to get some shuteye while they can. Let me know if you find anything. My phone is on buzz so no one can call at a bad time."

Brett sat back in her borrowed vehicle, thinking about what she would do next. Everyone was accounted for, and everyone was busy. Except her. She had some burglary skills, but she really didn't like cat burglary. People could be light sleepers, and violence might ensue, and she really didn't want to place herself in that position.

She needed to get on their computers, and computers had this annoying habit of beeping and making other sounds when turned on—all of which might wake the respective homeowners. She didn't know if she knew how to turn off speakers to get around such noises, and if she just stole the computers, their owners would know something was up.

Computers were the common denominator in this thing. Whatever *it* was. She had to do something, though. She drove to Robert's. She needed to see Allie.

Allie was reading a textbook by the light of her keychain penlight. She looked up as Brett approached the car. Brett grinned at this—that was her girl, always paying attention and always prepared.

"Hey, babe, what's up?" Allie said, lowering her window.

"I'm just checking up on everyone. Glad to see you're making use of the time here," she said, indicating the book Allie was reading.

"Well, yeah. And I figured the book would put me to sleep." She held up her wrist, indicating her watch. "But I've got my alarm set."

"I needed to see you. Tonight, that is. I needed to see you. And all."

"Is everybody following orders? Getting in the snooze while they can?"

"I just called Leisa, and she's trying to find connections with these folks. And you're my first stop."

Allie put her hand on Brett's, which rested on the windowsill. She caressed it lightly. "So you're just checking up?"

"Yeah. I need a clear visual of what we're dealing with."

"I hope you're planning on getting some sleep yourself. You get cranky and disoriented if you don't." She intertwined her fingers with Brett's. "I'll be watching you tomorrow, so I'll know. You don't eat when you're too tired."

Brett grinned and leaned over, touching her lips to Allie's, enjoying the softness, and the light moan that escaped from Allie's throat. She touched Allie's beautiful face, tracing it in the dim light, feeling her features like a blind person. "I'm sorry. I kept you out because I didn't want you implicated—"

Allie stopped her by catching her lips again. When they parted, Allie said, "I understand."

"I do love you, Allie."

"I know. Now go case the house, I know you want to."

Brett raised an eyebrow.

"I know you came here first, seeing what I'd let you do. These folks are bad, and they are cold-blooded killers. In my book, that means you can check them out—just not kill them."

"How do you know me so well?"

"I just do. You came here first, and you've got to know that Frankie and I are your most reliable and tested people."

"Thanks, babe."

"I wouldn't break in there myself. Looks like there's too much security, and I'm not as good as you."

"You thought about it?"

"Hell yes! They're fucking with my girl! I'm pissed as hell! But he's got some wicked security system there. See if you can do anything with it."

Brett put her hand over Allie's heart. "I love you." She leaned down to kiss her woman again, then lowered her hand to feel between her legs.

Allie swatted her hand. "Don't get me all worked up. Go, be your bad self and do your thing."

Brett started to walk away, then turned back to her. "Do you really think that?"

"What?"

"That I'm bad?"

Allie stepped from the car. Brett knew she hadn't done so before because they'd be more obvious if anybody looked out their windows. Allie pulled Brett into her arms. "Not bad the way you're thinking. I love you. And I know you're a good woman. You've done some things in the past that I don't like, but you're better now. And I'm pissed as hell about how you got yourself into this, but I know you didn't kill anyone." She pushed Brett away, but still held her at arm's length. "We'll have the argument about how you got into it after we've caught these sons-of-bitches."

Allie released her, and Brett went to check out the house. She saw flickering lights inside and quickly realized the security system was probably one she wasn't prepared to deal with. She hadn't seen it in operation nor seen this place in daylight.

She wasn't prepared for these odds. Especially not with Allie watching. She didn't want her to see a massive failure. It gave her stage fright. Funny that having her girl see her fail could be worse than being hauled off to jail in cuffs.

She stood in the backyard, holding her head in her hands. She loved Allie, she loved Victoria, she loved Storm. She didn't have enough people to cover everything. This growing miasma she was trying to keep track of had too many arms for her to cover. It was hopeless—beyond the hopelessness of her mixed metaphors.

But all these people were out in the middle of the night because of her, and she had to lead them, and she had to lead them with confidence. She had to at least appear to know what she was doing. She was surprised Allie was helping her at all. She had been . . . bad.

She walked back to Allie. "You're right. The security's too tight. And I'm thinking it's like that all over. And I'm a bit tired."

"You should go somewhere and get some sleep."

"No, you should. I'll keep watch here."

"You need sleep, too."

"I know. I also know that regardless, I won't get enough sleep, and I'll be cranky tomorrow. I don't want to take it out on you. So if you go someplace else to get your sleep, I can't take it out on you. Especially not if I force you there."

"So you want me to get a room?"

Brett shrugged. "That, or just find someplace to sleep. I'll call you. Just make sure your phone's turned on."

"We can be here together."

"If I get caught, I need someone who knows I'm innocent to track down the real killers."

Allie stared into Brett's eyes and realized that Brett was telling the truth. On all counts, in all ways. "Okay. Fine." Even though she understood, it still felt at that moment as if a wall went up between them.

After Allie left, Brett sat in her car, watching the house. She was too wound up to sleep. Too overtired. Too drained. Too emotional. Too much of everything all at once.

She checked her watch alarm and leaned her seat back. She needed to get some sleep, or else she wouldn't be any good tomorrow. Just a couple of hours. She relaxed her body, taking deep breaths. She tried to remember happy thoughts, things that would calm her. And she kept flashing through thoughts that maybe were dreams, maybe were reality, but she thought she was still awake.

She was wrong.

She was making love to a woman, but she couldn't see her face. She was fucking the woman with a strap-on, their sweaty bodies pressed together, sliding together, flesh-on-flesh. Their lips were locked on each other's, their tongues in each other's mouths.

Brett couldn't believe she herself was naked, but it all felt so wonderful. She loved the feeling of a woman's naked legs entwining around her, pressing them together, possessing her and owning her. Staking her claim.

"Oh, baby, fuck me, hard . . . harder . . ." the woman said. Brett still didn't know who it was, but that didn't stop her.

It only compelled her.

Brett yanked the woman's legs from about her, pushing her thighs upward, granting her full access while she pounded into the woman, again, and again, and yet again, the woman's cries of pleasure filling her ears, compelling her to go on and on.

She braced the beautiful thighs against her shoulders and body, keeping her wide open, and she dropped her fingers down to flick her swollen clit, playing with her, enjoying her wetness and liking that she was giving her such pleasure. It was a feast.

Brett tried to see her face, but couldn't quite make it out in the darkness.

Just then an ambulance raced by outside, bringing a bit of illumination to the scene, as well as an annoying buzzing.

The face beneath her seemed to change—from Gwen to Allie to Victoria . . . she couldn't tell who she was fucking . . . who was crying out in pleasure as she came . . .

She needed to know, dammit!

But that ambulance seemed to be circling them, getting closer and closer.

Brett started awake, finally turning off her watch alarm. The dream was already racing away from her, even as she tried to reclaim the joy she had felt in it, and the face of the woman she had been with.

Dammit. She'd be bugged by that damned dream all day. She hated when that happened.

Chapter Twenty-five

Once Diane got home, she e-mailed her fellows to let them know she had been followed. Heather had mentioned she'd lost a tail going to the restaurant, but if somebody was following Diane, then Heather hadn't been as successful at losing her tail as she'd thought.

They all figured Diane was the stupidest one of the bunch. They had no idea. She knew, once she spotted her tail, that they had probably already made her. They'd seen her tags, and probably could ID her from them. She knew she should have faked license plates.

But that was all blood under the bridge. Nothing she could do about it now, except warn her partners that someone was onto them.

She didn't spend much time on the phone, 'cause she didn't want to give whoever was watching her too many clues. They'd have to work to find out whatever they could.

The neighbors had asked Diane to watch their place. So she pocketed their keys, and wandered around her place, waiting until the man watching at her window went away. He didn't, so she pretended to send e-mails and played around online. She couldn't pace, she had to remain calm. She had to be boring.

She waited a while before getting up to get a beer. Whoever was watching her was tenacious. She glanced around at the windows, discovering there were two people lurking outside. That kinda made her feel like hot shit. The others didn't take her seriously, but these people did.

She was at her computer, and finally looked over her shoulder to see some light at the SUV parked across the street from her house. She saw two figures beside it and made her move. She turned out all her lights and snuck out her back door. She quickly moved across the yards to her neighbor's where she pulled up the garage door. She grabbed the car keys from where Jay and April always kept them. They'd taken Jay's Explorer, leaving April's second-hand Sundance. She kept checking for a tail, which would be quite obvious in the empty streets. She saw none.

She drove down highways fast, through alleyways slow, and she knew that if anyone was following her, she'd have seen him by now. She was clean.

She headed back to Lansing, and started cruising by all the houses she knew. Sometimes, people watching were apparent—they were sitting up, awake in their cars. Other times, they were asleep.

Finally, Diane drove by Doug's place, and found the all-too-familiar signs. She saw that his lights were out, so she drove around the block. She parked on a street at the rear of Doug's block and cut through backyards to his place.

She still had Doug's housekey on her ring, and she used that to soundlessly enter through the back door. She crept up to his bedroom. She put a hand against his mouth, to keep him silent. He was still a sound sleeper. She pinched him, and he jerked awake.

She kept him quiet and away from the gun he was trying to grab, while saying, "Shhhh . . . it's Diane. Your house is being watched." She waited till his eyes showed recognition before releasing him, though if he really struggled, she couldn't fight him. She knew that. It was one reason they weren't together any longer.

"Goddammit," he whispered urgently. "That fucking know-it-all bitch led them right to us!"

"Yes. She did. But she's also leading us to a fucking lot of money. So we have to figure out what to do right now." Diane had learned a lot with Dougie, and it was more than to watch her back, which she had also learned from her TV shows. Right now, she knew they needed to figure out how to get out of this, not point fingers. He was too passionate and angry, she had to be the one with a level head. She quickly filled him in on what she had learned in her late-night travels.

"Damn good thing there's a reason we're putting up with her shit," Doug said, sneaking over to the window and peering out between the curtains. "She told us this would all go like clockwork, it'd be a piece of cake. Well, Higgins pulling in enough folks to cover all of us wasn't in the game plan." He spotted the SUV and backed away. "I wonder if they saw my meeting in the park."

Diane shook her head. "I didn't know about it, so I couldn't check it out. Maybe you should call whoever you met with to tell them to watch out."

He shook his head as he paced. "I don't want to do that right away. I've got to decide if I want them to know about this—they might back down or somethin'."

Diane watched as he paced. She loved it when he focused. It was one of the reasons she had hooked up with him in the first place.

"How did this happen?"

"They followed Heather and found us."

"So we should probably call her." He picked up the phone and made the call.

"Hello?" Heather answered on the third ring.

"Don't turn on any lights."

"Huh? What?"

"This is Doug. Don't turn on any lights. Were you followed tonight?"

"Yeah, at the beginning. But I lost them."

Doug kept his temper down. "Did you turn on a light?"

"Yeah, I did, just before I picked up the phone."

"Okay, then go to the bathroom and then go back to bed. Turn your ringer on low."

"What's this about?"

"I'll call you back in a bit," Doug said, then hung up. He looked at Diane. "She said she was followed, but lost 'em. I'm thinking not."

"From what Heather said about this Higgins chick, it doesn't surprise me. Heather did seem to know her well. I mean, she was right on everything up till this."

"What she fucked up—majorly—was that she thought Higgins would either get rid of the body, run, or both."

Diane stood up, nodding, hoping pacing would help.

"She thought it would end at the murder," Doug said.

"She thought Higgins would take care of it for us. Especially with everything we went through to make the bulletproof frame."

"It seems our girl has changed. And she's brought friends, too." Doug turned to slam his fist against the desk, but pulled back at the last moment. Apparently he didn't want to draw any attention with loud noises. "So we just have to neutralize her and her crew." He grinned maliciously. Diane loved him when he was like this—so fiery, so sure of himself. She was also afraid of him when he was like this, but it did bring out her own animal urges. He could be bad, but she kept trying to be the wild animal tamer, able to restrain the beast. He occasionally got out of hand. But it was all so exciting, especially compared to her previous boring, humdrum existence. "We just need to show her who's in charge," Doug said, picking up the phone.

"Wait," Diane said, stopping him. "What are you doing?"

"I'm betting one of these stakeouts is Higgins' girl. I'm thinking we need to show her we mean business."

"Listen, that'd probably just really piss her off. I mean, Heather figured that making it look like Gwen was gonna tell the girlfriend about them would be motive enough for her to take Gwen out. Or at least, in the scheme."

Doug nodded. "Okay, so we might throw her into an all-out vengeance match, instead of scaring her off. Fine. But the only other way I can see is taking out Higgins and all her friends."

"But we'd have to make Higgins look like an accident or suicide. She kills all of them, then herself?"

Doug grinned at his one-time gal. "I take it you're still in the game, then."

"If these people are willing to do so much for Higgins, they must mean something to her," Diane said, pacing. "I gotta tell you, though, the guy outside here looked pretty big from what I saw."

Doug turned to her. "So they're not all women?"

"No. I think the one outside Heather's is, though. And I think mine was a guy."

"Was Heather's a blonde?"

"I couldn't get close enough to tell. Why?"

"Heather said Higgins likes blondes, so it would make sense if her girl was blonde. Was Higgins one of them?"

"No, she wasn't."

"Damn. If we knew where she was, we could just pop her and make it look like a suicide," Doug said, pulling on clothes. He had only been wearing boxers. "Although, given her reputation, I don't think anyone would be surprised that she got knocked off. How did you get here, by the way?"

Diane knew he'd want to check everything out for himself and was figuring a second eye wouldn't be a bad thing, so she quietly led him out the back and across the yards to where she had parked.

"Damn, I taught you good, huh?" he asked at the car. "Gimme the keys."

"Huh? It's my neighbors' car, I'm driving."

"Babe, I got to drive."

She went to the driver's side, unlocked it and got in. Then she unlocked his door. He tried to open her door, but she had already locked it. He glared through the window at her before climbing into the passenger's seat. She started the car. "I'm the only one who saw they were being tailed earlier. You're too hotheaded, so I have to be the driver. You can be the eyes. Where are we going?" She thought she was quite skillful at keeping him from lashing out and attacking her.

She knew he was impressed at how well she had identified their tails. She knew he had met with some guys after the meeting at the diner with Heather. He was just about itching to check their places as well, but didn't want her to know who they were.

They had gotten along well in bed, but he had been an abusive bastard. Still, it was through him that she got into all of this, which would probably provide enough cash to set her up for life on a nice tropical island somewhere.

Diane had set Doug up with Heather, and it was through his contacts they were selling Gwen's top-secret program to Alternities.

As they hid in the bushes near Heather's, Doug used binoculars to peer at the stakeout.

"I'm guessing it was Heather who led them to us all," Doug said. "She's such a fucking airhead. Unless she purposely turned us over to them."

"I don't think she did," Diane said. "I really don't."

"Okay, fine, but we still gotta decide what to do about her. And this situation."

"Well, this one isn't blonde, so she's not the one we want." Diane stared as Victoria talked on the phone then disappeared from sight as if she was lying down in her car.

"But if a woman, especially one that hot and sexy, is helping Brett—from what Heather said, she must be important to Brett, right?"

"Yeah, sure, so what?"

"We haven't seen a hot blonde woman yet, right?"

"What are you getting at?"

"I think we grab this one and maybe use her as ransom or something. Having one of Brett's buddies will help us get the upper hand. She's hot on our tail, and somethin's gonna happen."

"We just grab her, we don't kill her, right?"

"Yeah, yeah, whatever you say. Are you in?"

Diane sighed and sat back on her haunches. "What are you planning?"

"I think we wait a bit. They're not onto us, and it looks like she's catching some z's, so . . ."

"So we wait till she's really asleep. From what we've seen, everybody who's watching us is alone now."

"You got that right, babe. We wait till she's good and out, and we surprise her."

"The windows on her car look like they're up, though. And I'm guessing she locked it before going nighty-night."

"Hey, babe, remember who you're with here?"

"I don't think she's gonna give you time to jimmy her locks."

"I wasn't planning on that. It's quicker to go through the window."

"We need something big and heavy, though."

He reached over and ran his hand over her cheek. "You've learned some things. Good. Let's go to the car, see if we can find something good. If not, we'll play it by ear."

They got lucky. Diane's neighbors kept a toolbox in their trunk. One that had a hammer in it. They waited for an hour before making their move. She had to be asleep by then.

Doug bashed in the driver's window, then tossed the hammer over to Diane while he reached in to grab a startled Victoria. Diane bashed in the passenger's window and unlocked the door, reaching across to grab her.

With Doug's help, she forced a struggling Victoria's hands behind her back and secured them with a pair of cuffs Doug had brought along. She tied Doug's sock across her mouth to silence her.

Diane turned away when Doug repeatedly hit the woman across the head till she lost consciousness. They carried her limp body to their car. Diane made sure Victoria was secured, then sent Douglas back to move Victoria's car. They didn't want to be too easy to track.

Doug returned to the Sundance. "All taken care of," he said, leaning in to speak to Diane through the driver's window. "I made a few phone calls while I was gone."

"And?"

"I need to drive. We need to check out my contacts, and we might end up at one of them. You can't know who they are or where they live."

Diane stared up at him.

"Yeah, okay, I get it," he said. "You've changed and all that shit. But I'm serious here, I met these guys in the slammer, and they're not real open, okay?"

They moved Victoria's unconscious body to the back seat, and Diane sat next to her to make sure she didn't wake and cause trouble. Doug reached forward and said, "You can't know. Really. Just keep your hands on her." He tied his T-shirt around Diane's eyes. She went along with it.

She didn't really have a choice.

Doug drove by Robert's, and there was someone there. That bitch Higgins had even caught him. Steve had insisted his place was clear, and it was. Doug carried Victoria in, forcing Diane to hold onto him and follow.

He knew he couldn't totally keep Diane in the dark, but he did make sure she never saw Steve. She probably heard his voice from the other room, but before he took off her blindfold, he made sure she couldn't make an identification.

When they went back out to the car, she had her blindfold back in place.

He had a feeling she knew more than was good for her, but she was still necessary. He hated that she had been the one to notice all the tails they'd had on them.

Chapter Twenty-six

Day Seven

Brett woke at seven in the morning next to Allie. It was before she had told the others to wake. She was sure she had morning breath from hell. She found some breath strips in her pocket and used one. Didn't help. She knew it. She had an overnight pack in the back, but she didn't want to brush here. It would draw too much attention to her.

But she did call Maddy. She knew no matter who she called, she'd be waking them. She figured she'd start with Maddy, see if she had heard anything.

"Hello?" Maddy answered the phone.

"It's me. Heard anything?"

"No. All I know is that everyone has called in sick to work. We're all behind you, dear."

"Okay. Thanks." Brett hung up, then proceeded to call and wake her team. She figured the folks they were watching might be awake about now, so she had to make sure they were all up and ready. She hoped everyone could function on less than eight hours of sleep.

The only one she couldn't reach was Victoria. She was worried about that.

She went over to Heather's. Frankie had arranged for some old buddies of his, burglars by profession, to give them a hand. She hated burglary, but she felt better about it now since all their suspects would be out of their houses when they were hit.

This was much better. She was happy she thought of it.

When she got to Heather's and didn't see Victoria, she was worried—after all, she hadn't even been able to reach her on the cell phone earlier. She looked up and down the street and didn't see Victoria's car, but it looked as if Heather had already left for work, so Brett cautiously approached the house and glanced through several windows.

Heather wasn't home, but a car had driven by twice. Brett had a suspicion about the driver and didn't want to risk him going elsewhere, so while standing behind Heather's house, she called Frankie and told him to send in the burglar. She'd meet him behind the house.

Sure enough, the car came around again and parked a few doors down from Heather's.

Brett was very interested in seeing inside this house. Although she'd have liked to be in on all the searches, she couldn't have them all hold for her, so she chose this one to be a part of. She hoped Victoria had gone for coffee and a breakfast sandwich, or was tailing Heather, like she should be.

She didn't like the fact that she had really wanted to see Victoria and not just to check up on her.

She needed to nip that situation in the bud, even though it was already too late for that.

Randi was racing down the street on foot, chasing after bank robbers. She could hear the bank's alarms sounding in the distance. But they weren't quite right. And what was Ski doing next to her . . . trying to cuddle?

She suddenly sat up on the futon, throwing away the pillow she had been clutching and apparently smelling, thus leading her to imagine she was with Ski. She grabbed for her ringing cell phone. "Hello?" she said, trying not to yawn.

Her skin glowing from her shower, Ski walked past the futon room and into the kitchen. She was wearing a long white V-necked T-shirt and Red Wings boxer shorts. Randi watched her and just agreed with everything Greg Morrow said to her over the phone. When she hung up, she joined Ski in the kitchen.

"That coffee smells awfully good," Randi said.

"I'm in kinda a rush this morning," Ski said, as they moved around each other in the kitchen. "But I've got a variety of cereal and milk that's still good. And, of course, coffee."

"Coffee, black," Randi said, trying to keep her morning breath away from Ski. "I've got to get back to Detroit anyway. That was Greg. I need to get down there."

Ski laughed and led Randi back to the bathroom. "Toothpaste's in there." She reached into a hall closet and pulled out a toothbrush.

Randi took it. "Accustomed to a lot of overnight guests?"

"Cognizant of good dental hygiene. And I like sales and coupons, okay?" She smiled warmly.

"Oh, okay then. Thanks." Randi brushed her teeth vigorously and went back for coffee.

"So you have to go back to the office?" Ski said, as they brushed against each other, intentionally, while preparing a quick breakfast.

"Yeah. They need me there." Randi was quickly spooning Raisin Bran into her mouth.

Ski had found the Lucky Charms. "Do you think you'll hear from Brett and crew today?"

"I might. I will if they need anything." She jerked a thumb at Ski's cereal bowl. "Y'know, those aren't really that good for you."

"Yeah, but I like the marshmallows. And they make me feel like a kid, which is sometimes a *really* good way to start the day. You ought to try it sometime." She offered a spoonful to Randi, who accepted it with a goofy grin. "So, will you let me know what they want?"

Randi accepted a second spoonful before answering. "Yes. I will." The previous night they had compared more notes, and Randi had told Ski about the drugged blood Brett had sent her and each piece she was able to fit together. "I know you can't promise anything, but don't move too quickly on Brett."

"Randi, I can't—"

Randi pressed her lips against Ski's. "Just try, is all I ask. I gotta go."

While driving, Randi called Maddy to let her know everything she had learned.

Maddy called Kurt, then Allie, then Frankie. She updated them and checked to see how they were doing and what was happening. She needed to know if she could give Frankie's people the go-ahead to move in on a particular place.

Since everyone was now trying to single-handedly follow their subjects, they were all on the move. If anyone lost their subject, they'd try to pick them up at their place of employment and call in to Maddy.

She called Victoria's grandmother to let her know that all was well, then called Victoria. She knew Brett was already at Heather's, but she wanted to see how that was going. The phone rang four times, and Maddy was beginning to worry. She tried to reassure herself that maybe Victoria had turned the phone off because it was a bad time for it to ring, and that would be a good thing. But someone answered.

"Hello?" Maddy asked, when nothing was said. She could hear breathing on the other end. She said, "Victoria?"

"I'm sorry," a man's deep voice said, "but my cock's in her mouth right now, so she can't talk."

"Um, excuse me?"

"Oh, yeah, baby, just like that."

Had she misdialed? No, she had used speed dial. Part of her wanted to hang up. She found this deeply disturbing. She had to find out what was going on. "Yes, well, this is really quite terribly urgent. Please tell her Madeline is calling for her."

"No."

"Excuse me?"

"No. I won't tell her, and from now on, I won't talk to anybody but Brett."

"What are you saying?"

"Listen, bitch, if any of your little Scooby gang except Brett calls this number next, this little bitch'll die. And it won't be pretty. But I might send Brett her heart. Later."

"Who are you?"

"Brett better call me next. Got it?"

"I . . . I think so . . ."

"You'd better, or pretty little Victoria will go all to pieces. Literally." And he hung up.

Shaking, Maddy clicked off the line and called Brett's cell.

Brett let Frankie's friend Al lead the way into the house. He was the one who knew what to do, but she tried to pay attention for future reference.

"So we're safe now in here?" Brett asked Al.

"Yeah, we should be. So long's nobody saw us and calls the cops."

"Frankie told you what we're after?"

"Yeah."

"Okay, so you do your thing, and I'll do mine. Let me know when you're done."

"Gotcha." He started scoping the premises.

Brett wanted to ask what his objectives were, but realized she had to trust Frankie's instructions to them. She hated delegating, but maybe this basic shakedown would shake a few apples from the tree. She noticed the guy went right for the computer, so she looked around.

They both wore latex gloves to avoid leaving prints. Brett wandered around, just trying to understand, to figure out what had happened. There were framed pictures of Gwen and Heather around the place. The traces of their coupledom were obvious, now that Brett knew what she was looking for, what she was seeing, who she was seeing.

Heather had gone to great lengths to convince Gwen that she was really interested in her—and to convince everyone else as well. The scam touched every part of her life.

Her cell buzzed in her pocket. Considering how many bona fide hotties called her, she often thought about wearing it closer to her crotch, instead of in her jacket pocket. That way, she could get a thrill when one of these women called.

They were alone, so she answered. "Hello?"

"Brett, it's Maddy."

"Maddy, I'm—"

"We've got a problem. Victoria's been kidnapped, by the bad guys."

"What?" Brett felt the room tilt . . . she became dizzy and nauseous all at once. She remembered all those she'd already lost. She remembered Gwen's dead body in the bed next to her.

"Brett, Brett, get with it!" Maddy was screaming on the phone.

"NO!" Brett yelled back.

"Brett, I'm hanging up. Get to a pay phone and call me back. I am calling everyone to tell them not to call Victoria—so you don't till you talk to me!"

"Yeah . . ."

"Brett! No calls till we talk!"

"Yeah." Brett turned off her cell mechanically and yelled to the burglar, "Get what you need, I'm leaving."

"Yo, dude, what's up?"

"Get what you need. Follow orders. I am leaving. Now!"

"Gotcha." Later, Brett would realize that he had been properly trained and briefed on this mission.

Brett returned to her vehicle and drove halfway to a pay phone before she pulled over and broke down.

By the time she called Maddy, Maddy had called the rest of the team, and even the theatre and Victoria's grandmother, to let them all know not to call Victoria's cell for any reason. She quickly filled Brett in on the situation.

When Brett called Victoria's, she heard the phone answered, but no words were spoken. "I hear you been askin' for me," Brett said after a moment.

"This Higgins?"

"Yup."

"Hang up and call me back or the girl dies."

Brett followed the instructions.

"You know the limits. Follow them. Don't play with us, or the girl dies."

"Which girl?"

"Victoria Nelson. Pamela Nelson's sister. You might know Pamela better as Storm."

"Yeah, so fine, you know me. What's the deal?"

"The deal is we got yer girl, and she's gonna die unless you behave."

"Prove it to me?"

"What, that we will kill her?"

"No, that she's there and alive."

"Next call. Right now, I'm gonna tell you to get your buds off our asses. You're dealin' with shit you don't even know about, 'kay?"

"Like what?"

"Like, do you want me to tell you the plates, models, and makes of your friends' cars? Descriptions of the drivers?"

"Yeah."

"So you can trace?"

"I'm not tracing you."

"Call me back."

Brett did so. When the guy picked up, he read off a list of makes, models, plates, and driver descriptions. Asked for her number, and she gave it.

He called her back. "You get my drift."

"I still don't know she's even alive."

Victoria came on the line, "Brett, don't! They'll kill me any—" She was taken away.

"What do you want from me?" Brett asked.

"Turn yourself in," the guy said.

"That's still no assurance Victoria'll be okay."

"No, it isn't. But if you turn yourself in and call off your friends, she might be. And that's the best you can hope for, isn't it?"

Brett didn't want to admit defeat.

He continued. "At least then you'll know we won't come for the rest of your friends. I hear your girl Allie's a tasty bit."

Brett was silent, suddenly imagining all the people she loved being killed trying to save her.

"Just make sure you get on the news pretty quick," the guy said, then hung up.

Brett laid her head against the phone. Her hand was in her pocket, trailing her fingers through the change there. She pulled out a few more coins and called Maddy. Maddy could make it happen while she turned herself in. That was the only answer. So she called her.

"Hello?" Maddy sounded almost breathless.

"Maddy. Get in touch with everyone. Pull them off and out." They were made, and she couldn't risk any of her other friends for her own sake.

"Brett?"

"Yeah, it's me."

"Why?"

"We've been made. All of us. They took Victoria, and there's more than one of them. They gave me everybody's plates, makes, and models—even described the drivers. We're over and done with!"

"Oh dear lord! What are you gonna do?"

"I'm gonna track down Ski's ass and turn myself in to her. In the most public way possible, so it appears on the news as soon as possible!"

"What the devil is that going to accomplish?"

"The only way they'll let Victoria go is if I turn myself in. Confess to the murder."

"Brett. They won't let her go. She's seen them. The only chance she has is you."

"Maddy, you don't understand. Storm died because of me. I have to do all I can to save Victoria."

"The best you can do, only *you* can do."

"I can't get everyone else into it just to save her. And I can't sacrifice her."

"Brett, do you trust me?"

"What?"

"Do you trust me?"

"I don't understand!"

"It's a simple yes or no question, Brett."

"I get that, but—"

"Do you trust me, Brett," Maddy said softly.

"You know I do."

"Give me a number where I can reach you."

Brett read off the number on the pay phone.

"I'll call you back in ten minutes." Maddy hung up.

Brett used her cell phone. She called Randi.

Randi picked up on the first ring. "Hello?"

"Randi, it's Brett. I need Ski's number."

"Why?"

"I want to turn myself in."

"Are you on drugs?"

"I don't do drugs and you know that," Brett said, without thinking. She wasn't thinking, she was just doing. She was doing what had to be done.

"I do. Explain."

"I need Ski's digits 'cause I want to turn myself in. To her. Preferably with publicity."

"You don't like publicity."

"Doesn't matter. Nothing matters no more."

"Brett, what's going on? Is something up with Allie?"

"Allie's safe—for now," Brett yelled into the phone.

"Brett, someone's gotta talk to me. Can you call me back in ten minutes?"

"I can't wait that long. I'll just go to the station myself."

"Why don't you find out where a TV station is and turn yourself in there?"

"Fuck, yes! Thank you, Randi!"

"Brett!"

"Call me back in five—before!"

"No! Goddammit!"

"Call me back when you know where you're going!"

"What the fuck's up with you?"

"What you've said makes it sound as if Allie might be in danger," Randi said, trying to buy time. "Don't turn yourself in before we talk. Please?"

Brett could hear the plea in her voice. She knew Randi cared deeply for Allie. "Fine," Brett said.

Chapter Twenty-seven

Randi hit the line the desk cop had told her was waiting for her. "Maddy?"

"We don't have time, so listen and then question. Victoria's been kidnapped by whoever killed Gwen Cartwright. Brett feels responsible for Victoria's sister Pamela, Storm, being killed. And she's worried they'll kill Victoria—and Allie. And everyone else helping her. She's going to turn herself in. Randi, she cannot do this."

"Maddy, every bit of evidence we've found points directly to Brett. She is guilty."

"Randi, we have had dinner with Brett and Allie and Leisa together. I know you love Allie, or think you do, but that should not cloud your judgment. I cannot put more importance on this than saying that this is a key moment in your life. This is a judgment that will affect the rest of your life."

"Maddy—"

"Randi, you must call Brett back soon. So I have few moments in which to convince you."

Something about Maddy's tone, maybe it was that professorial bit, made Randi unable to interrupt her.

"Randi," Maddy said. It was as if she knew she had to keep saying Randi's name to keep her focused. "During our dinners together, I have been made fun of. I like it. It's all well and good. I'm the spooky woman who sees things. I see, and feel, more than I let on. I know already you'll hang up with me, and call Brett. Then you'll call Ski, whom you spent the night with . . . and that's where I grow foggy. But I do know you'll spill that cup of coffee on yourself in five minutes' time. And I do know Brett is good now and must not go to prison. So tell your girl Ski not to take Brett into custody."

"You're confusing the hell out of me."

"Do you love Allie?"

"Yes. Well, uh—"

"You want her. But she's not yours. Fine. You love her. Do you want her to die? Soon?"

"No!"

"The only way she will live is if Brett can save her. It's your choice. You have calls to make." Maddy hung up.

Randi's mind was swimming. She couldn't deal with this. She put her head down on her arms, unfortunately putting her head on her left wrist, right on top of her wristwatch, which beeped at her, drawing her attention to the time. She picked up the phone and dialed the number Brett had given her.

"Yeah," Brett answered. "Randi?"

"It's me. Why do you want to turn yourself in?" Brett took in a deep breath, and Randi could almost see the cogs in her brain turning around. *Watch. Protect Allie. And Victoria.* "Did you do it?"

"Yes. I killed Gwen Cartwright in cold blood with my three-fifty-seven. Now tell me where to confess, or I'm gonna walk into the TV station I'm parked outside of and do it myself."

"But did you do it?"

"Oh, yeah, fine, you're my friend and all, and trying to trick me on the phone."

"This isn't being taped."

"Then fine, I can say that Victoria's life is on the line here? And maybe Allie's as well? You're in love with Allie, aren't you?"

"But you didn't do it, did you?"

"This is stupid," Brett said, hanging up.

"Fuck!" Randi yelled, slamming the phone on the desk.

"Is something wrong?" Greg Morrow asked, walking by her.

"No, no sir. Just frustrated."

"About the right things, this time, I hope," he said, walking away.

Randi called Ski's cell. And let it ring and ring.

Finally Ski answered, "Dammit, I've got Higgins on the other line!"

"She's lying!" Randi screamed.

"She's confessing."

"Fuck!" Randi screamed as someone knocked her hand and caused her coffee to spill all over her. Maddy's desperate pleas from moments before hit her.

"What happened?"

"I . . . uh . . ."

"Randi, I'm trying to negotiate a plea bargain on the other line. Or something. She seems to be turning herself in."

"Don't."

"What?" then "I'm sorry Ms. Higgins, I am also trying to talk a suicide down at the moment."

"Ski. Joan. I am right now, here, willing to turn in my badge to protect that woman." Randi stood and pulled off her badge, which was a part of her. But she was suddenly realizing there were other parts of her. She was practically hyperventilating. "Whatever you do, talk her into tracking these SOBs. Do that like you're talking a jumper down. She looks at the world in black and white. She thinks she wears a black hat—"

"Are you telling me she's one of the good guys now?"

"Her record now speaks for itself." Randi walked toward the exit. Maddy's words rang in her head. But not like the feeling of Brett's hand around her ankle, when she saved her life. Or like the heat of the coffee burning her just now. "She cannot turn herself in, or others will die. We need to help her." She took Maddy's words at face value and ran with them. Ran with what she knew was right.

She hung up the phone.

Ski picked up her phone. "Higgins? Are you still there?"

"Yeah. I want this on TV and the radio."

"I'm not sure if I can arrange that."

"Goddammit! My picture's been everywhere, and my voice as well. This is Lansing! Little freakin' Lansing!"

"Brett, dammit—"

"What?"

"Randi McMartin . . . you do know her, right?"

"Yeah, I know her."

"She's been arguing for you for days. Saying you'd never let yourself be set up with this much evidence against you and if you'd done it, the body'd never be found."

"She's right."

"So why'd you do this? Like this?"

"I did it and that's all that matters. The world is black and white, and your colors lead you to know the good is with closing cases, right?"

Ski remembered Randi's words. "I want to know who did it."

"Fine. Then I did it. Come and pick me up."

Ski suddenly realized that all of Randi's crazy talk made sense. Everything was falling into place. "Brett, you know I could have easily traced this call by now, right?"

"Well, yeah, duh, that's the idea."

"I haven't."

"Ski, what do I need to do? I've got the addresses and shit on lots of TV stations. I could prance into one right now, into some nice daytime talk show, and turn myself in. I just thought you might like my ass yourself. You tell me how we're gonna play it."

"Why are you doing this?" Ski couldn't believe Higgins had just used the word *prance*. In a sentence. Regarding herself.

"I'm guilty. I did it. I killed Gwen. I just want to ensure that as much TV and radio time as has been applied to my alleged crime and my capture is devoted to my turning myself in. Okay?"

From everything Ski had heard, Brett was a quick-witted criminal who had never even been to the principal's office. None of this would have made sense before, but with Randi's phone call, and its oddities, she had to wonder. And realize that it made no sense. "Brett, tell me where you are, and we can go into the TV station together."

"I'm so not trusting you right now, Ski."

"Fine. Then tell me where to meet you?"

Brett thought back to her days as a media person in Lansing, and came up with the name of a live daytime TV talk show that was going to begin soon. She told Ski to meet her in the lobby of that building—and warned her to come alone. She'd come along peacefully so long as Ski was alone.

Brett strode into the lobby, wearing a black suit with a red and black tie, black shirt, and carrying a briefcase, doing her impersonation of a harried businessperson as she strode in talking on her cell phone to no one at all in an angry manner while signing into the building with an illegible scrawl.

She made sure to only enter at the time she had agreed upon with Ski, so as to bring even less attention to herself until she wanted it.

After she signed in, she glanced around and saw that Ski had positioned herself by the elevators so she'd see Brett as soon as she entered. Brett walked right over to her and hit the Up button for the elevator.

"Brett Higgins, long time no see," Ski said while they stood alone waiting for the elevator.

"Ski. I'd say the pleasure's all mine, but it's not."

"I have to ask why you're doing this."

"Go ahead and ask."

"Why are you doing this?" Ski asked as the elevator came and they got on. When someone tried to join them, Ski flashed her badge and said, "Police business."

Brett pushed the button for the fifth floor and said, "Because I don't have any other choice."

"What do you mean?"

"I. Don't. Have. A. Choice."

Ski slammed the stop button on the elevator. "Explain it to me."

"What do you care? You've been chasing me—before and now—and I'm ready to admit to everything."

"But you didn't do it."

"You don't think I did it? What the fuck is that now? You've been after me like a heroin addict looking for his next fix since Gwen got . . . since Gwen died."

Ski had been studying Brett's face during this. Carefully.

"What the fuck are you lookin' at, copper?"

"You really didn't do it, did you?"

"What the hell's gonna get through to you? I tell you I didn't do it, and you don't buy it—but now I'm tellin' ya I did do it, and you're not buying that either? What's gonna give you a happy, baby?" Brett was using her height advantage to back Ski, literally, into a corner of the elevator.

Ski looked up at Brett. "Finding whoever really murdered Gwen Cartwright."

Brett smirked down at her, then threw her hands up in the air. "Well, ya got her right here, baby. Yup, I did it. Fucked her brains out, then blew them out with my trusty three-fifty-seven." She opened her coat to show that it was with her even now.

Ski advanced on Brett, as if to show she was unafraid. "Yeah, right, you did it. You laid it all out for us to know it was you, and then, since we couldn't find you, you turn yourself in."

"Yup. Got that right home."

"But I don't see the game, Higgins. The game would be beating us against all odds, but you're not doing that. So what *are* you doing? All I can see is that you're setting yourself up for life in prison, and that really doesn't fit with what I've learned about you." Ski kept right on talking, not giving Brett a chance to cut in, even while she tried to slowly inch Brett into the opposite corner of the elevator from where she herself had just been cornered. "You're an animal, Brett, and going to prison for life would be the worst torture for you, don't you know that? So why are you doing this?"

"I don't have a choice, Ski."

"Why don't you have a choice, Brett?"

Brett looked down at the floor, and in that moment Ski really understood what people saw in Brett Higgins. When she looked back up, defeat was emblazoned across her face. "They have Victoria."

"Victoria?"

"Storm's sister, Victoria."

"Ummm . . ."

"You wouldn't understand. They made us last night—they identified everyone we had staking them out. I can't lose anyone else, ya gotta understand this, Ski."

Ski stepped back. "You're doing this . . . for the others?"

"Why the fuck else? Goddammit, Ski . . ." she turned away and put her head against the wall of the elevator.

"What?" Ski asked. If she actually was going to take Brett into custody, she would've told somebody and come with some backup. She hadn't. She had come knowing Brett was innocent, and trying to figure out why she was turning herself in when she was innocent.

She laid a hand on Brett's back. This fearless woman was afraid. Why?

Brett turned to face Ski. Her eyes were wet. "I loved Storm, but I let her down." She was leaning back against the wall. "She was murdered. My boss, Rick, was murdered." She stood to her full height and looked down at Ski. "Allie, Storm, Rick, Frankie, those were the only folks in my entire Goddammed life I loved. Then Victoria showed up, and wanted to kill me. She's Storm's sister. I can't let her down like I let down her sister, don't you get it?"

"Do you live in a soap opera?"

Brett grinned, her eyes clearing up. "Yes, Goddammit." She raised an eyebrow. "Haven't you figured that out yet? I live in a bloody soap opera—better'n even the Bard coulda written himself."

"So whoever really killed Gwen Cartwright has kidnapped Victoria?"

"Finally, ya got it, detective." Brett was advancing on Ski in the small space, forcing her to retreat further and further into a corner.

"They're going to kill her unless you give yourself up, in a public way?"

"Got it again." Ski would have thought that after these few years, and with Randi in the way, she would have gotten over Brett's sexual magnetism. She looked up at Brett, and felt her approaching as she backed herself into a corner.

"So you're doing this for Victoria?"

"Victoria . . . Victoria will die if I don't. I don't have enough time to stop them from killing her. And then, anyone else they can find, they will kill, till I turn myself in." She pushed closer to Ski. "Do you understand what I'm saying?" She laid her hands against the wall on either side of Ski's head. "The people who are helping me are the only people I know and . . . trust." She lowered her head till she whispered in Ski's ear, so Ski could feel her breath along that sensitive area, "These are the people who trust and believe in me, baby. I can't lead them to the slaughterhouse."

Ski pushed her way from the cocoon of Brett's body. "We have to move, then." She hit the emergency stop button so the elevator began moving again. "Here's what we do. I go on camera saying that you are in custody, outside. We'd like to broadcast your confession, but cannot."

"What the fuck you playing at, baby?"

Ski walked right up to Brett and said, "I'm a renegade cop, okay? I know you didn't do it, and I'm gonna do what I have to so I can figure this shit out, okay?"

"What the fuck you talkin' about?" Brett said, slamming the emergency stop button on the elevator again.

"Randi McMartin was ready to turn in her badge this morning to help you—"

"Okay, fine, sure, yeah, I saved her life."

"You dove off a Goddammed building to save her."

"Well, yeah. What's the big?"

"You saved her life!"

"She didn't do anything wrong. I just wanted to nail the assholes, 'kay? Nobody was 'sposed to get hurt."

It was like an untouching tango, they were dancing back and forth across the elevator, each pushing her lead, trying to end up on top. Brett would end up in prison for life. If she survived. "You risked your own life to save hers," Ski said, her back against the wall.

"I didn't think."

"I know you didn't. But underneath all your bullshit you're a good person who doesn't like to see innocent people die."

Brett put her leg between Ski's, not pushing, not yet. She met Ski's eyes. "Don't go givin' me all these noble motives. I'm here to save the people I love. The people who trust me enough to . . . to perhaps sacrifice their lives to me."

Ski braced Brett back, her hands against Brett's shoulders. She knew Brett well enough to suspect that the dark woman often used sex to help her when she was confused or cornered. A few years before, she might have let Brett seduce her, do her, take her on a magic carpet ride. But not now. "Brett, I want to go up there and say you've turned yourself in. I want to mention your record and say that. I don't want you to be on camera, or admit anything."

"Are you saying what I think—" Brett began, pulling back a bit, and apparently finally believing what Ski had been saying.

"You're innocent and I know that."

"You switching teams, babe?"

"No. I've always wanted to get whoever killed Gwen. And if they've kidnapped one of your friends, that means you're a lot closer than we are. I want to help you. I want us to work together."

Brett grabbed Ski by the shoulders and pushed her back against the wall. "What the hell sort of game are you playin' with me, Ski?"

"I'm not playing a game, Brett. I suggest we make it look as if you've turned yourself in, then we figure out how to rescue Victoria and capture the bad guys." She tried to pull out of Brett's grasp to no avail. "We will attract a lot of attention unless we get this elevator moving again."

"What are you going to get out of this, Ski?"

"The bad guys. Brett, you have to realize they're not just going to let Victoria go, not even if you turn yourself in. You're their biggest threat, so we need you to figure out why you're such a threat and who they are. You can't do Victoria, or Allie, or any of your friends any good if you're behind bars."

Brett pulled away and hit the button so the elevator started moving again. When they reached the floor of the studio, security guards met them, obviously suspicious because of the on-and-off movement of the elevator.

"Police. Everything's okay," Ski said, flashing her badge and pushing her way through. "I need to find who's in charge of this show. Police business."

After some haranguing, Ski was allowed to make an on-air statement. It helped that the producers of the show recognized Brett's face from the papers and TV news.

When Brett tried Victoria's phone after the announcement, she got voice mail.

Chapter Twenty-eight

The rest of the gang was in overdrive.

"There's at least one other person involved with them," Allie said. "He's got to be the key to where Victoria is!"

Maddy put the phone down. "That was Randi. She was able to track Victoria's cell phone." When everyone looked at her expectantly, she continued, "It was left in a field. Leisa, I need you to help me determine how we can receive a fax on our computer. Is that even possible?"

"Why?" Allie asked.

"Randi thinks she might be able to fax us a few items soon, so I need to determine how best that can be accomplished."

When Leisa and Maddy left the room for the computer, Allie paced, with Kurt's and Frankie's gaze on her. "What?" she asked, turning on them suddenly.

"What do we do now?" Frankie asked.

"I don't know," Allie said, sitting and burying her face in her hands. "I can't believe she's doing this! And she's turned off her cell phone so I can't even reach her!"

She felt arms around her. "She feels responsible for Pam's death, so she's doing all she can to keep Victoria alive," Kurt said, gently rubbing her back.

"But why the hell does she think they won't just kill Victoria anyway?"

"She's not really thinkin' too clearly, ya know?" Frankie said.

"For chrissake's, everybody knows that the bad guys never do what they promise to do!"

Just then the phone rang. Maddy yelled downstairs, "Don't pick it up!"

Allie stood up, unintentionally pushing Kurt away. "I wonder what's up?"

When the three of them entered the computer room, Maddy was printing pages from the computer. She looked up at them. "Randi's pulled some information for us about the major players."

Leisa glanced at the computer, which was apparently still receiving pages. "It looks like we have our work cut out for us."

"We're supposed to call her back if we need anything else," Maddy said. "If she's not there, then we can speak to . . ."

"Greg Morrow, her supervisor," Leisa finished.

Allie looked over Leisa's shoulder and punched some buttons on the computer, glancing through the pages that were coming up onscreen. The printer was a little behind. "I think we should print up several copies of these," she said. "So we can all look through everything. Some of us might catch things others might miss."

"Call Randi back," Allie said, still looking over the pages. "I want to see if we can find out where these guys went to jail and who their cellmates were."

Frankie's phone rang, he answered with a "Yo," and walked out of the room. He returned a moment later, covering the mouthpiece with his hand. "Yo, Maddy, my boys are startin' to call in. Okay if they drop shit off here?"

"Oh, yes. Certainly. Just tell them to try to be discreet. I don't want people thinking I'm running some kind of fencing operation."

Frankie grinned at this. "My boys are burglars. They got that down pat." He stepped out of the room again and Allie heard him giving directions.

"It should be interesting to sort through what they have to tell us," Allie said, looking up at the others.

"What's the plan?" Brett asked, climbing into Ski's car with her.

"I was hoping you had some ideas."

"Nope. No ideas here. You blew all of mine when you showed up."

"So all you had was turning yourself in?"

"Ayup. That was about it."

"And here I thought I was dealing with some sort of criminal mastermind."

Brett laughed. "Haven't been that for a long time."

"What were you doing before they got Victoria?"

"We were following everyone we could find who was involved."

"And who was on your team?"

"Frankie, Kurt, Victoria, and Allie. Maddy was call central, and I sent Leisa back home so she could continue researching during the night—after she lost the guy she was following. I never should've left each post with just one person!"

Ski pulled out her cell. "What's Maddy's number?" Brett told her and she dialed it. "It's busy." She handed the phone to Brett. "I'm just going to go over there. Keep trying her number."

"Aren't you even gonna ask who we were following?"

Ski shrugged. "Somebody kept calling Randi last night, asking about people."

"You spent last night with Randi?"

"She came back to my office with me. She didn't want to waste time getting back to Detroit to look up info on the plates, so she kept slipping behind my back to look stuff up. I caught her at it, and she showed me who you guys wanted to know about. So I think I know all the chief suspects."

"So you spent last night with Randi—go, copper, go!" She smirked and began trying to reach Maddy. She still hadn't gotten through when they pulled up to Maddy's and Leisa's house.

When Allie answered the door, she threw her arms around Brett's neck. "Oh my God, I love you!"

Brett buried her face in Allie's hair and neck, holding her close. She lifted her girl off her feet, enjoying the mix of shampoo, soap, and everything else that made up her smell. A scent she thought, just a few hours before, she'd never experience again.

"I thought you were going to turn yourself in," Allie said, still in Brett's arms. Tears were streaming down her face.

"Ski talked me out of it," Brett said, putting Allie back on the floor and moving aside so she could see Ski behind her.

"Oh."

"I come in peace," Ski said, putting up her hands. "I'm trying to help."

"What?" Allie asked.

"Don't look a gift cop in the mouth," Kurt said from behind Allie, putting his hands on Allie's shoulders.

Ski's phone rang and she pulled it out and looked at it, before putting it back in her pocket. "I went on the air to say Brett had turned herself in," Ski said, shrugging. "I'm just not telling the department about it, because then they might want me to actually bring her in."

"So who was that then?" Kurt asked.

"My boss. Wanting to know when I'm bringing her in. I think," Ski said. "Thank God for caller ID."

"Come on," Brett said, leading Ski into the house. "Where's Frankie?"

"He's in the guest room talking with . . . one of his . . . employees," Leisa said.

Brett shot her a questioning look.

Kurt grabbed Ski, saying, "Brett, you should go help him. Ski, let me get you a drink."

Ski pulled away from Kurt. "Brett, what's going on?"

Brett looked back at her. "Go with Kurt. Believe me. Let him get you something to drink." She went to meet with the only employees of Frankie's she could imagine him having over. Leisa went with her, while Kurt took Ski into the kitchen.

"Okay, so what've we got, Frankie?" Brett said, walking into the room.

"Who's this?" said a very slender Hispanic man with short, black hair and a dark scar cutting across his cheek.

"This, my friends," Frankie said, wrapping an arm around Brett, "is none other than Brett Higgins."

"Nice ta meetcha," a tall black man said, shaking her hand. "You got some balls on you for a chick and all."

Brett squeezed his hand hard while looking straight into his eyes.

"T-Bone," Frankie said. "You should know better than to ever call Brett a chick."

"Got that now," T-Bone said, withdrawing his hand and shaking it back to life.

A slender, petite woman with long black hair tied back in a ponytail and wearing tight black jeans, a black halter top, and a leather jacket, put out her hand to Brett. "You're a legend. I'd be happy to do anything else you need me to do." There was an evil twinkle in her eyes.

"But who's the other one?" the Hispanic asked, bringing Brett's attention back to him.

"A friend of ours," Frankie said. "Helping us out on this project. Leisa is a computer whiz. Brett, these here are a few of the independent contractors I hired—Carlos, T-Bone, Alphonse, and Cheryl."

"So what's going on?" Brett asked.

"They finished what they were doin' and came back here to fill us in."

T-Bone glared at Brett. "Here's the disks and shit, and the Polaroids you asked for." He handed them to Frankie, but kept his eyes on Brett. Frankie pulled out his wallet and peeled off a few hundreds to hand to T-Bone. But then he held onto them at the last moment.

T-Bone, unable to get the money, glared up at him. "Whatsa matter?"

"You didn't take anythin' else, did you?"

"No. I went in for a job an' I did it. 'Kay?"

"Good. Did you notice anything else?"

"No. Now can I get paid and leave?"

Frankie shoved the money into T-Bone's hand. "Leisa will take you out. You were never here and didn' see us—got it?"

T-Bone looked up at Brett. "Yeah. I got it."

Brett turned to look at the others. "You three did your jobs as well?"

"I'm a pro," Alphonse said. He was older than the other two, with white hair that made him look distinguished and respectable. But he also had a lean, hard look.

"I do the job I'm hired for." He pulled out some CDs and Polaroids from his pocket. "Strange job, but so long as you pay, I don't care and I wasn't ever there or here."

Frankie paid him, Carlos, and Cheryl, and had Leisa escort them out.

"I'm glad you've got Leisa taking them out," Brett said to Frankie.

"What, ya brought a cop with you?"

"Well, yeah, I did."

Frankie just shook his head. He picked up the disks and CDs and handed them to Leisa, who had returned. "I think this shit is yours." He picked up the Polaroids and handed them to Brett. "These are yours."

Brett flicked through them. "Good. These are good."

Allie, Maddy, and Ski were looking over the work they had done—the work they had all done.

"Is it just me, or is it weird that some of the different players work for different software companies?" Allie asked.

"I think that is . . . Well, it is an astute observation that bears further regard," Maddy said.

"Who are Brett and Frankie meeting with in there?" Allie asked.

"The burglars," Maddy whispered to her, obviously knowing they could be overheard.

"Oh," Allie said.

"I'm thinking I shouldn't even ask," Ski said.

"No, you should not," Maddy replied.

"Yeah. So, what was that about different people working for different software companies?" Ski said.

Allie showed her the information Randi had tracked down about their different players—Diane, Douglas, Heather, and Gwen all worked at CompuVisions, whereas Stephanski worked at Alternities, the competitor.

"Douglas and Diane were dating," Maddy said, "so that is the connection between them. But how about the others?"

Allie picked up the phone.

"What're you doing?" Ski asked.

"Calling Randi." When Randi picked up, Allie said, "Randi, can you pull down full records on the people you gave me info about? I mean, like where they've lived, who their cellmates were if they were in jail, where they've worked, that sort of thing."

"I thought I got you pretty good records so far."

"Yes, yes you have. But Stephanski works for Alternities, which is the company that suddenly caught up real quick with the program Gwen was developing for CompuVisions. There must be some connection between one of the people at CompuVisions and him."

"I'll get on it. We might have something there."

"I know that."

"Too bad we don't know anything about the guy you lost last night."

"Randi, we tried, okay?"

"Yeah. I know."

"Thank you Randi—for this, and bringing Ski over."

"Ski's there?"

"Yes she is. But you shouldn't know that. So behave."

"Yeah, okay, fine. I'll get this stuff to you as soon as I can. I do have a question, though."

"What is it?"

"If Ski's there, can't she be doing this?"

"I think she's kinda avoiding the police herself right now. She went on TV saying Brett had turned herself in, so they're expecting her to show up with Brett in cuffs."

"Oh. Okay."

Allie thought of something else. "Hey, can you also get me the full company rosters for both those companies?"

"Rosters?"

"I want to know the names, addresses, and phone numbers of everybody who works at either company."

"That's asking a lot, Allie. I'll see what I can dig up. You might want to check with Ski—she might already have that for CompuVisions."

"I'll do that."

Maddy and Ski had apparently been listening in because Ski said, "I've already got that for CompuVisions. It's in my car."

"Randi, Ski's got CompuVisions covered."

"Okay. Allie?"

"Yes?"

"Tell Ski I said hi, 'kay?"

Allie looked over at Ski. "Randi says hi."

Ski blushed, turned away, and said, "Hi back."

"She says hi back. I'll talk to you later, okay?" Allie wondered what was going on between the two detectives.

Allie hung up and turned back to the others. Frankie and Brett joined them then.

"What's up?" Brett asked.

"We've found a connection," Allie said. "Randi's seeing if she can find anything more on it."

"I'll go get my briefcase," Ski said as she headed outside to her car.

Allie filled Brett and Frankie in on what had just happened.

"Okay, so here's what we're gonna do," Brett said as Ski returned. Ski put her briefcase on the table and pulled out some sheafs of paper. "Leisa's analyzing computer information we gained from our suspects' computers." She looked at Ski. "Don't ask." She then pulled out the Polaroids. "We also got these. Allie, you should examine them. Maddy, Ski, keep looking at the profiles and information Randi's sent—and what she is going to send."

"What are you and Frankie going to do?" Allie asked.

"We're gonna hit the streets. Maddy, Ski—can we use your cars? The bad guys haven't made them yet."

"Where are you going?" Ski asked.

"I want to do the two-car approach, with radios, and check all our suspects' homes."

"I want to come with," Allie said.

"I'm not sitting around here looking over papers while you two are out there," Ski said.

"We need you here to let us know about anything that comes in," Frankie said.

"Listen, I'm a cop. I need to be out there with you two," Ski said. "If anything goes down, I need to be a part of it. This is my case, after all."

Everyone looked at Brett. Brett took Allie's hand and started pulling her from the room. "I need to talk to you alone."

Allie played along until they were alone in the guest room, but once Brett closed the door, she said, "You know I can take care of myself."

"Yes, I do baby. You're quick thinking and good in a bad situation."

"So what's your issue? I mean, this is about me going out with you and Frankie, right?"

Brett reached forward and took Allie's hands in her own. "I need you here, watching my back. I need you here, 'cause I need you all to find the needle in the haystack."

"You've got Leisa, Maddy, Randi, and Ski to do that."

"Randi's got to stay on her own job. We're lucky she can do what she's doing already. Ski seems like she's gonna wanna go out with us, and I can't stop her."

"Why not? This is your gig, right?"

"Yeah, but Allie . . ." Brett dropped her hands and began pacing. "This is Ski's case. If it weren't for her, I'd have turned myself in. She's out on a limb here."

"You're my lover, and I've supported you since day one." Allie could almost see Brett thinking of mentioning *except for when you went undercover to nail my ass.* But she was grateful Brett didn't.

Brett stopped and stared at Allie. "Don't you get it? Don't you understand?"

"No. I don't."

"Allie, I've always felt responsible for Storm's death. Now her little sister has been kidnapped because of me. I can't let anything happen to you as well."

"I know you love Frankie, too. What about him?"

"We'll have on Kevlar. And he's a big guy. No one goes against him without a second thought."

Allie wrapped her arms around Brett's neck. "What about you?"

"This is all about me. I need people looking over everything, and if anyone's gotta be out there risking their neck for me, I need to do it as well. I just can't risk you. I'll have to let Ski do it 'cause it's her game—but I can't endanger you. I love you too much for that, Allie." Brett wrapped her arms around Allie and pulled her in tight.

Allie decided against equating herself with Victoria, or Storm. This wasn't the time. "You know I can take care of myself," she said instead.

"I know that. You can be one big badass yourself when you want to be. I know this. But, before, with you, we were in it together. We got into it together. Most times. Now it's all about me, and someone I care about has already been taken. Frankie and I walk the same line, so we know what we're in. Ski does, too."

"I was a cop once as well."

"But you're my lover now. I just want you to be safe." She rubbed Allie's back tenderly before lifting Allie's chin to kiss her deeply and passionately. "I hope you can understand," she said, when their lips finally parted.

"No, Brett. I can't."

Brett pulled away. "I got into this through my own fucking stupidity, and I can't ask you to risk your life because of what I did. I have a lot to answer for already. I don't need your life on the line as well."

"So you admit it."

"Yes. I do. I'm an asshole, okay? You should just dump me and find someone who can make you really happy."

"Brett, you're the one who makes me happy. Even when you're driving me fucking crazy and being a total jerk."

"Allie, please just tell me you'll stay here?"

"I'll stay here. Unless you really need me."

"That's not what I asked."

"You can't help but try to protect me. I love you, moron that you are." A part of her wanted to add some other things, but she didn't. She'd save that for later. For now, she felt special, loved, wanted, and needed, in her lover's arms.

ꕥ

When Brett and Allie returned to the others, Leisa was there as well.

"Brett, your picture's been all over," Leisa said. "You can't go out."

"She'll be with me," Ski said. "She and I will be in one car, and Frankie in the other."

"She should still do . . . something . . . so she's not so recognizable," Leisa said.

"She's got a good point," Allie said with a smirk. "And I'd love to see you in that outfit you were wearing the other day."

Maddy was looking Brett up and down. "Actually, I think surfer boy Brett is more in order here. Come with me," she said, leading Brett upstairs by the hand.

Brett was amazed at Maddy's hand with makeup and her ideas on attire. Granted, Brett wasn't too pleased with the bleaching of her eyebrows, and she did have to call to Frankie to grab a vest from the car as Maddy dressed her, but she thought the overall effect worked quite well. Allie was even hesitant to give her a goodbye kiss because she looked so different.

When Allie's leg came up around her legs, Brett wondered why she ever looked elsewhere.

Chapter Twenty-nine

Brett and Ski were together in one car. Brett, the blond surfer dude, was driving. She hated the loud Hawaiian shirt she was wearing. She thought it'd call even more attention to her.

Frankie was tailing her. Kurt, Allie, Maddy, and Leisa were at the house trying to see if they could come up with anything else. Brett and Frankie were linked by radio. The others were calling in to Frankie to let them know what they found.

Brett was leading them around all their suspects' houses. They were carefully inspecting each residence, looking for anything out of the ordinary. Anything that might point to people being home, watching for them, or holding someone hostage.

They were at the last residence, Douglas Beauregard's, and Brett was seriously losing hope. She looked over at Ski. "We'll have to go back through them all," she said. "And this time more carefully. And I mean looking in windows."

"Brett, between you and me, I'm thinking you've had people look into these places . . . so . . . Victoria is obviously not being kept at any of them."

"What the fuck else can we do?"

Brett's radio crackled. "Brett," Frankie's voice came over. "They've found something."

Ski picked up the radio. "Frankie, there was a QD a few blocks back. Follow us there. We'll talk in the store while shopping."

"QD?"

"Quality Dairy. It's a convenience store."

Brett drove back to the store with Frankie following. She knew about QD from her days at Michigan State University.

"Yo, Jimbo," Ski said, when Brett and she entered the store, "I'm gonna get some munchies, 'kay?"

"I'll get the brew," Brett replied, understanding the game they were playing. She went to the beer coolers to look at her choices, and Frankie walked up next to her.

He slipped a piece of paper into her hand. "I hope you two know where it's at, 'cause I don't."

"Who is it?"

"There's a few connections 'tween the two companies. This is the hottest. An old cellmate of Stephanski's. Stephanski did some time with Douglas Beauregard." He pulled out a case of Miller from the cooler.

Brett grabbed a six of Sam Adams Oktoberfest.

"Diane dated Douglas," Brett replied.

"And a few years ago Di worked about two feet from Heather."

"Got it."

"They've got more if we need it."

"Cool. Get some more beer. And maybe some chips. Hopefully we'll have a celebration tonight." Brett went to the counter to pay for her beer. "Yo, babe, grab me a soda, 'kay!" she yelled over to Ski. Ski brought up non-alcoholic drinks, including Coke and Diet Pepsi. She wrapped her arms around Brett and leaned up to rest her chin on Brett's neck, as if they were a couple.

Brett paid for everything. They left. As soon as they were in the car, Brett passed her the slip of paper. "Please tell me you know where this is."

Brett drove slowly so Frankie could pick them up once he left the store. She didn't want it to appear that they were together, then she followed Ski's directions.

"Where are we going?" Ski asked.

"The missing link."

"What do you mean? Turn left."

"We lost someone last night. This might be him."

"Oh, turn right here. How'd you figure that out?"

"I didn't. The home team did—Leisa, Maddy, Allie, Kurt, and probably Randi. You like her?"

Ski blushed. "I like her. Oh shit, we just missed the street!"

"I thought you knew Lansing!" Brett said, rounding a block so two cars in a row wouldn't have to make illegal U-turns, which would be kinda obvious.

"I do, but not like every single side street."

"You have maps," Brett said, pointing out the maps Ski had pulled from her glove compartment to help her easily find any address.

"Stop."

Brett hit the brakes and pulled up to a curb. She checked her rearview mirror to see that Frankie had stopped at the other end of the block.

Ski looked over at her. "Do we want to do a drive-by, or closer inspection?"

Brett sat back in the driver's seat and took a deep breath. She let her instincts take over, and looked around at the seemingly quiet neighborhood. It felt as if . . . it was right. As if this was where she needed to be. "Closer. Me first." She picked up the radio connecting her to Frankie. "We're moving in. Me first, then Ski, then you. Usual signals." She put down the radio and moved toward the door.

" 'Usual signals'?" Ski asked.

"Screaming, yelling, gunshots . . . that sort of shit. I go in first, initial contact. I'll signal if you should follow. I'll give you a thumbs up if this is the place, and I'll raise fingers to let you know how long you should wait till you follow. Frankie knows his cues. You up for this?"

"Yeah."

"Good."

Ski laid a hand on Brett's shoulder before Brett could open the door. "Is Frankie?"

"He wouldn't be here if he wasn't." Brett got out of the car, looking down toward her hand as if she were double-checking some address she had written there. All her senses were on high alert. She had already checked her equipment, including the Beretta strapped to her ankle under her jeans; and the .357 in her shoulder holster, under her loud shirt as well as the picks in her trouser pocket, and the slender single-blade pocket knife in her back pocket. The shirt fell over it, covering it.

She went up to the front door and rang the doorbell. Then she waited. Nothing. So she knocked. And waited more. Then rang again.

Finally, a scruffy-looking fellow who needed a shave, shower, and change of clothes answered the door. "Yeah?" he asked, taking a drag off his smoke.

"Yo, dude, is Darla here?" Brett said, making sure to keep her voice deep.

"Buddy, ya got the wrong joint, ain't no Darla here."

"For fuck's sake, she told me if I was in Lansing, I should come by here!" Brett said, looking down at her hand, where she had penned this address.

The guy grabbed her hand and looked at it. "Looks like you got played, dude. Good for you! Ain't no Darla here, but I hope she was a good time."

Brett grinned up at him. "Oh, yeah, she was. She was, man."

"Sorry man," the guy said, closing the door.

Brett put her left hand at her side, palm toward where Frankie and Ski were parked, indicating that they should hold. She wanted to strip off the Hawaiian shirt, so she'd be wearing her black T-shirt, which would be a lot better than the loud flowery thing for this sort of activity, but couldn't risk any strangers seeing her taking off her clothing, or seeing her gun. That would be a bad thing. A very bad thing indeed.

Suspicious neighbors would call the police and she didn't need any more cops around. Ski was enough. She thought Victoria might already be dead. But she was thinking this was where Vickie was. Of course, if the bad guys really were here, they'd kill Victoria without a thought as soon as they knew Brett was around. All around, Victoria was dead or soon would be.

She really hated this crap.

She made her way around the house, carefully peeking into each room she could see. She figured that if Victoria was there, she'd be in the basement, or perhaps even the attic, but she wanted to know the territory before making her move.

Almost all Michigan houses had underground basements because the land was flat, and basements were perfect for hiding almost anything. Sound was muffled more in a basement than an attic.

She inspected the first floor, careful that her shadow and body could not be seen through the basement windows. She then crouched down low to see through the tiny basement windows set right at ground level, but she took her time and had patience.

Through one window, she saw several people. She wasn't sure who or how many were down there, but she was sure she saw Douglas. And Victoria. Tied to a chair. It looked like she was still alive, but Brett noticed what looked like blood on her face.

She kept watching for a moment. She was fairly certain she had not been seen. She wanted to bust in immediately, but instead she slipped to the front of the house. She looked toward the two cars occupied by Ski and Frankie, gave a thumbs up and raised five fingers. Five minutes. That's all she needed.

She returned to the backyard, took off the Hawaiian shirt and looked at the basement window through which she had seen

Victoria. She wanted to bust through it and surprise them. She was sure she could fit, but she'd get cut, and the moments that it took her to fall to the floor would make all the difference.

She went to the back door and pulled the picks from her pocket. Once inside, she inched along, knew the others would be following to save her ass quite quickly if need be. She pulled out her .357. She hadn't seen anyone on the first floor, but she spied what she figured was the door to the basement, just across from the back door.

She had to save Victoria. She couldn't let her down like she had let Pamela down.

She slowly crept across the aged floor, trying not to make a sound. She should've told the others to hold back for longer. She wanted to be the initial thrust, subduing everyone, claiming their attention and protecting Victoria before the others came in, guns blazing.

Victoria was the more important point. She chambered a shot, ready to shoot, to kill, to take a life. She reminded herself that anyone she encountered was a bad guy—someone willing to let Brett take the fall for a vicious murder, and ready to kill Victoria, an innocent bystander. If anyone should die, it should be her, Brett. Not Victoria.

Just then, the floor squeaked. She should've taken off her boots!

"What was that?" a male voice said from the basement.

"Fuck. The house is just settling," another male voice replied. "Higgins turned herself in. We have nothing to worry about."

"Then why don't we just kill this bitch and get on with it?" a woman, not Heather, said. Must be Diane, Brett thought to herself. Bitch. "How can we cover our asses if we're all not showing up to work?"

"We're keeping her alive in case any of the other Scoobies show up, or sniff around. She's our insurance policy. We haven't seen Higgins in cuffs, and that's what I want to see." The same male voice.

"I say we kill this girl, and it'll make our point to Higgins if she hasn't turned herself in, and if she has, it'll serve as a warning to the others." The woman again. She was ruthless.

"You might have a point, there."

"I'm checking upstairs," the first male voice said, and Brett heard footsteps on the stairs leading to the kitchen.

Brett ran to the door. She didn't know how many she had to fight off, but at least this would be one she could take out easily.

She ripped open the door at the top of the staircase, planting one hand on the railing on the right and bracing herself by placing her left hand against the wall. She swung her legs up, kicking forward. She pegged one guy upside the head. He flew down, his head hitting the wall and his body collapsing.

Brett finished her move, throwing her body down the stairs, but not landing on Douglas's neck. She turned toward the room in fighting position, gun in hand.

She met Victoria's eyes for an instant.

Stephanski shot. And kept shooting. The first bullet hit her in the heart, throwing her back against the wall.

Everything went black.

Ski wasn't patient. She climbed out of her car, and Frankie tried to stop her from moving in.

"She knows what she's doin'," he said.

"I'm her partner. Got it? Get it? Okay," Ski said, creeping around the house till she too saw Victoria in the basement, tied to a chair. She saw the size of the basement windows and signaled him to go for the front door. No way could he make it in through one of those windows.

But she knew she could. It wouldn't be easy, but she could. She pulled out her gun, knowing she could use it to bash through the glass if need be. Until then, she'd watch. See if Brett could pull off the magic she seemed to be known for.

She couldn't quite see everything that was happening, but when she saw a man move rapidly toward the stairs, she pulled out her police radio, knowing Brett had been discovered. She saw the guy hit the wall at the bottom of the stairs, and said, "Officer in trouble," and gave the address.

She twisted till she saw shots fired, and saw Brett's body slammed against a wall. She knew what she had to do.

She hit the window with the butt of her gun and took a shot to clear her path. Then she screamed and dove through. She hoped Frankie heard the scream.

She hit the floor, rolling over on her shoulder as she'd been taught at the police academy, her gun in her hand as she looked for a human target to shoot. But even as she aimed at Diane, she felt the barrel of a gun against her head.

"Do you want to die today?" a male voice said.

"I'm ready to die any day." Ski stopped moving.

"Yeah, right."

Brett was dead. Victoria was tied and gagged. All Ski could hope for was a last-minute reprieve from Frankie. If she could hold it off long enough, maybe the cops she had called might show up, but would they be in time?

Frankie quickly picked the front locks. Both the regular one and the deadbolt. Then he looked at the hardwood floor in front of him and kicked off his shoes to help keep his tread silent. He had heard shots fired. Then he heard glass breaking and Ski screaming.

He carefully made his way across the floor, hoping any sounds he made wouldn't be heard above the ruckus in the basement. He made it to the top of the staircase and looked down. Brett was sprawled out. He felt his heart leap into his throat.

She had to be alive. She just had to be.

He couldn't go on without her.

But then he saw her gun about a foot from her body and knew she'd never have let it out of her hand, her reach, if she was alive.

He couldn't finish that thought.

He needed to do something to . . . Nothing could make it right. But Brett would want him to save Victoria and Ski. So that's what he had to do.

Then he heard Ski say, "I'm ready to die any day."

At least Ski was still alive. Maybe even Victoria. He had to do what he could to help them, and avenge Brett. He didn't know how many he was going up against. He could only hope Ski and Brett had taken out a few of them.

He thought about how much he loved Kurt and threw himself down the staircase.

He was gonna die.

Victoria didn't want to see her wrists. Or ankles. She knew they were bloody. She had been working against her bonds for hours now. And her head throbbed from where Doug had hit her.

When Brett was thrown against the wall, she wanted to scream, to cry . . .

She cried out, and then somebody else burst in and then Frankie, and Victoria was confused but she knew she could pull out of the ropes. But did she still want to?

Frankie was hit full in the chest with a shot from Diane's rifle. He flipped through the railing of the staircase, his weight pulling it apart.

Part of Brett's mind knew all this shit was happening around her. It was like a bad dream. She waited till she knew she had control of her body, then in one fluid motion, she pulled herself up, pulled the Beretta from her ankle holster, and in two quick shots she hit the woman who had a gun to Victoria's head, then aimed at Ski's assailant. She hit them both straight through the forehead.

Ski whipped around to take aim at Diane, while Brett aimed at the last man. Both dropped their weapons and raised their arms.

Brett heard sirens in the distance. She figured they had all the bad guys, except for Heather, right there.

"Hands up, and keep them up," Ski said loudly. Brett risked a moment to look down at Frankie.

"Fucking Goddammed piece of shit," he said, slowly getting to his feet. "Where is that bitch? I owe her one."

"She's kinda splattered all over the basement."

"Dammit, I wanted to do her. That hurt." He pulled out his gun, helping to cover the two. Brett picked up her .357, holstered her Beretta, and moved to untie Victoria, pulling her up and into her arms.

"You have the right to remain silent," Ski began.

Epilogue

Some of the wonderful things about long hair are the way it can be flipped and the way it can cover two people making love. Brett loved the feel of silky hair against her face when her woman was on top. Brett loved long hair, especially when it came cascading down around her.

In the bar, Brett leaned back against the wall and watched the sway of Allie's long hair as she talked. Smiling, Brett relaxed and let her thoughts drift to the events of the past few months. She was off the hook now for Gwen Cartwright's murder. When caught with their hands in the cookie jars, all of the surviving conspirators were more than willing to testify against each other to lighten their own sentences.

Robert Stephanski had just been a janitor at Alternities. The connection between Alternities and CompuVisions was Douglas Beauregard, who knew Robert from their time in juvy together.

Diane Jackson and Heather Johnson were friends who both worked at CompuVisions, so one night during a party they started planning how they would spend the fortunes they would one day have.

They first planned what they'd do when they were rich. Then Heather, always the realist, the logistical computer person, wondered how they'd make these millions. She proceeded to drunkenly talk about all she had been through to get her degree and her job—and all she *was* doing to help her boss and eventual lover in the creation of this incredible new program that would put other business applications to shame and . . . One thing led to another.

Robert had been cellmates with Jacob Anderson, Alternities' head of security, which is how Robert got the janitor job. (Jacob had served time for computer piracy, and that's how *he* got *his* job. Who better to hire than the man who could cause you the most trouble?)

Douglas's girlfriend Diane invited him to the party, and he brought Robert. They liked that they were living so near each other. Old buds and all.

Robert knew a lot about Jacob, his boss. Including that he had the ears of the bigwigs in the company. As soon as he heard about the program Gwen was working on, he started doing the math . . . and knew Jacob might be interested. After all, CompuVisions was Alternities' biggest rival in the software world.

Jacob was interested. And he did get the ear they needed—an ear worth several millions to the co-conspirators.

Once they had that, it didn't take much to realize Heather had to become much closer with her boss, Gwen, in order to pull everything off. This was over everyone's heads, but Jacob was truly the mastermind behind it all.

Brett hated that Jacob and his bosses, who approved everything, *verbally*, were getting off scot-free. There wasn't enough evidence to charge them with corporate espionage, let alone Gwen's murder. No, that had entirely been Heather's idea after she'd had that chance encounter with Brett during the snowstorm.

This was a conspiracy that had arisen on a drunken night, from the lowest ranks. Brett had to distract herself from the hatred seething inside her that the ones in charge were being let go. But just talking politics these days could also drive her into such a frenzy as well.

She took a deep breath. All that really mattered was that none of them would be seen for a good long time.

Brett shook the thoughts out of her mind. She took a gulp of her beer and looked around, trying to distract herself from her anger.

She really liked women in dresses and skirts, because they were so feminine. They made her remember she was with women. And simple dresses could really draw her attention so well to what lay beneath.

Allie was across the room at the Rainbow Room, Brett's favorite Detroit lesbian bar, talking with old friends. And talking with Ski and Randi. She laughed, flipping her flowing blonde hair back over her bare shoulders.

Part of Brett wanted to go and break up the intimate conversation, but she cooled her jets, knowing she shouldn't be too jealous and possessive. Allie had told her that before, and recent events had proven that she couldn't call the kettle black. So she satisfied herself with leaning back with her beer, enjoying the sight of her lover. She couldn't help but think that she was awfully lucky. Allie had really let her have it after all the dust had settled. She'd been furious about the whole cybersex thing with Gwen and others. But Brett had groveled and promised to behave, and she'd bought five dozen roses and a diamond tennis bracelet to prove she meant what she said. She grinned at the memory of the hot lovemaking that had taken place afterward. God, how she loved that woman!

Allie was wearing an off-the-shoulder silk dress of royal blue. When they had walked in from the parking lot, Brett had noticed how the wind had blown the dress between her lover's legs, making the fabric wrap around them and drawing her attention there.

Brett loved off-the-shoulder tops and dresses. She adored collarbones and shoulders, and what Allie was wearing showed off both.

Exposed shoulders made real femmes seem innocent and exposed—and activated Brett's predatory instincts. She wanted to dominate.

Brett had always worried about Allie and Randi, and hoped Randi had something happening with Ski so she wouldn't have to worry on that score any longer. She didn't like the idea of Allie with another woman.

And to make sure that never happened, she knew she had to remain well and truly faithful to Allie, who was really a woman worthy of such fidelity. She glanced around the bar and realized no woman there was as beautiful as her long-legged partner, no woman could compare with her. The few somewhat attractive women had vacant or disdainful looks on their faces. They looked as bored as their companions. Brett could not imagine being with any of them.

She remembered how many girlfriends her brothers had had, and she remembered a few vague remarks made by aunts, uncles, family friends, and her mother while she was growing up—about what a charmer her dad used to be. These days the word would be "player." She really couldn't see it, but now she wondered if it was genetic, that she would always be restless. Would she always look at other women and wonder . . . what if?

But that sounded like a cheap excuse, and even she knew it.

Dad had always talked about what others had and he didn't.

Brett had to enjoy and appreciate what she had.

Allie laughed and leaned back against a pool table, so the slit in her skirt showed off an enticing slice of thigh. Slits in dresses gave you a glimpse of flesh, forbidden skin—as if it was an illicit peek beneath whatever the girl was wearing.

Even after all these years with Allie, Brett still felt the same way. The same love and desire that made her want to go and pull Allie into her arms and possess her with a kiss.

And so she did.